Rags to
RICHES

— HIS WISH,
HER COMMAND —

Rags to RICHES COLLECTION

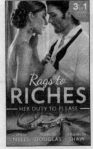

April 2017

May 2017

June 2017

July 2017

August 2017

September 2017

Rags to
RICHES

HIS WISH,
HER COMMAND

Nina
HARRINGTON

Annie
WEST

Laura Marie
ALTOM

Published in Great Britain 2017
By Mills & Boon, an imprint of HarperCollins*Publishers*
1 London Bridge Street, London, SE1 9GF

RAGS TO RICHES: HIS WISH, HER COMMAND
© 2017 Harlequin Books S.A.

The Last Summer of Being Single © 2011 Nina Harrington
An Enticing Debt to Pay © 2013 Annie West
A Navy SEAL's Surprise Baby © 2013 Laura Marie Altom

ISBN: 978 0 263 93101 3

09-0917

Printed and bound in Spain
by CPI, Barcelona

THE LAST SUMMER
OF BEING SINGLE

NINA HARRINGTON

Nina Harrington grew up in rural Northumberland, England, and decided at the age of eleven that she was going to be a librarian – because then she could read *all* of the books in the public library whenever she wanted! Since then she has been a shop assistant, community pharmacist, technical writer, university lecturer, volcano walker and industrial scientist, before taking a career break to realise her dream of being a fiction writer. When she is not creating stories which make her readers smile, her hobbies are cooking, eating, enjoying good wine – and talking, for which she has had specialist training.

CHAPTER ONE

'MARRY me. Come on. You know you want to!'

Ella Jayne Bailey Martinez tapped her finger on her lower lip and nodded her head several times as though trying to make up her mind.

Unfortunately Henri took this as an encouraging sign.

'I have my own set of wheels. You'll be able to motor anywhere you like in this town. What do you say, cutie? We could make some sweet music together!'

'Well… It is tempting. Although…Mr Dubois has already promised me the use of his senior citizen travel card. And it's hard to turn down that sort of offer.'

'Dubois? All promises. No action. Not like me, baby,' Henri replied with a saucy wink.

'Um. That's what I'm worried about. I'm a one-guy-at-a-time kind of girl, and I saw you two-timing me last night with the hotel receptionist. You handsome heartbreaker! Catch you later!'

Henri slammed his hand down hard on the arm of his wheelchair and muttered a vague expletive in French before shrugging his shoulders at Ella and replying in English.

'Darn! Busted!'

Ella smiled and ruffled up what was left of his hair, before sashaying slowly down the corridor back to the kitchen. Without looking back, as though she knew that Henri was still following her every movement, Ella broke step, gave two exaggerated tight bottom wiggles, then glanced back at the grey-haired Romeo just as he winked at her with a twist of the head. 'That's my girl!'

And with a nodding smile Henri swung his wheelchair around with a rim twirl, and sped off at a surprising turn of speed towards the conservatory dining room, where a peal of raucous laughter echoed around the walls as the automatic doors slid open, then closed behind him.

'I hope my guests are not making life too exhausting for you!'

Ella grinned back at her friend Sandrine, who managed the small hotel where she worked as cocktail pianist whenever she could—and occasionally helped out at lunchtimes.

'They're the best! I could talk to them all day about old-style jazz. I grew up with that sort of music. Did you know that Henri spent three years in New Orleans? *And* his pals have just wolfed down three of my apple tarts! Musicians are the same wherever you go in the world! Food comes a close second to the tune! Even in France.'

Sandrine wrapped one arm around Ella's shoulder and grinned. 'Are you kidding? Those charmers might claim that they don't have a sweet tooth in their heads, but once they take a look at the dessert trolley? No will power whatsoever! Thanks again for helping me out at short notice. I have my hands full!'

'No problem. I was glad to help. Are you still fully booked for next weekend?'

'Every room! I've never had forty guests staying for a complete weekend before.'

Sandrine gave Ella an extra hug before releasing her with a warm smile. 'And I know who I have to thank for that! Now don't look so coy. I know that you told Nicole that this was the only hotel you could possibly recommend for all of the guests who are flying in for her birthday party next week. This is true, of course! But thank you all the same.'

'Well, she did ask for my opinion! I'm just so pleased that Nicole decided to celebrate her birthday at the farmhouse instead of staying in Paris. She visits so rarely these days.'

'Isn't that one of the advantages of looking after a holiday home? You get to enjoy a lovely house all to yourself for most of the year while Nicole is in Paris or travelling?'

Ella closed her eyes and grinned contentedly. 'You're right. I love the house and couldn't imagine living anywhere else except the Mas Tournesol. We're so lucky.' Then her eyes flicked open. 'Nicole deserves the best birthday party the old house has ever seen and I'm going to do my best to make sure that she gets it! After all, you are only sixty years young once in your life.'

'Absolutely! And don't forget. You know where to come for anything you need.'

Ella air kissed Sandrine on both cheeks and gave her a swift smile.

'You're a star! But now I'm going to be late for Dan when he gets home from school. See you tomorrow!'

Time to make her escape before Henri finished his afternoon coffee and the caffeine rush inspired him to come up with an even better offer.

'PSN Media have come back with an even better offer but are still dragging their heels on the employee numbers. I'm not sure how far we can push them on the benefits package without impacting the overall deal,' Matt explained, his exasperation clear even down a cell phone.

Sebastien Castellano drummed the fingers of both hands on the leather-covered steering wheel of his low-slung Italian sports car and fought to keep his blood pressure down by focusing on the rows of grapevines that stretched out from his parking spot to the low green hills and shrubby *garrigue* beyond the isolated narrow country road in the middle of the Languedoc.

He had just worked through the night and most of Thursday with Matt and a negotiation team from PSN Media in a stuffy conference room in Montpellier to pull together a deal that could save the jobs of the hundreds of employees who made up Castellano Tech in Australia.

And PSN Media *still* refused to take him seriously!

Yes, they were the premier telecoms company in the field worldwide, but this was his private company. The company he had created from nothing.

He was not going to stand back while PSN Media tried to buy him out with no regard for the welfare of his workforce and their families.

Until recently he had interviewed every single employee himself, and many had been loyal to him from the early days when he risked everything on a crazy idea for a digital media company. His team had built Castellano Tech into the top media company across Australia. And he was not going to let them down for the sake of a few dollars. Loyalty went both ways.

Shame that PSN Media could not see it that way. And unless they were prepared to change their stance, he would not be signing the deal on Monday. The chief executive of PSN Media would have to sail his private yacht out of Montpellier empty-handed.

Seb took a long breath before replying.

'I know you're working hard on this, Matt, but we made our position perfectly clear. PSN Media either guarantees the workforce keep their jobs and the same benefits package for at least the next two years... Or I walk away. No compromise.'

His chief financial officer sighed on the other end of the telephone. 'It could cost you a lot of money, mate.'

Seb sighed out loud. PSN Media thought that every man had a price and that they could buy him off with money. Well, they were badly wrong if they thought that Sebastien Castellano's principles of looking after his staff could be bought, and he was the man who was going to prove it to them.

Seb paused before going on. Matt was only doing his job as Seb's second in command and doing it very well. He had lost just as many hours of sleep as Seb had over the past couple of weeks. They both needed a break.

'A few hours ago we told PSN Media that they had the weekend to come up with their final offer. Sorry, Matt, but nothing has changed during the time it has taken me to drive to the Languedoc. End of story.'

'As stubborn as ever!' Matt replied with a snort. 'Let me make the call. *Then* I suggest we both take time to do something different. Sleep might be nice, for example.'

'Best idea I've heard all day!' Seb added, trying to bring a lighter tone to his voice. 'Take the rest of the day off and I'll catch up tomorrow.'

'It's a deal! Maybe I'll go and see some of those wild flamingos you were telling me about. And say hello to Nicole for me. She must be thrilled you're in France in time for her birthday. Call you tomorrow!'

The cell phone clicked off, leaving Sebastien sitting silently cocooned in air-conditioned luxury and bristling with anticipation and frustration. This merger with PSN Media was the deal of a lifetime. Within six months the communication systems he had designed with his team in a converted garage in Sydney could be in use around the world!

He was so close to achieving his dream he felt like punching his fist into the air!

Yes. He could have gone global with his own design in

time, but merging with PSN Media was the best and fastest way to roll out his award-winning technology.

After ten years of long days and longer nights he was so close to the biggest deal of his life, he could feel it!

Of course, there had been a heavy price to pay for the punishing workload he had given himself. He had left a series of failed relationships and missed family events behind in Sydney.

But it had been worth it.

A few days from now Castellano Tech could be part of a global company and he would have a seat on the board of directors with new responsibilities and a brilliant business future ahead of him. He would be working from his existing company offices in Sydney—the vibrant and exciting city that had provided him with means and opportunities to put his plans into action.

And he would have the time and money to work on a very special project.

Income from the sale of Castellano Tech would provide him with the finance and the technical resources to fully fund the Helene Castellano Foundation. His pilot schemes all over Australasia had already shown that access to modern technology and communication systems could make a difference in the remotest parts of the world. And he *would* commit the time and resources to make those projects work.

His mother, Helene, would have loved the idea.

He could hardly wait to get back to Sydney and start work. The team was already in place, the plans scoped out—all that was needed was the final green light and a substantial part of the nine-figure sum that PSN Media were paying him for the merger.

But that would have to be fitted into next week's diary.

Today he had a much nicer assignment.

Today he was going to meet up with Nicole Lambert, the

lovely woman who had been his stepmother for twelve tumultuous years before she divorced his father and moved back to Paris from Sydney. He had given her plenty of trouble as a teenager but she had stuck by him and supported his career choice every step of the way—with not much in the way of thanks at the time. Their relationship had only really taken off in the last few years they spent together in Sydney—but he still had a lot of making up to do.

When he'd agreed to start secret negotiations with PSN Media he had not known that the company had made their European headquarters in the south of France and the city of Montpellier—and within driving distance from the old Castellano family house in the Languedoc where Nicole had arranged to hold her sixtieth birthday party.

For the first time in years, they would be in the same country within travelling distance at the same time.

Thinking back, he had to agree it was going to be a first.

He had barely managed to make it to her fiftieth birthday in Sydney after a major satellite disaster during a telecoms launch in Japan. Christmas and other family celebrations were out of the question, even before she divorced his father. So the fact that he was actually willing and able to attend her birthday party was something new.

Perhaps that was why he felt totally guilty about the fact that he was going to miss the party after all.

Nicole had been so delighted when he accepted her party invitation that she had insisted that he stay at the Castellano farmhouse rather than a grand hotel.

Of course, Nicole had not accused him directly of having his own agenda, but she must have suspected that something else was going on and he regretted not being able to tell her the truth about the business negotiations, especially when the meeting was brought forward a full week by PSN Media to coincide with the arrival of their CEO.

Which meant that if the deal went through as he hoped, a week from now he would be back in Sydney with a new job and a full workload. And not in the Languedoc helping Nicole to celebrate her birthday. But at least he could spend the weekend with her. That was *something*, even if he had to keep his cell phone turned on and be prepared to drive back to Matt at a moment's notice.

It was time to go and tell Nicole the bad news and apologise for missing her birthday. If he was lucky, she might forgive him. Yet again.

Free at last!

Ella pedalled a little faster for a few minutes to build up extra speed on the straight section of empty country road, then leant back on her bicycle saddle, stretched out both legs either side of the front wheel and lifted up her head to face the brilliant sunshine of an early July afternoon in the Languedoc.

The soft breeze cooled her bare arms and lower legs, and she could almost taste the salt from the Mediterranean only a few miles away to the south. The combination of sunshine and breeze was heavenly and she breathed a blissful sigh of sensual delight.

The familiar stillness and calm of the surrounding countryside acted like a stimulant to her tired head. Sandrine had called just after eight that morning to ask if she could come in to help serve lunch to a party of American jazz enthusiasts who were spending the weekend at the jazz festival in a nearby town.

How she wished she could go with them to the festival! It would be wonderful to spend time revelling in the thrill and excitement of the music she had grown up with—the music she had loved to sing and play professionally since she was sixteen. The music her parents still played for a living. Sometimes she missed her old life so much it hurt to think about it. It was easier to block it out of her mind and focus on the joy of living in this lovely place. Dan had to come first. He was all that mattered now.

The downside of being a housekeeper was that occasionally the owner of the house she loved actually wanted to live in it! Nicole was lovely, kind and generous and had given her a home and a job when she needed it most. For that alone she was prepared to work harder than ever to make sure that Nicole's sixtieth birthday party was a brilliant success. For the first time since they moved here, the house was going to be alive and bursting with fun and laughter! Wonderful.

And then Nicole would be gone for a week or two before returning for the traditional August holiday break. Leaving Ella to spend precious school holidays having fun with Dan.

A warm grin cracked her face and she took a moment to take in the orderly rows of trained grapevines that fanned out from the road towards the low pine-clad hills on one side and the sea on the other. Birdsong and the rustle of the plane trees on the side of the road filled her ears. With the extra flapping of a tiny flag that Dan had fastened with half a roll of tape to the side of his cycle seat.

The simple pleasures of a six-year-old. That simple pennant fluttering in the breeze as they whipped along gave him such pure joy it would have been churlish to point out that it was a Spanish flag from his grandparents and not perhaps the most politically correct item for the south of France. No matter.

This part of the Languedoc was not like Nice or Marseilles. There were no bright city lights, busy city streets or trendy bars or four-star restaurants. This was the working rural farmland that made France so very special. Even the tourist season was short here, and local small hotels like Sandrine's were only truly busy between May and October when visitors flocked into the area to enjoy the wonderful beaches and small villages in the Carmargue or east to Provence.

She wanted, needed, more time with Dan. He was growing up so fast. And now she was his only parent her little boy needed her so badly it broke her heart to leave him in the evenings so that she could bring in some much-needed extra cash working as a cocktail pianist in Sandrine's hotel. Of course he had the best babysitters in France catering to his every need, and it was only for special parties like this one, but she loved their time together in the evenings, especially when the weather was warm enough to sit outside with the dogs.

Only one more day to the summer school holidays! Fantastic.

A prickle of apprehension went through her and she shivered despite the warm breeze. The school holidays meant something else. Something she did not want to think about. Dan would be spending two weeks with his grandparents in Barcelona. The same grandparents who had fought so hard to take control of Dan away from her after his father died—and almost succeeded.

Oh, Christobal! You would have loved how your little boy has turned out!

She only had to look into Dan's eyes to see the man she had loved and married in a whirlwind smile back at her. And nobody was ever going to threaten to take Dan away from her again. She was going to make sure of that.

Even though it had meant saying goodbye to her professional musical career.

The road lifted in a small rise and as she dropped her feet back into the pedals the call of the local seabirds brought her back to the real world and the fact that school would be closing for the day in under an hour. Time to get pedalling!

Seb slipped out from the cool interior of his car to stand on the grass verge in the warm sunshine.

Facing him on the other side of the two-lane tarmac road were the narrow gateposts of the Mas Tournesol. The Languedoc farmhouse where he had been born and spent the first twelve years of his life.

It seemed a very long time ago.

Which probably explained why he didn't remember it being so narrow or overgrown, but perhaps his perspective was different as a boy of twelve from a man of thirty?

Back then there had been two matching heavy wrought-iron gates with the name of the farmhouse picked out in metal. *Mas Tournesol. The Sunflower House.*

Now one of the gates had been knocked off its hinges and was lying in the gravel and grass on the side of the path with weeds growing up between the filigree metal. The gate must have been lying there for months. There was no sign of its partner.

Memories of a childhood playing in these fields told him that there was a rippling river on the other side of the straight row of rustling shady plane trees to his left where he had spent many happy hours fishing with his dad. The hedges on the right formed the boundary to the vineyards and sunflower fields his dad had sold to their neighbour only days before they emigrated, but the branches were taller now, choked with bushes and flowering shrubs.

A rush of sadness swept over him as he thought of the last time he had travelled down this lane on his way to a new life and his breath came out of his lungs in a juddering rattle.

Perhaps he wasn't as prepared for this as he thought he was?

Closing his eyes for a second, he saw his mother's flower garden again in his mind's eye, and walked along its winding paths, their heady scent filling the air against the buzz of honey bees and birdsong. And for a few moments he was transported back to that one place on this earth that would always be embedded deep inside and to the happiest period of time in his life.

Before his mother died.

Seb slowly opened his eyes into the glare from the sun and adjusted his designer sunglasses.

He had resisted coming back to this house for so many reasons. He might have lived in Sydney since the age of twelve and adored his life there, but he was still a Frenchman with his heart rooted in a deep heritage of land and culture. That could not be denied.

But something else drew him here. And the feeling unsettled him. At first he had put it down to anxiety about the business deal, but it was more than that. It was a strange sense of dissatisfaction and nagging unease that he had managed to push under the surface of his life for the past six months.

In fact, ever since he found out that his dad could not be his natural father.

Yes, he had been shocked by the surprise of it. Yes, he was astonished and taken aback, but he had not allowed the earthquake of the revelation to shake his world to pieces. He had grown up in a loving family with two caring parents and travelling the world on his charity projects had shown him just how precious a thing that was to a child.

No matter what the truth of his birth, he was proud of his mother and always would be. She had put him first. Only... he could not help but wonder why she had not told him the truth. Especially at the end when they all knew that time was short and he had spent many hours alone with her while she was still lucid. *Just talking.* And she had kept her secret.

Of course these past months had been filled with frenetic activity in the business. This was his first opportunity to take a real break, even if it was just a few hours in between discussions with Matt or the PSN Media legal team.

It made sense to spend a few days with Nicole and put his mind at ease.

Seb raised his shoulders up towards his ears, then dropped them back down to help relieve the tension. He needed *something* to put his mind at ease!

Because now he was back where he started!

Back to the house that now belonged to his former stepmother, Nicole, who won this house in the divorce from his dad.

It was hers to do with as she liked, even if that meant only using it as a holiday house for a few weeks a year. Or as a venue for her birthday party.

Nicole probably didn't even realise that this was the same week as the anniversary of his mother's death. And that his precious mother had taken her last breath in this house.

Seb pushed back his shoulders and lifted his head higher.

He knew one thing.

He would never again allow himself to love one person and one place so completely. Not when they could be snatched away from him at a moment's notice and he was powerless to prevent it. Especially knowing what he knew now.

He didn't believe in focusing on the past—only the future. And that meant honouring his mother through the charity work that was changing lives *now*. His old life was gone. Over. And the sooner he got back to Sydney and started on the new projects, the better.

He was here to spend the weekend with Nicole, catch up with his emails, then get back to the negotiating table first thing Monday morning before flying home. And that was all. The sooner the better.

A few minutes later Sebastien gingerly edged his rented very wide, very red and very shiny Italian sports car between the posts and started slowly down the gravel path, which was becoming more and more familiar by the metre.

A splash of frustration at his own inability to control his anxiety and apprehension for this stretch of rough roadway hit Seb hard and fast as cold as the air conditioning and he straightened his back and revved up the engine, oblivious to the flying gravel on the paintwork and thrilling to the glorious roar from under the bonnet.

He only hoped the gardens would not be as overgrown as the driveway, but he would find out soon enough. Once around the next blind corner, he would be able to see the rooftops of the house.

He had been a fool to come here and expect the place to be the same.

The car picked up a little speed as he reached the corner, his eyes focused on the skyline looking for the house.

And then he suddenly slammed the brakes on so hard that the antilock brakes on the car activated and he came to a screeching halt on the loose gravel.

Something was lying in the road. Looking at him.

CHAPTER TWO

HEART thumping, it took a few seconds for Sebastien to catch his breath and unclamp his fingers from the steering wheel.

Knuckles still white, he flung open the car door, stretched his long legs out of the bucket seat and onto the path, the full heat of the afternoon sunshine hot on the back of his neck.

Laid out across the middle of the road only a few inches from the front of his car was a large grey and dapple brown dog who clearly had no intention of moving. Anywhere.

The dog was lying with its head on his paws, his shaggy coat thick with dust from the road and an extra layer of gravel that had been scattered by the car's sudden stop.

And it was not just any dog. It was a hunting griffon, just like the one the kids on the next farm used to have when he was a boy. There was no mistaking the whiskers and heavy grey eyebrows on an old bearded face. He had not seen a griffon for years and just the sight of those intelligent eyes looking up at him made Seb smile as he stepped closer to check the dog was not injured.

Seb breathed a sigh of relief and hunkered down onto the back of his heels to take a closer look at this strange beast, who simply pushed a brown nose into Seb's outstretched hand and sniffed heavily through wide open-flared nostrils before yawning widely, displaying a good set of teeth.

'Not the best place to choose to have a nap, old mate,' Seb

muttered as the griffon wagged his tail, then turned on his side to have his tummy tickled, completely unharmed and apparently oblivious to the heart attack he had almost given the driver of the car who had come close to running him over.

The dog clearly liked what he smelt because Seb's hand was given an experimental couple of licks before the ears twitched and the intelligent yellow eyes below the hairy eyebrows looked up into his face.

Then suddenly the griffon's head shot up and both ears lifted as he pushed himself into a sitting position.

'What is it, boy? What have you heard?' Seb asked in French, but before the dog could bark a reply a gaggle of energy and four legs burst through the bushes and undergrowth and leapt up, barking loudly, and struck Seb straight in the chest with enough force to send him flying backwards from the gravel path into the thick grass. And briars. And nettles. And whatever other bio matter the local wildlife had left there since it was last cut.

It took a few seconds for Seb to gather his wits and raise both of his hands to fend off the attack from a very wet tongue and even wetter fur ball, but it was too late to block the pair of wet muddy front paws dancing and prancing with delight on the front of Seb's couture south sea island cotton business shirt. He didn't want to think about his suit trousers. Not yet. From this angle the monster looked like a younger version of the dog on the path. The dog equivalent to a hyperactive toddler high on additives and sugar.

The grin and tail wagging said it all.

This was dog language for: *Look what I've found! Someone new to play with! This is fun! Shall we see what tricks it can do?*

Its older friend or relative decided that guarding the path was boring and took to hunting in the bushes.

Okay. Time to move.

Seb pushed himself up on one elbow and was immediately pounced on by the young hound, who had found a piece of stick for him to throw, his paws diving back and forward for attention.

Seb stared at it for a moment before chuckling out loud to himself.

This was turning out to be quite a day! Being knocked over by a playful puppy was nothing compared to a very long flight followed by two days of hard business negotiations and a short drive in a strange car on French roads he had last seen eighteen years earlier.

With a sigh he turned to the hopeful hound that was still prancing with his throwing stick and waved him away with one hand before speaking.

'Not a chance, fella. Let me get back on my feet first.'

Only he never got the chance since the dog suddenly dropped the stick and took off at great speed back down the lane towards the main road, leaving Seb alone with the older dog, who was shuffling towards him for an ear rub.

'Just you and me, mate? Where do you live? Um?'

'Milou doesn't speak English. And he lives with me, Mr Castellano.'

It was a woman's voice. Her words were spoken in perfect English with the same type of accent he had heard many times from his British colleagues at the Castellano Tech headquarters back in Sydney. This particular bodiless voice was coming from the part of the lane he had just driven down so that its owner was hidden out of view behind his car.

Great! The first person he met in his old home village and he was flat on the back in the grass. And he had already been recognised. So much for wanting to keep a low profile!

He wondered how long she had been there watching him.

Seb sighed out loud and shook his head at just how

ridiculous he must look at that moment. He had two choices. Start yelling about out-of-control hounds off the leash, which would hardly be fair considering that this was a private road in the middle of the countryside, or smile and move on.

By pushing himself up with one hand in a spot with the least number of stinging nettles, Seb managed to get himself to a sitting position without looking too much like an idiot, before paying more attention to the woman—who clearly knew who he was.

'Hello! Are these your dogs? They're quite a handful,' he asked in English.

A pair of straw-coloured espadrille shoes on the ends of slim tanned female legs appeared in the space between the gravel and the bottom of his sports car, then walked slowly around the front so that they were standing directly in front of him.

The ankle within touching distance wore a thin ankle bracelet with tiny ceramic flowers—but the lace in this shoe was green while the lace in the other was stripy blue.

Suddenly more than a little curious about what the rest of the outfit might look like, Seb tried not to ogle as he lifted his gaze up at a yellow and white sundress with thin straps, which hung from tiny collarbones to fall above dark green cut-off Capri pants.

The last time he had seen an outfit like that was at a Christmas charity concert his company has sponsored at a local primary school in Sydney.

He was looking at Peter Pan. Or perhaps it was Tinker Bell?

Lifting his sunglasses with one hand, he risked looking into her face and a pair of shockingly pale blue eyes smiled down at him above a button nose and bow lips.

Her straight light brown hair was tied back from a smooth

forehead with a broad green headband the same colour as her trousers.

He changed his opinion. Peter Pan was never this pretty, or petite. She was tiny! Tinker Bell.

And for a moment his voice did not seem to work as she took one more extra look at him without the slightest bit of concern, then turned to play with the dogs, who had clearly learnt not to jump up on the hand that fed them.

'Hello, gang!' she said in French. 'How are you doing? Sorry that I'm so late! Have you missed me?'

Her knuckles rubbed each of the dogs in turn, and then she flung the stick down the road away from the car—'Go on. Meet you back at the house!' Then stood back and smiled as they raced away.

Only then did this lovely apparition smile down at Seb and switch back into English.

'Don't worry. You can play with them later!'

Play. He had no intention of *playing* with them! Seb sighed out loud and shook his head. Her cheery tone was too infectious for him to be angry with her for the ridiculous position he was in.

'Are they always so...*welcoming* to strangers?'

'Oh, no. Only men. Especially men in suits. They just love men in suits.'

Her eyes locked onto his shoes then his trousers and she shook her head from side to side.

'On the other hand you are never going to get the stains out of those trousers. Maybe that wasn't the best choice of outfit for rolling about with the hounds!'

Choice! He hadn't been given any choice at all!

'Do you need some help with the car, Mr Castellano? We don't have a garage but I've cleared a space in the barn for you to use during your stay. There is a mistral forecast.'

Staying? How did she know that? Maybe there was more to this girl.

'What makes you think that my name is Castellano? Miss...'

'Mrs Martinez. Ella Martinez.'

She cocked her head to one side for a moment and gave him a smile that created little dimples in each cheek as though she could read his mind as easily as a book.

'Relax. I'm not a journalist, or a mind-reader. Just Nicole's housekeeper. This means that I've been dusting your photographs on top of the grand piano every week for the past three years.'

She paused, then glanced sideways at the sleek red car blocking the lane. 'My little boy loves the pictures with all of the pretty ladies from the Monaco Grand Prix, but Nicole prefers the yacht racing. Strange she doesn't have one of you sitting on your...best pants, in the grass. Shall I run and find my camera?'

Seb dropped his head towards one shoulder before snorting out a reply. Nicole had a housekeeper! That made sense.

'Pleasure to meet you, Mrs Martinez, and please call me Seb. As for a camera? Thank you, but no. In fact I am highly relieved that you do *not* have a camera. I am embarrassed enough as it is.'

She chuckled gently before replying.

'Don't be. In fact I can see you are quite comfortable there,' Ella replied with a small bow. 'So I'll meet you back at the house whenever you feel like it. Your room is all ready for you. Bye for now. And it's Ella!'

With one small finger wave she strolled back behind his car and pulled a very strange-looking ancient bicycle with a child seat through the bushes, gracefully pushed off with one foot on the pedal and calmly cycled down the lane towards the house, leaving him sitting there surrounded by birdsong, the buzz of insects, dogs barking somewhere close and the ping, ping, ping of condensation dripping onto hot metal from the air conditioning in the car.

He watched in silence as a yellow butterfly landed on his outstretched hand, cleaned its feelers, and then lifted away.

'Well, you are a long way from Kansas now, Toto,' he mumbled before chuckling to himself, then chuckling louder, the ridiculous nature of his position hitting him right in the funny bone.

So much for the millions in his private bank accounts! Thank heavens the 'suits' at PSN Media could not see him now! They might think twice about buying a company from a farm boy.

This was turning out to be quite a day! And he had only just arrived.

It was almost a shame that he would not be staying long enough to find out more about Nicole's housekeeper!

A few minutes later, Seb stepped out from the car and felt the small hairs at the back of his neck stand on end.

The outside of the house had not changed that much in eighteen years. The farmhouse had been built from sandstone, which he already knew took on a golden-pink hue at dusk in the long summer evenings. The long wooden shutters that covered the windows and patio doors used to be painted a lavender-blue shade that he had never seen anywhere else except in this part of the Languedoc. Now they were dark blue with a pale yellow trim, which to his untrained eye was too harsh a colour contrast below the old terracotta tile roof spotted with patches of moss.

Any fears he might have had about his old home being a ruin were gone, replaced by a general sense of unease that brought a crease of tension to his forehead and a strange quiver of anxious fear in his gut matched with a cold sweat in the small of his back, despite the warmth of his shirt and suit jacket.

He had not expected to feel this way.

He had formed his own company, which had grown into an international multimillion-dollar business, he thought nothing of giving presentations to hundreds of strangers and yet here he was, standing in the warm sunshine, and nervous of taking those few steps through the tall and, oh, so familiar wooden door that led inside the house where he had grown up.

Suddenly a light breeze picked up through the resin-heavy poplar and plane trees and carried the scent of lavender, roses, honeysuckle and sweet white jasmine. Instantly his mind was flooded with so many memories that he sucked in a breath to help steady himself.

Thousands of moments and images that all called out the same message.

You've come home.

After almost a lifetime away from the country of his birth, this area, this village and this farmhouse…he was home.

And the very thought shocked him more than he thought possible.

Home was the apartment in Sydney with the stunning views over the city where he slept some of the time and kept his clothes. Sydney was his home. Not here. Not any more.

He had decided eighteen years ago that he would never again rely so much on one person for his happiness. The agony of being dragged away from this house had destroyed that kind of childish sentimentality for good.

He did not do sentimental.

Indeed the notion shocked him so much that when Ella sauntered around the side of the house and stood next to him looking up at the window, he barely noticed her presence until her light sweet voice broke the silence.

'Has it changed much since you were here last?'

He half turned and blinked in confusion as he fought to regain the connection between his brain and his mouth. *Had she been reading his mind?*

She tilted her chin upward and looked at him eye to eye. 'Nicole told me that you grew up here. I was just wondering if the house is still the same as you remember. That's all!' And with that she turned away to pick off dead flower heads from the cascades of stunning blossoms billowing from two giant stone urns that stood either side of the main door, giving Seb a chance to put together a sensible reply.

'Er, no. Not much. I noticed the gates are down—' he sniffed '—but the house itself looks pretty much the same.' He raised one hand toward the shutters with a nod. 'The colour scheme is different. Not sure it works.'

There was an exasperated sigh from Ella who twirled around to face him and planted a fist firmly on each hip.

'Thank you! Nicole hired an "interior designer"—' at this point she lifted her hands and made quotation marks with her fingers '—to remodel the old place in the spring.'

Ella nodded towards the shutters and shuddered with her shoulders. 'He was a lovely charming man who had a wonderful eye for textiles but had *no* clue about the local style. I mean none. Zip. *De nada.* Zero.'

She bent towards Seb as though confiding in him. 'I may be from London but I have lived here long enough to know that this house does not need navy-blue shutters!'

Then she stepped back to the flowers and expertly snipped off a perfect half-open pink rose bud with a few glossy green leaves with a fingernail.

Before Seb could reply she skipped up, stood on tiptoe and slipped the rose into the buttonhole of his made-to-measure suit jacket, smoothing it into place on his soft cashmere collar with the fingertips of one hand.

'There. That's better. No thorns, you see. I planted a rose without thorns. Do you like it?'

Ella raised her brows and looked Seb straight in the eye with an intense look and suddenly her mouth twitched as if she was only too aware that as he looked down to admire the new addition to his wardrobe he had a delightful view down the front of her yellow and white sundress.

For a few moments he completely forgot his troubles as he admired the tanned skin and soft curves under the thin yellow and white cotton. A white lacy bra peeked out either side of the dress, which had slipped down over one shoulder, and he felt the sudden urge to lift the strap of her sundress back into position. But that would have meant touching her skin and finding out if it was truly as soft and smooth as it looked.

It was very tempting but also totally prohibited.

Oh, no. Not going there. Bad idea! He liked city-smart women who knew how to run multimedia servers and could make orbiting satellites obey his commands. Not elves in green pants. Especially when she released her hand from his jacket and he saw a diamond and sapphire wedding band on her left ring finger.

Mrs Martinez! A married housekeeper. Okay. Very prohibited! That made sense. He vaguely recalled that she mentioned a little boy. *A married woman with a family.* The perfect housekeeper and gardener and maintenance man team to look after the house when Nicole was away.

Mr Martinez was a very lucky man.

He brought his attention back onto the trellis of roses above her head before croaking out a reply. 'I do like it. It's a stunning display. Thank you, Mrs Martinez.'

She gave his jacket a small final pat and smiled back at him before dropping back onto her heels.

'You are most welcome. The main rose garden is still at the back of the house.' She paused for a second, then gestured to the car and flashed him a half-smile. Then it was back to business. 'Even in that mobile sofa you call a car, you must be tired after your long drive. Ready to see what he did to your old bedroom?'

This *had* been his room. The ancient bathroom with the cracked enamel basin had been in the room next door. The wall must have been knocked through to create this stylish tiled ensuite. But the room itself had not changed that much and the floorboards certainly creaked in the same places.

The rush of memories threatened to overwhelm him again as he looked out from the square window onto the walled garden at the back of the house where he had played and learnt to love life.

And then it hit him.

Ella Martinez had made up *this* room for him. Not the spare room his grandmother had used when his mother was terminally ill, but *his* old room. How had she known that this had been his room?

He turned back towards the door. Ella was standing at the top of the stairs simply watching him and her smile was like sunshine inside the dark cool shade of the corridor.

Seeing the look on his face, she said, 'I worked it out,' then pointed to the wall behind his back. 'From the wallpaper.'

Then she grinned and took pity on his confusion. 'Relax. I'm not psychic. When the decorators stripped off the layers of wallpaper they found some interesting blasts from the past.'

Ella glanced back over each shoulder, and then peeked down the staircase, as though checking that they were not being overhead, before leaning closer.

'I'm sure lots of teenagers back then plastered their bedroom walls with posters of their favourite pop groups. In fact—' and at this she leant back, pursed her lips, and nodded before going on '—I'm willing to bet that you would sing along to your favourite records holding a hairbrush as a pretend microphone. Am I right?'

Seb felt the back of his neck flare with heat and embarrassment, only then he looked at Ella and the laughter that had been teasing the corner of her mouth bubbled through into a full warm giggle.

Nobody had dared giggle at Sebastien Castellano for a very long time, only there was something in Ella's voice that told him that her comments were not insulting or meant to embarrass him. She was simply sharing a joke.

And suddenly the irony of his old posters being found almost twenty years later hit him hard and he made the mistake of looking back at Ella. He started to laugh, really laugh, the sound so unfamiliar to him that he realised with a rush that he had not laughed like this for a long time.

'Quite wrong,' he eventually managed to reply, wiping the tears from his eyes. 'It wasn't a hairbrush. It was a can of my grandmother's hairspray. And the old wardrobe had a full-length mirror so I could admire my new denim outfit in its full glory.'

'In that case consider yourself lucky. My parents are full-time musicians and I was actually born above their jazz club in London. Can you imagine what the noise was like every evening?' Ella paused and looked up at the ceiling before sighing out loud. 'Actually it was amazing and I adored it.' She shrugged her shoulders. 'Hey ho. On with the show. I'll leave you to get settled. If you need anything I'll be in the same place as the coffee and cookies.'

Seb nodded. 'On with the show? Okay, that sounds good. One question. What time are you expecting Nicole today? I need to catch up with her as soon as she gets back.'

Ella's brows came together and her mouth twisted in surprise. 'Nicole? Nicole isn't here. Didn't she tell you?'

Seb's frown deepened as he looked up at Ella.

'Not here? I don't understand. She emailed me a few weeks ago to make sure that my plans had not changed. Has something happened? Is she okay?'

Ella raised and lowered both hands. 'Fine. As of this morning she is just fine. A little wet maybe, but fine. What is not so fine is the weather in Nepal. The monsoon rains have come early and she is finding it slow going walking back from Everest Base Camp. They've already missed their original flight. So, you see, Nicole won't be back for at least another few days.'

Then she added with a small shoulder shrug, 'Until then you are stuck with me.'

CHAPTER THREE

ELLA peeped out of the kitchen window to see if Seb had woken from his nap yet.

She had hoped that he would be awake in time to move the very fine example of Italian design he called a motor vehicle that was still half parked, half abandoned, on the round driveway at the front of the house, before Dan's schoolteacher tried to squeeze her tiny car through.

Everything in the garden was quiet and tranquil. A normal summer afternoon.

Strange. From what Nicole had told her, Sebastien Castellano was used to living life at top speed. Rushing here and there, always looking for the next project or the next business deal where he could have fun bringing modern communications to a company or even a city! Burning the candle at both ends with his remarkable workload and high-profile fund-raising events.

She had not been joking about the silver-framed photographs on the piano that needed regular dusting and polishing. Nicole had built up quite a collection.

Although there was something odd about the photographs. Something that she had never mentioned out of respect for Nicole's personal life.

The collection did not have one single photo of Sebastien with his father or with Nicole. Not one family picture. Seb wasn't even on Nicole's wedding photo, and he must have been in his late teens when Nicole married Seb's father.

It had always seemed strange. Especially compared to her own personal albums of photos. She treasured the family photos with her parents and Dan. Christobal's family loved formal portraits taken by professionals in a studio, and she was so grateful that she could show Dan what his father had looked like, but she was happy with a spur-of-the-moment shot taken with a cheap pocket camera.

Not for Nicole.

Of course, there was one great advantage in being the person responsible for polishing Sebastien Castellano's face every week. She could allow her imagination to run riot about what the man himself was like in the flesh. Nicole was not the only one thrilled when Sebastien accepted the invitation to her birthday party—out of the blue!

Ella chewed her lower lip. She had hardly believed her eyes when she saw who owned the car blocking the driveway. How could any man look so handsome sitting on his bottom in the hedge playing with Milou and Wolfie?

Although it did make her wonder what he truly was doing here. From what little Nicole had told her, Seb had gone out of his way to *avoid* coming to see her in the past, and he never took a holiday so it was more than a little odd that he turned up like this. Perhaps Nicole was correct and he had his own agenda for being in this part of France?

Ella shook her head with a smile.

Silly girl. Speculating her life away!

It was such a lovely day she could hardly blame Seb for taking time away from work to relax and enjoy the garden of his old home after the long flight from Australia.

While it was time for her to get back to work and for one of her favourite tasks, which Dan adored helping her with. Shelling peas under the trees.

Ella went through the house to the kitchen, picked up her colander and a basket of fresh peas in the pod from the local market, and carried them out to the patio table.

And stopped abruptly, the peas skidding in the basket.

Seb was lying on a recliner with a beaker of now-cold coffee and a home-made cookie from Dan's stash on a tray on the low table next to him.

Fast asleep.

His chest lifted gently up and down under a once crisp formal shirt, now smudged with dog paw marks.

Ella leant as quietly as she could on the edge of the hardwood table and looked at him. *Really* looked at him.

Dappled sunshine flickered over his skin as the light breeze moved through the branches of the trees, lifting the wide leaves to create a mosaic of light and shade on the patio lounger.

The strong handsome face was a road map of luxurious places where the very rich and powerful people liked to visit in their drive to become richer and even more powerful.

Places where sensitive souls like her own would burn up in the intense heat of that fire and driving passion. And from what she could see Sebastien Castellano was at best a little scorched and at worst exhausted from fighting back the flames.

His dark brown eyebrows were thick, wide and set into a powerful broad brow, which had been designed by nature to make his look fierce and intense even when asleep on the lounger.

His dark brown hair was expertly cut into a formal business look—but just a little longer than the average, leaving dark strands falling across his brow and collar.

He had a strong nose, and as she peered closer a sprinkle of sun-kissed freckles made her smile. Probably from his days spent yacht racing in the tropics. Or scuba-diving trips to the

Great Barrier Reef. Something like that. Nothing as mundane as shelling peas in a farmhouse in the Languedoc.

A five o'clock shadow of dark brown stubble stretching down from his sideburns and across his upper lip softened the fierce-looking square jaw, which could have belonged to a prize fighter or matador, rather than a self-made entrepreneur.

His bottom lip was narrow compared to a sumptuous upper lip that photographers loved to capture at prestigious award dinners or business functions.

She could not resist a small sigh. *Oh, how she envied him his lifestyle!* She had loved her old life on the road! Travelling with her parents from town to town, playing jazz and classical concerts wherever they could. She had lost count of the number of weddings, birthdays, festivals and fairs where the Bailey trio had shared their passion for music.

She had spent so many years on the road since she turned sixteen the countries that they visited sometimes blended into one. Spain and Portugal had been amazing, but it was the three months they spent in southern India that she remembered the most. The colours, the energy, the dusty roads that choked you just before you had to sing for two hours! She remembered every minute. And was grateful that she had those memories to look back on.

That life was very far from this safe farmhouse where she could give Dan the benefits of a settled life.

Yes. *You are a very lucky man, Seb Castellano.*

Only at that moment Seb's mouth moved in a charming little twitching action at the side and it hit her hard that Dan did exactly the same thing when he dozed off sometimes.

Ella smiled to herself.

Not exactly the image of the intimidating power-hungry master of Castellano Tech that Nicole kept cuttings about from business magazines!

So this was Nicole's celebrity stepson! Or was that infamous?

He had reacted so oddly when he found out that Nicole was not going to be back until Monday at the earliest. From what Nicole had told her, they were not close and never had been, but he did seem genuinely concerned that she had been delayed.

What was it that he wanted from her friend and employer that he could not ask over the phone, or in an email? What was he here for?

Whatever the reasons, this real live version of Sebastien Castellano looked as though he needed a good meal followed by decent sleep in a soft bed.

Failing that, a power nap in a warm garden would do him good.

Which meant two things; first she had to head off attacks from both the dogs who had disappeared once they had been fed, and her son who should be arriving home from school at any minute.

Turning carefully on the balls of her feet, Ella lifted her basket of peas as quietly as she could—and almost dropped them when Seb's cell phone started ringing.

He stirred twice, sighed loudly, and sat up, quickly grasping onto the cell phone, flicking it open and saying, Yes, before his eyes had even come into focus.

The image was of someone living on a knife edge and suddenly her envy was replaced with pity.

The familiar ring tone broke the deep sleep Seb had been enjoying and he yawned widely and uncreaked his neck muscles as he checked the caller identity and blinked a few times.

'Matt? How are you doing? Oh. Insect bites? Ah, yes. The infamous Camargue mosquito. Should have warned you about those. Sorry, mate.' He chuckled briefly with a closed mouth before getting back to business. 'I take it you've had a call from PSN Media?'

Seb's left hand rubbed vigorously along the line of his powerful jaw and the longer-than-normal designer stubble, then his mouth curved into a knowing smile. 'I knew they would come around on the employee benefits in the end. You've done a great job, Matt. What's that? His private yacht? Trying to impress us, is he? Interesting.'

His hand lifted, then dropped onto his knee. 'If Frank Smith wants to fly a corporate lawyer down from Paris on Monday morning so that we can sign the contract on his yacht, then I'm happy to turn up and enjoy his hospitality—providing the numbers add up.'

Then a sniff. 'Right. In that case, we'll go through the fine print Sunday evening before dinner. Close the deal Monday. Thanks. You too.'

The fingers of both hands clenched hard into his palms as his brain reeled with the implications of the news.

Yes! PSN Media had come up with a compromise on the benefits package. And the chief executive of PSN Media was remarkably choosy when it came to inviting people onto his private yacht. This was a first. It was actually going to happen!

And he knew exactly who to share it with.

In an instant he swiped his finger across the touch screen on his top-of-the-range cell phone, found the contact number he was looking for, and the call was answered in his Sydney office within three rings.

'Hi, Vicky. Seb. It's good news. You've got the green light to start planning the phase two Foundation projects.'

Seb smiled at the shriek of delight and laughter that burst out from the talented project manager he had hired to look after the Helene Castellano Foundation.

'Thought you'd like that. I'll be back in the office next

Wednesday and want to see the projected timelines and budgets some time before Friday's meeting. Think you can manage that? Thought so. What else are weekends for, right? Thanks, Vicky. You too. Yes, it is brilliant news.'

Seb closed his eyes, shook his head with a relaxed grin, then stretched out the length of his body on the lounger like a cat waking from a long sleep, with both arms behind his head.

Vicky was the best in the business and one of the most passionate and enthusiastic people he had ever met. She had chosen to spend her retirement making best use of the contacts she had made during forty years in investment banking. This time next week she would have a dream budget to work with and Seb could get on with the hands-on work implementing the communication systems.

All he had to do was ensure that the offer on the table was signed with no last-minute problems.

Then he would really feel like celebrating. It might be winter back in Sydney but he didn't see any reason why he could not take his team down to the beach for the day! They had worked for this just as hard as he had. They deserved a decent party before the real hard work kicked in. He could not wait to get back to Sydney and get the ball rolling!

He allowed himself a smile.

Then spun around, suddenly conscious that he was not alone, and for a few seconds he had to work out where he was. Then his fists clenched in anger at the intrusion into his private business and thoughts.

He had let his guard down for a moment. Stupid!

Ella recoiled for a second with Seb's sudden movement. A handful of pea pods fell onto the patio stones and she leant down to scoop them up.

Only as she did so Ella recognised that three things had become quite apparent.

Two of them were attached to her chest and she was pointing them quite brazenly under strained cotton and a low-cut sundress at the man whose eyes were now at the same height as her own.

Idiot! She was not used to having men around the house. She really had to think about her clothing for the next week if she wanted to avoid this happening again.

And then came number three. Sebastien Castellano was looking at her.

Amber eyes the colour of beech trees in autumn met hers, flashed with startled energy and widened slightly in surprise that he was being observed so closely. And then those eyes seemed to warm as though melting in the summer heat.

Suddenly she understood what the fuss in the gossip columns was all about.

His eyes were not just amber, they were the deepest dark caramel brown flecked with gold, with a dark centre that pulled you in, like pool of deep, deep water so dark she would be scared to dive into it for fear of never reaching the bottom. Or of never being able to swim back to the surface.

She had seen a tiny glimpse of that look when he had looked down the front of her dress earlier—which had been completely her own fault. And he had been gentleman enough to look away as soon as he could. But now she was taking in the full blast and the depth and intensity were only too clear.

Ella could feel the beat of her heart in her neck and wrist respond to the power of something very primal that came from a very masculine man who had started to relax once the tension of answering the call had ebbed away, warm and stretching sensuously in the sunshine only inches away from her.

He didn't say anything, or move from his recliner, he simply turned his head and looked back at her. The moment stretched until she could feel it like an elastic band pulled tighter and tighter until she was frightened about what would happen when all of that energy was released.

Heart racing, she opened her mouth to speak but didn't get the chance, because in that fraction of a second doors started slamming all over the house, a car crunched away on the gravel drive and a distinctive voice called out in the local French dialect, 'Mum-m-m! Milou got out again!'

Seb stared at the dog-shaped apparition that joggled towards him to make sure that he was not still dreaming, and blinked hard a couple of times.

Nope. He was awake.

The child's voice had emerged from behind the huge armful of dog that had grown tired of being carried, and the bundle of fur and paws had now decided to come alive and was struggling like a wild thing to be free now he was home.

The child made it as far as the table before he released the furry creature that dropped into a heap of low woof and flying fur and dust onto the patio tiles.

Seb wasn't dreaming after all. And the creature looked remarkably like the old griffon hound that had almost ended up under his tyres on the path.

The cherub of a dark curly-haired boy who emerged tried to brush some of the dog hair from his school shirt, looked at the mess and claw marks, then looked up in astonishment as he realised that there was a strange man lounging on one of the recliners.

'Daniel Charles Bailey Martinez. You. Have not been doing your job.' Ella was bending forward now, her head tilted to one side as she spoke to her son.

The child looked up from the dog towards Sebastien, and

then back to his mother, shrugged and turned around, dropping his shoulders.

'Sorry, Mum.'

'Don't apologise to me, young man. He made it as far as the traffic this time. If Mr Castellano here didn't have good brakes on his car, your old pal Milou might have been injured, and you—' she was pointing now '—you would have to explain how Milou came to be taking a nap in the middle of the road. And that would be. Serious. So, you know what to do.'

She gestured with her head over one shoulder towards Seb, and nodded.

The cherub moved slowly forward with his head down, sidled one step at a time until he was standing in front of Seb, shuffling from side to side, his hands stuffed deep into the pockets of his school trousers.

'Thanks for not killing Milou.'

Seb looked at the little boy's head, then at the dog lying on his back at his feet, waiting to have his tummy tickled. Seb was so used to people around him showing due deference he was not accustomed to a child's version of an apology. He quickly recovered as best he could and replied with a, 'No problem,' in English, before wondering how that translated to child talk.

The child glanced up and whispered in an excited voice, 'Did you have to screech your car? I mean, did you have to skid and everything?'

'Dan!'

His head dropped again.

'I was just asking!'

Dan glanced up at Seb and gave him a toothy smile, which would be breaking hearts in the very near future. It was a signal between boys.

'Matter of fact I did have to screech my tyres. Grit was

flying everywhere. It was like being in one of those rally cars. Even had to skid a bit along the grass.'

'Cool!'

'Oh, I give up. Boys!' Ella turned back to her peas while Milou chose that moment to issue a loud yawn and settled down to sleep after his exciting adventure.

Dan sidled up closer to Sebastien and looked once at Ella, who gave him one single nod before asking in a low whisper, 'Is that *your* car outside? It's the biggest I've *ever seen*.'

Seb bent down from the waist so that he was at the same level as Dan. Interesting. Apparently he had just been given security clearance from Ella.

'Yes, it is my car, but your mother is right, mate.' Seb shook his head. 'I would have felt just awful if I had hurt your dog. I only just managed to turn away in time. Were you supposed to be making sure he didn't make it to the road?'

There was a nod but, from the way the boy's bottom lip was quivering, Seb took the initiative and moved to a different question. He was not used to children at the best of times and he certainly didn't have the training to handle tears.

'Tell me about the other dog. The younger one. Where does he live?'

The little boy glanced back towards Ella and Milou, twisted his mouth from side to side, made a decision, and replied in a big gush, 'Milou is really old now, but Wolfie is a puppy and lives next door at the farm and comes to see us sometimes. Want to see where Wolfie gets through the fence?'

Dan's eyes brightened and he clutched at Seb's sleeve. 'Maybe you can help fix the fence? That way Milou won't squeeze out in the gap? Can you? Can you fix it? Please?'

'Dan! Please don't pester Mr Castellano,' Ella whispered in a kind voice, but Dan had taken firm hold of Seb's sleeve and clearly needed a reply.

Seeing as a working knowledge of hand tools and do-it-yourself carpentry were not skills that Seb considered priorities in software and communication systems design, he decided that mending fence panels was not a job he was qualified to undertake. Besides, Mr Ella Martinez would probably be back from his day job or whatever other task took him away from home on a Thursday afternoon, and could no doubt do a far better job.

So he replied with the first thing that came into his head.

'Why not wait for your dad to come home and then you can fix the fence together? I'm sure he'll do a far better job than I can.'

There was a sudden intake of breath from the tiny brunette sitting at the table, and as Seb glanced up her hands had stilled over the peas and her lips were pressed tight together as she stared intensely into the basket.

This was not a good sign.

Then Dan was shaking his head at him and tugging at his sleeve more urgently, demanding his attention.

'My daddy is in heaven! And Milou is very naughty! Aunty Nicole is having a party. And there are going to be lots of cars and vans and things and that means...*big trouble*.'

Dan sighed twice between these two final words and released Seb to lift both hands in the air.

Seb paused for a second in appreciation of the simple, devastatingly logical thinking of a small boy. Whose daddy was in heaven. And whose fence was broken, and probably had been broken for quite some time.

Perhaps he could apply the same simple childlike logic to the simple request for help? This was Nicole's house. He was Nicole's former stepson. In a strange way that sort of made him responsible in Nicole's absence. Not that he *wanted* to be responsible but...?

Decision made. Seb swung his legs down from the recliner and nodded. 'I can see that could be a problem. How about you show me how Milou made his escape? Then maybe between the two of us we can come up with a plan to keep him safe from now on. What do you say?'

The little boy glanced back towards Ella and Milou, twisted his mouth from side to side, made a decision, and said, 'My name is Daniel. What's yours?'

'Well, back in Australia my friends call me Seb. How about that?'

'Okay,' Dan replied with a shrug as he meshed his little fingers into Seb's open hand and tried to drag him off towards the barn.

Seb stood in silence and glanced down at Dan's small fingers clasped tightly around his. He hadn't been expecting that. Some of his team were married with children but the majority of the technical experts who worked with him in design were single men. He was not used to having children around him in his workplace or his daily life.

Especially children who insisted on holding his hand. He could not recall that ever happening before.

This was going to be a first. But he was up for new experiences. He could handle it.

'Come on, Seb,' Dan called out, and tugged at his hand. 'Or Wolfie will break Milou out again.'

Ella watched as Seb paused for a second, dumbfounded, before closing his fingers around her son's relatively tiny fist and walking slowly back out to the sunlit garden. Dan's little dark head kept glancing up as he chatted nonstop about the fence and the gaps between the trees, and how his mum and Yvette had fixed them high on one side, but Wolfie had jumped on the fence when he came to see Milou and it all just went squish, and…

Seb nodded but did not reply. He had opened up a personal organiser one-handed and was probably looking for the telephone number of a local odd-jobs man at that very minute. This of course was what *she* should have done. If she had thought of it.

How could he get a word in? Dan had said more than enough for both of them.

Oh, Dan.

Ella hadn't been expecting that outburst about his dad. Dan was wonderful with adults he knew, but he sometimes found it difficult to approach men. Especially strangers he had never met before.

She sat and watched the unlikely pair for a few seconds in silence. The tall business executive in the designer clothing, wearing shoes that cost more than her week's wages, was giving his full attention to a little boy who was revelling in the simple fact that he had a man to talk to for once.

A man who did not have other children to deal with and play with.

A man Dan could talk to and keep all to himself. Even it was only for a short while.

And her heart broke for her fatherless child who would never know the love his father had felt for him. One day she might find someone who loved both her and Dan, but in the meantime she could only hope that Dan did not become too attached to Seb in the short time that he was going to be with them.

Perhaps having Seb in the house for a few days was not such a good idea after all?

CHAPTER FOUR

SEB turned over in bed, pulled an overstuffed pillow over his head and decided that there was no way he could go back to sleep.

His body clock was still set on Sydney time, and it was too dark and quiet in his old room for his brain to calm itself long enough for sleep. His mind was still racing with the exhilaration of the events of the last two days and he had tossed and turned most of the night. Twice he had reached out to the bedside table and typed a couple of notes on his personal organiser.

He was totally exhilarated at the prospect of completing the deal with PSN Media—but more than a little frustrated that he had come all the way out here to see Nicole only to find her still on holiday. Both of which had conspired to rob him of sleep.

Seb tossed aside his pillow.

Back in Sydney Nicole was famous for being the least sporty person he had known, which was quite an achievement in *that* city. And now she was trekking in Nepal? She certainly had changed in the last three years—it would have been nice to catch up. But unless Nicole managed to get back to France in the next thirty-six hours, he was going to leave without seeing her. And he was sorry for that.

But now it was time to make a move.

Untangling himself out of the mess of twisted bedcovers, Seb tested the temperature of the cool floor tiles on his bare feet and shuffled across the room in his T-shirt and shorts to open the window. It would not take him long to repack his hand luggage.

It had made sense for him to stay here overnight but he could work a lot more effectively back in Montpellier with Matt and a hard wire connection to the Internet rather than a wireless telephone connection.

Warm sunlight slanted in, startlingly bright and welcoming, then blinding him with the brilliance of a summer sunrise as he pushed open the shutters.

In an instant his old boyhood bedroom was transformed in that unique quality of light in the Languedoc that reflected back from the tall ivory-painted walls.

The honey-coloured armoire, which had seemed so bizarre and antiquated the previous evening, now looked perfect set against the pastel colour scheme that had been chosen for the textiles in the room.

He ran his forefinger along the faded floral stencils of leaves and pale pink flowers and wondered what gentle hand had worked the design with such care and detail.

One thing was for sure.

This furniture and this decor had certainly not been here eighteen years ago. Back then this house had been clean, comfortable, and a home. Now he felt as though he had just spent the night in some theatre set for a typical French country house.

All the pictures were perfectly parallel to the floor and every square centimetre of exposed wood had been sanded and waxed to create one uniform sheen. Imperfections were clearly not allowed.

But it *was* beautiful. Stylish and what you would expect to find in this part of France.

For a hotel room.

Pushing harder on the shutters, he leant forward onto the stone window sill and looked out across the garden at the back of the house. Some things had not changed.

And his senses reeled at the sensory overload.

The early morning sun shimmered hot above the terracotta roof tiles, distorting the cobalt blue of the sky with ripples and waves of colour. Any cloud had already been burnt away to leave a pristine expanse of unbroken clear sky.

He breathed in the air, fragrant and clean. Somewhere in the distance dogs were barking and he could just about detect the rumble of traffic on the nearby road he had driven down the previous evening, but apart from that there was only birdsong.

And the sound of a woman's voice singing somewhere in the garden below.

It was such a sweet sound that at first he thought it must be a radio station or recording, but as he listened the song was broken up by snatches of humming and a gentle sniff followed by a strange sequence of made-up words and tunes.

The sound was so intriguing, bizarre and interesting that he could not help but smile just hearing it. It was somehow—joyous. As though the owner wanted to express out loud her love of life and living and music.

And that spirit and energy was so contagious there should be a health warning!

The vague headache that had been nagging him for days seemed to lift away as he listened and he could feel his shoulders unclench.

Suddenly he didn't want to stand inside and look *out* at the warmth and the sunshine. He wanted to experience it for himself. He wanted to immerse himself in this place he used to know so well for a few more moments before he headed back to the city and the luxury of a five-star hotel conference room.

Getting dressed could wait. His normal urge to turn on his laptop and log onto his international Wi-Fi connection. Could wait. *Well, for now anyway. He would be back on the road in an hour.*

It took only a few minutes for Seb to skip down the stone stairs, draw open the wide front door and stroll out barefoot onto the golden sandstone paving that curved around the side wall of the house to the part of the patio that was bathed in sunlight.

Seb's brain tried to assimilate the intensity of the colours he was looking at. And failed.

Lavender bushes lined the paths and exploded in long swathes in huge clipped hedges, mixed with what looked like pale blue bellflowers and pink peonies in full bloom. Rambling roses covered the stone wall above glossy dark green leaves.

Dominating the garden was the old pollarded plane tree that had been planted when the house was built. Large flat leaves provided perfect dappled shade over the patio area outside the kitchen door all summer.

Birdsong filled the air. Mixed with the lapping of water on stones from the nearby river. Otherwise there was only the hum of bees on the flowers.

It was so quiet it felt as though he were the only human being for miles.

Perhaps he had imagined that musical voice and was still half dreaming after all?

The warm breeze was fragrant with the scent of flowers and herbs. And something else—a scent that was unique to this special garden. Rich and sweet and spicy. Like cinnamon apples, only sweeter.

One sniff of that scent and he was taken back to his life in this house. Dozens of white rose blossoms cascaded out of the urns and trailed in profusion up into a white-painted trellis on the wall of the house where the rose branches were intertwined with sweet white jasmine to create a heady aroma.

Musk rose and jasmine. It was wonderful. Magical. His mother would have loved it.

A bristle of discomfort shivered across his back.

Helene Castellano was the only mother that he had ever known. The fact that she might not be his birth mother did not change the close bond that they had shared. He was so proud of her and everything she represented.

Except that, as he looked around this garden, the thoughts and concerns he had pushed to the back of his mind since he had found out that his dad was not his father started to slip through gaps in the barriers he had put in place. Each fresh memory of his life in this house rose like a bubble to the surface, bringing with it fresh concerns.

Seb sucked in a deep breath of the fragrant warm air.

Despite his best intentions, he was still infuriated with his dad for refusing to discuss the matter of his parentage with him. And he simply did not understand why he did not want to tell him the truth. It was illogical. They were adults and it had all happened thirty years ago.

He could at the very least have told him whether he had another father, or whether he had been adopted! He would not have judged his mother any differently if she had a previous relationship before marrying Luc Castellano six months before he was born. Everyone made mistakes in life. And she had been a wonderful mother to him.

What if he had been adopted? Perhaps there was a family out there looking for him? He did not need one, but it was something to consider.

Unless of course there was something about his real parents that his dad did not want him to know. Something that could be damaging to him, and possibly even his career? That was possible—but if anything it made his need to find out the truth even more pressing.

Perhaps their hasty emigration to Australia had been because of his real father?

He had so many questions and so few answers.

Seb closed his eyes and fought to calm his racing mind.

This was not what he was here for. That was in the past. *He would persuade his dad to tell him when he got back to Sydney.* Perhaps he could take some photos of the place before he left? Just to remind his dad of their happy family life in this house? It could be just the extra ammunition he needed to help change his mind.

This was probably why Seb stepped out from under the shade of the patio onto the hot stone and pressed his bare toes onto the warmth beneath his feet.

The heat seemed to radiate upwards like energy from the earth until it reached his head and he leant backwards to take in the maximum amount of the glorious warmth on his head and throat.

The balmy breeze caressed his face, shoulders and exposed lower arms.

With one breath he closed his eyes and wallowed in the moment.

Serene. Tranquil. Warm. Heaven. He could stay like this for ever. Arms outstretched.

He was instantly transported back to another time in this very garden and his life as a boy. Memories flooded into his head. Memories he had not even thought about for many years, memories buried deep down inside his private life, which the paparazzi would never know about or expose to the public world.

Memories of gentle hands and kind adult voices saying how sorry they were, and how much they would miss her. His grandmother in black. Friends and neighbours, school pals.

His mother had died in her favourite month of the year. And that was more than sad. She would have enjoyed this garden.

His reverie was broken by a snuffling noise coming from the direction of the kitchen to his right, followed by the unmistakeable sound of the same woman's voice, humming along to an old show tune.

Seb slowly opened his eyes, dropped his arms in alarm like a teenager caught with his hands in the cookie jar, and whipped around to check that nobody had seen him so exposed. His neck flared red with embarrassment at the thought that Ella Martinez and her son were probably both awake and sniggering at him through the bedroom curtains!

He had already embarrassed himself enough talking to Dan about his dad without adding to the humiliation.

Of course there had been no way of knowing that Dan's father had passed away, but it was still an awkward moment and he felt for the boy and his mother. He knew what it was like to lose a parent and Dan was so young. That was tough.

As it was he had barely spent more than an hour with Ella and Dan the previous evening before excusing himself to a couple of intense hours spent in the company of his laptop, a two-day backlog of emails and a delicious meal Ella had delivered to his room on a tray.

This probably explained his grumbling stomach in need of breakfast.

Time to find the source of the singing! And something quick to eat so that he could get packed and back to civilisation—and away from these unsettling memories.

By following the sweet voice Seb strolled slowly around the patio, his bare feet finding an occasional piece of loose gravel, but it was worth it.

Ella Martinez was standing just inside the kitchen door,

whisking something in a large ceramic bowl. She was dancing and jiggling her head from side to side. A telltale pair of white headset wires trailed down to the pocket of her pink pyjamas.

Her right arm was beating in tune with the song she was humming, which sounded as if it should be from a classical musical, but he could not place it.

Her hips and shoulders twisted and turned and as he watched she lifted a wooden spoon and conducted a virtual orchestra on the other side of the kitchen window, so caught up in her world that he felt guilty at the very thought of intruding.

The sunlight was on one side of Ella's face, flashing the copper and gold highlights in her long brown hair that fell about her shoulders. She looked rapturous and as innocent as the day.

It was a moment and a view he knew would stay with him. No photograph could have captured it. The smell of the flowers early in the morning, the tang of the pine trees, the sound of songbirds in the trees.

And a pretty brunette dancing in a country kitchen.

It was all combined into one magical moment in time.

A familiar heat welled inside him, and despite his best intentions Seb wondered how a grown woman old enough to have a little boy like Dan could look so sexy and desirable in pyjamas with pink rabbits on them.

She was so totally different from the kind of woman he normally was attracted to, but somehow, in this house and this garden, she was perfect.

He envied her total sense of relaxed serenity and the calm lifestyle that came from living in a country farmhouse. Her day might be spent within the small world of this house and garden but he could think of worse places to live.

It was not Sydney. It couldn't be. His apartment was within

walking distance of world-class restaurants and entertainment. But calm? No.

One more reason for him to get back to his own world as soon as he could. No doubt about it. This place was seriously unsettling, even if he did enjoy the view.

Ella was humming as she moved between a long pine kitchen table and the granite worktop of a very modern-looking professional-standard kitchen.

Ella Martinez was not just pretty. She was unspoilt, unsophisticated and completely charming. And disarming. Part of him wanted to know more about the woman behind the façade of mother and housekeeper.

Which unsettled him even more.

Perhaps it was this house that was the cause of such thinking?

And yet…the attraction was there.

He should ask her if she had heard anything from Nicole. Keep it formal and fast.

Then he remembered that he was in boxers and a T-shirt. Unshaven and in need of a shower. Perhaps not his best look. Time to make a discreet retreat back to his room to get changed.

Too late. Just as he turned Milou snuffled his way across the patio from the direction of the barn and the woods, saw him, stopped dead, ears up, then hurled itself in Seb's direction, tail wagging. And started barking furiously.

Seb groaned and the dog jumped up onto his scanty clothing trying to make purchase on thin cloth not designed for dog claws but this time he managed to stay on his feet by sitting on the edge of the patio table. Oh, no, not again. And ouch.

Instantly he heard a low whistle and looked up as Ella strolled out of the kitchen, her wooden spatula dripping in one hand. Milou leapt towards his food bowl, leaving Seb to try and salvage his dignity and modesty with a bright, 'Good morning, Mrs Martinez.'

Exposed.

Ella wondered how long he had been watching her.

A flush of the heat of embarrassment flared at Ella's neck under the hairline and she shook it off. It was done now.

And it might have been worse. Some days she only wore the T-shirt! Nicole usually brought a female friend to stay or a gentleman guest who made himself scarce in the most discreet way.

And Sebastien Castellano was going to be here for a few days!

With a bit of luck his early-morning wander around the garden was the exception rather than the rule.

She loved her music and this short time before Dan woke was so precious, she claimed it for herself. For an hour or so each morning she could indulge in her passion for her music without waking Dan by playing the piano in the salon or singing too loudly.

Ella swallowed down her embarrassment, lifted her chin and smiled politely as though she were greeting a garden-party guest and waved at him as graciously as she could with her wooden spoon, especially considering that they were both in their nightwear.

'Good morning to you. And it's Ella, remember?' she replied. 'I hope that you slept well. It's a lovely morning.'

The smell of warm earth, the garden flowers and a salty citrus tang of man sweat and whatever body spray he used hit her hard, then hit her again as she moved closer to shake his hand. Except one of her hands was holding a mixing bowl and the other was sticky with splashes of batter from the wooden spoon.

His dark eyes under darker eyebrows flickered with

something close to amusement as she changed her mind and simply gestured with her spoon instead.

Even in shorts that revealed long powerful legs and a taut waist, Sebastien was every inch the sophisticated city millionaire businessman. And he was tall. At least a foot taller than she was. But there was also a presence about Seb. A gravitas that screamed loud and clear that this was a man who was used to giving orders and seeing them through.

The main effect it had on her was to make her gabble to fill the silence between them.

'And if you don't like Ella some of my friends call me Cindy. You know—Cinderella. Like the fairy story. But I'll answer to either Ella or Cindy. You choose.'

She looked into his slightly stunned face and wondered if her Beatrix Potter T-shirt and pink pyjama bottoms were too much for that time in the morning. And she wasn't wearing anything underneath.

And she had messy unbrushed bed hair.

Oh, no. Not exactly the best look. The village was used to her creative dress sense. From the look on her employer's stepson's face, Seb was clearly not.

'Ella,' he said, sounding out the letters, 'is perfect. But only if you call me Seb.'

She opened her mouth to suggest Bastien or Sebby or Bast, and changed her mind. If this man wanted to be called Seb she could live with it.

Seb was staring into her face so intently that she wondered if the pancake batter had splashed on her cheek or there was a pillow feather sticking out of her hair.

'Thank you. Seb. Was the room okay? I am sorry if I woke you with my crazy singing this morning. I'll try and remember to be quiet in the future.'

'The room was fine. And you are free to sing any time

you like. This is Nicole's house and your home. Speaking of which, have you heard from Nicole?'

Ella felt the tension in the air lift to match the sudden stiffness in his shoulders. And his dark eyebrows grew even more hooded.

'Not yet, but I haven't fired up my computer yet this morning. I'm just about to get dressed then make some breakfast, Seb. Would you like to join us in, say, twenty minutes and I can check my mail? Then I need to bring you up to date about the birthday party.'

She paused and sucked in a breath. 'Things are going to be a little *interesting* around here today.'

The first thing Seb heard when he walked down the corridor to the kitchen was a series of big sighs followed by groans. Perhaps that was what Ella had meant by 'interesting'.

The shower had been hot. His suit trousers and business shirt were relatively uncreased and as he tied the laces in his shiny black shoes his uniform was complete and his brain more or less back to the state he was used to.

In control and focused on the task in hand.

His ten minutes of madness in the sun were over. He had things to do and people to see and a full agenda of work to get through—depending on when Nicole was expected back from holiday.

Perhaps Nicole could meet them at the airport?

What was really annoying him was that he didn't have the information he needed at his fingertips. Yes, of course Nicole would make contact with her housekeeper as first point of call, but he found it surprisingly frustrating to be kept out of the loop.

He checked his watch. Twenty minutes. Precisely. Ella should have logged on by now and picked up any emails.

So he was not quite prepared for the sight of Dan sitting

at the kitchen table with his chin in his hands, his face only inches from the screen of the oldest TV Seb had ever seen in his life.

'Mu-u-um, it doesn't work, Mum. I can't see Aunty Nicole *at all*!'

'I'll be right there, sweetheart. Just enjoy your breakfast.'

Ella had changed from kids' pyjamas into slim-fitting cherry-coloured trousers and a sleeveless candy-stripe top in pinks and yellows. It was a riot of colour and he felt oddly drab and sombre. Perhaps he should have packed some casual clothing? He only ever carried hand luggage on business flights, which did not leave any room for casual clothing, but he just might be a tad too formally dressed for a French farmhouse.

It was only as he moved closer that Seb realised that the TV was connected to a huge computer case with a well-worn keyboard and mouse attached.

This wasn't a TV. It was a personal computer. And, from the age of it, was probably powered by a steam engine.

Another long sigh came from Dan and the little boy's shoulders dropped even lower as Ella placed a brightly coloured plate with delicious-looking billowy fruit pancakes and a glass of milk in front of him.

'Hello, Dan.' Seb smiled down at the face that was twisted into a curious expression as Dan chewed. 'What have you got there?'

Dan gulped down his bit of pancake and waved the remaining portion towards the monitor, scattering soft crumbs onto the keyboard and table as he did so.

'Aunty Nicole sent a letter and pictures of elephants! And big mountains with snow.'

'And where exactly are these mountains, Dan?' Ella asked.

His lips twisted for a second and then he nodded with a big grin. 'India. The elephants are in India.'

Ella glanced once at Seb, then shrugged. 'Close enough. Well done for remembering.' She gestured to the table. 'Please join us, Seb—I will have some scrambled eggs and ham ready in two minutes.'

'Wonderful,' he replied, his stomach growling in agreement, but as he looked at the display of large-size pancakes, croissants, preserves and baguette laid out for a more adult breakfast at the end of the long table furthest away from Dan Seb made his second executive decision of the day and sat down in the chair next to the little boy and leant forward so that they could stare at the screen together.

The Internet browser did have emails, but the photographs attached to the message were taking so long to open up that Dan would be in school before he saw anything.

'Um, see what you mean. Mind if I have a go?'

'Mum. Is it okay if Seb touches the 'puter?'

Seb glanced up at Ella, who was still stirring eggs, and she smiled at him and nodded. 'Only if he promises not to break it,' she replied with a smirk, her teeth pressed into her lower lip to block the laughter.

'Oh, I promise,' Seb replied earnestly, and Dan looked at him, nodded once and passed him the mouse so that he could concentrate on holding his beaker of milk with both hands.

It had been a very long time since Seb had seen such a decrepit piece of equipment with the processing speed of a small slug. In fact his mobile phone had better connections.

Just as Ella was bringing the pan of eggs towards the table, Seb pushed back his chair. 'Back in a moment, please start without me.'

In fact it took him a good few minutes to jog up to his room, slip back to the kitchen with his laptop and forward the email to himself so that Dan could read the message on the laptop instead of the TV screen.

'Here you are, Dan.'

'Where's the clicky mouse?'

'Inside. You press on here instead. And that little box sticking out of the side means that I can connect to the Internet wherever I go in the world.'

Dan's eyes widened in delight. And he yelled out loud and clapped his hands together as a brightly coloured photo of a woman smiled back at him with a dramatic backdrop of ice and mountains.

'Look, Mum—it's Aunty Nicole.'

Ella took a second to spoon the creamy scrambled eggs onto ham and toasted sourdough bread on Seb's breakfast plate, then lifted the hot pan away from Dan's head and peered over his shoulder.

'It certainly is. Look at that lovely hat she is wearing! Thank you, Seb. That was very thoughtful. Please. Feel free to read the message. It's not private.'

Dan nodded several times as he chewed and mumbled his thanks through a full mouth.

Seb smiled back. 'You are most welcome.' And then his smile faded. 'She's not due back in Paris until Monday evening, and then plans to fly south late Tuesday.'

He sat back and pursed his lips. 'Well, that's a shame. I was hoping to see Nicole but I have to fly home late Monday.'

Seb glanced up at Ella. 'My apologies, Mrs Martinez, but in that case there is no reason to stay here any longer. I'll drive back to Montpellier later this morning.'

Dan's eyes widened in astonishment. 'You have to leave? Already?'

Ella kissed the top of Dan's head, her hands on his shoulders, but the smile had faded from her mouth. 'Don't you remember what Aunty Nicole said? This is Seb's work. He lives in Australia and that is a long way from here. Now. Time to check on Milou and get ready for school. Okay?'

Dan nodded furiously while sliding off his chair, a pancake clutched in one hand, but stopped to pat Seb on the arm.

'Can I send you a mailey message on the 'puter? Please? Can I?'

'Sure,' Seb replied, between mouthfuls, and then shot a glance towards Ella. 'If it's okay with your mum.'

Ella looked from Seb to Dan, then grinned. 'Maybe later.'

Ella sat down opposite Seb as soon as Dan had skipped up the staircase and exhaled loudly before she poured two cups of fragrant coffee.

'I am so sorry about that,' she said in a low voice. 'Dan seems to love anything to do with computers and technology. I have no idea where he gets that from.'

Then she looked up at him with a faint smile. 'I am sorry that you have to leave so soon. I know Nicole will be very disappointed to have missed you. She was so looking forward to having you here.'

Seb took a long sip of the delicious coffee, and savoured the aroma and flavour with a satisfied sigh.

'As am I, but I do have a question. You are clearly an excellent cook, Ella, but you are also a busy mum. I'm surprised that Nicole asked you to organise her birthday party. That's a lot of work for one person.'

Seb reached into a pocket and pulled out his personal organiser. 'If it helps, I could make amends for my absence by arranging for an events management company to take care of the party. I would be happy to do it.'

Ella replied with several quick shakes of the head.

'Thank you, but no, Seb. Nicole didn't ask me to organise her birthday. I volunteered. I asked *her* to give me the chance to do it.'

* * *

Just as Ella was about to tell him the long list of reasons there was a sharp knock on the kitchen door and a small dark-haired older woman with bow knees sauntered in, nodded at Seb, deposited a basket of what looked like apricots on the kitchen floor, then kissed Ella on each cheek before heading back to the breakfast table.

Ella's friend was wearing blue dungarees and old boots set off with a jaunty wool scarf. She leant against the sink and slurped down the coffee as Ella dived into the box.

'Oh, these are fantastic!' Ella squealed in perfect French with enough of the local accent that Seb could not help but be impressed. Unless you had been born and raised in this area, most people did not notice the subtle differences between the dialects in the different towns of the Languedoc. But Ella seemed to have picked it up perfectly.

Then she looked up and remembered that Seb had no clue as to who their visitor was.

'Oh, sorry. Introductions. Yvette. Do you remember the Castellano family who used to live here? This is Sebastien Castellano visiting from Sydney.'

'Of course I remember,' Yvette replied and nodded once. 'You're Helene's son. Used to play football with my boys after school when we had the farm.' She scanned his business clothing for a few seconds before adding, 'I heard that you've done well for yourself.' Then she slurped down what was left of the coffee, grabbed another pancake and waved one hand in the air with a friendly goodbye and was gone before Seb had a chance to reply.

'What was that all about?' Seb asked in a dazed voice.

'Actually that was quite a speech for Yvette,' Ella replied. 'The forecast is for a mistral storm over the weekend and I need to bring in the cherries today or risk losing them.'

She stopped rummaging around inside the basket and glanced back towards the kitchen door before whispering in

English, 'Yvette is a wonderful babysitter and totally brilliant with the garden, but I am a bit worried that she'll try to help me out from the top of a wobbly ladder in the orchard, so, would you mind doing me a huge favour?'

Ella licked her lips a couple of times. 'Could you keep Yvette talking and away from ladders until I get back from the school run? I don't want any accidents, but I promise that I won't be long and you can get on your way the minute I get back.'

Then she gave him a lopsided grin. 'I was forgetting! This is your chance to catch up with all of the gossip. Won't that be the best fun?'

CHAPTER FIVE

BEING interrogated by Yvette for almost an hour about every detail of where he had been, what he had studied, what he had done and where he had travelled in the past eighteen years had not been what Seb called fun.

And she had made him work. By the time Ella wheeled her bicycle around the corner of the house, he had emptied three wheelbarrows of plant clippings, heard potted histories of most of his old schoolmates and made rash promises to welcome assorted members of Yvette's extended family to Sydney.

So he was more than happy to hand over the reins to Ella, who vanished into the kitchen with Yvette the minute she got back, leaving him trapped outside on the patio.

At last! It was finally time to get packed and on his way back to the business world he understood.

So he had to find a way into the house that did not involve going through the kitchen. The fastest way would be to sneak in through the sitting room and what had been his mother's *salon*.

Sebastien glanced through the open patio windows of the long wide room and stopped dead in his tracks—his feet frozen to the floor.

Hanging above the heavy stone mantelpiece of the original

fireplace was a photograph he had never seen in his life. Of his mother.

Tears pricked at the corners of his eyes, startling him with their intensity, after the shock of seeing her picture, life size, smiling back at him.

Hardly believing his eyes, he clenched his toes hard inside his made-to-measure shoes and breathed out slowly through his nose before taking a step across the threshold onto the marble tiles.

Only the fireplace was familiar in this strange mix of a room that had originally been two rooms—the formal parlour and the *salon*. The dividing wall was gone and the long sitting-room windows had been replaced by wide glass doors that opened out into the garden and allowed light to flood into what had been a rather dark space.

That light seemed focused like a spotlight on his mother's image. She must have been in her twenties when the photograph was taken and the photographer had captured her in a moment when every aspect of her beauty and grace were at their height.

She looked stunning. More like a film actress or professional fashion model than the woman who had kissed him goodnight and made his favourite chocolate cake every Friday—just because she felt like it.

How had he forgotten how very beautiful she had been?

Her sparkling hazel-green and amber eyes shone out from the flat surface behind the glass, as bright as her perfect smile that could light up any room in seconds. Even now this simple colour photograph dominated the room.

She was wearing a pale pink dress with the slight shimmer of silk in the ruffles on the collar, and a single string of pearls he knew that his father still kept in a wooden box in his bedroom that Seb was not supposed to know about.

On one shoulder was a corsage of white and pale pink

rosebuds chosen to match the exact same shade as her dress and she had raised her left hand towards it. She was wearing a ring with a large heart-shaped diamond-cut pink stone on the fourth finger—but it was not a ring he recognised.

Intrigued and fascinated by the maelstrom of emotions whirling around inside him, Seb moved closer to the fireplace until he was within touching distance of what was obviously an amateur photograph.

One thing was clear. She was looking straight into the lens of the camera and at the person taking the photograph with a look in her eyes that was absolutely unmistakable. It was the look of love. Because if Helene Castellano had a flaw, this was it.

She was incapable of hiding her true feelings—about anything.

She might have told him that the garden frog he had presented her with when he was seven was the best she had ever seen, but he had only had to look at her face to know the truth. And she had released the poor frog back into the river by morning.

He had loved her so very much. When she was taken ill, he had felt so powerless to do anything to help her that her last weeks were a whirlwind of kind words and fierce anger and frustration, which he took out on everyone and everything around him.

In life she had taught him about respect and hard work. Her death had taught him what it felt like to love someone so much and then have that love snatched away from you.

Her heart had been an open book.

His heart was locked tight closed and was going to stay that way. Other men might be foolish enough to risk falling in love and start a family. Not for him.

The blood pounded in the veins in his neck.

The photograph could have been taken by Luc Castellano,

the man he had called his father for the first thirty years of his life. But it could equally have been a friend or relative at the same party. He simply could not know! And yet this photograph had been deliberately left behind when they emigrated!

Possibilities raced through his mind in tune with the blood pounding in his heart. What if his birth parents had been in the same room when this photograph was taken?

This photograph could be the clue he had not even acknowledged that he had been looking for. The first step to finding the answers to so many questions he had buried deep inside about his parentage.

Questions which now *burned* to be answered.

He had been a fool.

The growing feeling of unease and anxiety that had sat on his shoulders ever since he found out that his dad could not be his natural father suddenly made sense.

It had nothing to do with the business deal, and everything to do with understanding who he truly was, and the decisions his parents had taken to give him a safe family life.

Instead of feeling elation and exhilaration that he was within sight of the greatest business deal of his life, standing at that moment in front of his mother's portrait, all he could feel was a hollow emptiness that needed to be filled.

The Helene Castellano Foundation meant everything to him going forward and he refused to let that work suffer because he was preoccupied with his heritage and his past. He *had* to put that behind him.

He had come here to ease his mind before starting work on the greatest adventure of his life. Nicole was not around. So he would have to do the job himself.

It was time to face the facts and get the answers he needed.

* * *

There was a rustle of movement behind Seb and he swung around, his mouth hard with emotion and resentful at the intrusion.

Ella bustled happily through the patio doors, her arms wrapped around a china bowl packed with a stunning arrangement of fresh early sunflowers and green foliage, which she carefully lowered onto the low coffee table in front of the sofas, turning the bowl from side to side to give the best viewpoint.

Only when she was satisfied did she stand back, nod once, and then march over to the *dressoir* sideboard and start rummaging around in a long bottom drawer.

'Thank you for staying and looking after Yvette. Do you like the portrait? I found your mum's photograph in a box in the attic. Nicole's designer had some modern abstract above the fireplace but it was totally wrong. Doesn't she look wonderful?'

Her words had emerged with such a gush and a rush that Seb had to take a second to form an answer.

'Yes, she does,' he replied, turning back to face the portrait so that Ella could not see his face as he composed himself. 'I've never actually seen that picture before. I don't have many family photographs so it's quite a surprise.'

Ella shoved the drawer closed and pushed herself back onto her feet with a satisfied sigh. 'Here is the original print. These were all in the same box in the attic.'

Seb stared at the brown card wallet that Ella was holding out towards him and steadied himself to accept it from her, only they both stepped forwards at the same time and for a fraction of a second their fingers slid into contact, a gentle stroke of skin against sensitive skin.

Instantly a burst of hot energy ran through Seb's hand, then arm and body, like a small electric shock. It was so unexpected and surprising that he half coughed out loud, breaking the heavy weight of silence. The awkwardness of the moment made him look up from the folder into Ella's blue, blue eyes. And found that she was staring back at him. Wide eyed. Startled.

In a blink she sucked in a breath, waved her arms to the air above her head and squeaked. 'More in the attic. I'll go and, er, try and find them for you.'

Before Seb could reply Ella fled away into the corridor, her sandals making a light pattering on the wooden staircase.

Clearly he had not been the only one to feel the connection.

Mentally shaking himself for being so obvious in front of a widowed single mother, Seb sighed heavily.

More photographs? He didn't even know that these photographs existed, and here they were. For *strangers* to see.

He flicked open the folder, and quickly sorted through the jumble of mostly black and white prints he found inside.

Some of the faces were so familiar to him they were like friends he vaguely remembered but could not name. His grandmother and his parents were in many of them, but in others strangers smiled back from locations and events from a very different world he knew nothing about—a world called the past.

Then he found it. A small colour print with his mother smiling out. Her beauty and life force captured in two dimensions for all time. Only as he picked it up he saw that there was writing on the back.

His heart skipped a beat as he read the faded words in French. *'Engagement Party. 26 May. André's house.'*

That was all. No indication of who had been celebrating their engagement. Or who André was. A friend? A relative?

Perhaps André was one of the young people in the bundle of photographs he had just glanced at? Someone who had known his mother as a young woman and who could tell him who his birth parents had been and what had happened to them.

He had so many questions. And way, way, too few answers.

Seb dropped the folder of photographs onto the sofa and started pacing up and down the room between the fireplace and the garden.

He had known the old house would have mixed memories for him, but this was something new. Something he could not have expected.

Hot resentment flashed through him and his fingers clenched into his palms. His dad had left these precious photographs of his mother and his heritage behind in his rush to abandon everything and leave for a tiny apartment in Sydney.

Seb stopped pacing and picked up the colour print. How could he do it? How could he have left these pictures behind for strangers like Ella Martinez to sort through? Maybe even throw out or burn in the fire? He could easily have made room for these few precious pieces of paper.

Back in Sydney he had three photographs of his mother. Three worn, faded and torn prints, the surface coating worn away by the rubbing of his fingers over the years. His dad had one single wedding photo in a silver frame in his bedroom, which Seb used to sneak in and look at. He never got tired of grinning back at the pretty dark-haired girl in a long white dress and carrying a huge bouquet of flowers that trailed almost to the ground, standing next to his dad in his best banker's smart suit, as they both smiled for the camera.

Four photographs. And yet here in this house he had already seen more photographs than he ever knew existed.

It was almost as if his dad had deliberately kept these photos from him. Was he trying to hide something? Trying to protect him?

Not any more.

Change of plan.

He was here now. He had the means and the opportunity and he could spare a few hours of personal time. In a few days he would be back to Australia. This could be the only chance he might have.

The more he thought about it, the more decisive he became.

He had used his tenacity and determination to take his business to the top. Now it was time to apply that same energy and drive to do some digging into his own past.

Decision made.

He had a new mission. *He was going to find any and every scrap of evidence of his family's past.* Even if it meant turning this house upside down to find them.

Starting with the attic.

Because whatever he found from now on, he had every intention of claiming for himself. This was personal and had nothing whatsoever to do with Nicole or her housekeeper. Nothing at all.

Ella tried to wind her way through the jumble of unwanted furniture and assorted objects that had accumulated in the attic. And fought a sudden urge to kick them out of the way. Hard.

Stamping her foot, she squeezed her eyes tight shut, dropped her head back and counted to ten. Backwards. The furniture was bashed enough without her adding to the knocks and scrapes.

They said that bad things came in threes. Well, her Friday was certainly turning out to be a lot more challenging than she had expected. First was the news about the mistral. A summer storm was the last thing this garden needed a few days before a garden party. And it could last for days!

As for the second? It was obvious to her now that Sebastien

Castellano never had any intention of staying around long enough to attend Nicole's birthday party. And that was just cruel.

How could he do that? How could he promise to be here then change his mind?

She simply did not understand that at all. He had travelled halfway around the world for a business trip, only to take off again without seeing Nicole!

How could he be so selfish? Surely he could put Nicole's needs in front of his own for once? And what was so urgent back in Sydney that he could not stay for a few more days?

And then there was the killer. The thick letter stuffed into her trouser pocket that had been waiting for her when she got back from the school run.

The very sight of the Spanish stamps made her heart sink into her deck shoes.

To a six-year-old, Barcelona might just as well have been next to India and not just a few hours' drive away. Not that Christobal's parents came to see them very often. They hated staying at Sandrine's clean but simple hotel and made repeated comparisons with their luxury villa complete with indoor heated swimming pool and every possible item of the latest technology.

They truly could not tolerate the fact that their grandson was being brought up in a tiny French village while their daughter-in-law worked as a housekeeper for a wealthy woman.

She did not even drive any more.

Christmas had been a nightmare. As soon as Dan had gone to bed they had bombarded her with their elaborate plans for his education—all the time making her feel like a completely selfish mother by not providing personal tutors and modern computer games and the like so that Dan would not feel left out at the expensive private schools he would soon be attending.

Yeah. Boarding schools. Right. Like she was going to let that happen! Except of course by selfishly keeping Dan here with her she was ruining his chance of a good education and a career. Guilt. Guilt. Guilt.

Ella groaned, then shrugged and sat down on the curved cover of an old trunk and opened the letter under the light beaming in through the dirty glass-covered skylight in the attic roof.

Then hot tears burned the corners of her eyes, blurring her vision.

Two return train tickets to Barcelona. First class. For Monday next week! Two days. She only had two days before she had to hand her baby boy over to his grandparents.

Oh, no. Of course she had known that they wanted to see Dan during his summer school holidays, but the first week! The Martinez family took their holiday in August, not July! And Dan had been so looking forward to Nicole's party. If she used these tickets, she would be forced to leave him there on his own while she scurried back here to work every hour she could to create this very special birthday party for Nicole.

So what if she had been putting on a brave face in front of Sebastien Castellano? He didn't have to know that she was secretly panicking. Swan on the water did not come close.

No. She would simply reschedule the dates and... Ella scan-read the letter that came with the tickets. His grandparents had already booked more tickets for a whole programme of special trips and wonderful treats for Dan, which she knew that he would adore.

The energy and the fight drained out of her.

She couldn't reschedule the trip without throwing all of those plans away.

They were Christobal's parents! Of course they wanted to

see Dan and give him a wonderful time. Dan was all they had left of their son. Chris would have wanted this. Of course, Chris would also have liked them to welcome her as well. But that was a lot more difficult.

Her fingers clenched around the paper. What choice did she have? They knew that she did not have the money to give Dan the things they could. Playing the piano at Sandrine's at the weekends was not going to be enough to even buy a new computer. She was lucky to have Sandrine's old machine so that she could keep in touch with her own parents and they were in no position to help her financially.

In their eyes she had made a total mess of her life. A wandering musician without a stable home. She had no investments or resources to provide her son with the type of education that his father had enjoyed. She had never even been to university!

The beam of sunshine focused through the skylight on her hand and she watched tiny motes of dust float in and out of the narrow cone of intense light. Dust particles going where the breeze took them. Without direction.

Then the sound of a dog barking echoed up from the garden and the old house creaked around her. Solid and reassuring.

'Stupid girl,' she said out loud, wiped her eyes with a not-so-clean finger and sniffed loudly. She was *not* without direction or friends. 'Let's get this show on the road. Things to do and people to see.'

'Do you have a saying for everything, Mrs Martinez?' a man's voice asked, and Ella practically jumped off the trunk in shock.

Seb watched Ella stuff a letter into her trouser pocket. He had seen enough for him to know that something had upset her very badly.

'I'm sorry if I startled you,' he added, then glanced around the attic room and blinked several times as his eyes became more accustomed to the dim light in that part of the attic. 'Although I am surprised that you can see anything at all.'

He turned sideways and stumbled over a box of tools as he reached for the light switch but Ella was already on her feet and faster, and as their hands connected his mind and senses were filled with the image of the girl with her hair down he had seen in the garden that morning. The girl whose touch made the hairs on the back of his arm prickle to attention.

A hard fluorescent strip light crackled into life above his head creating hard shadows and dark corners. Ella instantly snatched her hand away as though she had been stung, but her pale blue eyes were still locked onto his. In this light the planes of her face were in hard contrast to her plump, soft-looking skin.

He was the first one to break eye contact and glance around the long narrow room where he had spent many happy hours exploring as a child.

'Wow,' he said. 'Well, this is going to be rather more of a challenge than I expected. It never used to be this messy.'

Ella found her voice. 'The roof was repaired last autumn. And then the designer needed somewhere to store all the bits and pieces he moved from downstairs. There are several families of mice living in the barn, and...'

She left the end of that sentence unsaid with a simple tilt of her head and Seb picked up on it. 'Everything ended up in here instead. Got it.'

Ella pointed to a large wooden crate with the name of a well-known champagne house on the side. 'That was the box where I found your mum's photo. There are a couple of photo albums in there mixed in with the other paperwork. It's too heavy for me to lug down those narrow stairs. I know there are more, but they've been pushed right to the back by the furniture.'

'Here. Let me pull them forward.'

'Are you sure?' Ella choked, flapping away the dust she was stirring up, which only seemed to make it worse. 'It's going to make a horrible mess on your clothes.'

Seb glanced down at his outfit and frowned. A designer-suit-and-bespoke-shoes combo was not perhaps the best choice for scrambling around in dirty attics, but seeing as he had not packed any casual clothes he didn't have a lot of options.

And he was on a mission.

A few items of damaged clothing were a small price to pay to find some clues to his personal history.

'I'll live,' he replied, trying to squeeze his way between unrecognisable lumps of old chairs and bookcases to reach the stack of boxes in the dark corner of the attic.

'Oh, no,' Ella exclaimed, reaching into the first box she had pulled forward. 'The frame is cracked. What a shame. I've often wondered why you didn't take these photos with you. I mean, if you didn't want them any more, you could have given them away to the rest of your family instead of leaving them here for the mice.'

Seb took the photograph from her and pressed his fingers onto the glass for a moment.

'When we left for Australia,' he replied in a low voice, 'I was allowed one suitcase and whatever I could carry in my rucksack. That was it.'

He tried to keep the hard reality of his dad's decision out of his tone but failed.

'I was twelve and leaving the only home I had ever known.' He looked up from the photograph and shrugged like the Frenchman that he always would be in his heart. 'I was far more worried about leaving my dogs and my pals behind to even think about the personal stuff, but…that was a long time ago.'

He carefully lowered the broken picture onto the pile of paperwork and photos and old birthday cards and goodness knew what else inside the wooden wine box.

'I'm actually surprised that this much has survived all of the tenants who lived here over the years. They mustn't have been very curious. Or there was nothing worth selling.'

When Ella didn't answer immediately he turned back to find her looking at him with a confused expression on her face.

'Actually there was only ever one tenant. A retired couple from Marseilles who only ever used the house during August. The house had been empty for over a year when Nicole and I moved in. Didn't you know?'

He stared at her hard, the words resonating inside his head before words burst out of his mouth from a place of anger and resentment. 'That can't be right. There was a family living here right until the day the divorce papers were signed.'

The hard words echoed around the small space, and the temperature seemed to drop several degrees.

Ella licked her lips, squeezed them hard together, crossed her arms and stretched up almost onto tiptoe so that she could stare Seb straight in the eye.

'Mr Castellano,' she said in a calm low voice, and her chin lifted another couple of inches. 'I may only be the house-keeper here, but I do not appreciate being called a liar.' She paused, took a breath then carried on, her shoulders lifting and falling as she spoke. 'So. Make your mind up. Do you want me to help you? Or not? Because if you do, you're going to have to change your tone. And fast. Have I made myself perfectly clear?'

Her lips formed a single line, her arms wrapped tighter across her chest and she just stood there, covered in dust and grubby marks, holding her ground and waiting for him to say something.

Seb responded by sitting down on the next box. Not caring about the damage to the fine fabric of his trousers or the indentations being poked into his skin.

It had been a very long time since anyone had dared to confront him face to face and ask—no, demand—that he change his tone.

His tone! His tone was just fine. It was his temper that was the problem.

She did not know what he had gone through. How could she? How could anyone understand when the only person who knew the truth was his dad? Luc Castellano was the person he should be challenging.

As for Ella Martinez? Ella Martinez was simply magnificent.

He had misjudged her. She had clearly been upset about a letter he had seen when he came into the attic, and perhaps that had made her oversensitive. The laid-back serene woman he had seen singing that morning had her own issues to deal with and he had no right to make them any worse by shifting his hot temper onto her shoulders.

Seb inhaled a deep breath, formed a thin-lipped and restrained smile and saw the tension in her jaw relax just a little.

'Quite right. You have made yourself very clear and I can assure you that I won't use that tone with you again.' He gave her a closed-mouth smile. 'I am pond scum. Please accept my sincere apology.'

Her lips twitched slightly, but he had already guessed that she was not going to let him off the hook that easily. 'What kind of pond scum?'

'Green slime.'

'Um. Okay.' She released her arms and leant back on one

of the chairs so that she was at about the same height as Seb. 'But I'll only accept your apology if you tell me why it was so hard for you to accept that this house had been standing empty. Because it really was. I know because I had to clean it!'

The power of her simple words combined with a steady and trusting gaze bored into his skull. She was telling the truth and he was the biggest idiot in the world. He had believed his dad. Suddenly he was tired of all the lies.

She deserved an explanation. No. More than that. She deserved the truth.

It had been years since he had felt the need to explain himself to anyone and Seb sniffed away the apprehension that came with finding himself in such an unusual position. Perhaps it was this house? The challenges just kept coming.

He had two choices. Stand up, walk out and jump into his car. Or stay and see it through.

Which was probably why he stretched out his long arms in front of him, hands palms together.

'I will tell you what I do know. I know that a few years ago I offered my dad a very large sum of money in exchange for this house at a time when he needed the cash to pay for his divorce and early retirement. I know that he refused to sell it to me at any price. When I asked him why, he told me that he had a sitting tenant who he had no intention of throwing out onto the street.'

Hot anger flushed at the back of his neck and his breathing raced. Pulling himself back, he added, 'So you can see that I was rather confused when Nicole was given the Mas as part of the divorce settlement a few weeks later. So, yes, I am somewhat annoyed.'

Then he twisted his mouth into a quirky grin. 'But that is my personal problem and I have to live with it. You do not. Hence my apology, Mrs Martinez.'

'Oh. Well, I find the direct approach works best.' Then her face brightened. 'Why don't you just call him up and ask him?'

Ask him? Ask him what? Ask him why he had lied about the fact that Seb's parents were not his real parents? Or perhaps ask him why he had married the first Frenchwoman he met in Sydney and expected Seb to make Nicole his new mother? And now this.

No, thanks. He had stopped asking and started making his own choices a long time ago.

'Maybe another time. Right now I'm far more interested in collecting together as much of my family history as I can before I leave today.'

'Well, in that case, you had better start with these photos of your parents' wedding.'

Ella pressed a leather photo album into his hands. 'Your mother looked so beautiful. She obviously loved being pregnant.'

CHAPTER SIX

Two hours later Seb was pacing the length of his bedroom and in danger of wearing a track on the surface of the fine wool rug.

He had not left the Mas Tournesol. He couldn't. He was far too agitated to drive anywhere except into the nearest solid brick wall or large tree.

The only good news was that he now had the answers to *two* of his questions.

He had not been adopted after all.

There was no doubt now that his mother had been pregnant when she married his dad. The wedding photographs Ella had found in the attic were wonderful—it was a delight to see his mother laughing and happy, surrounded by family and friends she loved. And without the huge bouquet of flowers to hide her baby bump, she was very definitely pregnant.

Ella had recognised the fact instantly when she had seen those photographs.

While he had been kept in the dark all of these years!

Okay. He could deal with that and stomping around his old bedroom was not going to help. It had always been a possibility that his mother had been in a previous relationship and it certainly did not change his deep connection to her.

Which left the missing piece of the puzzle. *Who was his father?*

And now he had a possible answer.

Because he had a name. *André Sebastien Morel*. Only this André was not a friend or some relative. André Morel had been his mother's fiancé.

Clutched in his left hand was a crinkled and faded clipping from a Montpellier newspaper he had unearthed from the second box of Castellano family records he had hauled down from the attic.

The edges of the clipping were torn because whoever had cut the announcement had used pinking shears from a young woman's sewing box.

The photograph in the living room had been taken at his mother's engagement party to celebrate her engagement to André Sebastien Morel some fourteen months before she married Luc Castellano.

There was no doubt. Both the date and the year on the newspaper clipping matched those on the photograph from the living room.

His mother had been engaged to André Sebastien Morel.

It did not mean that André was his father, of course, but it was a start.

Screwing up the ragged scrap of faded newsprint, he pushed it deep into his pocket, marched over to the window and clenched his hand over the narrow ledge, his fingers and knuckles white with the effort, desperate to breathe in some cool air.

He felt totally bewildered at the fury of questions and implications that showered out of this discovery.

There were two more boxes to sort through and the weight of what he might find there was starting to bear down heavily. He would do it. He had to.

But suddenly he felt constricted, trapped in this tiny room. He needed to walk some of this tension out of his body. And fast.

Perhaps a change of scene would help him to come up with a plan?

He needed to find out everything he could about André Morel. At the very least André had known his mother at a crucial time and could help track down his father. And at worst? His mother would not be the first girl to find herself pregnant and engaged to the man she loved—only to find herself a single mother. Either way, he needed to know.

Seb snatched up his carryon bag and started stuffing it with paperwork and photographs—but it was far too small.

The knock on the door startled him and he jogged the few steps to yank it open in frustration, only to find Ella peeking in towards him, carrying a small wooden tray complete with a white lacework napkin and a steaming beaker of the most delicious smelling coffee.

'Sorry to disturb you, but delving back into the past can be hard work. Do you need milk or sugar? I noticed you took your coffee straight at breakfast but I can always dive down and get you some. And how about a pastry? You look like you need a pastry. Oh. You're packing.'

The look on her face of simple interest and calm concern hit him like a bucket of cool fresh water, dousing out the flames of his anger and discontent.

She was gabbling. Nervous…for him.

The gesture was so genuine and caring that it grabbed him and shook him hard out of his grave state of mind.

He gently laid one hand on her arm and she stopped gushing and gabbling and looked at him. Really looked at him. As though she could see into his mind and untangle the turmoil of questions and answers that lay within. 'Are you okay?' she asked, the concern in her soft voice making it tremble.

The coffee was starting to slosh and the whole tray threatened to shake out of her hands so he carefully took it from her hands and lowered it onto a stack of old magazines. Almost instinctively his hands reached out to take hold of hers, but he caught them in time to push them firmly down into his trouser pockets.

'No. I'm not okay, and, yes, I am packing. Except that I am going to need several more bags,' he replied, his gaze on the assorted documents that were spread out all over the bedroom floor, close to Ella's feet.

Ella was wearing blue lace-up deck shoes and a green ribbon tied around her left ankle.

A small sigh escaped from her mouth and there was something about it that touched him. He barely knew her, but she was as transparent as glass. Which was probably why he startled both of them by looking into her blue eyes and asking, 'How about you? Are you okay?'

She breathed in through her nose and her chin tilted back a little as she rocked back on her heels.

'Been better,' she whispered, 'since you ask.'

Then her lips came together and for one, horrible moment that filled him with dread Seb thought that she was going to start crying on him.

Instead, she blinked several times as though clearing her mind, smiled and gestured with her head towards the corridor.

'It seems to me that you need a job to keep your mind busy. I need someone who is taller than I am and not frightened of heights. Yvette has gone home for the day and, to be perfectly honest, you look like you could use some fresh air. Interested?'

'You have a job for me?' He snorted in disbelief. 'I'm sorry, Ella, but I have more than enough on my mind right now.'

He flung his arm out over the jumble of papers and boxes. 'I need to get to the city and find myself a large conference table and a fast computer. Databases. Old newspapers. Anything that can give me the background data I need. Starting with my birth certificate. How do I get hold of a copy in a hurry? I've never seen an original.'

Ella peered around him at the crates. 'How do you know that you don't have one buried in those boxes that you have not opened yet?'

His eyes narrowed and he glared at her. 'I don't want to be rude but I need to get back to work. So if you'll excuse me, I'll finish packing. I'm sure there is someone else who can help you in the garden.'

She pursed her lips and watched him for a few seconds as he snatched up clothing and tried to cram it into the holdall. Without success.

Ella took advantage of a pause to step close enough for him to stop what he was doing and turn his head towards her.

'I'll trade you one hour of *my* time sorting through all of these boxes in exchange for one hour of *your* time in *Nicole's* garden. You do remember *Nicole*, don't you? She's the woman whose birthday party you are going to miss, even though you promised her that you would be here.'

Ella tilted up her head and twitched her button nose as she peered at the wedding photos Seb had spread out across his bedcover. 'Nice photos. Pity that you cannot spare a few days out of your *so* busy schedule to find out your family history. Or are you too busy making money to wonder who you really are?'

She glanced at her watch and folded her arms. 'But please make up your mind because I don't have all day.'

'Matt! How are you doing, mate? Having a great time by the pool?'

'Pool? I wish. I'm back in Paris,' Matt replied with a sigh. 'No rest for the wicked.'

Seb's eyebrows joined as his face darkened. 'What do you

mean, you're in Paris? Montpellier not exciting enough for you? Or is there a problem with the deal?'

'Nothing for you to worry about. The PSN Media lawyers need me to go over some fine details on the contract and it made sense for me to fly up to their offices. I'll be back on Sunday. Job done. Ready to sign the papers. Okay?'

Seb paused before swallowing down regret that his friend was not only out of town but also working on the deal while he had just wasted the last hour reading through farmhouse accounts and village sporting achievements. And failing to find a copy of his birth certificate.

'Do you need any help?' Seb offered. 'I don't want to be having all of the fun!'

'All taken care of. You enjoy yourself and I'll see you at the hotel Sunday evening. Then back home on Monday. Can't wait!'

A great whoosh of air jetted from Seb's lungs as Matt disconnected.

He still had to decide whether to stay an extra day and visit the local records office to get a copy of his birth certificate, or head back home with Matt. Even with Ella's help he had found little extra information in the photos and documents. Perhaps this was all a wild goose chase after all, brought on by lack of sleep and too much caffeine?

In the meantime he had to waste an hour doing gardening jobs for the woman he had barely spoken to since agreeing to accept her help.

She was infuriating! Especially when he could not argue with her common sense.

A deal was a deal. And he had lugged two boxes of paperwork back to the attic before calling it a day.

Seb strolled out into the warm sunshine and was greeted by birdsong and the sound of bees on the lavender and herbs in the kitchen garden.

A flash of colour appeared at the side of the house and he turned the corner just in time to see Ella trying to drag a set of very large, heavy ladders out of the barn, a basket hanging from the crook of her arm. From the huffing and puffing going on, the ladders were heavier than they looked, and Milou was playing around her legs at the same time.

'I had better help you with that before it falls on your foot and breaks some toes.'

'I can manage, thank you,' she blew out. Only at that moment her basket fell onto the patio as the ladder slipped and Ella veered towards it as her weight shifted. Seb ran forward and caught her arm just as she was about to lose her balance.

'So I can see. And when was the last time you pruned these trees?'

Ella raised her eyebrows and looked quizzically at Seb as he calmly took the ladder and opened it in one swift move.

'Hello! I am a London girl. Brought up above a jazz club! A window box was just about my limit. Yvette did prune the apples last winter but I can't remember her touching the cherries.'

Seb smiled and braced the ladders into a stable position against the trunk of the nearest cherry tree.

'If these are the original trees, I seem to remember that these cherries are good.'

'They are sweet. Dan loves them. And I'm hoping Nicole and her guests will too. At the moment my plan is to serve cherry frangipane tart as part of the dessert menu but I'm still fiddling with the recipe.' She took a sharp intake of breath. 'And there is no way you are going up that ladder in those shoes!'

Seb stopped and looked down at this black lace-up meeting-room leather designer wear.

'What's wrong with these shoes?'

'Nothing. They are excellent for a boardroom or fancy restaurant. But those leather soles are way too slippery to be safe. I hate to say it but I wouldn't be able to catch you if you fell. So…thank you for the help, but I'll take it from here.'

And before Seb could stop her, Ella had dived in front of him and was already skipping up the ladder. Until she reached three steps from the top and reached out towards the nearest branch, which was still way above her head. Then she stopped, dropped her arm, closed her eyes and clutched onto the wooden frame for dear life as the ladder slipped an inch, then another, before juddering onto a firmer spot. A very Anglo Saxon expletive escaped under her breath.

'Um,' Seb replied as she slumped forward onto the ladder. 'Good effort. Can you make it down?'

Her reply was a whimper and a gentle nod. 'I just need a minute,' she replied in a faint voice.

'Okay. I am going to put my hands on your waist. So don't be startled. It's just to hold you steady on the way down. Are you ready?'

Seb stood behind Ella and gently spread his hands both sides of her waist and pressed gently.

'I've got you now. One step at a time. Steady. That's it.'

A fast-beating heart pulsed below the fragile ribcage under his fingers. Fast like the caged finch he used to have as a boy. Only this was no bird. This was a soft and warm person trembling in his hands. A thin layer of fabric separated his fingertips from her skin and as she slowly extended one leg down to the next rung he breathed in a luscious smell of flowers and baking and the sweet fruit on the ground under his shoes and above his head.

He did not do intimate. And this was the closest he had come for longer than he cared to recall.

And he would have a lot of explaining to do if someone caught them like this, because, like it or not, when Ella reached the bottom of the ladder, she turned to face him. And leant forward with both palms flat against his chest, resting her forehead on the backs of her hands, so that he was looking down onto the top of her shiny brown hair as she caught her breath.

Connection. Deep, real and not to be denied. Connection and attraction. The kind of attraction that meant that he had no desire whatsoever to remove his hands from her waist.

Which was totally crazy!

He had felt unsettled earlier in the day when their hands had touched, but this felt deeper and more fundamental and so far out of his comfort zone it was not funny.

He swallowed down a moment of spiralling heat, then slowly released his hands from her waist and stepped back. Time to take control.

He was a tourist here with every intention of leaving at the first opportunity and he had better remember that fact. Perhaps he could find the time to take some lunch, but then he would be on his way. Job done.

'Are you okay?' he asked, looking into her face, and was rewarded with a hesitant smile.

'Much. Thank you. I, er, really should know my limitations, shouldn't I?'

'I'll trade you a basket of those cherries—' he pointed at the highest point on the tree, red with ripe glistening fruit '—for one of those tarts and that lunch you promised me. And I will be careful in my slippery shoes. Do we have a deal?'

Ella pushed out her lower lip and pretended to think about it for a second, then nodded and reached out to shake his hand once. The texture of her skin was dry. The palms calloused. A worker's hand. He liked that, which was bizarre. Perhaps he didn't like smooth-skinned girls with immaculate manicures as much as he thought he did? Either way, Ella was making his head spin.

'Deal.' She nodded firmly. 'I did promise you lunch. Provided you can do it now, of course. No time like the present.'

'Is that another of those English expressions you are so full of?'

'One for every occasion. Didn't you know?' Ella replied with a faint smile, her breathing back close to normal. 'I had better sort out that recipe. And don't forget that you owe me an hour. Best get to work!'

And with a wave of her hand she turned back towards the house, and Seb and Milou stood next to each other for a second watching the slim figure negotiate the patio.

Seb glanced down to see a pair of yellow eyes looking back at him.

'Well, we best get busy then, mate.'

There was a low sigh in disgusted response and the dog settled himself into comfort in the shade of the cherry trees.

'Good idea—you just stay there on guard duty! That's it. I'll do the work.' *And try and work out what I have just got myself into in more ways than one.*

An hour later, Ella looked out of the kitchen window at the sound of Milou barking.

Seb was pacing up and down the patio stones, wagging the fingers of his right hand and gritting his teeth while chatting away to someone on the cell phone.

Intrigued, she strolled outside just as he closed the call, drying her hand on the towel tucked into her apron waistband.

'Problem?'

He noticed her, and a slight flush of embarrassment flared on his neck, as though he had been caught doing something naughty.

The naughty Sebastien. Now that thought was enough to bring a smile to her face.

There were pieces of twig and dead leaves caught in the tight curls of his hair, his right forearm was scratched below his rolled up shirt sleeve and cherry juice was spotted all along one broad shoulder.

Strange how it suited him perfectly. The naughty Seb.

'The wasps,' he sighed. 'Took exception to my stealing their food. And my friend Matt has just found a legal technicality which will keep him in Paris until late Sunday. Looks like I am on my own.'

'Oh, thanks a lot! What a lovely compliment. Let me take a look at your sting.'

He held his hand above his head and gave her a look of disbelief.

'I can handle a wasp sting, thank you all the same. Even if it does smart.'

Ella raised both of her hands. 'I was simply going to offer you some antihistamine cream. But if you prefer to suffer in silence like a macho hero? Well, that's up to you.' She folded her arms and waited. Patiently.

He pursed his lips and sniffed. 'Antihistamine I can use. Pass it over.'

Ella gestured with her head toward the kitchen, unfolded her arms, then picked up the basket of cherries. 'Follow me.'

The first thing Seb saw when he walked into the kitchen were two family-sized open fruit tarts.

'Wow. You weren't joking. Are these a trial run for Nicole's party?'

'Partly for Nicole's party but I also need to get baking for the end of year fete at Dan's school this afternoon. I volunteered to help out with the entertainment. And most of the desserts! I made the fresh apricot and vanilla cream last week, but the cherry is a new recipe. The cherries I picked yesterday are so sweet and juicy it seems a shame to spoil the flavour with too much almond.'

Seb sat down in front of the two desserts which had already been cut into large segments. They smelt wonderful.

'Oh you mean the kermesse? Everyone loves the end of year party.' Seb smiled with a shake of the head as a long forgotten memory wafted into his mind. 'I vaguely remember dressing up as a tiger in primary school. Or was it a bear? I think we had too much fun running around in costumes to think about the food.'

'Then this could be your lucky day. I need a human taster to help me decide which of these two beauties would be best for a summer dessert. Think garden party on a hot evening. Think nice dresses and smart suits. No gloppy sauces allowed. The children and parents at the fete won't mind, but Nicole's guests might.'

Ella kept on talking as she loaded a plate with a large slice from each tart, slid it across the table towards him and popped the tube of antihistamine cream next to it.

'This is your lunch, so please help yourself while they are still warm. I know you won't hesitate to tell me the truth.'

Seb picked up the nearest fork and broke off a piece from the soft deep cherry tart. As he raised it towards his lips the overwhelming fragrance of sweet almonds, butter pastry and warm tart cherries had his mouth watering even before his lips closed around the food.

His eyes closed.

Wow. He was tasting summer.

Crisp pastry melted in his mouth as the rich ground almond paste soothed his tongue and, just when he thought it could not get any better, his teeth squeezed into a whole pitted cherry, and the warm juices burst onto his tongue.

It was the most amazing cherry tart he had ever eaten. No, the most amazing, delicious dessert he had ever eaten! Which was quite an achievement considering that he was on first-name terms with chefs at famous-name restaurants all over Australia.

He had been brought up to believe his grandmother was the finest cook in the world, but she had never made anything like this.

Seb flashed open his eyes and took another generous forkload. Suddenly hungry for more. Just to make sure his senses weren't deceiving him.

As he bit into another cherry it took him back in an instant to the happy long days when he was a boy in this very kitchen.

Cherries, almonds, apples, apricots. Sitting in the garden on hot summer days, eating sun-warmed strawberries direct from the plants. Being scolded then hugged when he was caught with fruit-stained shorts and skin.

The flavours linked for ever in his mind and memory to this house and to this land. And the people who had made it special.

It was the taste of home cooking and fresh fruit. These days his meals tended to be fine food in hotel restaurants or a sandwich while he was working, but that was it.

When had he forgotten what real food tasted like?

Food made with love in a home with a family around the table.

It had been years since he had remembered so vividly what it had felt like to be part of a warm loving family. And it had taken a stranger to do it. A crazy Englishwoman had given him back that memory. And it meant a lot. Perhaps one day he would have a family of his own, but until then he was grateful for the memory.

Seb turned around in the chair to thank her just as Ella bent over from the waist to offer Milou a plate of what looked like broken pastry. The old dog almost jogged over from his water bowl to gobble up the crisp trimmings as Ella rubbed his head in tune with the wagging of his tail. For a few seconds woman and dog were framed in the sunlit doorway.

His eyes flashed up her long slim trousers to her trim waist and the sun-touched lower arms as she chatted to Milou, who had decided to try his luck by never leaving her side.

She looked happy. At home. Serene. Normal. And so very, very beautiful.

And the thought startled him so much that he coughed.

Beautiful? Where had that come from?

He instantly glanced away as the kettle came to the boil and tried to calm his breathing as he watched her stir the hot water into the ground coffee and savoured the delicious aroma.

God, this woman was good. Even the coffee was excellent.

His eyes moved to her left hand as she brought the coffee over to the table. The pale blue sapphires had no doubt been chosen to match the colour of her eyes by her late husband—whom she was probably still crazy about.

A tinge of something approaching jealousy sneaked into Seb's mind so quietly that he did not notice it until too late. Ridiculous!

One more reason to finish his packing and get back to his solitary life.

Ella looked up from Milou as he laughed out loud, and she sat down opposite Seb as she dried her hands.

'What's so funny? Don't you like it?'

He sat back in his hard wooden chair, hands behind his head, and stretched out, unaware that in doing so he had exposed a healthy section of bare midriff complete with muscular abs covered by a band of dark hair.

'Oh, please, not at this time of the day.' Ella covered her

eyes with one hand in dramatic horror. 'Put it away—it's putting me off my lunch.'

Seb glanced down, realised what she was referring to, and dropped his arms. For the first time in many years a flash of real embarrassment made him feel awkward and he busied himself pouring the coffee.

'Is there any place or time of day when it wouldn't be a problem?'

Had he really just said that out loud? Because for a second it sounded as though he was flirting—and he did not flirt. Ever.

'Well. Maybe there is.' Ella smiled closed-mouthed across the table as she accepted the coffee. 'But it usually involves swimming pools and drinks with umbrellas in them, and since we have neither...'

'I'll keep my shirt tucked. Got the message.'

He took a small sip of coffee, then sighed in pleasure.

'This is great coffee. Did you buy it around here?'

She shook her head.

'Montpellier. I'm pleased that you like it. Nicole finds it way too strong. And my parents prefer tea.'

Seb shuddered in response. 'I never got used to tea. Do you see your parents very often? Back in London?'

Ella took a long drink of coffee. 'No. They gave up their home in London years ago and bought one of those huge mobile homes. They're still working as jazz musicians and usually find gigs across Europe during the summer, then drive south for the winter. They pop in whenever they can.' She looked over his head towards the sunlit garden and smiled. 'But I wouldn't have it any other way. Especially for Dan.'

She glanced down at his plate, then looked up at him, her eyes dancing. 'You chose the cherry tart. What do you think?'

'Really delicious. And it would be perfect for a summer party. Nicole and her guests are going to love it.'

Ella slowly lowered her cup to the table. 'Good. Then you won't mind if I ask you a question?' She looked up into Seb's face, suddenly serious and full of understanding. 'Does Nicole know that you never had any intention of staying for her birthday party?'

Seb frowned. 'I knew that I was going to be in the area for a few days and we agreed to spend some time together for once. As it happened my business meeting was brought forward a week. I am sorry to have missed her, but there will be other times.'

'You do know that Nicole is my friend as well as my employer?' Ella replied. 'I hate to think that you are here to hurt her. Is it because of the divorce? Because I think she has suffered enough over that one.'

'No. It's nothing to do with that. I have every intention of apologising the first chance I get.'

Ella's focus was still on her coffee cup and when she replied her voice was cracked with sceptical concern. 'Then why are you still here, Seb? You were quite ready to leave this morning, but as soon as you saw your mum's portrait something changed. Can you tell me why that was? What did you find in that picture today that was so important to you?'

Seb paused before replying, her question resonating inside his head.

He had survived the traumatic events in his life by keeping everything personal bottled up inside himself. But here, in this kitchen, it somehow made perfect sense to give Ella the explanation she needed. And perhaps by talking through the issues out loud, he might make sense of them. Just as he had planned to do with Nicole.

This could be the only chance he would ever have to tell his story to a disconnected person and know that it would be heard sympathetically. Somehow, somewhere in the last day, he had found someone he could trust with his personal problems. And that was special.

Ella watched Seb's heavy dark eyebrows come together, his frown as deep as his heart.

She might have pushed him too far.

And in that instant she reached out and touched his hand and smiled to break the tension.

'I am the nosiest person in this town. Please excuse me.' Ella laughed. 'You are a guest in this house and your personal reasons for staying around are none of my business.'

In a moment she was on her feet, reaching out for the cups and plates and desperate to change the subject. 'Would you like to try the apricots before you leave? Yvette picked them at dawn.'

Only Seb caught her hand and kept it, calm and still. Something flicked across his face as though he was struggling to come to a decision.

'Six months ago my dad—' and at this Seb sighed a little too loudly '—had what the doctors described as a mini-stroke.'

She gasped and sat back down again. 'Oh, no. I'm so sorry. Is he okay?'

He nodded slowly. 'It was very small, and he was back on his feet in a few days.'

He looked up at her and his upper lip twitched. 'It shook me up, I can tell you. My job demands regular health checks, but nothing specific. Nothing where I needed a detailed family history and blood work.'

Seb's eyes were focused now on the palm of Ella's hand and he spread out her fingers, moving his fingertip along the life line on her palm before speaking again. 'I asked my company doctor to test me, in case there could be any hereditary problems. He's a friend. A good friend. So when he came to my office and closed the door behind him I knew it must be something serious.'

Ella thought that her own heart was going to stop. 'Oh, no. What did he say? Please?'

Seb meshed the fingers of one hand through hers as he resisted saying the words out loud.

'He said that I needed to talk to my dad. Because he had been through our blood work three times and there was no mistake. Luc Castellano cannot be my biological father.'

CHAPTER SEVEN

'WHAT did you do?' Ella whispered. 'I mean, that must have been a terrible shock.'

Seb nodded. 'It was. There were two options. I had either been adopted, or my mother had a relationship with someone else before she married my dad. Either way I knew that I had to ask my dad face to face and ask him to tell me the truth.'

'Of course! The wedding photographs! She was pregnant with you when she married.' Ella paused. 'But you didn't expect that, did you? What did he tell you?'

Seb sat back in the hard kitchen chair, arms stretched out on the table, but his fingers slid out from hers.

'I waited until dad was out of hospital and recovering back at home for a few days. He was feeling good and planning a holiday. And trying to pass his health problems off as just some minor problem. Anything to avoid the real issue.'

He made a rough chuckle in the back of his throat. 'As if I didn't know what he was up to. So I bypassed the chit-chat, showed him the lab-test results and mentioned the fact that I was old enough to hear the truth, and would rather hear it from him.'

Seb rose and started pacing the floor. When he turned back to Ella his face was dark, controlled anger only too visible.

'He told me to leave it alone. Water under the bridge. And he did not want to discuss it ever again.' He snorted and shook his head. 'I told him that I had no intention of leaving it alone. He told me that I was a stubborn fool and that I should get on with my life.'

Seb was holding onto the back of his chair so tightly that his knuckles were white in sharp contrast to the thunderous look on his face. 'And then we had a fight. I blamed him for taking me away from everything I loved to a country where I didn't even speak the language. He blamed me for driving Nicole away. And then it got worse.'

He flexed his fingers for a few seconds, trying to restore some of the circulation. 'I won't bore you with what happens when two Frenchmen start an argument where neither of them have any intention of backing down, but it was lucky that a couple of his friends turned up to play golf before things got out of hand.'

He shrugged. 'I admit it. I was angry. He had completely refused to answer any of my questions. So I told him he was a coward. His final words of comfort and consolation were along the lines of: "You can't bring her back," and then he slammed the door behind me. That was the last time we spoke.'

'Oh, Seb. That's horrible. You haven't spoken to him since?'

He raised his head and stared at her in disbelief. 'What would be the point of that? I know my dad. He won't change his mind. If I want to know who my father is then I'm going to have to find out on my own.'

'And that's why you want to follow up what you found today?' Ella raised her hands. 'Because he is right, you know. You'll have to decide what to do with any information you do find. There is a good chance that your father may not want to be part of your life, even if you want to be part of his.'

Seb nodded in agreement. 'I know it. There is a very real chance that André Morel let my mother down. But I don't want to make that judgement without knowing the facts. Perhaps she left him to be with my dad? It might help to explain his reaction.'

'Wait a moment. Did you say that his name was Morel?' Ella asked in a voice bright with curiosity.

Seb reached deep into his trouser back pocket and tugged out the newspaper clipping he had found that morning and passed it to Ella, who was now standing next to him as he looked out of the window into the garden where the trees were swaying wildly in the wind.

She scanned the few words, then let her shoulders drop. 'André Morel. Well, that cannot be a coincidence.'

Ella's hand slid down and her fingers clasped around Seb's, forcing him to glance down at the sudden sensation of her fingers on his as she spoke.

'I think that you had better come with me. There's something that you need to see!'

Ella half dragged Seb the few steps from the kitchen to the living room, then used her free hand to rummage around in a wicker basket of cards of all sorts.

'Mind telling me what I'm supposed to be looking at?' Seb asked impatiently as he tried to slip his hand away from hers, but she was not having any of it.

'This,' Ella replied, waving a party invitation in the air. 'I'm working this evening at my favourite hotel in town. Private birthday party for…wait for it: Madame Morel and family,' and she held the invitation behind her back. But Seb just scowled at her from his great height and lifted the card from her fingers.

'Is this for real? And what do you mean when you say that you are working at the hotel?'

'It is absolutely for real. And you may recall that my parents are professional musicians. Well, until I had Dan I earned my living as a performer. So tonight I am going to be playing and possibly singing for my supper and Madame Morel. *And*—' she shrugged her shoulders '—Sandrine told me that the Morel family are originally from Montpellier but have retired to their holiday home around here. I know that they *might* be a completely different family and it could lead to nothing, but isn't it worth taking the time to ask a few questions?'

'Maybe,' Seb replied hesitantly. 'And this is all going a little too fast for me to keep up. You are a professional musician working as a housekeeper, in the middle of nowhere. Is that right?'

'My choice. And no, I had not made the connection between the name Morel and your family until you mentioned it.'

Ella waited, watching his face, begging him to agree to follow this up. But patience was never her strong point, so she leapt in while he was still thinking about it.

'Come to the party tonight as my guest. I'll introduce you and tell the family that you are trying to trace an old friend. See what happens! There could be someone there who can put you in touch with this André Morel or may even have known your mother in person. You don't have anything to lose except a few hours in the city.'

Seb slid his hand from hers, and sank down onto the sofa. Ella perched next to him and brought her bare feet up onto the sofa cushions. Waiting.

Seb slowly raised his head to look up at the portrait of his mother before turning back to Ella.

'I can't be satisfied with the fact that my parents loved me.' He shook his head. 'That's just great. What an idiot, eh?'

Ella tapped her bottom lip a few times, then slapped her hand on the coffee table. Startled, Seb jumped forward.

'What?'

'Seb Castellano. I have a proposition for you.'

The surprised look on his face was replaced in an instant with a cunning smile.

'Oh? But we have only just met. I thought you English were so reserved!'

Ella smirked. 'Yes, very funny. You should be so lucky. This is serious. So please try and pay attention. Nicole Lambert has been a very good friend to me. I know how hurt she would be if I tell her that her stepson Sebastien, who she talks about constantly, had never intended to stay for her birthday celebrations in the first place—'

Seb sat forward but Ella gestured him back down with the flat of her hand. 'Please sit, I'm not finished yet.

'Okay. It goes like this. You stay here until next weekend and help Nicole celebrate turning sixty—which she totally hates the idea of, by the way—and in return…' She paused and breathed in through her nose. 'In return I will do everything I can to find out about this André Morel. I know everyone in this village and the hotel is the local meeting spot for the retired population who would love to have a detective job like this to work on. I can soon get the network going on tracking him down. What do you say?'

Seb reached out, grabbed her hand and kissed her knuckles before Ella could grab her hand back, if she wanted to. She didn't want to, and the natural wide grin on Seb's face said it all.

'I would say thank you for the offer, but I can't stay. I have to head back to Sydney on Monday, then Tokyo at the end of the week…what? Why are you shaking your head? Those tactics are not going to work on me.'

'You know, I never took you for a quitter, Sebastien Castellano.'

Seb bristled. 'Quite right. I'm not.'

'Then why are you making excuses? You know, Nicole

came back from Australia with a suitcase of photos of her amazing stepson. She was all alone in the world but she made sure she had your photos with her. How do you think she is going to feel when you leave the country before she gets back from holiday after…when was the last time you saw her, exactly? Two years? Three?'

Seb's scowl deepened. 'Three. We met at a charity concert in Sydney.'

Ella hugged her legs and rested her chin on her knees and smiled at Seb with such a sweet and innocent expression it was impossible for him to be angry with her. 'You know, I was explaining to Daniel on the way to school this morning how marvellous laptops and wireless Internet connections were. Some people work from home *all the time*. Without the need to travel at all.'

She shrugged and pretended to be examining her cerise toenail polish. 'Of course, after what you have just told me, I would understand if you feel compelled to travel to the other side of the world to talk to men in suits about computers instead of finding out who your real father is.'

Seb moved forward so that their heads were only inches apart. If he expected Ella to shuffle away as he moved into her personal space, he was thwarted because she did not budge.

'Monday. I'll stay until Monday.'

'Tuesday,' Ella retorted immediately. 'My final offer. But as an added incentive, we can start this very afternoon at Dan's school fete. All the parents will be there and there is bound to be *someone* who knows about the Morel family. *Then* you can go to the party. Just to make sure that we don't miss *any* possible leads.'

They looked at one another for a few seconds, the air between them crackling with electric tension.

But before Seb could open his mouth to reply, there was

an almighty crash from the kitchen and Ella leapt to her feet and sped down the corridor.

She slid to a halt at the door, hand on chest, so that Seb had to slide past and take in the damage.

Seb's laptop computer was lying face down on the hard tiles, surrounded by pieces of broken fruit tart, which Wolfie and Milou were gobbling up in delight.

'Oh, no,' Ella gasped in horror. 'I am so sorry. I should have closed the outside door. Bad Wolfie! Bad Milou! Is it broken? Please say that it is still working!'

Seb blew out a long breath and picked up the laptop and they both stared in silence at the smashed Wi-Fi attachment.

Ella cringed inside, and prepared herself for the onslaught! This was Seb's work! His precious laptop! She had totally blown it by being so careless. He had to leave now, whether she liked it or not. There was no way she would be able to convince him to stay and see Nicole now this had happened.

To her astonishment, he simply checked that the monitor and keyboard were still working in complete silence before turning back to her with a nod.

'It's okay. We build computers with cases designed to be pretty indestructible. Even against dogs and hard floors. I should be able to wire it into your telephone line through a modem. But my dongle is shattered.'

'I couldn't have put it better myself.'

'Slave driver! Have you seen my thumb? I may never type again. A few balloons you said. Nothing about 200 helium crocodiles.'

Seb waved his right hand in Ella's direction, but she was still luxuriating in the soft leather passenger seat with her eyes closed.

'Just part of the service,' she replied with a grin. 'Come to the Languedoc for wonderful new experiences. Thanks again for helping Dan with his pirate costume by the way. The eye patch idea was inspired. He looked terrific!'

She tipped her sunglasses higher and shuffled higher in her seat so that the light breeze lifted her hair down around her shoulders as Seb drove the open topped sports car along the quiet coast road.

'No problem,' Seb replied, smiling to himself, despite his frown. 'I had forgotten how much fun you can have at a school fete. I was actually in danger of enjoying myself a couple of times.'

'I noticed. You only answered your cell phone three times during the costume parade and you even put it away while you scoffed my quiche and salad. I take that as a compliment!'

'Oh more than that! I actually turned it off while you were playing piano at the old folks' home.'

'Wow!' Ella hissed. 'The school choir is not that good this year, but I did notice you charming the old ladies. You rogue.'

'Two of my school teachers actually remembered me! But not an Andre Morel. He was obviously not a local boy.'

'Oh, sorry. Even if that does explain the bright orange lipstick on both of your collars.'

'Oh, what?' Seb replied as he screwed his face up so that he could inspect his dress shirt, and then shrugged. 'It was worth it for the fringe benefits.'

'Oh? Do go on. Are you calling the bingo numbers tomorrow?'

He snorted a chuckle. 'I have the pleasure of escorting a pretty lady home while the young master of the house and his pirate crew are terrorizing the local cinema on a school outing. Even if the lady is taking me on a wild goose chase.

He started out at the countryside. 'Are you sure this is the right road?'

'And you a local boy!' Ella pointed to a signpost on

the deserted dusty road. 'Turn right here and all will be revealed.'

Seb frowned but gently swung the car down the single track road for a few minutes before the road ran out in a sand swept empty car park. The air was suddenly tangy with salt and the smell of the sea and as he swung out from the car his mind seemed to turn back the years with every caress of the wind on his cheeks.

They were deep in the Camargue. The huge flat plain of marshland and fresh and salt water ponds created by the river Rhone as it wound its way slowly to the sea over the centuries was laid out in front of him with only the sea in the distance.

Ella was already out of the car before he realised and automatically reached for his hand as though it was the most natural thing to do in the world, before dragging him through the rickety wooden gate and onto the loose sandy dyke which held back the water.

'Not a wild goose chase. A wild flamingo chase!'

And just as Seb was about to reply there was a low rustling and rhythmical beat of black and crimson wings above his head as five long necked flamingos flew across the tall grasses and landed perfectly in the shallow water with a quick back brake of soft pale pink wings. They honked and hooted as they flew, louder than geese, but so beautiful it took his breath away just to watch them.

Wild flamingos! *Flamants roses*!

Seb stood in silence with the warm sunshine on his face and watched the tall reeds sway in the sea breeze. Snowy white egrets and grey herons picked around the edge of the brackish pond, but it was the clusters of stunning flamingos feeding in the rich water on their red stick legs that captivated his attention. There were hundreds of flamingos just meters from the shore.

There was no sign of human life. No cars or houses. No laughing groups of primary school children having fun.

Simply sea, sky, birdsong and the rustle of tall grasses against the back of his hand.

And Ella. Captured in a moment in time with the wind in her hair and the sun on her skin.

Seb sucked in a breath to steady his heartbeat then exhaled slowly.

And it felt as though all of the tension that he had been holding in his clenched shoulders these past few months building up to the negotiations suddenly released all at once like smoke spiralling into the air.

His shoulders dropped away from his ears. The creases in his forehead relaxed away and the dull ache at the back of his head which had been bothering him since the long flight from Sydney simply drifted away on the warm tangy wind.

He would have been content to stand there for hours, but Ella released Seb's hand so that she could shuffle onto the warm sand and wrap her arms around her knees. Once in place she rested her chin on her hands and gazed in delight at the flocks of wading and flying birds on the pond.

Seb smiled down at Ella as she shirked off her pretty daisy sandals and squeezed her toes into the sand with a soft sigh of delight.

Then he glared at his dusty black business shoes and the tight black high socks which were digging into his calves below black business trousers. And felt totally ridiculous!

Without hesitating, Seb collapsed down on the sand, loosened his laces and shocked his bare feet by exposing them to the sunshine for the first time in months. He vaguely recalled the beach barbecue party he had set up for his design team in Sydney at New Year, but not the reason he had been called away at the last minute.

He wiggled his toes a few times to make up for lost time. It felt wonderful.

And then it hit him out of nowhere. Like a meteorite falling onto his head.

He had turned into a time poor cliché of a bloke who had all this money in the bank but no time to enjoy it!

How totally crazy was that!

It was so ridiculous that the laughter that burst through without warning came from a place deep inside his body, low in his abdomen. It was the kind of laughter that made his jaw ache for a few seconds before he was able to sniff and wipe his eyes.

Only then did he dare to turn his head towards Ella.

She smiled at him closed mouthed for a few seconds before shuffling over in silence then faced forwards so that they could both stare out at the flamingos, side by side and only inches apart. Their world encased in a cave of grasses and low shrubs.

Seb felt the sun and warm wind on his face and toes, and a strange sense of contentment and something close to joy filled his heart and his mind. Mingled with regret.

There had been a time when he loved to experience every new sensation with such pleasure and delight. When had he lost that ability?

And it had taken an English girl to help him to reconnect to this world free from high tech communications—and to make this moment something truly special.

'Sometimes I like to cycle down here out of season. Just to find some peace. I hope you don't mind?' Ella whispered.

He reached out for Ella's hand, raised it to his lips and grinned at her. Strange how he kept a tight hold of her hand and they sat huddled together in comfortable silence, just smiling. And she did not seem to mind at all.

* * *

'You could have warned me that I would have a reception committee,' Seb whispered to Ella as she hooked her arm around his and wound their way through the assembled guests towards the piano at the back of the room.

'What? And spoil the fun of seeing you charm the ladies?' She chuckled. 'You're quite the celebrity guest!'

Then she squeezed his arm a little tighter and joked, 'Sandrine has already ordered a fattened calf!'

Seb almost choked on his fizzy water. 'I'm hardly the prodigal son,' he spluttered.

'Um. I wouldn't be so sure about that,' Ella replied, dabbing with a napkin at the droplets of water he had sprayed onto the sleeve of his beautiful suit jacket. 'It was very kind of you to offer to take a look at Sandrine's Internet connection for her. I know she relies on those online bookings. It's not often they have a tame computer tech guru at hand.'

Before Seb could reply, Ella glanced over his shoulder and nodded. 'Speaking of shouting, I'm getting the nod from Sandrine. The buffet is about to be served, which is my cue to start work. I hope you like piano music!'

Ella slipped onto the piano stool and moved her hands swiftly up and down the keyboard, creating a stream of gentle lyrical sounds that seemed to Seb's untutored ear to be based around the melody of a familiar song but transformed under Ella's fingers into a tapestry of elegant and emotional music.

She might have told him that she had trained as a professional, but to his untrained ear she was superb!

'Are you improvising?' he asked in amazement.

She laughed out loud, but her focus remained on the keys. 'That's the whole point. Sandrine could have played a compact disc through the music system. My job is to create the background music which is special to this event.'

Ella raised her head for a second and nodded towards the

elegantly dressed lady who had greeted Sebastien so warmly after he had apologised for being a gatecrasher.

'The Morel family specifically asked for a combination of smooth jazz and some classical ballads from her favourite musical shows.'

Her hands slowed a little, the right hand picking out a theme he recognised from a very old Hollywood movie. Except that Ella was somehow playing the lyrics in the form of a musical expression so soft, smooth and warm that he was stunned by how every scrap of emotion was teased out in a few notes on a keyboard.

'You've done this before.' He smiled, and moved to the other side of the piano so that he could look at her face, suddenly delighted that he had agreed to come to this small hotel on a wild and windy evening.

Her nose wrinkled into a smile. 'Since I was about twelve. I love it, love it, and love it. Did I mention that I love it? I would play even if they did not pay me—but please do not mention that to anyone.'

Seb nodded sagely. 'Your secret is safe with me. But I do have one question. Why a cocktail pianist?'

'People watching, of course! Oh, you would be surprised what you see from behind a piano!'

She looked up over the lid of the piano towards the guests who were chatting away in clusters around the buffet table.

'After a while you merge into the background and that's when people reveal who they truly are.' She smiled up at him, then focused on a complex fast run up and down the keyboard using the lightest of touches. 'Any minute now, Madame Morel is going to make her way over and invite you to join her party at their table. Now, play nice! Who knows, by the end of the evening you may have discovered a whole *new* set of relatives!'

Sure enough, only seconds later Ella nodded and continued

playing as their hostess whisked Seb away. From her position, she could only sympathise as within minutes he was being introduced to the assorted aunts, uncles, cousins, nieces and nephews that made up the Morel family. And from what she could hear in random snatches, several of the men were either called André or had other Morel relatives by that name in Montpellier.

Poor Seb. This situation had to be bewildering for him.

As her hands moved through sequences of key strokes her muscles had learnt years ago, Ella glanced up from time to time.

Her eyes were drawn inexorably to the tall handsome man in the couture suit who had dominated the room from the moment he followed her inside.

Sandrine had taken one look at Seb and switched from being a professional hotelier of advanced years into a giggling schoolgirl who blushed at his every compliment.

Internet access! Sandrine! What a pathetic excuse. *The shame!* She was going to tease her friend mercilessly about that feeble excuse to keep Seb to herself for a few minutes.

It had given her just enough time to introduce herself to Madame Morel and her family and explain why there was an uninvited guest in the room. Who just happened to be the CEO of Castellano Tech.

Delighted did not come close!

Sebastien Castellano was at their little party and looking for one of the Morel family?

How exciting.

Make that *two* fatted calves, Sandrine.

As for Seb?

Sebastien Castellano had entered the room with all of the persona and confidence of someone used to achieving whatever they set out to do.

Plus he had two distinct advantages.

Firstly he had switched on his full-on charismatic charm offensive for anyone within speaking range. And then of course he was dressed for success. His dark suit was cut to perfectly emphasise broad shoulders and slim waist and hips—the same broad chest that she had pressed against so pathetically in the cherry orchard that morning.

Her fingers missed a key change and she quickly masked her error by turning the mistake into a jazzy flourish and carried on. That dazzling smile and those heart-stopping dark good looks had worked their power on more than Sandrine and their hostess!

The simple touch of his arm on hers had been enough to set her heart racing and head spinning. Despite her sweaty palms and dry mouth, she had managed to conceal her physical reaction to him...until now.

Working with Seb for the next few days until Nicole returned from holiday was going to be far more challenging than she had imagined.

From that very first moment when she caught sight of him sitting on the grass she had felt that certain, telltale, spine-tingling prickle of attraction that refused to go away.

Of course she had tried to rationalise it. She had seen his photos and imagined what Seb would be like in person. Meeting him, arguing with him, learning more about his reasons for coming home...that had simply helped her to understand the man himself.

Her fingers hammered out the dramatic phrasing from a powerful ballad.

Who was she kidding?

She was smitten.

Which was just about the silliest idea she had heard in a long time.

Looking at Seb now as he effortlessly worked the room,

the hopelessness of that attraction shook her by the shoulders like a good friend and demanded that she snap out of it.

He was a tourist who would be gone in a few days. Just passing through like a whirlwind destined to churn up everything in his path. Here was a man who only yesterday had no intention of keeping his promise to Nicole. Selfish perhaps? But also vulnerable when it came to his own family.

It was a powerful combination.

She was far too old to have a summer fling. Wasn't she?

Ella had been right. The gentle ebb and flow of the piano music blended seamlessly into the bright background chatter and laughter from around the room as Madame Morel introduced Sebastien to her extended family and friends.

Yes, there were several André Morels in the family, but André Sebastien Morel from about thirty years earlier? Cue puzzled faces and questions about places and dates he had few answers to. He had quickly accumulated a list of names and telephone numbers to follow up.

Friendly promises to ask around and get back to him mingled with the excellent food and drink to create a genuinely warm and welcoming sense of community and family.

His greatest challenge was refusing the delicious wine that a local winemaker had supplied for the evening. His apologies ended in a mass exodus of the men, and a few of the ladies, to the car park to admire his sports car. Only the howling cold wind prevented several test drives and they agreed to continue their heated debate on the relative merits of French and Italian motor manufacturers back in the warm comfort of the bar.

Where Seb had his first real opportunity to observe Ella as she worked.

The woman was a revelation! Just when he thought he was

starting to understand her, she came up with something even more remarkable!

The elf who had challenged him all morning had been replaced by an elegantly dressed beautiful woman with immaculate grooming.

Her dress was a shimmering blue silk cocktail gown with a matching gossamer wrap that drifted around her shoulders like candyfloss. The shade of the silk was a little darker than her eyes, but fitted perfectly onto her sweet rounded curves. It was an inspired choice. Elegant but not stuffy.

The bed hair was twisted up into a French chignon, leaving the smooth line of her neck clear for a small row of pearls.

Combined with natural looking make-up, which seemed to make her pale blue eyes sparkle even more than normal, the overall effect was stunning.

He had met and escorted many beautiful women and professional fashion models over the past few years whose artifice in making themselves attractive for the cameras evaporated a few hours later. Ella was a natural beauty, as easy in her own skin whether she was cycling along a country lane or baking in a country kitchen, or, now, elegant and sophisticated.

Ella Martinez the single mother, hard-working housekeeper and young widow was gone. Replaced by Ella Jayne Bailey. Solo pianist.

She simply took his breath away.

He was totally attracted to Ella Martinez and everything about her, and this new side of her personality and talent only added to his confused feelings.

Which meant that he was in deep trouble.

Seb gulped down the recognition of what he was thinking and feeling and quickly looked around the room to see if anyone had noticed him growing hot and heavy.

He did not do holiday romances, or short-term affairs.

But it did make him wonder about her choices.

What was Ella Bailey doing here in the middle of the Languedoc when she had so much talent?

Did she love her late husband so much that she wanted to hide away from the world with her son in the countryside? Perhaps she had wanted somewhere safe and secure where she could grieve in peace?

But perhaps it was more than that?

He leant against the wall as the other guests shuffled to the dessert trolley.

For now he was happy to watch the most beautiful woman in the room as her small hands moved effortlessly over the keys, her attention focused completely on the sound she was creating. Now and then her shoulders swayed from side to side with her head as she moved with the melody.

No sheet music. No written notes.

Yet the music soared into a tapestry of emotional, uplifting and inspirational sound.

This was her passion. Her delight.

He had always been fascinated by the work of skilled craftsmen, whether they were the expert cabinet makers who designed and made the dining-room furniture in his Sydney apartment, or the software engineers who saw their virtual designs take shape on mobile technology used around the world.

This was why every part of him knew that he was looking at a true artist.

Ella was superb. The music was perfect. *She was perfect.*

Except that she was playing the piano in a dim corner of the room, being ignored by the party guests as they chatted and sampled the delicious food. Guests like himself, for example.

He had been to so many parties and events over the years where there had been a cocktail pianist playing in the background, and, thinking about it now, he was shocked to recall that he had not once gone over to speak to the musician or even made a note of their name.

Ella was happy to stay in the background playing the piano while he worked the crowd for information about André Morel. In much the same way, Ella seemed happy to stay hidden away from the world in a remote farmhouse while he travelled the world!

His high-profile lifestyle would horrify Ella. What girl would want to have every aspect of her personal life and past history trawled through by journalists looking for a juicy headline?

And she was a single mother with a son.

Putting all of those aspects together, there was only one conclusion he could make.

He and Ella lived in completely different worlds with very different priorities and the sooner he realised that, the better. For both of their sakes.

Right now he had to focus. He needed to know a lot more about the Morel family before the evening was over.

Over an hour later, Seb was noting down the telephone number of an older lady whose cousin was called André Sebastien when he noticed that the music had stopped.

He calmly promised to call the next day, expressed his thanks, and then turned back to the piano.

Ella was standing now, her cell phone pressed firmly against one ear, her right hand squeezed against her mouth, and from the look on her face whatever she was hearing was not good news.

Seb instantly made his excuses and crossed the room to take her arm.

'What is it? Is everything all right?'

Ella shuddered and shrugged into her jacket. 'That was Yvette. She was reading to Dan when the lights went out. It has happened once before in a mistral and we lost power for a couple of days.' She clutched at Seb's arm. 'Can you take me home, please? I wouldn't normally leave a party before the guests but this is an emergency.'

'Sure. But I don't understand… Is it Dan? Is he frightened of the dark?'

Ella grabbed her bag, then pressed her hand onto her chest and took a breath. 'Not frightened of the dark. Terrified. I'm hoping that he will grow out of it, and I've tried everything but right now…he's going to be panicking. I need to get there and fast.'

'Of course. Let's go.' Seb grabbed her hand and led her through the hotel guests who were crowding in to chat about the music. Ella would have been lost in the crush but with Seb in the lead they were in the porch before Sandrine could reply to their quick 'farewells.'

Seb flung open the front door to the hotel and it was snatched immediately out of his hands by the gale-force winds that howled as loudly as the howls of protest from the hotel guests who were being buffeted by the freezing cold draught. By turning his shoulder to the wind, and protecting Ella as best he could with his body, Seb managed to shuffle their way across the car park and open the passenger door of his car for Ella, bracing it against his back long enough for her to throw herself into the seat before the wind slammed it closed.

By the time Seb collapsed into the driver's seat and pulled his door closed, he was freezing cold, exhausted and shaking with physical effort.

'I had forgotten what the mistral wind feels like!' Seb murmured to Ella, who had taken a firm grip with one hand on the grab handle on the car frame and was holding her seat belt extra tight with the other.

He slowly unclamped her hand from around her seat belt.

'Relax. You are surrounded by six air bags, Ella, and

the same safety technology used in racing cars. You are quite safe.'

'Then why do you need six air bags?' she squeaked as the powerful engine roared into life.

'Not all drivers are as experienced as I am,' Seb replied with a hint of a smile on his lips, trying to reassure her, while thinking of some task to keep her mind busy. 'But I do need some help. Would you mind checking for fallen branches on the road? There is not much clearance between the road and our seats.'

Ella could only look ahead in terror as Seb carefully edged the car down the main road, the powerful headlights lighting up the thrashing trees and bushes either side of the road.

It was going to be a bumpy night.

CHAPTER EIGHT

ELLA came to a dead stop at the top of the staircase.

Dan was sitting huddled on the bed in his room, one arm wrapped tight around Milou's neck while his other hand was clasped firmly around the handle of their biggest torch.

The light was pointing upwards and reflecting from the ceiling so that the bottom half of his small face was white and the rest in shadow. Thick church candles burnt brightly inside glass flues, but their light was ineffectual compared to the giant electric torch.

The hard light contrasted so powerfully with his sweet striped pyjamas and towel dressing gown that her heart constricted with the sight of it. Dan had always been scared of the dark but she had not seen him looking so pale and terrified for a long time.

Ella forced herself to lift her head for the last few steps and skip lightly into Dan's room. She had to be positive for her son's sake—she just had to get him through the night.

'Hello. Are you still awake? This is exciting, isn't it? Did you hear the big wind? Oh—you found the torch from the kitchen! Good thinking.'

Ella flung herself down on the bed next to Dan and gave him an extra warm cuddle.

'What a clever boy you are. And thank you for helping Yvette.'

'I had to help find the torch,' he finally managed to reply. 'But then the wind got a bit scary.'

'Well, seeing as you have been so brave, I think you can come downstairs for a few minutes and tell Seb all about the excitement.'

In an instant Dan was shrugging the duvet from his legs and sliding out of bed.

Ella grabbed hold of his hand and used the torch to guide their way to the hall, which was flooded with light from the driveway. Yvette had already driven off home, but Seb had left his car headlights on so that the powerful beams pointed straight onto the house and the glass panel above the front door.

She could have kissed him on the spot.

An even brighter light came walking out of the living room—the beam so powerful that Ella shaded her eyes.

'Hey, guys. Hope you don't mind that I lit the fire. And what do you think of this new torch? Cool, eh?'

Dan shone his torch onto the carpet, then looked at Seb. 'Yours is better than mine,' he said with a quivering-lip voice. He looked back and forth between the two torches and said, 'I need one like that.'

'Well, how about a swap? Here, try it out. I should warn you, though. It's pretty heavy!'

Dan ran forwards to take the handle from Seb, then blew out hard. 'Really heavy!' Then he started waving it about. 'Look, Mum. Now I can see everything.'

'That's wonderful. In that case you can guide our way to the kitchen. I fancy some hot chocolate. And you'll never guess what happened to me tonight?'

Dan lifted his head towards her, eyes wide and suddenly curious.

'Did your lights go out too?'

'No, they didn't. But Seb gave me a scary ride home in his sports car. What do you think of that?'

'Hey! It wasn't that bad! I didn't go *that* fast.' Seb laughed and winked at Dan, whose mouth curled up into a grin. But as Seb strolled down the short corridor, Ella realised that it was Seb's fingers Dan sought rather than hers, his tiny hand engulfed inside Seb's palm.

And it broke her.

Hours later, Dan's head lolled on Seb's shoulder as Seb carried him back to his toy-filled bedroom, with Ella carrying the torch to guide their way up the narrow old staircase.

They had shared hot chocolate made in a pan on a gas ring fed by a bottle of propane, then huddled in front of a roaring fire in the living room. Seb had drawn the heavy curtains, but nothing could block the howling wind on the other side of the glass and the draughts that blew the smoke right back down the chimney, making them all choke and splutter and laugh.

Dan had been given the task of holding the big torch while Seb fed the fire and lit a cluster of scented candles so they could see where the cups of hot chocolate were.

It had seemed only natural for Seb to divert Dan with stories about the hot and dusty places he had visited and all of the exotic plants and birds that he had seen during the previous month in the North of Australia.

Tales of kangaroos and Koala bears and kookaburras and remote towns where people had to drive for hours before they saw another house or person.

Places where people needed computers and clever phones to keep in touch, and even go to school. Places where the software and communication systems that his company made came into their own.

An hour later Dan was cuddled against Milou and his

mother on the couch, half asleep and yawning his head off, despite calls for more stories about the kangaroos.

Seb lowered Dan slowly onto his warm bed as Ella held back the quilt, and then tucked him in.

'Doors, Mum. The doors.'

Dan's eyes fluttered open and Seb turned away as Ella opened up the big wardrobe door and shone the powerful torch inside so Dan could see the neat shelves of clothes and toys.

And absolutely no monsters.

Ella bent over to kiss Dan, wish him goodnight, and stepped quietly onto the landing.

Just as Seb went to follow on, Milou tried to jump onto the bed, but was not quite up to it without Dan helping him up, so Seb did the honours instead, and as he did so Dan tugged at his sleeve. 'Have you looked inside? Over there? Cause I can't see over there. I don't want to worry Mummy.'

Seb glared at the dark spot next to the cabinet, reached out and turned on the powerful torch from the car, grateful beyond measure that the batteries were new and unused.

The whole bedroom flooded with light and Dan peered out over the top of the bedcovers before snuggling down again with a sigh of contentment.

Seb popped the torch onto the bedside table. Just in case Dan needed it again.

Then without thinking or hesitating, he whispered, 'Night, Dan. Sleep well.'

And a sweet child's voice answered, 'Night, Seb.'

The living room was still cold despite the fire, which had started to ebb down, and Seb quickly tossed dry wood onto the burning embers.

'I suppose power cuts are one of the downsides of living

in a remote farmhouse. Some things clearly haven't changed,' he said in a positive voice, then looked around for Ella.

He was shocked to see a tearful, anxious little face staring back at him, her skin pale even in the warm amber glow from the fire.

Ella had wrapped an old patchwork quilt around her shoulders and was sitting hunched up with her knees to her chest, hugging the quilt tight around her body.

She looked cold, shivery and terrifyingly, achingly sad and empty. As though all of the joy had been drained out of her. When she spoke she asked him the most ridiculous question he had ever heard.

'Am I a bad mother, Seb?'

He was so shocked that instead of answering he simply turned back to the fire to hide his own rush of emotions, stoking up the wood into bright flames.

Seb did not have to look at her. Her anguish was only too clear in her voice. The type of anguish that no bland denials and complacent phrases could eradicate.

'I love Dan so much and want him to be happy,' Ella continued in a low tremulous voice, 'but maybe Christobal's parents are right? Maybe I should move back to Barcelona? He will have a better education and money and… He would never have to worry about the lights going out in a storm and being scared again.' She paused for a second before her voice faltered in a few halting words. 'He was so frightened! I don't want him to be scared. *Not ever.*'

She was crying now, the tears running down her cheeks as she fought and lost the battle to hold back her fears and regrets.

Which was why Seb did the only thing he could do. He sat down next to her on the sofa and wrapped his arm around her shaking shoulders, gathering her close to his side so that she was cuddled all along the side of his body, cocooned inside the quilt.

The contrast between the Ella he was holding and the Ella who had been playing and laughing only a few hours earlier was so sharp that Seb took a moment to close his eyes and try and clear his head. He revelled in the glorious sensation of holding her in his arms, but immediately felt guilty for taking advantage of her sudden vulnerability.

His chin pressed onto the top of her hair and he hugged her closer, wrapping the quilt around her back, desperate to share his warmth with her. Her perfume was fainter now, mingled with the soft fragrance of lavender from the quilt and Ella's own sweet scent. Unique, powerful and totally compelling. A scent that pulled him in so fiercely that he never wanted to let her go.

She snuggled closer. Just a tiny inch. And his heart soared in delight. It had been so long since he had been in such close physical contact that the gentle thump of her heartbeat inside the ribcage beneath his hands seemed magnified. Loud and fervent.

He did not do intimate. Ever. Yet here he was, holding this wonderful, amazing woman while a little boy slept above them. How had that happened?

They barely knew each other and yet he felt so connected. Perhaps it was this house? These four walls, now cast in deep shadows, which made the rest of his life suddenly come into sharp focus.

Or was he simply in the right place at the right time to offer her some comfort? Any port in a storm? No. It did not feel that way at all. This was real. And so was her concern.

Seb slowly pressed his cheek to her hair before speaking in a low and soft voice.

'I've only been here for one whole day but I already know that Dan is a very, very lucky boy. You have given him so much more than any amount of money can buy. He's a remark-able young man. You should be proud of your son...' and at this point he lifted some strands of her hair behind her ear '...and what you have achieved.'

Seb slid slightly to one side and tilted her chin up towards him, only to find her looking up at him, her eyes focused on his in the flickering firelight, as though seeking the confirma-tion that the words were real and for her.

He raised his right hand and his palm cupped her chin as he gently wiped away the trace of a tear from her face with his thumb. Her skin was soft and her colour was already starting to return, bringing a flush of life to her cheeks.

'You are a remarkable and wonderful mother, Ella. Don't let anyone *ever* tell you any different. Okay?'

He looked into her eyes now, and felt her chest rise a little under the quilt.

Seb tried to ignore the overwhelming urge that swelled from deep within him to caress and protect her—an urge that was threatening to break down his resolve not to become even more connected to Ella.

Except at that moment Ella seemed to take his uncomfort-able squirming as a signal that she could move to a better position so that she could argue with him, and made an effort to wriggle out of her quilt. He recalled the dress that she was wearing and decided that it would be better for both of them if she stayed wrapped inside her quilt, so he held her even tighter against his body until she conceded.

'Okay,' she whispered, and her mouth curved up at the sides into a timid smile that was so warm, trusting and caring that any shade of doubt he might have had was blown away in a fierce blast of red-hot attraction.

Only this time it was Ella who surprised him by wriggling her left arm free on top of the quilt and laying it on his chest as she snuggled closer into his shoulder and gave a gentle sigh.

A sigh of contentment that hit him hard and hit him again as his own body responded to her touch.

His heart raced to match hers, the blood hot in his veins. The gentle pressure of the side of her face on his chest flicked on switches he'd thought were long burnt out. Switches connected to a tangled set of wires labelled with words like trust and caring and commitment.

Caring? His mind reeled at the very concept. This was impossible. Ridiculous! He could not be falling for this lovely woman he first met only yesterday. He just couldn't! Could he?

What about the small matter of the fact that the worlds they inhabited were not only continents apart, but her world was based around Dan and the simple life in this house, whereas his…? He had renounced love and chosen the type of frenetic lifestyle where no second of the day was wasted in relaxation.

They might be breathing the same air, but apart from that they had so little in common it was crazy.

He glanced down at the gentle rise and fall of her chest against his in the warm glow from the now-hot fire. She was dozing. This beautiful, fragile, clever and funny woman was using him as a pillow.

And he absolutely adored it.

He was doomed.

And where did that leave him? Leave all three of them?

Only one way to find out.

'I don't know how to say this, so I'm simply going to say it anyway.'

His jaw seemed to tighten and as she looked into those wonderful amber-brown eyes they smiled back at her as though he was looking for reassurance that what he was about to say would not be rejected.

'You are a very attractive woman, Ella Bailey Martinez. The kind of woman a guy like me could fall for very easily. And cause a lot of damage in the process.'

His hand slowly lifted up her fingers to his mouth, and his warm lips pressed against each of her fingertips, one by one, sending delicious shivers of tender longing sweeping through her.

It was the sweetest tender touch she had been missing, and the instant Seb lowered her hand and released her fingers she knew that she wanted him to do it again. And again.

It had been so long since she had been held like this, touched and caressed like this, even before Chris died when their love life had died down to the point of a few absent-minded pecks on the cheek when he remembered.

There had been nobody else since.

Seb was like water in a desert. And she wanted to drink her fill.

'I need to know if you feel the same way,' he asked. 'Or is it only me?'

She had sensed the attraction since the moment they had met on the dusty road, but putting it into words was harder than she expected.

He needed her to tell him how she felt.

He *needed* her.

And it was terrifying. What was going to happen? Was it possible that they could have a future together? Could she let this man into her life and take the consequences? For herself and for Dan?

Yes, Seb had been kind to Dan, and she had been surprised that her little boy had taken to Seb so quickly, but her simple life in rural France was poles apart from Seb's high-flying world.

What had her mother always said when she struggled to

learn how to sing a new ballad? 'Go with your heart first. Follow your heart.'

Her fingers stroked his cheek and his eyes fluttered in pleasure before opening with such desire that every cell in her body screamed, *'This one. Choose this one.'*

She grinned and lifted her shoulders into a slight shrug. 'I'm scared.'

Seb must have been holding his breath because he shuddered out a half-smile before hugging her closer. 'Me too.' His hand caressed her waist and she sensed the air change a little before he braced himself with the big question. 'Are you scared for Dan? Or is it Dan's father?'

She closed her eyes. She'd never talked about Christobal to anyone. Certainly not to Nicole or Sandrine. As far as they knew she had been a devoted wife who was still mourning the loss of her soulmate. The truth was too hard. And way too difficult.

Only now that she tried to recall the personal conversations with Seb in the short time she had known him, she realised that her husband had never come up. Seb had no way of understanding how she felt about the man she had loved once.

Her stomach cramped in anxiety and he instantly seemed to sense her resistance.

'You don't have to talk if you don't want to. Being a single mother is hard enough. I know that Dan has to come first in your life.'

Now he was being sympathetic! This was totally wrong. She did not want sympathy from Seb. Just the opposite. And she especially did not want him to think that memories of Chris were still influencing her choices.

'No. It's okay. After Chris died in a car crash, my life was in turmoil.' Ella focused on a spot in the pattern of the patchwork quilt as Seb squeezed her hand once more in encouragement. 'But you know the hardest part? I knew that

I was lying to myself and everybody else. Christobal and I were so in love when we married. It was a magical time for both of us, and I will never forget it. He was really making a name for himself as a conductor around the world and I loved travelling with him to rehearsals.' She flashed a smile at Seb before refocusing on moving her hands in his.

Her head fell onto Seb's chest. 'Only… Once I got pregnant I couldn't go with him on long overseas tours, and we…we drifted apart.'

Ella sucked in a breath and concentrated on the sound of the crackling fire and Seb's heart beating under his shirt to steady herself enough to go on.

'Chris adored Dan and we both agreed that he had to come first. We were both professionals. We had no illusions about how hard it was going to be when he was away so much. We just didn't expect our marriage to fall apart so completely and so quickly in the process. The truth is…' And her voice faltered, before she steadied herself to explain, 'The truth is that for the last two years of marriage we were living more like brother and sister.'

Her head lifted in emphasis. 'Oh, we cared about each other. Very much! And he loved Dan! We never stopped being friends, and I think we made a good show of pretending to be a happy couple, but in private we both knew that our marriage was over.'

Seb kissed her forehead before replying, 'I am so sorry.'

She sighed and nodded once. 'Me too. Christobal was a wonderful man who had a brilliant future ahead of him, and I still mourn him and miss having him in my life. Only, not so much as my husband, but more like the best kind of brother a girl could wish for. He was great company. Funny. Talented. He was the best friend I ever had. I miss him every day.'

'I don't understand. You are still wearing your wedding ring and answering to your married name,' Seb replied, and

Ella could feel a new awkwardness between them and he moved slightly back on the sofa, creating a physical as well as a mental barrier.

'I was proud that he chose me as his wife and the mother of his child. As for now?' Ella shook her head. 'People know me as a grieving young widow and my efforts at making a new life haven't gone too well, so I let them believe it for Dan's sake as well as mine. I hate being such a hypocrite.'

'You have nothing to be ashamed about,' Seb replied, his brows coming together into a frown. 'People change. It doesn't mean that you didn't care about each other or your son.'

'I feel more disappointment than shame. I knew all about touring! How hard a life it was! But I believed that we would have a marriage like my parents. They have been married thirty-five years and are still so much in love it hurts. They can't bear to be separated.'

Tears started to prick the back of Ella's eyes now, and she straightened her back on the sofa and tried to slide away, but Seb brought his legs up, blocking her escape.

'I'm right here. And I'm not going anywhere until you get those demons off your chest.'

'What if I don't want to talk about it?' Ella replied, her voice bumbling with more indignation and frustration than she had intended. 'I'm not proud of having a failed marriage. And I'm even less proud of pretending to the world that it was perfect. Because it wasn't at the end.'

'You shared a wonderful few years together. Is that right? Is that true?'

She hesitated, already sensing where Seb was going with this question. For years she had felt the pain of never knowing what might have happened if Christobal had not jumped into that *particular* taxi cab on that *particular* day. Her feelings were so mixed up. Guilt. Regret. Disappointment. And fear. But one thing she was clear about was the answer to that question. She had loved Christobal and for a precious time he had loved her. 'Yes. Yes, that is true.'

Seb slipped off the sofa and leant on the rug in front of the fire so that he was facing her directly. 'Then celebrate that fact. And move on.'

Her mouth dropped open. 'Move on? How do you propose I do that when I have a six-year-old little boy to take care of? If you want to feel sorry for someone, save your sympathy for Dan. He is the one who will never know his dad!'

She was shaking now, her voice harsh and angry despite being little more than a whisper. 'Dan needs me to be strong for him. I'm all he has.'

Seb reached forward and clasped her hands in his, before she could move them out of reach. 'How old was Dan when his father died?'

Ella looked into Seb's eyes and the tenderness and caring in them almost broke her. 'Eighteen months. No more than a baby really. We were living in Barcelona with his parents back then. Chris was in Mexico on tour when his taxi was broadsided by a truck. No brakes. He died instantly.'

A photo of the crash flashed into her mind and she instantly closed her eyes and squeezed them together to block out the terrible images, suddenly angry with Seb for making her see it again. For taking her back to those dark days of oblivion and pain when she was so very, very alone.

'It must have been horrible for the whole family. His poor parents!'

'Oh, yes, his poor parents!' Ella replied with so much venom in her voice that she pulled her hand away from Seb's grasp and slapped it over her mouth.

Horrified by what she had said, Ella spun her legs over the edge of the sofa and tried to stand, only to fall back dizzily, light-headed, her heart pounding.

Instantly Seb was holding her upright in his arms,

supporting the back of her head with one hand as his other held her firmly against him, close enough for her sobs to be soaked up by the fabric of his shirt.

'Oh, that was so unfair! Please forget I just said that. I am a horrible person for even thinking that way!'

'No.' Seb's reply was muffled by her hair. 'You are not a horrible person. Far from it. But something happened to upset you. You have come this far, Ella. You can tell me. Why is there such a rift between you and the Martinez family?'

Ella felt Seb lift up her chin so that she could see him smile down at her as his hand caressed her lower back, holding her in his arms, taking her weight. Supporting her. Those strong arms giving her the strength she needed to tell him the truth.

'They…' And she swallowed down hard and clamped her eyes shut as she clutched Seb even closer. 'They tried to take Dan away from me. And they almost succeeded.'

CHAPTER NINE

SEB pulled the collar of Ella's fleece jacket a little higher to ward off the chill wind that was still howling outside the kitchen door. The skin at the back of his fingers lingered just a little too long at the base of her neck as he flicked the hair from under the collar and smoothed down the soft, cosy fabric.

And he sealed it with a gentle touch of his lips to the hollow just below her ear.

His reward was a smile as warm as the steaming tea he set before her on the kitchen table. A ring of beeswax candles lit up the centre of the kitchen, their flickering flames creating an intimate dome of light, just bright enough to light the gas ring without accidents.

'You don't need to tell me anything else, Ella. I know that you are a wonderful mother. You've made a life for yourself and Dan. That's all that matters.'

Ella nodded and sipped her tea. 'That's true. But it's okay, I want to tell you.' She looked at him with such trust and innocence that he slid back onto his seat and waited for her to begin.

The confident and joyous woman he had admired only a few hours ago was starting to return. And if telling him the truth made it easier, then he would listen. 'I haven't talked about this to anyone. Not even Nicole or Sandrine. But I have to go back to Barcelona with Dan next week, and maybe it is time to sort out what happens to Dan in the future.'

She sighed once, then gritted her teeth as painful memories hit hard.

'After Chris died in the accident…well, I was a mess, Seb. So when Chris's parents offered me a home with them for as long as I wanted, I was truly grateful. I really was. Everything was such a blur. My parents came to Barcelona for a few weeks but they had already given up the jazz club in London and bought a motor home to help with their touring. It was not designed for a young baby. As the months went by I started to feel…I don't know. Trapped, I suppose. I like Barcelona, it is a beautiful city with a wonderful live music scene. But that made me yearn so much for my old life on the stage.'

'And perhaps a little desperate to get your life back on track?' Seb added, wanting her to know that he understood, only too well, how it felt when your world was turned upside down because of events you felt powerless to control.

She shrugged. 'I did something stupid, and booked a gig at one of the local jazz festivals Chris and I used to go to together with our musician friends. It was just a couple of hours on a lovely July afternoon.' Then a smile crept back onto her mouth and Seb realised just how much he had missed that. 'Dan slept through the whole thing at the side of the stage under the fierce protection of my Spanish friend and her mother.'

Ella closed her eyes and her smile dropped. 'The fallout was horrendous. I was accused of being irresponsible and, well, a poor mother, for taking an infant into that sort of environment. I tried to explain that he had the best babysitters in the city *and* I could see him the whole time, but it was no good. As far as they were concerned I could not be trusted to look after their grandson.'

Her hands clamped tight around the beaker of steaming tea. 'So they called their lawyers. Who took me to the cleaners.'

Ella focused on the flickering shadows from the candlelight and her voice was harsh now. 'You can imagine the kind of picture their lawyers painted.'

She sighed and half smiled up at Seb. 'Until I got married I had basically lived most of my life as a nomad. Apart from a few years of formal education in London I had been educated and had grown up on the road. Touring from town to town. Making a living as we went.'

She lifted her hands and pointed from finger to finger. 'I don't have any formal qualifications, even if I do speak several languages and can sight-read, play and sing just about any piece of music first pass. No savings, of course. No pension. No insurance. And no way of earning a living to support myself and my son. Oh—and I had no home to go to.'

She dropped her hands onto her lap. 'Put that all together and any judge is going to think very hard about whether the child's grandparents should have custody instead of this flakey, messed-up girl sitting in front of him.'

Seb took her hands in his so that their faces were only inches apart.

'What did you do to change their minds?'

A warm and coy smile beamed back at him. 'I did something I had never done before. I fought back. It was tough.' She snorted. 'Make that very tough. My parents helped with professional references and somehow I managed to convince them that I could support myself without handouts. But it was still hard.'

She looked down at Seb's hands and turned them over so that she could trace the life line across his palm with a fingertip. He sucked in air as delicious shivers moved up his arm and into the part of his heart he had thought was closed off from the world and all it had to throw at him—closed off with the barriers of work and a relentless drive to succeed.

Now this seriously amazing little woman was doing a pretty good job of tearing them down.

'I didn't blame them, you know. I've never blamed them. They had lost their son and wanted the best for Dan. Or maybe that was the best for them at the same time. I don't know, but it was all about Dan in the end.'

'And what about you, Ella? Are you saying that they wanted Dan to grow up in an ivory castle without his mother?'

'Maybe. But I understand why his parents did it. Never more so. It just took me a few years to catch on.'

'Are you justifying what they did?'

'No.' She shook her head. Her voice lowered an octave. 'Focusing on what was best for Dan made me grow up in a hurry. Suddenly I had to prove to the local authorities that I had the ability to take care of a child on my own and pay the bills. A safe home. School. Medical care. That meant a regular income from a full-time job. Maybe even a bank account with some money in it.'

She bared her teeth in a grimace. 'That would be new. Believe me. Pensions and savings were for other people who had regular jobs.'

'You didn't have any savings at all?'

Ella shook her head then blew out, hard.

'They were the hardest six months of my life but eventually I left Barcelona a different person from the girl who was going to sing every night of the week just for the love of it, to please myself and my family, then move on to the next venue. I had changed. A lot.' She paused and her eyes flicked up at Seb as he held his breath for what she was about to say next.

'I had gone from being a girl who was always ready to take off for the next thrill at a minute's notice to a single mother who was at home with a child who was going to get all of my attention if I wanted to keep him. I had to find a job. And fast.'

'And then you met Nicole.'

She nodded. 'Actually I met one of Nicole's friends at the Avignon Jazz Festival. My parents had a three-set gig so I brought Dan on the train from Barcelona. She asked me if I knew anyone who might be interested in working as a housekeeper for her friend who had a holiday home. Ta da! I loved to cook. I could learn to clean. Two days later I had a roof over our heads and a regular income. And we never went back.'

She blew out dramatically and dropped her head back. 'And there you have it. A brief introduction to the life and times of Ella Jayne Bailey Martinez.'

Her head came back up and she squeezed Seb's hands. 'I am so sorry. I never intended to bore you silly. Can I blame it on the mistral? It does make some people melancholy.'

'And perhaps a little scared about what the future might hold?'

Ella bit her lip and swallowed, her face quiet and still, but her eyes were on fire.

'I'll remember the good times Chris and I shared together but I can't control the past. Only the future.' And she smiled at him. A smile that lit up her eyes and mouth and face. 'Right?'

'Absolutely. Does that mean you might be ready to go on your first dinner date in…how long has it been? Over four years? Well, that just has to be wrong!'

He took one look at the stunned expression on her face and grinned. 'I understand that there is some form of music festival in the area at the moment. I will be out for most of the day in Montpellier following up a few leads on André Morel, but I was wondering if you would care to join me tomorrow evening? Oh. Sorry, later *this* evening for some dinner and musical entertainment? It sounds like a fine excuse to start looking forward instead of backwards, and possibly even enjoy yourself.'

'You want to take me out to dinner?' She squeezed her eyes half closed. 'No. Not if it is out of pity for the sob story you just squeezed out of me. Is it?'

Then he tapped her gently on the underside of her chin with his knuckles.

'It's been a long time for me too, Ella.' His voice was gentle and warm. 'But now I'm asking you to trust me. Can you try and do that? Trust me as much as I want to be with you?'

And before Ella had a chance to answer he shifted his head and brushed her lips with his, the tip of this tongue moistening her soft mouth. Begging her to respond as he moved slowly to her chin and neck, kissing her soft skin with all of the tenderness his heart could bring. Desperate not to break the deep connection he knew bonded them together.

His mouth brushed along the length of her cheek, the stubble on his chin rough against the soft warmth of her skin, and tasted the salt of dried tears.

Drawing back, he gazed at her in wonder for a few seconds before brushing away the teardrops that had fallen from the corners of her eyes with his thumbs as he cupped her face in his hands.

'I am going to take that a yes. Was that a nod? Excellent,' he said and he moved to kiss her again.

Only at that second the electricity came back on in a blinding brightness against the relative gloom of their cosy nest and Ella buried her face in his shirt to escape the glare.

'I think that's a sign.' Seb chuckled, and hugged Ella closer. 'You did warn me this morning that it was going to be a very *interesting* day! I can hardly wait to see what tomorrow will bring!'

* * *

Seb switched off the car engine, dropped his head back against the fine leather, and closed his eyes.

He was exhausted. Physically and mentally.

After the traumatic events of the previous day, he had found it impossible to get to sleep in the early hours of the morning and after a few hours of tossing and turning, listening to the wind howling outside the bedroom window, his mind burning hot with thoughts of Ella, he had finally admitted defeat and turned to the never-ending barrage of emails that had arrived from all over the world through a much slower connection than he was used to.

News about the PSN Media offer had still not broken but it would not take long. On Monday morning the financial papers would be looking for interviews and press statements. And, of course, he would have to tell his staff before then.

Matt had pre-recorded a simple video but that was nowhere good enough to reassure the people who worked for him. They needed details and facts. And it was his job to provide them.

So spending almost a whole day driving around the Languedoc from one Morel family to another was a luxury he could ill afford, even if his cell phone had never stopped ringing. Yet, somehow, finding out the truth about who he was and the father he had never known seemed more important than ever before.

Holding Ella in his arms last night when she told him about her past had opened a window for him on his own questions. He *could* hire a private detective and start a detailed investigation, but he knew that the Morel family would be much more likely to tell him the whole story about André Morel if they met him in person as Helene's son.

And he was right.

It had taken him several hours to put together the snatches

of thirty-year-old memories from each individual he had spoken to and create one complete picture.

But now he knew *what* had happened. And *why*. And *when*.

He could not wait to share what he had discovered with Ella.

There was no one else he *wanted* to tell.

Her trust had forged a link between them that was not going to be broken when he left for Sydney.

He slowly opened his eyes and released the tension in his shoulders.

His news could wait. *His problem. His past.*

There was one more piece of information he *could tell her*—but it could wait until tomorrow. The woman deserved one night of happiness before hard reality crept back in.

He had promised Ella Bailey an evening out and that was precisely what he was going to deliver. Time to find out if she was ready to be spoilt!

Seb strolled around the side of the house as the sun began to dip below the top of the plane trees. He could hear cicadas in the vineyard, and a nightingale on the river bank nearby. And a smooth jazz piano melody.

Ella was sitting at the piano in the living room with her eyes closed, her hands moving effortlessly across the keys. She was humming and singing along to the music that drifted out into the garden through the open patio doors, so enchanted by the song that she had not even heard his car glide up at the front of the house.

She sang in such a sweet, tender tone that he stopped, happy to simply listen to her beautiful voice.

It was such a magical sight that his senses filled with the serene beauty of the moment.

And his heart swelled to bursting just looking at her.

Ella was wearing a sleeveless blue dress the exact same colour of her eyes. Luminescent pale china-blue eyes the shade of a spring morning. It seemed to be gathered just below her breasts in the perfect place to make his blood pound and his heart beat even faster. There were flowers and beads in trailing patterns all over the short skirt that billowed out each side of the piano stool.

By Ella's standard it was positively modest and sedate.

She looked stunning.

This was the Ella who had dominated his mind every minute since he had left her that morning after spending an hour on the computer with Dan, showing him all the places where his charity projects were making a difference. Seb sucked in a breath of the sweet garden air. Somehow this amazing woman made him feel and do things that were so unexpected that they startled him.

He had never played computer games or worked on education with children before and had felt so far out of his depth it had been ridiculous—for the first ten minutes, before he had started to share the joy and excitement of a six-year-old seeing new worlds for the first time.

He was not used to acting on impulse. And he certainly wasn't used to sharing his past with people he barely knew.

But with Ella?

She made him feel that he could act differently. And that was more than unsettling.

Perhaps he was being selfish wanting to share the evening with her?

In two days he could be on a flight back to Sydney with several years of frantic project work ahead of him—and no plans to return to France.

So where did that leave him?

The implications of what he was getting into were only too clear when he thought about her little boy, whom he had become so fond of in such a short period of time. The new owner of his power torch was living in the house he grew up in, playing with the kind of dogs he used to play with. It had been such a pleasure to show Dan the wonders of the technology that was so commonplace in his own life, but seemed somehow magical to a six-year-old. The few hours he had spent with Dan had been the most fun he had experienced in a long time.

There was no way he could break Dan's heart with broken promises.

The public persona his media team had created for Sebastien Castellano was a carefully constructed myth created by experts keen to exploit the young sexy image of a man whom the cameras loved—exactly the kind of man investors wanted to know was in control of their communication systems. He could talk to TV reporters; he could walk up red carpets. But his personal life was another matter and one he never talked about.

The truth was far simpler. The truth was that he had only ever dated single girls who knew that he was not interested in a long-term relationship.

That policy had made him a very rich and successful man. And alone. There was no one waiting for him to come home to in Sydney. Or Perth or Tokyo or whatever city needed his skills. All he had waiting for him back in Sydney was an amazing high-tech apartment with every possible luxury. And emptiness.

Ella had helped him to remember how it felt to be part of a close and loving happy family.

Strange how he had been denying it to himself all of these years as he filled every second of every day with frenetic activity then went home alone to an empty apartment.

Only now? More than once that afternoon he had seriously considered driving back to Montpellier and calling Ella to say that he had to deal with a company crisis and someone would collect his bag and it would not be far from the truth. There was always some project that could use his expertise should he want to use it as an excuse. He had his passport in one pocket, his organiser in the other. He could go anywhere in the world he wanted simply by making one telephone call. He could always tell Ella that Matt needed him.

Instead he had driven back to this house. To this woman. Knowing that in his heart he wanted a few more minutes with Ella and her son when he could pretend that they were *his* family.

It would be a whole lot easier for both of them if he left now, and blamed the negotiations for dragging him away.

Walking away would be the sensible thing to do. And until now he had always been the sensible one.

Except this was Ella and Dan he was talking about. There was no way that he was prepared to lie to either of them.

And it had been worth it. Looking at Ella now, seeing her so happy, any doubts he might have had about their date or his reasons for being here were quashed.

Ella was here. Now. In this moment. That was all that mattered.

He wanted to find out if the skin on her neck and arms was as smooth as he remembered. To kiss her lips. Her stunning hair. To savour the precious time he could hold her in his arms.

He felt almost guilty looking at her when she was so caught up in the music; she was completely oblivious to anything and anyone around her.

He would have been content to stay watching her for hours except at that moment she swung her slim legs off the piano stool and raised her arms out above her head in a delicious cat stretch. And saw him. Watching her.

With one flush of embarrassment she slid her feet into

high-heeled slingback shoes and flicked her hair back over
one shoulder as she stepped lightly over to the music system
and pressed the play button. Classical jazz echoed out from
the speakers in the living room.

'It's the other Ella Jane. Ella Jane Fitzgerald. Maybe one
day I will be able to sing half as well!'

As he strolled over to join her he noticed that hanging down
tantalisingly between her breasts was a necklace made up of
an odd assortment of objects. Shells, beads, precious stones
set in silver, a collection as unique as she was. It suited her
perfectly.

Then something sparkled and he focused again, while
trying not to ogle at her bosom.

A thin circle of gold inset with diamonds and sapphires
hung from one of the loops of her necklace. A quick glance
at her ring finger confirmed it.

She had taken off her wedding ring.

Something inside him suddenly felt light and in the mood
to join in the singing, preferably something with hallelujah
in it.

'I like your necklace,' he said, trying to sound calm and
casual.

Her lips pressed together for a fraction of a second in recognition and understanding. 'Thank you, it's new.' Only then
she tilted her head to one side like a curious bird as she moved
her shoulders from side to side in tune with the music. 'You
look very pleased with yourself. Are you going to tell me
where you went today? You do know that I will wangle it out
of you eventually, don't you?'

The joyous, playful tone of her voice was so contagious
that Seb could not contain a tiny bubble of happiness, which
emerged as a chuckle. And then another.

'That's for later. And where is the man of the house?' he

asked, pretending to look over her shoulder into the garden and then the house. 'I come with date gifts.'

'Gifts? A box of lovely chocolates would be nice. Or perhaps a new fairy godmother to provide some glass slippers?'

Seb snorted. 'Please! As if I was that predictable?' He swung a large heavy plastic bag from an upmarket electrical store onto the patio table. 'The store didn't do gift wrapping. I hope Dan likes it.'

Ella peeked inside, looked at Seb with a puzzled expression, then pulled out two large cartons from inside the bag.

'How *very* thoughtful of you, but, er, what are webcams?'

Seb shook his head. 'Dan told me that he was going to visit his grandparents next week, and I thought you mind find these useful. Think of it as a video camera attached to your computer. If you both have webcams, you can see each other and talk live. Every day if you like. Perhaps I had better set it up for you in the morning?'

'I think you had better,' Ella replied as she read the information on the side of the box. 'Wow. I can see and talk to Dan through the computer any time I like? Well. That is, without doubt, the nicest date present I have ever received. Thank you; they are just what I have always wanted. Wait until I tell Dan! He already thinks that you are totally cool!'

'I aim to please.' Seb laughed and pulled out a wrist corsage with a single fresh pale orchid blossom from inside his jacket pocket. 'I know. I am hopelessly old-fashioned. But I hope you like it. Sorry it's a bit crushed.'

Ella sucked in a breath and held her whole body still for a moment as she stared at the orchid as though it were an object from a distant planet.

Seb's face fell. 'You hate it.'

'Oh, no, nothing like that,' Ella replied with a smile, trying to quickly reassure him. 'It's just that it has been a long time since a man bought me flowers. I didn't realise until right now just how much I missed that. Thank you. I love it.'

She quickly popped the flower onto her wrist and held out her arm to admire it.

'Perfect.'

'Um. I would have to agree,' Seb replied, only his gaze hadn't left Ella's face. 'Is Dan here?'

'Oh, young mister Daniel is currently enjoying the delightful company of his school friends at a party at Sandrine's. Apparently there are two birthdays to celebrate next week.'

She grinned. 'Yvette will be bringing him home later and either playing with Dan or trying to get him to bed, depending on the amount of sugar and artificial colourings he has stuffed himself with. I suspect industrial quantities of ice cream and cake will be involved so he will probably still be bouncing when we get back.' Then she added,' I did warn her that it could be a little late.'

'Wise move.' Seb nodded. 'I understand that these musical soirées can sometimes go on after ten in the evening,' he added in a mock serious tone. 'How shocking!'

He looked behind him from side to side, then whispered, 'And there might even be dancing, but please don't tell anyone I said that.'

'Of course not.' Ella frowned. 'Actually I am not one for dancing. I know it's weird.' She shrugged. 'I adore the music but the feet don't move where they should do.'

She stuck out her legs and twirled her ankles. 'I think it comes from being left-handed. I move left and everyone else moves right. Which is the other left, if you know what I mean, which I know you don't? Then my face goes as red as my partner's toes.'

She shook her head. 'I'll be quite happy just dancing along by myself. Disco style. Much safer for all concerned.'

Seb snorted in disbelief. 'Disco! You are the most musical

person I have ever met, so your pitiful excuses do not work on me.' And he strolled up to her and extended both hands palm upwards. 'May I have the honour of this dance, *mademoiselle*?'

CHAPTER TEN

ELLA bathed in the heat of Seb's gaze as he smiled down at her, clearly determined to make her dance. He looked sexier and even more handsome and any resolve *she* might have had to stay on her piano stool seemed to melt like ice.

In seconds they were on the patio under the moonlight.

Her senses were so alive when he was close like this. The garden suddenly seemed full of the sound of birdsong and insects. Bees from the honeysuckle, thyme and lavender were the soundtrack to the beat of her heart and the soft music playing in the house. It was magical. Tonight they sang for her. And for Sebastien. And only for them.

She simply could not resist him. And it had absolutely nothing to do with the fact that he looked every inch the same multimillionaire businessman whose photos she had been polishing for months. No. It was the man under the suit.

Oops. She had a vision of Seb minus his clothes. Big oops.

Ella willed down the intense blush she could feel on her cheeks as she felt Seb clasp hold of her fingers and draw her to him.

'Thank you, sir. How kind of you to think of us poor wall-flowers. All alone and overlooked.'

'Um. Right. You have never been a wallflower in your life, Miss Bailey. You look amazing. That dress...' He exaggerated a shiver then hissed, 'Amazing,' making Ella's blush even hotter. And with one swift tug on her hands she was in his arms. One hand slid strategically onto her waist, the other clasped firmly around her palm. And her body...her body pressed tightly against his chest.

'Exactly what kind of dance is this?' she dared to ask, her nose about two inches away from the open neck of Seb's shirt, so that she could see the dark hairs on his chest below the St Christopher pendant. He smelt of expensive cologne and something musky, spicy and arousing—something that was uniquely Sebastien. A flash of something horribly close to desire ran through her body, startling her with its intensity.

Her back straightened and her head lifted away as she tried to regain her self-control, only to become suddenly aware that the music compilation she had selected for Nicole's party had changed to a lively upbeat rhythm of a South American tango.

Instantly Seb drew her even closer, so that his hips moved against hers, swaying from side to side. Taking her with him. She had no choice but to follow his actions, his broad chest and strong legs pressed so close to the thin fabric of her silk dress that she felt glued to him along the whole length of his body.

'Latin, of course,' he replied, his voice close to her ear and muffled by her hair. Rough, urgent. She was clearly not the only one who was starting to become rather warm. 'Lots of shuffling and stamping. Leg twisting and dipping comes later...although.'

He stopped talking and Ella took a deep breath and asked 'Although?'

His hand moved sinuously up her back as the pace increased and his legs started moving faster. 'Perhaps not in that dress. It is...' and he sighed, the implications only too obvious as his fingers splayed on the bare skin of her back and his grip tightened '...far, far too tempting.' And without warning he leant forward from the waist, so that she moved backwards chest to chest, both of his hands taking her weight with effortless ease and agility. Except that she had been so captivated by his words that she had not seen the move coming and her arms clenched hard around his neck to stop herself from falling backwards and she cried out in alarm.

With a gentle movement Seb slowly brought her back to a standing position, his hands drawing her closer and holding her against him as she dragged in ragged breaths of air in a feeble attempt to calm her heart rate.

'Sorry,' she eventually managed to squeak out, feeling like a complete idiot. She knew that Seb would never let her fall. She had overreacted, her body once more letting her down.

Seb paused and released her long enough so that they could look into each other's eyes as his fingers spread wide so that they could caress her skin in delicious soft circles.

His forehead pressed against hers so that his voice reverberated through her skull. Hot, concerned, tender and understanding.

'You have to trust me and let me lead, Ella. Can you try?'

Ella closed her eyes and tried to calm her heartbeat and failed. Her mind was spinning as his words hit home, all the while Seb's body was pressed close to her, filling her senses with his masculine scent and the sheer physicality of him.

She knew that he was talking about more than placing her faith in a dance partner. And part of her shrank back from the edge.

She had never truly allowed anyone to lead her. Not deep down. In fact the more she thought about it, the more she knew that she had always danced to her own beat.

His breath was hot on her face as he patiently waited for the answer that would decide where they went from here. And not just for the evening. He was asking her to trust him with nothing less than her heart. Was he also asking her to trust him with her future and her dreams?

'I...don't know,' she whispered, her heart thumping so hard that she was sure that he must be able to hear it, but not daring to open her eyes. It would be too much.

'Then perhaps I can persuade you?'

Gentle pressure lifted her chin and, although her eyes were still clamped tight shut, she felt every tiny movement of his body as his nose pressed against her cheek, his breath hot and fast in time with the heart beating against her dress.

A soft mouth nuzzled against her upper lip and she sighed in pleasure as one of his hands slid back to caress the base of her head, holding her firm against him.

The stubble on his chin and neck rasped against her skin as he pressed gentle kisses down her temple to the hollow below her ear. Each kiss drove her wild with the delicious languorous sensation of skin on skin.

He was totally intoxicating.

The tenderness and exquisite delicacy of each kiss was more than she could have imagined possible from Seb. More caring. More loving... Loving. Yes. They were the kisses of a lover. *Her* lover. And it felt so very right.

Which was why she did something she had believed until a few short days ago would never happen again. She brought her arms even tighter around Seb's neck and notched her head up towards him.

And with eyes still closed, Ella kissed him on the mouth.

His hands stilled for a moment and she paused to suck in a terrified breath, trembling that she had made the most almighty mistake. Until now *he* had kissed her. This would change everything. What if she totally misunderstood what he had told her? And he only wanted to lead? Not share.

She felt him shift beneath her, and, daring to open her eyes, she stared into a smile as wide as it was welcome, but then his mouth pressed hotter and deeper onto hers, blowing away any hint of doubt that he wanted her just as much as she needed him with the depth of his passion and delight.

A shuddering sigh of relief ran through her and she grinned back in return and buried her face deep into the corner of his neck. His hands ran up and down her back, thrilling her with the heat of their touch as his lips kissed her brow and her hair.

Kisses so natural and tender it felt as though she had been waiting for them all of her life.

Every sensation seemed heightened. The warmth of the fading sun on her arms, the touch of his fingertips on her skin, the softness of his shirt under her cheek and the fast beat of his heart below the fine fabric.

It was Seb who broke the silence. 'Now will you trust me?' He was trying to keep his voice light and playful but she knew him too well now, and revelled in the fact that she was the source of his hoarse, low whisper, intense with something more fundamental and earthy.

The fingers of one of his hands were playing with her hair, but she could feel his heartbeat slow just a little when she chuckled into his shirt, then turned his face towards the sun.

'Well, I just might. We are talking about dancing. Aren't we?'

His warm laughter filled her heart to bursting.

'Of course. Although I do have one request. I have an appointment with a very special lady who I haven't visited for eighteen years. And I'd like you to come and meet her. Do you mind if we stop in on the way?'

* * *

Sebastien Castellano stood in silence at the foot of the grave in the tiny village cemetery and gently lowered the bouquet of his mother's favourite white roses from the Mas Tournesol onto the engraved granite monument.

Stepping back, he wrapped one arm around Ella's waist, then slowly read out the words chiselled into the hard stone surface out loud.

'Helene Laurence Castellano. Beloved daughter, wife and mother.'

He closed his eyes for a second and thought about the portrait hanging in the living room back at the house that had been their home. And the lovely woman smiling back at him, captured for ever in a moment in time.

Nothing to indicate the devastation her death had brought to all of her family.

His father had suffered six months of agony before packing their bags and putting them as many miles as he could from this peaceful, beautiful Languedoc village where Helene had made her home.

Even if that meant dragging his angry and confused twelve-year-old son with him all the way to Australia. He would probably have chosen a remote island in the Pacific if the international bank he worked for had been able to transfer him there!

'My father chose the inscription. He said that there were not enough words to describe the wonderful person my mother had been. And he was right. How do you put into a few lines the joy and laughter and energy of such an amazing, smart, pretty, funny and creative woman I was lucky enough to know as my mother? It's impossible. All you can do is remember her how she was and hold that memory every day of your life.'

'Oh, Seb. I am so sorry.'

Sebastien sighed as Ella wrapped her arms as far around his waist as she could, and leant her head on his jacket.

'How did it happen?' she asked quietly after a long drawn out silence.

'Brain tumour. I remember coming home from school a few times and she was lying down with a headache. She blamed it on too much sun and rosé wine with lunch.' Seb lifted his head and swallowed down the lump of pain that had built up. 'She never complained. Then one Saturday morning my father came in from the garden and found her lying on the kitchen floor having some sort of seizure.'

Seb looked up into the poplar trees. 'I remember that day so clearly. I was helping out at my grandmother's and we were all meeting up for lunch. It was a lovely spring day, birds were singing and we had been laughing and messing about. Just having fun. Only when we got to the Mas the ambulance was outside.'

He did not dare look at her. 'They thought it was a stroke at first. She could still talk and get around and keep up the pretence that everything was okay, but later the seizures got worse. In the end there was nothing the hospital doctors could do to help her. She asked us to take her home so that she could spend her last days in the one place she loved more than anything.'

Ella sucked in a breath. 'The Mas. Did she…?'

The words were left unsaid but Seb simply nodded. 'We set up a bedroom in the room next to the kitchen where the living room is now. Eighteen years ago, today, my dad and I sat with her for the last time. She was looking out of the window and smiling at the roses—these white roses—so I ran out and snipped off a blossom to give to her, and when I got back inside…she was gone. Oh, Mum, I am so sorry. So very, very sorry.'

Tears were running down his cheeks now, and Ella turned around and gathered him to her, holding him tight until his head fell onto her shoulder and his body relaxed enough for his arms to embrace her. The taut muscles in his chest quivered with such deep emotion that her own eyes filled with tears.

His mother had passed away in the house where she cleaned and cooked and was bringing up her son. How could he *not* feel conflicted? And Nicole was his stepmother. Who used the Mas Tournesol as her holiday home. As somewhere she could hold parties in the summer.

Ella winced. *Oh, no.* The realisation hit her so hard that she lifted her arms and reached around Seb's neck, her fingers caressing his head. Nicole was holding her birthday party only a few days after the anniversary of Seb's mum's death.

Oh, Nicole. Do you even know how important this date is to Seb?

She stood on tiptoe to press her lips against his full mouth, and then his cheek, and his arms tightened into a warm hug, as though he needed to wrap himself in her understanding and sympathy.

If only it could be enough!

'I found out who André Morel is today. It turns out that I was right after all. He did let her down, only not in the way I had imagined.'

'Oh, Seb,' she replied, taking his hand in hers.

'André was nineteen when he asked my mother to marry him. Apparently a few weeks before the wedding he told his parents that he couldn't go through with it. He wasn't ready to settle down and be a husband and work in the bank like his own father had done.'

Seb turned slightly and braved a small proud smile. 'And my mother let him go. She didn't want him to feel trapped and she loved him enough to let him leave her and set off around the world without her.'

'She must have been a remarkable woman,' Ella whispered. 'And what about Luc Castellano? How did she meet him?'

'Luc was André's boss and a good friend to both of them. He was going to be the best man at their wedding. The Morel family suspected that he was in love with her. What they didn't know was that he loved her enough to offer her marriage when she found out she was pregnant. Do you know the strangest thing? As far as his family are concerned, it was a teenage romance and my mother fell into the arms of her friend Luc Castellano to console herself on the rebound. She never told André about me.'

'So he never knew he had a son. What are you going to do?'

He stared at her hand, fascinated by the pattern her fingers and his made as they meshed and twisted and turned. 'I could make the calls. Find an address for André and his new family in Canada. But I won't. I already have a father. And it turns out that he is a damn good one. One of these days I might even tell him that to his face.'

'Oh, Seb. He loved you, even though you were someone else's son. And he still does.'

Her fingers moved below the hair on his neck and closed around the links of a fine chain. Sensing the pressure, Seb released his bear grip and stood back a little to lift one arm and released the St Christopher that was hidden beneath his business shirt.

Ella fingered the small oval medallion hanging from the chain in silence, waiting for him to speak.

'The last time I stood in this spot was with my maternal grandmother. She hung it around my neck and told me that it would keep me safe on my travels until I was ready to come home. I've worn it every day since. I suppose it is a little old-fashioned but it means a lot.'

Seb looked down at Ella and smiled a crooked, lopsided smile. 'The women in my life have a very annoying habit of being right. I suppose I had better get used to that.'

Ella's heart skipped a beat. 'What are you saying, Seb? Am I part of your life?'

His smile widened and he turned away slightly so that he could grasp hold of her hand. Ella sighed in silent contentment as they stood side by side looking out across the stunningly pretty cemetery, past the poplars and yew trees to the rows of sunflowers and vines that stretched out to the low green hills beyond the village in the fading light.

'I haven't been here for eighteen years. And I chose you to share this moment with you. Does that answer your question, Ella?'

Ella smiled and looked down at the roses, their petals fluttering in the warm breeze, and hot tears pricked the corners of her eyes as her throat closed. Seb's fingers meshed between hers, giving her strength as she fought the intensity of the feelings that bound them together. Her only answer was a sharp nod and a whispered, 'Yes. Yes, it does.'

He kissed the top of her head and turned back to face her, then lifted her knuckles to his lips. 'I'll turn the car around. See you in a minute.' And with one small kiss on her forehead he released her hand and strolled back down the grass towards the narrow lane leading up to the church, leaving her bereft. 'Be right there,' she said under her breath, overcome with a riot of sadness and tenderness and devotion and something she had known only once in her life. Something she imagined that she had lost for ever.

She was falling in love with Sebastien Castellano.

Which was just about the craziest thing she had ever done—crazy even by her definition of normal. In a few days Nicole and her sixtieth birthday party would be a happy memory, Dan would be in Spain with his grandparents and Seb would be thousands of miles away in, well, in whatever country he was working in at that moment. Whether it was

Sydney or Seattle one thing was certain. It would not be here, in the village where he grew up.

Ella rearranged the flowers on the granite and smiled down at the monument to a woman who had loved her son as much as she loved her own little boy.

Perhaps his grandmother had only been partly right. Yes, Seb had come home, but perhaps he had only come home for a visit. Not to stay. Not to rebuild a life for himself. Just passing through.

Like a tornado leaving destruction in his wake.

Which made going out on a date with him this evening an even crazier decision!

'Yvette? Are you still awake?' Ella whispered, peering into the living room, frightened of waking Dan, as she yawned widely. She had dozed off for a few minutes in the warmth of the car with her new smooth jazz CD playing on the impressive car music system. And Seb sitting next to her chatting happily away.

Still smiling languorously at the memory of one of the most amazing musical evenings of her life, Ella grinned as Yvette rustled in from the kitchen, very much awake and dressed in her outdoor clothing.

'Ella? Is that you? Have you seen Dan?'

'Dan?' Ella repeated, suddenly alert. There was something in the tone of Yvette's voice that sent a cold shiver down her spine, but she shrugged it off. A windy night with his mother away was bound to unsettle him. 'Is he still up watching cartoons? Not to worry, I'll soon get him settled.'

'Dan isn't watching cartoons, Ella. He's not in his bed. I think he's gone out looking for that stupid old dog.' Yvette reached out and grabbed Ella's arm. 'I am so sorry. This is my entire fault.'

At two a.m. Ella might not have been at her best, but the

words seared into her brain like a shower of icy water. Not in his bed?

She grabbed her friend around both shoulders, forcing her to make eye contact, even though they were both shaking.

'When was the last time you saw him? Please,' Ella managed to get out through a closed throat.

'I checked him about one. He was fast asleep!'

Her head dropped onto her chest. 'I settled down to read the paper,' and her voice came now as a trembling rush, 'and like the old fool that I am I must have dozed off long enough for the boy to slip past me.' Yvette looked up at Ella with tears in her eyes. 'I am so sorry.'

Ella ran upstairs and flicked on the light in Dan's bedroom. The nightlight was still on. The wardrobe doors were open. His boots and jacket were missing. So was the new power torch that Seb had given him.

Suddenly aware that she was wearing thin sandals, Ella fled back to the hall, shrugged on a waterproof jacket and her gardening clogs, flung open the front door against the strong wind, and ran into Seb's arms.

He held her trembling body against his before lifting her fearful face in both hands for a second and asking in a voice so loving and caring that she almost lost it, 'Hey! What's going on?'

'It's Dan. He's gone missing.'

CHAPTER ELEVEN

Dan! Seb's heart contracted and he took a moment to calm his breathing.

If anything happened to that little boy he did not know what he would do! If this was what being a full-time parent was like, it was terrifying!

Seb held Ella against his side, the trembling of her fragile body forcing him to make decisions before she started to panic. 'He won't have gone very far. Not in the dark.'

He turned back to Yvette, who had started to sob.

Oh, no. Time to take charge and use the quick brain and problem-solving skills he was famous for, even if he did feel like floundering.

'Yvette. I know this is hard, but please try to remember,' he said in a quiet calm voice in the local dialect, trying to quell his own anxiety as much as Ella's. 'Did Dan give you any clue that he was going outside?'

'He told me that Milou was still inside the barn, and the wind was howling and he was frightened that he would not be able to get to sleep without his dog. I told him that Milou would be okay and he could see him in the morning. He seemed to accept that...' Her voice trailed off.

Seb kissed the top of Ella's head so that his words were muffled by her hair but still sounded clear and echoing across the silence of the hallway. 'The barn? That's as good a place as any to start. Did he take the new torch?'

His arm slipped from around Ella's waist as she answered with a quick nod, and she almost snatched at it, the loss was so great. 'Ella, you are with me,' he replied, bustling them both into the kitchen and passing Ella the small torch. 'Yvette. Why don't you make a start on the hot chocolate? We'll be back as fast as we can.'

Seb turned back to face Ella and he took a firm hold of both of her forearms, demanding her attention so that when her eyes locked onto his Seb's words were focused on her and her alone.

'We're going to need more light. You make a head start towards the barn, and I'll bring the car around and catch up as soon as I can,' and with one hot, hard kiss on her lips he was out of the door and into the night.

'I like him,' Yvette whispered through a choked throat. 'Helene would have been proud of her boy.'

'I like him too,' Ella sniffed, 'but I don't know what I'm going to do about that.'

'You'll think of something. Now get out there and find Dan. Those torch batteries won't last all night and he could get scared.'

The rumble of a powerful car engine reverberated around the silent kitchen. The beautiful shiny red sports car edged its way onto the patio across the grass like a cruise ship coming into harbour. Only this ship was knocking over the stone flower urns as it went, destroying the bodywork in the process.

Ella ran out into the garden as Seb swung the car around so that the powerful headlights illuminated the top part of the barn doors, which were closed tight shut. She tugged hard at the latch but it refused to move, and Ella's chest heaved with tears of frustration as she struggled against the wind and the heavy wooden latch, terrified about what she might find inside and furious that she could not reach Dan.

'The wind has blown the barn doors tight shut,' Seb called, jogging behind Ella so that they tugged at the heavy latch on the door at the same time. The door flew backwards in the force of the gusting wind and they both lunged inside.

Looking back at them from the seat of an old stuffed chair was a little boy with his arm around his dog sitting warm and cosy under Ella's old quilt and reading his cartoon book by torchlight. A bottle of juice and an empty biscuit packet lay at his feet.

'Hello, Mummy. We're having a midnight picnic. Seb's torch is so cool. Will you read me a story?'

Ella leant against her kitchen table and closed her tired eyes. So much had happened since she had left Dan with Yvette that it felt as though *days* had passed rather than merely a few hours. A few *precious* hours when she had been able to spend time alone with Sebastien on a simple dinner date and concert.

Only nothing was simple where Sebastien was concerned.

Deep pain cramped around her heart when she thought about what could have happened to Dan when he was out alone in the night.

Part of her was proud that her little boy was strong and brave enough to go out in the dark in a storm to find his old dog, but the cold, gut-wrenching fear of that moment when she found his bed empty overwhelmed her once again, and Ella collapsed down onto the kitchen chair and wrapped her arms around her raised knees, not caring that it would cause serious creases in her best party frock.

She had only been gone for a few hours! And look what had happened!

Tears streamed down her face, ruining the clever make-up she had taken an hour to perfect so that she could look great on her first date in years.

The emotions of the evening were finally starting to take their toll and she now knew what being twisted around inside a tornado must be like.

The wonderful, magical evening she had spent with Seb had been turned on its head, and now? Now she barely knew her own name.

One thing, however, was crystal clear. She was never going to be selfish and put her own needs ahead of Dan again.

It had been *her* decision to stay out and enjoy herself a lot longer than she had planned, and Yvette had encouraged her to do so, but the impact of that decision had consequences.

Dan needed her to take care of him. She was the only family he had. His two sets of grandparents were either travelling on tour in some remote part of the world where health care was a distant dream, or holed up inside their luxurious town house in Barcelona, trapped inside walls of loss and grief.

No. Dan was her responsibility. And tonight…tonight she had failed him.

For a few hours she had been given a glimpse of her old life and she had loved it. And now she was paying the price. Her instincts had been right. She could not combine the role of single mother with life as a performer. It simply did not work.

There was a shuffle in the doorway and her traitorous heart skipped a beat in both pleasure and guilt as Sebastien stepped into the kitchen and drew her up out of the chair and into the warmth of his embrace.

'Dan is fast asleep. That little man has had a big day. And so has his mum.'

Ella looked into Seb's lovely eyes and tried to smile through a trembling jaw.

He instantly seemed to pick up on her distress and wrapped his arms around her back, pressing her head into the warmth of his chest, his love and devotion only too clear.

Ella blinked away tears of happiness as he dropped a kiss on the top of her head and rubbed the small of her back.

'I know you were scared. But he is fine. Just fine.'

Her voice trembled with delight at his touch. 'I know, it's not Dan. It's me. I was the one who was terrified this time.'

Seb held her tighter for a second and then his arms relaxed and he guided her gently back into a chair.

He sat down opposite her and stared into her eyes as he brushed a strand of hair back behind her ear with his finger-tips, the delicious sensation so hypnotic and so welcoming that she felt like sighing in delight.

'You can't blame yourself,' Seb said in a low voice. 'You did everything you could to keep him safe. But you have one very determined little boy.'

He reached across the table and took one of her hands in his, caressing her palm with his thumb.

'I've just talked to him man to man about sneaking out late at night on his own without telling anyone where he was going and scaring the living daylights out of his mum and his babysitter. He won't be doing that again.'

His wry smile melted her resolve and she managed a gentle grin as she pushed her shoulders back with a shudder.

'Thank you for that. And for helping me to look for him. I just keep thinking that I should have seen it coming. He knows that his grandparents love him, but being away from home for two long weeks is a big deal when you are six years old.'

'How about when you are twenty-eight?' He paused for a second, then took both of her hands in his, and focused completely on her face, forcing her to give him her total attention.

'I spoke to Nicole this afternoon. The flights are booked out so you should expect her Tuesday. And she did tell me something else. Something important. Nicole is thinking of selling this house so that she can start a new life for herself. And it could mean a new fresh start for you and Dan at the same time, Ella.'

Blood surged to her brain, making her dizzy and light-headed. Her mind tried to cope with the meaning of the words while fighting to reject them at the same time and started spinning downwards in a spiral of terror.

'Nicole can't be selling the house. She told me that she loved it here!'

Ella's head reeled with the implications and she slid her fingers from Seb's and pushed herself onto her feet, using the edge of the table to steady herself as she shook her head and stared at Seb in disbelief.

'Wait a moment. Did you just say that you spoke to Nicole this afternoon? You knew! You knew what she was planning and you never said a word all evening! How could you do that, Seb? How could you not tell me that I was about to lose my home?'

'Because I didn't want anything to spoil our evening together. You have so little time for yourself, Ella. You deserved a few hours away from reality.'

She clasped tighter onto the hard, well-worn wood, her knuckles white with the pressure. She wanted to be happy for Nicole but every part of her screamed out at her own loss.

'You don't understand. This house is not just my job. I love it here.'

Glancing frantically around the room, Ella raised one hand towards the watercolours she had painted of the garden and Dan's artwork on the refrigerator. 'This is the only home Dan and I have ever truly known. These walls are my rock. I need this, Seb. I need this house. And so does Dan.'

She closed her eyes and a glimmer of hope flicked through her brain. 'Perhaps the new owner needs a housekeeper. Nicole can give me a good recommendation. That's a possibility, isn't it?'

There was so much doubt and fear in her voice that Seb walked swiftly around the table and gathered her into his arms, soothing her with calming words before pressing his forehead gently against her brow so that he could smile into her tear-filled eyes.

'There is another option. I know this has come out of the blue for both of us but there is another option. I want you to come away with me. You and Dan. We can make it work, Ella. I know we can.'

His words stunned her with a sense of such wonder and delight that she took a step back and battled to sort through the confusion of thrill, excitement and terror.

'What do you mean…come to Montpellier with you tomorrow, or come to Sydney with you?'

'Sydney, of course,' he replied, raising both hands in the air and glancing around the kitchen. 'I realise that my penthouse won't be quite as exciting as a farmhouse without electricity or midnight picnics in a storm,' he added, grinning, 'but I think you would love it. Being with you and Dan these last few days has shown me what I have been missing in my life. We can be a family, Ella.'

The excitement and enthusiasm in his voice beamed out in the kitchen, filling it with energy and power and vitality. His hands moved to stroke her face and his smile bored deep into the core of her soul with such love and fierce passion that it broke her heart, but that did not make it any easier to slip out of his arms and step across to the open kitchen door.

She needed to clear her head. And fast.

Seb followed her and she wallowed in the wonderful sensation of his arms wrapped around her waist as he laid his head on her shoulder so they both looked out onto the moonlit garden where they had danced together only a few hours earlier.

'Come to Australia with me. And be my love.'

She breathed in the heavy scent of him mingled with the night-flowering nicotiana, the musk roses around the door and what remained of her precious perfume. His words were liquid honey on her frayed nerves, soothing and so welcoming and warm that she allowed her senses to revel in them.

There was no sound. The fierce winds had died down to a breeze and as they stood there, clasped together, a nightingale sang out from the plane trees that bordered the river, filling the night air with its wonderful song.

Calling her with music and joy because it was singing its own true song.

Her heart broke because now she knew that she had the strength to say what she wanted for herself and Dan.

She forced herself to turn inside the curve of his arms and took hold of his face with both of her hands and held it steady, so that she could force out the words that she needed to say before her courage failed her.

'I am happy for you, Seb. I truly am. You deserve every success and I know that you are going to do wonderful work with your charity. But I can't come with you to Sydney. My home is here. In this small village in the Languedoc. Not in the city.'

His handsome face twisted in confusion and he replied in a voice crackling with hesitancy.

'I know this has come fast and it's a lot to take in, but you know that you and Dan will never want for anything. Dan will get the best education and his wonderful, amazing mother can have her choice of singing coaches and start performing again anywhere she likes. In a few years you could rebuild your career. It would be great.'

Ella smiled through her tears in understanding. 'I know that you mean well. You can offer us the best that money can buy. But there are other things we need which will be harder to find in the city.'

She paused as the impact of what she was saying hit hard, and deep crease lines appeared on his brow as he shook his head.

'What do you mean? What other things?'

She bit her lip. Seb had created an ideal picture for their life together in the city, which was brilliant, and yet it all seemed suddenly too much to take in all at once. She had already been through this situation when Christobal's parents had planned her life in Barcelona without consulting her. They had acted out of love, she understood that now, but trying to fit into another person's lifestyle and rules in a modern city had almost destroyed her.

'Peace. Tranquillity. Calm. A garden where I can pick fruit from the trees. Somewhere for Dan to play and run around all day. A community where he feels safe and welcome and his grandparents are within driving distance. And his dog, of course. And something else. Something even more important than any of those things.'

Ella looked hard at him. Could she take that risk in another city with Seb? And what would that do to Dan? He adored Seb. But was Seb ready to be a father to her little boy?

'Can you give us yourself, Seb? Your time and your love and your heart? Not money or possessions. Dan needs people, not possessions. I need you. Can you put us ahead of anything else in your life? Because otherwise I will be repeating exactly the same mistake that Luc Castellano made after your mother died.'

His lips came together and the dark eyebrows twisted more fiercely but he allowed her to continue without interrupting.

'How did you feel when you were wrenched thousands of miles away from this house and your life without having any say in the matter? Don't you see? I would be doing exactly the same thing to Dan as your father did to you. And that is just not fair to Dan.'

Seb inhaled a deep breath and tilted his head, but his smile had faded.

'So you want to stay here and settle for a life without passion in it? Is that right? Have I understood correctly?'

'Of course I would love to travel and work but this has to be my decision!'

He shook his head. 'You're forgetting something. I may only have met you a few days ago but I know you, Ella Bailey. I know the girl who played the piano at Sandrine's the other night. I saw the way you loved the music more than the people around you. You were born with a passion for music and performing. Not settling for some comfortable life. Don't you see? You have made this house and this life a nice safe cage. A fantasy life complete with a child and a pretend family of friends and neighbours.'

She tried to move away but he held her firmly in his arms before going on.

'You can try and deny it as much as you like, but you are the one who asked for the truth. Remember? Well, I'll give you the truth.'

He reached forwards and lifted up her charm necklace with one finger.

'As far as I can tell you have used that wedding ring and your child as a barrier to any form of relationship with any other man after Christobal. That wedding ring screams out, *"Look at me, the poor single mother, and the poor young widow!"* Well, I've seen through that charade, Ella, and I'm telling you that you have just as much passion inside of you as you ever had!'

His voice softened.

'You can do anything you want. If you want to stay as a cocktail pianist, watching other people having fun from your place in the background, then fine! Do it! But if you want to take back the life you deserve for yourself and find the kind of happiness where you are the one out front on the stage— then you are going to have to learn to trust yourself.'

'What do you mean?' she asked hesitantly. 'Trust myself?'

'I watched you tonight at the jazz concert. Chatting to the other musicians and improvising on the piano just for fun. You have such a wonderful talent, Ella. Even I can see that. You were meant to be out there on a stage! Singing! Playing! Living the music—and trusting yourself to be wonderful. Because you are wonderful. You are beautiful. Talented. A joy. And the world should have a chance to see that for themselves.'

'You think I'm good?'

'I think you're better than good.'

He smiled and flicked his finger under her nose. 'And now you are fishing for compliments. I take that as a good sign.'

Seb's arms wrapped around her, snuggling her closer, his hands running up and down her back, his long fingers finding every sensitive spot.

'Will you do it? Will you take the risk? All I want is a chance to prove how much you mean to me.'

Her head lifted long enough for him to smile back at her before collapsing down against Seb's shoulder.

'I am scared. It has been such a long time.'

'I know you are. And not just about performing in public.'

He played with a strand of her hair as his cheek moved against her head.

'Sorry I raised my voice. Strange how my bad temper only surfaces when it comes to people I care about. I do care, Ella. I care very deeply. And, yes, I heard what you said. Would moving to Sydney with me be so very terrible? I'll buy us a real house with a garden where Dan can have as many dogs as he wants, right next to the beach. I have a great life there and it would be wonderful to share it with the two of you.'

'This is all too much, too fast. And it has been quite a day!'

'You don't have to make a decision now. But will you think about it? I have to go to a meeting tomorrow but I'm coming back to see Nicole. Can we talk again in a few days? Yes? Then goodnight, sweetheart. Goodnight.'

He tilted her head and kissed her with all of the love and devotion he could bring, a kiss from the heart. Because he was leaving her with his heart and his future in her hands.

Ella closed down the lid on Dan's suitcase and pressed the palm of her hand flat against the cartoon characters. She had never been apart from Dan except for occasional sleepovers at the homes of school friends and now, of all times, when she needed to be with him so badly, she knew that it was time to let him go.

Time to put the past behind her.

Time to make peace with Christobal's parents.

Of course, they were still in pain and always would be. They had lost their only son.

Ella's heart flinched at the very idea of losing her little boy. It was too horrible to even imagine. Christobal lived on through Dan and he should spend time with his grand-parents and through them come to know more about his father. The very human, talented young man she had fallen in love with.

Seb was right.

The Martinez family treasured and loved Dan and she knew that he could not be in safer or more loving care. She was the one who had to learn to accept that the only thing they had ever been concerned about was Dan's welfare. And she totally respected that.

All she had to do was trust them to believe in her. By showing them that she was the best and only mother that Dan could want.

Milou barked a rough call to Wolfie in the garden below Dan's window, and she looked out onto the sunlit flower beds that made up the safe, small world she had created for herself and Dan.

Was she a coward? Too terrified to leave the nest for fear of falling to the ground?

Perhaps she was. And all of the security she had worked so hard to build was simply an illusion to be blown away in the sea breeze.

In a few days Nicole would be back to celebrate her birthday—and Seb had promised to stay in France until she returned. Then she would have to face Seb and give him her answer.

Could she do it? Could she pretend that she was not thinking about him every waking second? Caring about him? Wondering what he was doing and where he was at that moment?

Because once he had made his peace with Nicole, then there would be nothing to keep him in this small French village full of painful memories.

The sound of barking echoed up the staircase and she smiled, inhaled deeply, slung an overstuffed bag over one shoulder and grabbed the small suitcase.

Dealing with the fallout from Seb was one thing, but keeping it together and helping Dan was something else altogether. Especially when they were about to spend several hours on a train taking him away from this house, which had been the only home he had ever known.

Ella deposited the luggage in the hall and strolled casually through the kitchen and leant against the doorpost, arms crossed. Dan was sitting with his back against the stone table, hardly looking at Milou and Wolfie, who were playing happily in the early morning sunshine. They were completely adorable and she knew that at any other time he would be out there rolling in the grass with them.

Dan had something in his hands that she could not make out, but as she walked casually over to him and kissed the top of his head Dan turned his face up towards her and his loss was marked so clearly that it almost broke her.

He misses Seb. *So do I.*

The question that had haunted her dreams played now like a record stuck on repeat. Perhaps she should have accepted Seb's offer immediately? For Dan's sake if not for hers? Perhaps they could have found a way to be happy in Sydney?

No. She had tried that in Barcelona and it had crushed her spirits. She had to be sure.

'Hey, sweetie. Ready to go and see Grandma and Grandpa in Spain? Aunty Sandrine's car will be here soon to take us to the station and we don't want to miss the train!'

Dan sniffed and his lower lip quivered.

Oh, no, don't do that! Please. Or we will both start weeping.

'Don't want to go. Want to stay here.'

Okay. She dropped down and sat next to Dan on the stone patio so that when he snuggled next to her she could wrap one arm around his shoulders and hold him tight.

Being man of the house was tough for a six-year-old.

'You know that Seb had to go to work. But what have you got there?' she asked as Dan looked down at the fine chain wrapped around his fingers. The metal glinted in the sunshine. Seb's St Christopher! The one he had shown her at the cemetery.

Ella closed her eyes and swallowed down the tears that had been threatening to force their way to the surface from the moment the tail lights of his sports car had blinked around the corner of the drive.

Seb had given her little boy something that meant a great deal to him.

'Did Seb give you that yesterday? When he came to say goodbye?'

Dan nodded twice, then hesitated for a moment and then his words gushed out in a great rush. 'He said that his grandma gave it to him when he had to leave and go all the way to where the kangaroos live. It kept him safe when he got scared, but now he doesn't need it any more.'

Wide dark amber eyes looked up at her with such love and Ella struggled to keep in control.

'In the night I got scared about the dark and the torch was downstairs and then I put this on my neck and I felt better. I didn't get scared any more. Can I wear it all the time, Mummy? Can I?'

'Of course. Here. Let me fasten it around your neck for you. That was very kind of Seb, wasn't it? Because now you are ready for anything! Taxis. Fast trains! Meeting up with all of your Spanish cousins.'

She hugged Dan closer for a moment before sitting back and pretending to straighten the St Christopher on the front of his T-shirt.

'Grandma and Grandpa are so looking forward to seeing you again. It's been such a long time since Christmas. And you know so many Spanish words; they are going to be so impressed!'

'I'm a bit scared about being there without you, Mummy.'

Me too.

'And what if Milou forgets about me?'

'Hey! Are you forgetting about the magic computer camera that Seb showed you yesterday? Well, there is one for Grandpa, so that I can talk to you and watch you on Grandpa's computer, and Milou can see you too, every day. I promise. Okay? It's only two weeks. Then we have the whole summer to have the best fun together. Isn't that wonderful? Maybe Grandma and Grandpa Martinez could come and visit us here? Then you could show them your room and your school and everything. How's that for an idea?'

He thought about it for a few seconds then nodded furiously, his interest sparked.

'Okay. Do you remember what Nana Bailey says?' Ella asked.

'Time to get the show on the road?'

'That's right! Let's get ready to go on the road. Hands washed!'

Ella helped Dan to his feet and watched him stroke Milou a couple of times before he walked slowly inside, dragging his feet. Milou wagged his tail in delight as Ella rubbed the special point on his ears.

'I did not think it would ever be this hard. It hurts so much without Seb. So very much. I'm going to have to survive without him, but I don't just know how I'm going to do it.'

CHAPTER TWELVE

THE hot afternoon sunshine bounced back from the rippling azure Mediterranean Sea and the shiny polished chrome trim on the stunning white luxury yacht.

Seb caught his tanned but haggard reflection in the mirror-like glass of the main cabin window and ran both hands back through his hair.

So this was what a billionaire looked like.

He had worked all his life for this. It was the crowning achievement the like of which he could not even have dared to dream of as a boy growing up in the Languedoc.

The negotiations had lasted all of Monday and well into the night, but the deal had finally gone through. In two days, Castellano Tech would be part of PSN Media, and every one of his own employees had been guaranteed work or an amazingly generous early retirement package if they wanted it.

And he was going to become the youngest member of the PSN Media Board of Directors with the salary, status, shares and perks to match.

More. The Helene Castellano Foundation had just become a reality.

Shame that he had never felt so lost and miserable in his life.

He missed Ella and Dan so much it hurt. Perhaps that was

why he had worked so feverishly all night to block out any other thoughts except work.

He had never needed people before.

Ella should be standing on this yacht right now helping him celebrate, not clean-shaven men in smart suits popping fine champagne while Matt checked that the lawyers had printed out the final contracts for him to sign.

A massive press conference with television interviews was planned for the afternoon followed by an executive party on the yacht for the new management team.

Ella was the one he wanted to share his excitement and passion. Share his life. Share his future.

It had not taken him long to realise that of course he had been kidding himself. He *had* expected Ella to sacrifice her friends and the pretend family she had created for herself and Dan and replace it with what? A lovely home with everything she could possibly want in education and facilities for Dan. And not one person Dan could call family. Grandparents on the other end of an Internet connection did not play football or come over for birthday parties.

He had wanted her to make all of the sacrifices and compress her life force into a pretty cage he had created for her, while he didn't change a thing.

Ella deserved better than that no matter how much he loved her.

Love? Where had that come from?

His breath caught in his throat as the realisation of what he had done crushed down on top of him with a heavy weight.

He was in love with Ella Jayne Bailey and he loved her precious boy as though he were his own son. Luc Castellano had taught him that it was possible for a man to love someone else's son but he had never imagined knowing how that felt firsthand. Until now.

The thought terrified him, excited him, filled his heart and head with so much light and joy that he should be floating right now.

But he had never told Ella how much he truly cared and how very special she was.

He had come close the night he gave Dan his St Christopher, but had not dared take the final step and make promises to a little boy and his mother he did not know that he could keep.

He would never do that.

So overall he had been a complete idiot.

Suddenly he was aware that Matt was nudging him and Frank Smith, CEO of PSN Media, was looking up from the long glass table, pen in hand.

In an instant he accepted the pen from Frank's hand, scribbled his name in three places, and slapped his new boss on the shoulder.

'Sorry, mates. Have to go. I'm late for a date.'

Ella peered over the dashboard of the very solid and safe estate car her parents-in-law had bought for her within hours of her telling them that she was finally ready to drive again, and tried not to scratch the paintwork on the bushes that lined the familiar lane from the road down to Mas Tournesol.

She had missed this lane so much it felt as though she had been away for two weeks instead of two days.

It was worth the trauma of getting behind the wheel again to be able to drive home to the house she loved so passionately, and the man she knew she was destined to be with.

She was not going to lose Sebastien. And if that meant fighting for him, then so be it. He had filled her dreams and thoughts from the moment they parted and all she longed for was to be with him again.

A familiar bark echoed along the lane and she slowed the car down to a halt. Some things had not changed!

Milou was lying in the road in his favourite spot, stretched out in the sunshine and yawning widely, then wagging his tail as fast as he could muster as soon as he recognised her.

Ella had just bent down to stroke his head when a familiar very red but rather dented sports car raced up the lane from the house and screeched to a stop just short of Milou's tail.

Seb jumped out and walked the few steps towards her before snatching off his sunglasses and gazing at her as though he could not believe his eyes.

They both stood in stunned silence for a few seconds, her heart racing in tune with his breathing, and then he smiled and lowered his hands to his hips.

'I'm sorry, *mademoiselle*, but Milou does not speak English. Can I help you?'

His lower lip was quivering so hard as he fought to contain his laughter that she relaxed enough to pick up on the joke. Anything to ease the heartache of simply seeing his face again.

'Hello.' She swallowed hard. 'I'm looking for the Sunflower House. Am I on the right road?'

'Just carry on. It's the end of the lane. Miss?'

'Bailey. Ella Jayne Bailey.'

'Hello, Miss Ella Jayne Bailey,' he answered with a smile. They grinned at each other for a second.

'Is Nicole here?' she asked tentatively.

'Just arrived.' His hand slid across the side of her car as he stepped closer. 'Nice wheels. Do they do it in red?'

Her eyes never left his smiling face as she replied.

'A present from Dan's grandparents.' And then the intensity of his smile burnt through her hesitation and she shuffled one step nearer. 'Is everything okay?'

Are you okay?

There was a low gravelly sigh. 'I collected Nicole from

the airport. And we talked. Really talked. I was on my way to Barcelona to convince you to change your mind.'

Ella shook her head. 'I was on my way back from Barcelona to persuade you to change your mind. But I don't understand. What made you reconsider?'

'André Morel let the most precious people in his life slip away from him because he was too scared—scared of settling down as a husband. Scared of taking the responsibility. I'm not repeating that same mistake.'

Seb reached into the pocket of his denims and pulled out a familiar set of long ornate keys, and he moved a few steps closer, so that his other hand was only inches from Ella's.

Her head lifted and she focused on his face.

'Nicole is building a new life for herself in Paris and London, so I made her an offer she couldn't refuse, with the promise of a warm welcome any time she liked.'

Seb lowered the keys into the palm of Ella's hand and slowly closed her fingers around them.

'Nicole sold you the house?'

'This is the home I always wanted to come back to. If I am honest, I carried it with me every step of the journey back here. Now I know that I couldn't live anywhere else in the world.'

'Why? Tell me.'

'Because you are here.'

Seb's hands came up slowly to support her face, his long fingers tenderly caressing her skin as he leant in towards her, his deep brown eyes burrowing into hers as their bodies touched.

Ella could feel his warm breath on her skin as he whispered the words she had longed to hear, his voice low and trembling.

'I need you, Ella. I love you and I love Dan as though he was my own son. I can work *anywhere*. Go *anywhere*. And if you feel the same I'm happy to make my home right here. Just say the word. Are you willing to give us a chance for happiness together?'

Ella pressed her lips gently against his, desperate to reassure him. 'I am. More than ever. I never thought that I would feel this way again, Seb. I love you. I love you and I want to share your life, no matter where that might take me. You have brought me so much happiness in these last few days.'

His broad grin made her heart sing. 'This is a first for me. You hit me hard, Ella Jayne, and I'm still reeling. I don't want to lose you, Ella. You or Dan.'

His forehead pressed against hers. 'I have a new job. There will still be some travelling, but I can make sure that the dates match up with weekends and school holidays and we can make them family trips.'

His voice trembled with excitement and happiness. 'Can you imagine taking Dan into the jungle or swimming on the Great Barrier Reef? Seeing kangaroos in the wild for the first time? And he would be meeting some great kids from all walks of life on the way. I'd love to have you both with me!'

She laughed out loud and grinned at him, crazy with wild emotion. 'Dan and kangaroos! You might have to buy a farm for all of his new pets.'

His hand moved behind Ella's head so that he could whisper the words.

'Then be with me, Ella, and make my house a home again. We might even have a party to celebrate. Starting today.'

AN ENTICING
DEBT TO PAY

ANNIE WEST

*For dearest Claire whose hard work,
exuberance and sheer talent are an inspiration.*

With love.

Growing up near the beach, **Annie West** spent lots of time observing tall, burnished lifeguards – early research! Now she spends her days fantasising about gorgeous men and their love-lives. Annie has been a reader all her life. She also loves travel, long walks, good company and great food. You can contact her at annie@annie-west.com, or via PO Box 1041, Warners Bay, NSW 2282, Australia.

CHAPTER ONE

'I'M AFRAID THE latest audit has thrown up an…irregularity.'

Jonas looked across his wide, polished desk and frowned as his Head of Finance shifted uncomfortably in his seat.

What sort of *irregularity* could make Charles Barker palpably nervous? He was the best. Jonas made it a policy only to employ the best. He didn't have patience for underperformers. Barker ran his part of Jonas' business enterprise like a well-oiled machine.

'A significant irregularity?'

Barker shook his head. 'Not in overall financial terms.'

Since the company's total assets figured in the billions, Jonas supposed he should be relieved, but watching Barker loosen his tie, Jonas felt a prickle of foreboding.

'Spit it out, Charles.'

The other man smiled, but it turned into a grimace as he passed his laptop across the desk.

'There. The top two lines.'

Jonas noted the first entry—a transfer of several thousand pounds. Below it another, much larger entry. No details were provided for either.

'What am I looking at?'

'Withdrawals against your original investment account.'

Jonas' frown became a scowl. He used that account now only to transfer personal funds between investments.

'Someone accessed my account?' But the answer was obvious. Jonas hadn't made these withdrawals. He managed day-to-day expenses elsewhere and, though large by normal standards, the withdrawals weren't significant enough to match his usual personal investments.

'We've traced them.' Of course, Barker would make it his business to have an answer before he fronted Jonas with the problem.

'And?' Curiosity rose.

'You'll remember the account was originally set up as part of a family enterprise.'

How could Jonas forget? His father had given him chapter and verse on how to run a business, pretending he, as head of the family, was the senior partner in the enterprise. But they'd both known it was Jonas' talent for spotting a sound investment, and his ruthless hunger for success, that had turned the floundering investment company around. Piers had simply been along for the ride, revelling in the novelty of success. Until father and son had parted ways.

'I remember.' Memory was a sour tang on his tongue.

Barker shifted again. 'The withdrawals were made using an old cheque book—one that had supposedly been destroyed.' Jonas looked up, catching a faint flush on the other man's cheeks. 'The records show they were accounted for but this one of your father's…'

'It's okay, I get the picture.' Jonas let his gaze drift across the unrivalled view of the City of London.

His father. Jonas hadn't called him that since childhood when he'd discovered what sort of man Piers Deveson was. Despite his bluster about honour and the family name, Piers had been no model of virtue. It shouldn't surprise Jonas to learn the old man had found a way to access his son's assets illegally. The wonder was he hadn't used it earlier.

'So Piers—'

'No!' Barker sat straighter as Jonas turned back to him. 'I'm sorry, but we've reason to believe it wasn't your father. Here.' He passed some photocopied pages across.

Jonas scanned them. Two cheques with his father's familiar flourishing signature.

Except they *weren't* Piers Deveson's signature. They were close enough to fool a stranger but he was familiar enough with that scrawl to spot the differences.

'Look at the dates.'

Jonas did and to his surprise felt a punch to the gut that winded him.

Bad enough to think the old man had pilfered funds. But this was—

Jonas shook his head, his lungs cramping as unexpected emotion filled him.

'The second one is dated a day after your father died.'

Silently Jonas nodded, his heart slowing to a ponderous beat. He knew the date, and not just because it was recent.

For years his father had been a thorn in his side, a blot on the family—living in gaudy luxury with his scheming mistress. They'd flaunted themselves among the rich and notorious, uncaring of any hurt they'd caused. When Piers died Jonas had felt nothing—neither regret nor an easing of the tension that had gripped him since Piers' defection had taken its ultimate toll. He'd expected to feel *something*. For weeks there'd been nothing, just an emptiness where emotion should have been. Yet now—

'Not my father then.' His voice was calm, belying the raw emotions churning in his gut. Beneath the desk his hands clenched.

'No. We've traced the perpetrator. And she's not too clever, given the obvious anomaly with the date.' Barker spoke quickly, obviously eager to get this over. 'It was a Ms Ruggiero. Living at this address in Paris.'

Barker handed over another paper. It bore the address of the exclusive apartment Piers Deveson had shared for the last six years with his mistress, Silvia Ruggiero.

Jonas paused before reaching out to take the paper. His fingers tingled as if it burned him.

'So.' Jonas sat back. 'My father's whore thinks she can continue to milk his family even after his death.' His voice was devoid of emotion, but he felt it deep inside like the burn of ice on bruised flesh.

How could the woman think she'd get away with this after all she'd done to the Devesons? Surely she wasn't stupid enough to expect mercy?

His pulse thudded as he thought of the woman who'd destroyed so much.

He remembered Silvia Ruggiero as clearly as if he'd seen her yesterday, her voluptuous figure, flashing eyes and froth of dark hair. Sex on legs, one of his friends had said the first time he'd seen Silvia, who was then the Devesons' housekeeper. And he'd been right. Not even a drab uniform had doused the woman's vibrant sexuality.

That had been mere weeks before Jonas' father had turned his back on family and responsibility, let alone respectability, by running off with his housekeeper to set her up in a luxury Paris apartment.

Four months later Jonas' mother was found dead. An accidental overdose, the coroner had said. But Jonas knew the truth. After years spurned by the man she'd loved, his public repudiation had finally been too much. His mother had taken her own life.

Jonas breathed deep, pulling oxygen into cramped lungs. Now the woman responsible for his mother's death had struck again. She had the nerve to think she could continue to steal from him!

The paper in his hand crackled as his fist tightened slowly, inexorably. Fury surged, tensing every sinew. His jaw ached as he clenched his teeth against a rising tide of useless invective.

Jonas never wasted energy on words when actions were so much more effective.

For six years he'd spurned the idea of revenge. He'd risen

above that temptation, burying himself in work and refusing any contact with Piers or his gold-digging mistress.

But now this—the straw that broke the camel's back.

The blood raced hot and sharp in his veins as for the first time Jonas allowed himself to contemplate fully the pleasures of retribution.

'Leave this to me, Charles.' Jonas smiled slowly, his facial muscles pulling tight. 'There's no need to report the fraud. I'll sort it out personally.'

Ravenna surveyed the apartment in despair. Most of the furnishings she knew now were fake, from the gilded Louis Quinze chairs to the china masquerading as period Limoges and Sèvres.

Mamma had always been adept at making ends meet, even through the toughest times.

A reluctant smile tugged Ravenna's lips. Life in a swanky apartment in the Place des Vosges, one of Paris's premier addresses, hardly counted as tough, not like the early days of Ravenna's childhood when food had been scarce and the winters cold without enough blankets or warm clothes. But those early experiences had stood her mother in good stead. When the money began to run out she'd methodically turned to replacing the priceless antiques with copies.

Silvia Ruggiero had always made do, even if her version of 'making do' lately had been on a preposterously luxurious scale. But it was what Piers had wanted and in Silvia's eyes that was all that mattered.

Ravenna tugged in a shaky breath. Her mother was far better off in Italy staying with a friend, instead of here, coping with the aftermath of Piers' death. If only she'd told Ravenna straight away about his heart attack. Ravenna would have been here the same day. Even now she could barely believe her mother had kept that to herself, worrying instead about disturbing Ravenna with more trouble!

Mothers! Did they ever believe their children grew up?

Silvia had been barely recognisable when Ravenna had arrived in Paris from Switzerland. For the first time her gorgeous mother had looked older than her age, worn by grief. Ravenna was concerned for her. Piers might not have been Ravenna's favourite but her mother had loved him.

No, Mamma was better off out of this. Packing up here was the least Ravenna could do, especially after Piers' generosity when she most needed it. So what if it meant facing creditors and selling what little her mother had left?

She returned to her inventory, glad she'd organised for an expert to visit and separate any valuable items from the fakes. To Ravenna they all looked obscenely expensive and rather ostentatious. But since her home was a sparsely furnished bedsit in a nondescript London suburb, she was no judge.

Jonas pressed the security buzzer a second time, wondering if she was out and his spur of the moment trip to Paris had been an impetuous waste of time.

He didn't do impetuous. He was methodical, measured and logical. But he also had a razor-sharp instinct for weakness, for the optimum time to strike. And surely now, mere weeks after Piers' death, his father's mistress would be feeling the pinch as creditors started to circle.

Static buzzed and a husky, feminine voice spoke in his ear. 'Hello?'

Yes! His instinct had been right.

'I'm here to see Madam Ruggiero.'

'Monsieur Giscard? I was expecting you. Please come up.'

Jonas pushed open the security door into a marble foyer. He ignored the lift and strode up the couple of floors to what had been his father's love nest. Suppressing a shiver of revulsion, he rapped on the door of the apartment.

It swung open almost immediately and he stepped past a slim young woman into a lavishly furnished foyer. Through an open door he glimpsed an overfull salon but no sign of the woman he'd come to see. He moved towards the inner room.

'You're not Monsieur Giscard.' The accusation halted him.

He swung round to find eyes the colour of rich sherry fixed on him.

'No. I'm not.'

For the first time he paused to survey the woman properly and something—surprise?—rushed through him.

Slim to the point of fragility, she nevertheless had curves in all the right places, even if they were obscured by ill-fitting dark clothes. But it was her face that arrested him. Wide lush mouth, strong nose, angled cheekbones that gave her a fey air, lavish dark lashes and rather straight brows framing eyes so luminous they seemed to glow. Each feature in her heart-shaped face was so definite that together they should have jarred. Instead they melded perfectly.

She was arresting. Not pretty but something much rarer. Jonas felt his pulse quicken as heat shot low in his body.

He stiffened. When was the last time the sight of a woman, even a uniquely beautiful one, had affected him?

'And you are?' She tilted her head, drawing his gaze from her ripe mouth to the ultra-short sable hair she wore like a chic, ruffled cap. Another few weeks and she'd have curls.

He frowned. Why notice that when he had more important matters on his mind?

'Looking for Madam Ruggiero. Silvia Ruggiero.' It surprised him how difficult it was to drag his gaze away and back to the apartment's inner rooms.

'You don't have an appointment.' There was something new in her voice. Something hard and flat.

'No.' His mouth curled in a smile of grim anticipation. 'But she'll see me.'

The young woman strode back into his line of sight, blocking his way to the salon. Jonas catalogued the lithe grace of her movements even as he told himself he didn't have time for distractions.

She shook her head. 'You're the last person she'd see.'

'You know who I am?' His gaze sharpened as he took in her defiant stance—arms akimbo and feet planted wide, as if she could prevent him if he chose to push past! She was tall, her mouth on a level with his collarbone, and she stared up at him with complete assurance.

'It took me a moment but of course I do.' A flicker of expression crossed her features so swiftly Jonas couldn't read it. But he watched her swallow and realised she wasn't as confident as she appeared. Interesting.

'And you are?' Jonas was used to being recognised from press reports, but instinct told him he'd met this woman before. Something about her tugged at half-buried memory.

'Forgettable, obviously.' Her lips twisted in a self-deprecating smile that ridiculously drove a spike of heat through his belly.

Jonas blinked. She wasn't smiling at him yet he reacted.

Annoyance flared. He drew himself up, watching her gaze skate across his shoulders and chest.

'She's not here.' The words tumbled out in a breathless rush that belied her aggressively protective stance. 'So you can't see her.'

'Then I'll wait.' Jonas stepped forward, only to come up against her slim frame, vibrating with tension. He'd expected her to give way. She surprised him with her determination to stand her ground. But he refused to retreat, no matter how distracting the sensation of her body against his. His business with Silvia Ruggiero was long overdue.

He looked down and her golden brown eyes widened as if in shock.

'I'm not going away,' he murmured, suppressing an inexplicable desire to lift his hand and see if her pale face was as soft as it appeared. The realisation threw him, making his voice emerge harshly. 'My business won't wait.'

Again she swallowed. He followed the movement of her slim throat with a fascination that surprised him. The scent of her skin filled his nostrils: feminine warmth and the tang of cinnamon.

Abruptly she stepped back, her chest rising and falling quickly, drawing his attention till he snapped his eyes back to her face.

'In that case you can talk with me.' She turned and led the way into the salon, her steps a clipped, staccato beat on the honey-coloured wood floor.

Jonas dragged his gaze from the sway of her hips in dark trousers and followed, furious to find himself distracted from his purpose even for a moment.

She settled herself on an overstuffed chair near a window framed by cloth of gold curtains. Hoping to put him at a disadvantage with her back to the light? It was such an obvious ploy. Instead of taking a seat Jonas prowled the room, knowing that with each passing moment her unease increased. Whoever she was, she was in cahoots with Silvia Ruggiero. Jonas wouldn't trust her an inch.

'Why should I share my business with a stranger?' He peered at an over-decorated ormolu clock.

Was there nothing in this place that wasn't overdone? It reeked of a nouveau riche fixation with show and quantity rather than quality. His cursory survey had revealed the best pieces in the room to be fakes. But that had been his father—all show and no substance. Especially when it came to things like love or loyalty.

'I'm not a stranger.' Her tone was curt. 'Perhaps if you stopped your crude inventory you'd realise that.'

To Jonas' surprise unfamiliar heat rose under his skin. True, his behaviour was crass, calculated to unnerve rather than reassure. But he felt no need to ingratiate himself with his father's mistress or her crony.

He took his time swinging around to meet her eyes.

. 'Then perhaps you'll do me the courtesy of answering my question. Who are you?'

'I thought that would be obvious. I'm Ravenna. Silvia's daughter.'

Ravenna watched shock freeze Jonas' features.

You'd think after all these years she'd be used to it, but still it struck her a blow.

She'd been a gawky child, all long limbs and feet and a nose it had taken years to grow into. With her dark, Italian looks, exotic name and husky voice she'd been the odd one out in her English country schools. When people saw her with her petite, ravishingly beautiful mother, the kindest comments had been about her being 'different' or 'striking'. The unkindest, at the boarding school her mother had scrimped to send her to—well, she'd put that behind her years ago.

But she'd thought Jonas would remember her, even if she'd worn braces and plaits last time they'd met.

True it had taken her a few moments to recognise him. To reconcile the grim, abrasive intruder in the exquisitely tailored clothes with the young man who'd treated her so kindly the day he'd found her curled in misery behind the stables. He'd been softer then, more understanding. To her dazed teenage eyes he'd shone like a demigod, powerful, reassuring and sexy in the unattainable way of movie stars.

Who'd have thought someone with such charm could turn into a louse?

Only the sex appeal was unchanged.

She looked again into those narrowed pewter-grey eyes that surveyed her so closely.

No, that had changed too. The softness of youth had been pared from Jonas Deveson's features, leaving them austerely sculpted and attractively spare, the product of generations of aristocratic breeding. He wasn't a chinless wonder of pampered privilege but the sort of hard-edged, born-to-authority man you could imagine defending Deveson Hall astride a warhorse, armed with sword and mace.

From his superbly arrogant nose to his strong chin, from his thick, dark hair to his wide shoulders and deep chest, Jonas was the sort to make females lose their heads.

How could she find him attractive when he oozed disapproval? When his barely veiled aggression had kept her on tenterhooks from the moment he stalked in the door?

But logic had little to do with the frisson of awareness skimming Ravenna's skin and swirling in her abdomen.

Steadily she returned his searching look. No matter how handsome he was, or how used to command, she wasn't about to fall in with his assumption of authority.

'What's your business with my mother?' Ravenna sat back, crossing one leg over the other and placing her hands on the arms of the chair as if totally relaxed.

He flicked a look from her legs to her face and she felt a prick of satisfaction that she'd surprised him. Did he expect her to bow and scrape in his presence? The thought shored up her anger.

'When will she be back?' No mistaking the banked fury in those flashing eyes. For all his outward show of calm his patience was on a short leash.

'If you can't answer politely, you might as well leave.' Ravenna shot to her feet. She had enough on her plate without dealing with Piers' privileged son. Just confronting him sapped her already low stamina. The last thing she needed was for him to guess how weak she felt. He'd just railroad her into doing his bidding—he had that look about him.

She was halfway to the door when his words stopped her.

'My business with your mother is private.'

Slowly she turned, cataloguing the harsh light in his eyes and the straight set of his mouth. Whatever his business it spelled trouble and Mamma wasn't in any state to deal with him. She was floundering, trying to adjust to the loss of the man she'd loved so ardently. Ravenna had to protect her.

'My mother's not in Paris. You can deal with me.'

He shook his head and took a pace towards her. It ate up the space between them alarmingly, bringing him within touching distance.

Did she imagine she felt the heat of his body warm her?

'Where is she?' It wasn't a request but a demand. 'Tell me now.'

Ravenna curled her fingers into tight fists, her nails scoring her flesh. His high-handed attitude infuriated her.

'I'm not your servant.' By a miracle she kept her voice even. She knew the guilt Silvia had suffered for years because of this man's refusal to reconcile with his father. 'My mother might have worked for your family once but don't think you can come here and throw your weight around. You have no power over me.'

Anger pulsed between them, so strong she felt it throb hard against her chest wall.

At least she thought it was anger. The air between them clogged with tension that stole her breath and furred the nape of her neck.

'But I do have power over your mother.' The words were silky soft, like an endearment. But it was suppressed violence she heard in that smooth baritone, a clear threat.

'What do you mean?' Alarm raised her voice an octave.

'I mean your mother's in serious trouble.'

Fear clawed at Ravenna's throat and she swallowed hard, taking in the pitiless gleam in his silvery eyes.

Understanding hit. 'You're not here to help, are you?'

His bark of laughter confirmed the icy foreboding slithering along Ravenna's spine.

'Hardly!' He paused, as if savouring the moment. 'I'm here to see she goes to prison for her crimes.'

CHAPTER TWO

RAVENNA LOCKED HER knees as the room swirled sickeningly.

She reached out a groping hand to steady herself and grabbed fabric, fingers digging claw-like as she fought panic.

The last few months had been tougher than anything she could once have imagined. They'd tested her to the limits of endurance. But nothing had prepared her to confront such pure hatred as she saw in Jonas Deveson's face. There was no softness in his expression, just adamantine determination. It scared her to the core.

Shock slammed into her and the knowledge, surer with every gasping breath, that he was serious. He intended to send her mother to prison.

A hand covered hers to the wrist, long fingers encompassing hers easily, sending darts of searing heat through her chilled flesh.

Stunned, Ravenna looked down to find she'd grabbed the only thing near—the lapel of Jonas Deveson's tailored jacket. Now he held her hard and fast.

'Are you all right?' Concern turned his deep voice to mellow treacle. She felt it softening sinew and taut muscle, easing her shocked stasis enough that she finally managed to inhale. The spinning room settled.

She tugged her hand away. Worryingly, she felt cold without that skin-to-skin contact.

Ravenna spun on her foot and paced to the window. This

time when she clutched fabric it was the heavy gold swag of curtain. It was rich and smooth under her tingling fingers, but not as reassuring as the fine wool warmed by Jonas Deveson's body.

She shook her head, banishing the absurd thought.

'Ravenna?'

Her head jerked up. She remembered him calling her by name years before, the only time they'd really talked. In her emotionally charged state then she'd imagined no one but he could ever make her name sound so appealing. For years her unusual name had been the source of countless jibes. She'd been labelled the scrawny raven and far, far worse at school. It was disturbing to discover that even now he turned her name into something special.

'What?'

'Are you okay?' His voice came from closer and she stiffened her spine.

'As okay as you can expect when you barge in here threatening my mother with gaol.'

For a moment longer Ravenna stared out of the window. The Place des Vosges, elegant and symmetrical with its manicured gardens, looked as unchanged as ever, as if nothing could disturb its self-conscious complacency.

But she'd learned the hard way that real life was never static, never safe.

Reluctantly she turned to find him looming over her, his eyes unreadable.

'What is she supposed to have done?'

'There's no *suppose* about it. Do you think I'd come *here*—' his voice was ripe with contempt as he swept the salon with a wide gesture '—if it wasn't fact?'

Ravenna's heart dropped. She couldn't believe her mother had done anything terrible, but at the same time she knew only the most extreme circumstances would bring Jonas Deveson within a kilometre of Silvia Ruggiero. There was hatred in his eyes when he spoke of her.

'You're too angry to think straight.' At her words his lowering dark brows shot up towards his hairline. Clearly this was a man unused to opposition.

She drew another, slower breath. 'You've despised my mother for years and now you think you've found a way to make her pay for the sin of falling in love with your father.'

The sizzle of fire in his eyes told her she'd hit the nail on the head. Her hands slipped onto her hips as she let righteous indignation fortify her waning strength.

'I think you've decided that, without Piers here to defend her, she's easy prey.' Her breath hitched. 'But she's not alone. You'd do well to remember that.'

'What? She's moved on already?' His voice was contemptuous. 'She's found another protector to take his place? That must be some sort of record.'

Ravenna wasn't aware of lunging towards him but suddenly she was so close she saw his pupils dilate as her open hand swung up hard and fast towards his cheek.

The movement came to a juddering halt that reverberated through her as he caught her wrist. He lifted it high so she stretched up on her toes, leaning towards him. Her breasts, belly and thighs tingled as if from an electric charge as the heat of his body, mere centimetres away, burned hers.

His eyebrows lowered, angling down straight and obstinate over eyes so intent they seemed to peer into her very soul.

His scent—clean male skin and a hint of citrus—invaded her nostrils. Abruptly she realised she'd ventured too far into dangerous territory when she found herself inhaling and holding her breath.

A shimmy of reaction jittered through her. A reaction she couldn't name. It froze the air in her lungs.

Instinct warned he was dangerous in ways that had nothing to do with her mother.

Ravenna tugged hard but he refused to release her hand. Leaning up towards him like this, almost touching along

the length of their bodies, Ravenna became fully aware of
the raw, masculine power hidden beneath the designer suit.
The clothes were those of an urbane businessman. The burning stare and aura of charged testosterone spoke instead of
primitive male power, barely leashed.

She breathed deep, trying to douse rising panic, and registered an unfamiliar spicy musk note in the air. Her nerves
stretched tighter.

Never had Ravenna felt so aware of the imbalance of
physical power between male and female. Of the fact that,
despite her height, she was no match for this man who held
her so easily and so off balance.

'Nobody slaps me.' His lips barely moved, yet Ravenna
felt his warm breath on her face with each terse word.

'Nobody insults my mother like that.'

Even stretched taut against him, her mind grappling with
a multitude of new sensations, she refused to back down. She
stared into those glittering, merciless eyes and felt a thrill
of fear, realising he was utterly unyielding.

'Then we're at an impasse, Ms Ruggiero.'

Did he tug her closer or did she sway towards him? Suddenly keeping her balance was almost impossible as she
teetered on the balls of her feet.

'In which case there's no need for the macho act. You can
let me go.' She paused, deliberately going limp in his hold.
'Unless you feel you have something to prove.'

Relief gushed through her as he released her.

Rather than let him see it, Ravenna bent her head as if
examining her wrist for bruises. There wouldn't be any. His
touch hadn't been brutal, but its implacability had scared
her.

'Let's get one thing straight,' she said finally, looking
up into his arresting, aristocratic face. 'My mother loved
your father.'

'You expect me to believe that?' Jonas shook his head,
his lips curling in a sneer. 'I'm not some callow kid who be-

lieves in fairy tales. She was on the make—out to snare a rich lover. It was obvious to everyone.' He raised a silencing hand when she would have spoken. 'She flaunted herself every chance she got.'

'My mother never—'

'He was years older, with a wife, a home, a family. He had an extraordinarily comfortable lifestyle, the respect of his peers and a social life he revelled in. You think a man of my father's disposition would give all that up unless he'd been lured into it by a clever gold-digger?'

Ravenna hesitated, as ever torn by the knowledge of how many people had been hurt by Piers and her mother. But loyalty made her speak up.

'You don't believe in love, then?'

'Love?' He almost snorted the word. 'Silvia pandered to his desires in the most obvious way. I'm sure he loved flaunting her just as he loved showing off his other possessions.' His gaze raked the room, lingering on a Cézanne on the far wall that Ravenna knew for a fact was a copy of an original sold just last year. The derisive twist of Jonas' lips told her he knew it too.

'And as for her...' Wide shoulders shrugged. 'He was just a meal ticket. They had nothing in common except a love of luxury and an aversion to hard work. Why should she toil on as a housekeeper when she could be kept in style for simply letting him—'

'That's enough!' Bile blocked Ravenna's throat and she swallowed hard, forcing it down. 'I don't want to hear any more of your poison.'

His brows rose. 'You're hardly a schoolkid any more, Ravenna.' This time when he said her name there was no lingering warmth and no frisson of subtle reaction. 'You can't pretend.'

'Leave it!' She put up her hand for silence. 'We'll never agree, so leave it.' She hefted in a deep, steadying breath. 'Just cut to the chase and tell me why you're here.'

* * *

Fury still sizzled in Jonas' blood so he took his time slowing his breathing and finding his equilibrium. It wasn't like him to lose his cool. He was known for his detachment, his calm clarity of vision even in the most potentially dangerous of commercial ventures.

And in his personal life…he'd learned his lesson early, watching his father lurch from one failed love affair to another. He'd seen the ecstatic highs of each new fixation, then the boredom and disappointment of each failure.

Jonas wasn't like his father. He'd made it his business to be as different from the old man as humanly possible. He was rock steady, reliable, controlled.

Except right now his hands shook with the force of his feelings. He swept the gilded room with a contemptuous glance and assured himself it was inevitable his father's flashy love nest would evoke a reaction.

'Well? I'm waiting.'

At her husky voice he turned to survey her.

Ravenna Ruggiero. He'd never have recognised her as the tear-stained girl he remembered. Then she'd been lanky with the coltishness of youth, her features still settling and her hair in ribbons, as if to remind him she was still a child. Only her mouth and her stunning eyes had hinted at beauty. And the low register of her voice that even then had unsettled him with its promise of sensuality to come.

It had come all right.

Silvia Ruggiero had been a stunning woman in her prime. But her daughter, even dressed in sombre, loose clothes, outshone her as a flawless diamond did a showy synthetic gem.

There was something about Ravenna. Not just a face that drew the eye as a magnet drew metal so he'd had to force himself not to stare. But an elegance, a grace, that contrasted with yet magnified the earthy sexuality of her voice, and that sassy attitude of hers…

The feel of her stretched up against him, her breasts almost grazing him as she panted her fury in defiance of his superior strength, had stirred something long dormant.

Suspended in a moment of sheer, heady excitement, he'd revelled in the proximity of her soft curves and lush mouth. There'd been a subversive pleasure in her combative attitude, in watching the sparks fly as she launched herself at him.

For the first time in his life Jonas, who preferred his pleasures planned, wondered about being on the receiving end of such unbridled passion. Not just her anger, but—

'Did you hear me?' Fingers clicked in the air before him, dragging his attention to her flushed face.

The colour suited her better, he realised, than the milky pallor he'd noticed earlier. Then he cursed himself for the stray thought.

'You want to know what your mother's been up to?' It was easy to thrust aside his unsettling distraction and focus on familiar ire. 'She's stolen money. My money.'

He had the satisfaction of seeing Ravenna's eyes widen.

It galled him that she'd had the temerity to defend Silvia when they both knew the truth about her mother. Like a magpie with an eye for a pretty, expensive bauble, she'd feathered her nest with his father's wealth.

Jonas recalled the day he'd come home unexpectedly to Deveson Hall from London and found the housekeeper in his mother's suite, in front of a mirror, holding an heirloom choker of sapphires and pearls to her throat. Instead of embarrassment at being caught out, she'd laughed and simply said no woman could have resisted the temptation if she'd found the necklace lying there. Without turning a hair she'd put it down on the dressing table and turned to plump the cushions on a nearby settee.

'No.' This time Ravenna's low voice sounded scratchy as if with shock. 'She wouldn't do that.'

'Wouldn't she?' He looked around the over-stuffed room, wondering how many of the pieces were what they appeared.

Money had obviously been tight enough for his father to cash in the more valuable pieces.

'Of course not.' Ravenna's certainty tugged his attention back to her. No longer flushed but pale and composed, she stared back with infuriating certainty.

'Then how do you explain the fact she forged my father's signature in a cheque book she shouldn't even have had access to?'

'Why blame my mother?'

'No one else had access. Piers would have kept it safely by him, believe me.' He let his gaze rove the room. 'I'm sure if we search the apartment we'll find it.'

'There'll be no searching the apartment. And even if it was here, what's to say it wasn't Piers' signature? His handwriting could have changed when he got ill.'

Jonas shook his head. 'That would have been convenient, wouldn't it? But it won't wash. Unless you can explain how he managed to cash a cheque the day after he died.'

Her eyes widened, growing huge in her taut face.

'I don't believe you.' It was a whisper but even that was like a flame to gunpowder. How could she deny her mother's wrongdoing even now?

'I don't care what you believe.' It was a lie. Her blind faith in the gold-digging Silvia was like salt on a raw wound. Perhaps because he'd never known such loyalty from his own parents. Why should she lavish it on a woman so patently undeserving?

Piers had been an absentee parent, finding plenty of reasons to stay in the city rather than at the Hall. As for his mother—he supposed she'd loved him in her own abstracted way. But she'd been more focused on her personal disappointment in marrying a man who loved not her but the wealth she'd brought with her.

Jonas slipped a hand into his jacket pocket and withdrew the photocopied cheques.

'Here.' He held them out, daring her to take them. 'I

never lie.' His father had been an expert at distorting the truth for his convenience. As a kid Jonas had vowed never to do the same.

He watched Ravenna swallow, the movement convulsive, then she reached out and took the papers. Her head bowed as she stared at them.

The sound of her breath hissing in told him he'd finally got through to her. There was no escaping the truth.

The papers moved as if in a strong breeze and he realised her hands were trembling.

In that instant guilt pierced his self-satisfaction. Belatedly it struck him that taking out his anger on Silvia's daughter was beneath him.

His belly clenched as he reviewed their encounter. Even given his determination to make Silvia pay for her crime, he'd behaved crassly. He'd stalked in, making demands when a simple request for information would have done. Worse, he'd been too caught up in own emotional turmoil to spare a thought for the shock this would be for Ravenna.

'Do you want to sit down?' The words shot out like bullets, rapid and harsh with self-disgust.

She didn't say anything, just stood, head bowed, staring at the papers in her shaking hands.

Hell! Was she in shock?

He leant towards her, trying to read her expression.

All he registered was the stiff set of her jaw and the scent of warm cinnamon and fragrant woman.

And the way she bit her bottom lip, pearly teeth sinking deep in that lush fullness.

Jonas breathed in slowly, telling himself the heat whirling in his belly was shame, not arousal.

The idea of being turned on so easily by any woman was anathema to a man who prided himself on his restraint. When she was the daughter of the woman who'd destroyed his mother… Unthinkable!

'Ravenna?' His voice sounded ridiculously hesitant, as if the ground had shifted beneath his feet.

She looked up, her eyes ablaze as they met his. Then her gaze shifted towards the window.

'You're mistaken.' Her voice sounded wrong, he realised, tight and hard. 'Silvia had nothing to do with this.'

'Stop denying, Ravenna. It's too late for that. I've got proof of her forgery.'

'Proof of forgery, yes. But not Silvia's.' She shifted, standing taller.

Jonas shook his head, weary of the unexpected emotional edge to this interview. 'Just tell me where she is and I'll deal with her.'

Those warm sherry eyes lifted to his and he stilled as he saw how they'd glazed with emotion.

'You don't need to deal with her. She had nothing to do with it.' Ravenna tilted her chin up, her gaze meeting his squarely. 'I did it. I took your money.'

CHAPTER THREE

RAVENNA'S PULSE KICKED as Jonas stiffened. Her throat dried so much it hurt to swallow. But she didn't dare turn away. Instead she met his stare unflinchingly.

She feared if she showed even a flicker of the emotions rioting inside, he wouldn't believe her.

He had to! The alternative, of pinning the theft on her mother, was untenable.

With Jonas' revelation so much fell into place—Piers' remarkable generosity in not just covering her medical costs these last months, but funding the long convalescent stay at an exorbitantly expensive Swiss health resort.

Only it hadn't been Piers making that final, massive payment, had it? It must have been Silvia—breaking the law to help her daughter.

Ravenna's heart plummeted as she recalled her mother's insistence that she needed total rest to recuperate. That without the health resort there was a danger of the treatment failing. Ravenna, too weary by then to protest when all she wanted was to rest quietly and get her strength back, hadn't put up much resistance.

She'd never sponged off Piers' wealth, and had silenced her protesting conscience by vowing to pay back every last euro. It was only when she'd arrived at the Paris apartment the other day that she realised they were euros Piers and her mother could ill afford.

Guilt had struck Ravenna when she saw how much they'd sold off. But she'd never for a moment thought her mother had purloined money that wasn't hers!

Oh, Mamma, what have you done?

Through the years Silvia had gone without again and again so Ravenna could have warm clothes and a roof over her head. And later, so she could go to the respected school her mother thought she needed. But to take what wasn't hers…!

'You're lying.' Jonas' frigid eyes raked her face and a chill skimmed her backbone.

Ravenna smoothed damp palms down her trousers and angled her chin, trying to quell the roiling nausea in her stomach.

'I don't lie.' It was true. Maybe that was why she hadn't convinced him. Her muscles clenched as desperation rose.

She couldn't let him guess the truth. Already a broken woman, Mamma would be destroyed by the shame and stress of gaol.

For a moment Ravenna toyed with blurting out the whole truth, revealing why her mother had stolen the funds and throwing them both on Jonas Deveson's mercy.

Except he didn't have any mercy.

That softer side he'd once shown her years before had been an aberration. In the six years Silvia and Piers had been together, Jonas hadn't once condescended to acknowledge his father's existence. He had ice in his veins rather than warm blood, and a predilection for holding a grudge.

Now it seemed he had a taste for vengeance too.

That might be ice in his veins but there was fire blazing in his eyes. It had been there since he shouldered his way into the apartment, prowling the room with lofty condescension as if his father's death meant nothing to him.

His hatred for her mother was a palpable weight in the charged atmosphere.

He blamed Silvia for his father's defection. He'd sided

with the rest of his aristocratic connections in shunning the working-class foreigner who'd had the temerity to poach one of their own.

Ravenna had to keep this from her. If Mamma found the theft had been discovered she'd come forward and accept the penalty. Ravenna couldn't let her do that, not when she saw the violence in Jonas Deveson's eyes. She couldn't condone what Mamma had done but could understand it, especially since she must have been overwrought about Piers.

'You haven't got it in you to do that, Ravenna.' He shook his head. 'Theft is more your mother's style.'

Fury boiled in her bloodstream. She didn't know which was worse, his bone-deep hatred of her mother or that he thought he knew either of them when at Deveson Hall family hadn't mixed with staff.

His certainty of her innocence should have appeased her; instead, tainted as it was by prejudice, Ravenna found herself angrier than she could ever remember. Rage steamed across her skin and seeped from her pores.

'You have no idea of what her style is or mine.' Her teeth gritted around the words.

His damnably supercilious eyebrows rose again. 'I'm a good judge of character.'

That was what Ravenna feared. That was why she had to work hard to convince him.

Maybe if her mother had a spotless reputation she'd ride out a trial with nothing worse than a caution and community service. But sadly that wasn't the case.

Years before, when Silvia had been young and homeless, kicked out by her father for shaming the family with her pregnancy, she'd resorted to shoplifting to feed herself. She'd been tried then released on a good behaviour bond. That had terrified the young woman who'd been until then completely law abiding.

Much later, when Ravenna was nine, her mother had been accused of stealing from the house where she worked.

Ravenna remembered Mamma's ravaged, parchment-white face as the police led her away under the critical gaze of the woman who employed her. It didn't matter that the charges had been dropped when the woman's daughter was found trying to sell the missing heirloom pieces. Silvia had been dismissed, presumably because her employer couldn't face the embarrassment of having accused an innocent woman.

Mud stuck and innocence didn't seem to matter in the face of prejudice.

Look at the way Jonas already judged her. If she went to trial he'd dredge up her past and every scurrilous innuendo he could uncover and probably create a few for good measure. His air of ruthlessness that chilled Ravenna. His lawyers would make mincemeat out of her mother.

Ravenna couldn't allow it. Especially since her mother had stolen to save her.

Hot guilt flooded her. How desperate Mamma must have been, how worried, to have stolen this man's money! She must have known he'd destroy her if he found out.

Which was why Ravenna had to act.

She stepped forward, her index finger prodding Jonas' hard chest. It felt frighteningly immovable. But she had to puncture his certainty. Attack seemed her best chance.

'Don't pretend to know my mother.' Furtively she sucked in air, her breathing awry as her pulse catapulted. 'You weren't even living at home when we moved to Deveson Hall.'

'You're telling me you masterminded this theft?' His tone was sceptical. 'I think not.'

'You—' her finger poked again '—aren't in a position to know anything about me.'

'Oh, I wouldn't say that.' Warm fingers closed around her hand so that suddenly she was no longer the aggressor but his captive. Tendrils of sensation curled up her arm and made her shiver. 'I know quite a bit about you. I know you hated school, especially maths and science. You wanted to run away but felt you had to stick it out for your mother's sake.'

Ravenna's eyes widened. 'You remember that?' Her voice faded to a whisper. She'd assumed he'd long forgotten her teary confession the day he'd found her wallowing in teenage self-pity.

'You hated being made to play basketball just because you were tall. As I recall you wanted to be tiny, blonde and one of five children, all rejoicing in the name of Smith.'

It was true. Living up to her mother's expectations of academic and social success had been impossible, especially for an undistinguished scholar like Ravenna, surrounded by unsupportive peers who treated her as a perennial outsider. For years she'd longed, not to be 'special' but to blend in.

'And you didn't like the way one of the gardeners had begun to stare at you.'

Ridiculously heat flushed her skin. That summer she'd been a misfit, neither child nor adult. She hadn't known what she wanted.

But she hadn't minded when Jonas Deveson looked at her or, for one precious, fleeting moment, stroked wayward curls off her face.

Ravenna blinked. She wasn't fifteen now.

'You remember far more of that day than I do.' Another lie. Two in one day had to be a record for her. Maybe if she kept it up she could even sound convincing.

Did she imagine a slight softening in those grey eyes?

No. Easier to believe she'd scored her dream job as a pastry chef in a Michelin-starred restaurant than that this steely man had a compassionate side.

'You haven't changed that much.' His deep voice stirred something unsettling deep inside.

'No? You didn't even recognise me.' She pulled back but he didn't loosen his grip. He held her trapped.

For a moment fear spidered through her, till she reminded herself he had too much pride to force himself on an unwilling woman. His hold wasn't sexual, it was all about power. The charged awareness was all on her side, not his.

She had no intention of analysing that. She had enough to worry about.

'You've changed a lot.' Her tone made it clear it wasn't a compliment. At twenty-one he'd been devastatingly handsome but unexpectedly kind and patient. She'd liked him, even more than liked him in her naïve way.

Now he was all harsh edges, irascible and judgemental. What was there to like?

'We're not here to discuss me.' His eyes searched hers. Stoically she kept her head up and face blank. Better to brazen out her claim than show a hint of doubt.

Yet inside she was wobbly as jelly. The past days had taken their toll as she saw how grief had ravaged her mother, making her seem frail. Ravenna had sent her away from the apartment so ripe with memories of Piers. She'd offered to pack up the flat and deal with the landlord, but even those simple tasks were a test of Ravenna's endurance. Now this...

'We're here to discuss my money.' Jonas' fingers firmed around her. 'The money stolen from my account.'

Ravenna swallowed hard at his unrelenting tone.

Just what *was* the penalty for theft and forgery?

Jonas felt her hand twitch in his.

A sign of guilt or proof she lied about being the one who'd ripped him off?

Her soft eyes were huge in her finely sculpted face, giving her an air of fragility despite her punk-short hair and belligerently angled chin.

Jonas wasn't sentimental enough to let looks mar his decision-making. Yet, absurdly, he found himself hesitating.

He didn't *want* to believe Ravenna guilty.

Far easier to believe her rapacious mother had organised this swindle. After years keeping his emotions bottled up he'd almost enjoyed the roaring surge of fury against his father's mistress that had borne him across the channel in a red-misted haze.

But what bothered him most was the recognition he didn't want it to be Ravenna because he remembered her devastating innocence and honesty years ago. He didn't want to reconcile that memory with the knowledge she'd become a thief.

Jonas' lips twisted. Who'd have thought he still had illusions he didn't want to shatter? He'd been too long in the cut-throat business world to believe in the innate honesty of mankind. Experience had taught him man—and womankind were out for all they could get.

Why should this revelation be so unwelcome?

'You say you wrote the cheques?'

Again that jerk of tension through her. Her pulse tripped against his palm and he resisted the absurd impulse to caress her there.

She nodded, the movement brief but emphatic.

'How did you get access to the cheque book?' Piers would have been canny enough to keep it close at hand, not lying around. 'Were you living here with them?'

'No, I—' She paused and her gaze shifted away. Instinct told him she hid something. 'But I visited. Often. My mother and I have always been close.'

That at least had the ring of truth. He remembered her misery in her teens, not simply because she hated school and the vicious little witches who made her life hell there, but because she didn't want to disappoint her mother by leaving. She cared what her mother thought.

Enough to learn her mother's ways in seeking easy money from a man? Had she modelled herself on Silvia?

The notion left a sour tang of disappointment on his tongue.

'You're hurting me!'

Jonas eased his grip, but didn't let her go. He was determined to sort this out. Until then he'd keep her close.

'Why did you need the money?'

Her eyebrows arched and she tilted her head as if to inspect him. As if he weren't already close enough to see the rays of gold in the depths of her eyes.

'You're kidding, right?' Her tone of insouciant boredom echoed the attitude of entitlement he'd heard so often among wealthy, privileged young things who'd never worked a day in their lives. Except something in her tone was ever so slightly off-key.

Suspicion snaked through him.

He pulled her closer, till her body mirrored his. He felt the tension hum through her. Good! He wanted her unsettled.

'A girl needs to live, doesn't she?' This time there was an edge of desperation in her tone. 'I've had...expenses.'

'What sort of expenses? Even shopping at the top Parisian fashion houses wouldn't have swallowed up all that money.'

Her gaze slid from his. 'This and that.'

A cold, hard weight formed in the pit of Jonas' belly. He was surprised to feel nausea well.

'Drugs?'

She shook her head once, then shrugged. 'Debts.'

'Gambling?'

'Why the inquisition? I've admitted I took your money. That's all that matters.' Her gaze meshed with his and a jagged flash of heat resonated through Jonas. It stunned him.

How could a mere look do that? It wasn't even a sultry invitation but a surly, combative stare that annoyed the hell out of him.

Yet aftershocks still tumbled through his clenching belly and he found himself leaning closer, inhaling her warm cinnamon and hot woman scent.

This couldn't be happening.

He refused to feel anything for the woman who'd stolen from him. Especially since she was Silvia Ruggiero's daughter. The thought of that family connection was like a cold douche.

Deliberately he chose his next words to banish any illusion of closeness. 'Why steal from me when Piers would have indulged a pretty young thing like you? I'm sure he'd have been amendable to *private* persuasion.'

'You're sick. You know that? Piers was with my *mother*. He had no interest in me.' She drew herself up as if horrified. Either she was a brilliant actor or she drew the line at men old enough to be her father.

'In my experience he wasn't discriminating.'

Ravenna yanked her hand to free it from his grasp but Jonas wasn't playing. He wrapped his other arm hard around her narrow back, drawing her up against him.

Just to keep her still, he assured himself.

It worked. With a stifled gasp she froze. Only the quick rise and fall of her breasts against his arm where he still held her hand revealed animation.

'Speaking from personal experience, are you, Jonas?' Her voice was all sneer. 'What are you doing now? Copping a feel?'

His jaw ached with the effort to bite back a retort.

Unlike his father he'd never been a sucker for a pretty face and a show of cleavage. Sure, he appreciated a sexy woman. But he was discriminating, private in his affairs and loyal to whomever he was with. His intellect and his sense of honour took precedence over cheap thrills.

When he married there'd be no shady liaisons on the side, no whispered rumours and knowing looks to embarrass his family. None of the pain to which Piers had subjected them.

Jonas stared down at the firebrand who'd managed to tap into emotions he'd kept safely stowed for years. In one short interlude she'd cut through years of hard-won self-control so he teetered on the brink of spontaneous, uncharacteristic, dangerous action. He almost growled his fury and frustration aloud.

He wanted to lean down and silence her sassy mouth, force those lush lips apart and relieve some of his frustrated temper in steamy passion and a vibrant, accommodating woman.

She'd be receptive, despite that accusatory look. That was what made the idea so tempting. Ravenna might hate him for making her face what she'd done. But it wasn't merely anger she felt for him—not by a long chalk.

'Oh, I choose my women very carefully, Ravenna.' His voice was a low, guttural burr. 'And I never take anything from a woman that's not offered freely.'

Dark satisfaction flared as he assessed her reaction with a knowing eye.

He read her rapid breathing and the flush that began at her cleavage and highlighted her cheeks. The way her tongue furtively slicked her lower lip. The indefinable scent of feminine arousal.

'Really?' Her breathless challenge didn't convince. 'Well, keep that in mind. I'm not offering you anything.'

Jonas was torn between wanting to kiss her senseless and wanting to put her over his knee. He leaned in a fraction and heard her soft exhale of breath. A sigh…of surrender or triumph?

Suddenly it hit him anew that he was in danger of succumbing to the allure of a Ruggiero female. Of an unprincipled thief who threw her crime in his teeth.

Who enticed with her soft body and tell-tale physical signals.

'Is that so?' he murmured, knowing he had her measure.

She'd use any tactic to thwart his retribution. Did she aim to play him for an easy mark, as her mother had targeted Piers?

The realisation stilled his impetuous need to taste her. Yet he couldn't draw back. He was trapped by a hunger sharper and more potent than he'd known in years.

That infuriated him even more than the missing money. He burned with it, the fire in his belly white hot with a virulent mix of lust and self-disgust at his weakness.

Keeping one arm around her back, he released her hand and let his fingers drift. She didn't flinch, didn't move, her eyes daring him to do his worst. Because she thought herself immune or because she assumed he wouldn't rise to her challenge?

His fingers brushed her soft, high breast and moulded automatically to that sweet ripeness. The hard nub of her nipple pressed into his palm and arousal seared his groin. A spasm of something like electricity jerked through his body.

For a breath-stealing moment she stood rigid as if about to lambast him for groping. Her eyes widened in shock, then dropped in heavy-lidded invitation. Her lips parted on a silent sigh. A moment later she shifted, melting against him.

'Tell me to stop and I will.'

He prayed she wouldn't.

She opened her mouth but no sound emerged.

The weight of her in his palm, the press of her body, the heady sense of promise thickening the air between them, sapped his resolution.

He was ready to take her up on her unspoken invitation. His body was rock hard with a hunger that was all the stronger for being unexpected. Why not take a little something for himself after she'd taken so much from him? Clearly she expected it, wanted it, if the tremors in her pliant body were any indication.

But that smacked of history repeating itself. The little thief would think he kept his brain between his legs, as his father had when he'd run off with her mother, leaving his responsibilities behind.

Jonas couldn't let Ravenna enjoy the illusion of triumph. He had too much pride.

He was nobody's gullible mark.

As she'd learn to her cost.

Gently he squeezed her breast, just enough to elicit a delicate shudder in her fine-boned body and a throaty sigh of delight.

The hairs on his arms prickled and his blood rushed south at the sound of her pleasure. But he refused to respond to the urges of his suddenly intemperate body.

'You like that, do you, Ravenna?'

Slitted now, her eyes had a glazed look that told its own story. She swallowed convulsively, drawing his attention to the slim length of her pale throat. The collar of her dark jacket sat loose, giving her an air of fragility at odds with the pulse of vibrant life he felt as she arched against him.

He'd pull back soon. In a moment. When he'd allowed himself a single taste...

Cinnamon and feminine spice filled his nostrils as he dipped his head, nudging aside her collar and nipping gently at the sensitive spot where her neck and shoulder met. She shook in his hold, her hand grasping his between them as if for support.

'No. Please I—'

Her words cut abruptly as Jonas laved the spot, drawing in the sweet taste of her warm skin.

Too late he realised his error, as he angled his head hungrily for a better taste, pressing kisses up her arching throat, past the throbbing pulse to the neat angle of her jaw.

She was addictive. Scent or taste or the feel of silky soft flesh, or perhaps all three, had Jonas ignoring the voice of reason and losing himself in the moment. In the luxury of caressing Ravenna.

He'd never come across a woman who tempted him so easily.

Her free hand cupped his neck, holding him close, and he pulled her tight against him, enjoying the slide of her body as she bowed back to give him free rein.

He stroked his tongue along the scented skin behind her ear and had to tighten his hold when she slumped against him as if her knees had given way.

She was so responsive, inciting a surge of arousal that swamped all else. Blood roared in his veins, primal instinct taking over. His focus blurred, his mind racing frantically with the practicalities of getting her horizontal as soon as possible.

He nipped lightly at her ear lobe and she turned her head restlessly as if seeking his lips.

Triumph hummed through him as he pressed a kiss to the corner of her lush mouth.

One quick taste then he'd find that preposterous gilded sofa and treat them both to sexual release so intense it would shatter them. Already he was hard as a rock. Carrying her across the room would be torture but he wasn't letting her go till he'd had his fill. Till they were both limp and the urgent hunger gnawing at his vitals was appeased.

His ears rang with the force of his blood rushing. He ignored it and tilted his head to take her mouth.

Except her eyes were open now and that dreamy expression had faded. Stark horror flared instead in those dark gold depths.

Jonas frowned. She wanted him. He knew it. He felt it with every muscle and sinew as she pressed herself against him. Yet—

The ringing sounded again. This time he realised it came from somewhere outside his head—the front door.

'Let me go.' Her voice was so hoarse he read her lips rather than heard her. Jonas blinked, trying to make sense of the abrupt shift in mood.

She pushed against him with both hands. 'I said, let me go!' Her gaze slid from his as if she couldn't bear to look at him. Because he'd made her forget her little game of temptation? Because she'd been the victim of unexpected lust this time instead of the temptress?

Something soured his belly. Memory. Disillusionment. The realisation that despite his vaunted immunity he'd fallen hard and fast for what she offered: hot sex with a gold-digging opportunist.

Just like his father before him.

He released her so quickly she wobbled and he reached out a hand to steady her.

'Saved by the bell,' he murmured and watched heat flush her cheeks. Not for the life of him would he let her see how she'd knocked him for six. That was his private shame.

She knocked his hand away, rubbing her palm over the place he'd held her as if to erase his touch. But he wasn't fooled by her show of antipathy. She'd lost control too. It was that latter truth that cut him to the core, tapping the long-dammed reservoir of fury so it finally broke free.

He watched her spin away from him, her steps uneven as she headed for the foyer. With each step he cursed himself for his weakness. He'd seen what she was. She'd *told* him. Yet he hadn't been able to resist her.

'If that was you being unaffected,' he drawled, 'I look forward to seeing what you're like when you put a little effort into sex.' He drew a slow breath, watching her stumble to a halt. 'I was willing to test the waters to see how far you'd go. And I wasn't disappointed.'

Her shoulders hunched but she didn't turn around.

For a moment something like sympathy hovered. Jonas had a ridiculous urge to cross the room and pull her close to comfort her.

He shook his head.

What was it about Ravenna Ruggiero that got under his skin despite what she'd done?

Was there a family weakness after all? Something in the Deveson genes that made them putty in the grasping hands of the Ruggiero women?

He gritted his teeth against a howl of fury and, worse, disappointment that now he'd never have her in his arms again. He couldn't trust himself with her. How sick was that?

He buried the knowledge behind a wall of disdain.

'Do let me know, if you decide you have something to offer me after all. I might even consider being a little less *discriminating* just for the novelty of it.'

CHAPTER FOUR

RAVENNA STARED AT the mellow wood of the floor, wishing the old boards would part in a yawning void and suck her away into nothingness. Anything to escape the sarcastic lash of Jonas Deveson's contempt.

As if she should be so fortunate! This past year there'd been no good luck in her life. Except the unexpected gift of the rest cure in Switzerland. But now it turned out that had an awful catch. An enormous debt to be paid.

And a big, ruthless debt collector to make sure she paid in blood.

She shivered, cold to the bone, yet her skin crawled with a clammy heat that matched the nausea twisting her insides. She fought it, refusing to be ill in front of him.

Could anything be more humiliating than this?

She felt sullied by him. It was far worse than facing a dressing-down by the head chef at work, whose explosive tirades were legend. As for the torments of her school years—they'd been nothing to this excruciating shame.

For this time every word was deserved. She'd behaved like some slut, eager for the touch of a man who despised her. For the first time she hadn't behaved like the sensible, careful, self-contained woman she was.

She'd acted like a hormone-riddled stranger with no scruples or self-respect.

The doorbell rang again and she dragged herself into the

foyer, propping herself against the wall with a shaking hand as she pressed the intercom.

'Monsieur Giscard?' The words were so faint she cleared her throat to try again. The response from below was garbled in ears that still thrummed with the pulse of arousal.

Nevertheless, she pressed the button to let the visitor in downstairs. Whoever it was, he couldn't be more devastating than Jonas Deveson.

She felt his eyes on her. Her skin prickled and heat drilled her spine. She could pinpoint the exact place between her shoulder blades where that penetrating gaze scored her. If she found later that his laser-sharp gaze had scorched a hole in her jacket she wouldn't be surprised.

Ravenna struggled to swallow the hard knot of emotion blocking her throat.

What had got into her to behave so utterly out of character?

Taking a deep breath, she tried to centre herself but instead inhaled the remnants of his tangy, hot citrus scent. It had impregnated her very pores.

Never in her life had attraction been like that—instantaneous and absolute. Consciously, to her thinking mind, there'd been no attraction—just fear and shock at his revelations, and a determination to divert his thunderous anger from her mother.

But something had happened when he'd touched her. Something unheralded.

She'd heard of animal attraction. She had some experience of desire.

But this... This had been a tsunami obliterating reason and doubt and anything like resistance. She'd stood like a rabbit spotlighted by a hunter, watching his eyes cloud with desire as he touched her. Excitement had stormed through her.

Part of her brain had screamed for her to move, to slap his hand away, but she'd stood, rooted to the spot, eager for more. When he'd bitten her neck in that delicate tasting, she'd gone up in flames.

How was it possible?

Brushing off male attention had never been hard. Yet she'd practically begged for more from him as carnal heat melted her insides and left her a quivering, pathetic wreck.

Where was her backbone? Her sense of self-preservation?

The doorbell rang and she stumbled forward. Her legs felt like melted wax and she fumbled at the door with shaking hands.

On the threshold stood a man of middle years, exquisitely dressed and sporting a rosebud in his lapel.

'Mademoiselle Ruggiero?' He pronounced her name with the softened consonants of the French.

'Monsieur Giscard.' She held out her hand. 'It's a pleasure to meet you. I appreciate you coming so quickly.' She led him into the apartment, carefully keeping her gaze from the far side of the salon and Jonas' watchful presence.

If she could she'd eject him from the premises, but he wouldn't leave till he was good and ready. They had too much to discuss.

At least having the antiques expert here gave her something else to concentrate on, and a chance to regroup after that devastating embrace.

Despite her best intentions her gaze slid across the room to lock with eyes the colour of impenetrable mist. Jonas' face was blank but his words echoed in her ears, making heat scorch her throat and cheeks.

Beside her the dapper Frenchman started forward eagerly, his arm outstretched as he introduced himself to Jonas Deveson. For a moment Ravenna thought the two must have met before but it appeared Monsieur Giscard simply recognised him from press reports.

Ravenna spun away on the ball of her foot. Jonas Deveson even managed to usurp the position of authority now, without trying. Her visitor was fawning over him like a long-lost son. Or a wealthy potential client.

'I have an inventory of furnishings here, Monsieur Giscard.' Reluctantly he turned towards her, and then nodded.

'Perhaps, Mr Deveson, we could meet later today to conclude our discussion?' She had a snowball's chance in hell of fobbing him off but she had to try. The idea of him watching them trail around the apartment, sizing up her mamma's possessions, made her skin crawl.

'I think not, Ravenna.' He deliberately dropped his voice to a pseudo caress on her name. To her consternation and shame she felt her skin tingle and her nipples harden.

It was as if she were programmed to respond sexually even to the cadence of his voice!

'I'm afraid Monsieur Giscard and I will be busy for some time—'

'Don't let me disturb you.' His open wave of the arm, as if graciously giving them permission to continue, made her grit her teeth. 'I'm happy to wait.'

As if to emphasise his point he sank onto a gilded chair and nonchalantly crossed his legs, his hands palm down on the arms in a pose that screamed authority. His tall frame in that delicate chair should have looked ridiculous. Instead he looked…regal.

For a second Ravenna toyed with the idea of calling for the police to eject him as an unwanted intruder. Until she realised the police were the last people she wanted. Her mother's crime loomed over her like a leaden storm cloud.

Fear sank talons deep into her vitals. This impossible situation could only get worse, given this man's implacable thirst for vengeance. Her body stiffened, adrenalin surging and heart pounding in an unstoppable fight-or-flight response. Chaotic thoughts of disappearing out of the front door and not coming back raced through her brain.

But she couldn't do it.

Ravenna was hardworking, dutiful, responsible. It was

the way she was made, reinforced no doubt by watching her mother slave so long and hard to support them both.

Besides, if she disappeared, Jonas would go after Mamma.

Drawing a slow breath, she squared her shoulders. If there was one thing the last months had taught her it was that she had the power to endure more than she'd ever thought possible. She'd pay the debt somehow, save her mother from his destructive fury, then get on with her life.

'As you wish. Feel free to make yourself comfortable.' She shot him a dazzling smile and had the momentary pleasure of seeing him disconcerted. Then she turned to Monsieur Giscard, gesturing for him to precede her from the room. 'I thought we might start in the study.'

Why Piers had needed a study was beyond Jonas. The old man hadn't worked for years, merely living off what was left of his investments.

Jonas had been at the helm of what had begun as a Deveson family investment company. He'd cut the old man from his life and manoeuvred him from the business when he'd left and destroyed Jonas' mother, never once expressing regret.

Shifting in the uncomfortable chair, he cast a scathing look around the room. It didn't improve with familiarity. The few good pieces were overwhelmed by the clutter of showy ornamentation.

Piers had been a magpie, attracted by the bright and shiny, displaying his wealth in the most obvious way. That went especially for women.

Jonas raked his hand through his hair. Had Ravenna Ruggiero's dismay been genuine when he'd suggested she should have used her feminine wiles to get money from Piers?

More important—what on earth had possessed him to touch her?

He was appalled by his reaction to her, but fascinated. He

couldn't remember being fascinated by anything other than an exciting investment opportunity in years.

Jonas shot to his feet, unwilling to sit on the sidelines.

He found them in a large room dominated by a massive desk. They were examining ornate snuffboxes.

'This is a passably good piece. You might manage a hundred euros for it.'

The antique dealer, Giscard, had his back to the door so Jonas couldn't see what he held. But Ravenna's disappointment at the words was clear. Her shoulders slumped and her whole body sagged.

'Really? I'd thought perhaps this at least might be worth more.' Her voice had an edge of desperation.

Giscard turned and Jonas watched him hesitate, his brisk manner softening as he took in her barely concealed distress.

'Well, perhaps a little more. I tend to err on the side of caution, Mademoiselle Ruggiero.' He turned back to the item in his hands. 'After a closer look I think it possible we could do better. If you like I can undertake the sale personally. I have some contacts who might be interested.'

'Really?' Ravenna's eyes shone hopefully and she leaned towards him. 'That would be wonderful, Monsieur Giscard.' Her voice was soft with hope and Jonas felt his skin contract as if she'd brushed her fingertips over him.

He clenched his jaw, furious yet intrigued at the power of that throaty voice.

'It is the least I can do in the sad circumstances.' The dealer moved closer as if drawn by her tremulous smile. 'Perhaps, in the circumstances, you should call me Etienne.'

Jonas' grip tightened on the doorjamb as the pair continued their conversation, oblivious to his presence.

Distaste was a pungent note on his tongue as he watched the older man respond to Ravenna's artful show of vulnerability. That was what it was, he realised, his lips thinning in a grim smile.

The woman who'd made such a point of confronting him

with her crime was no innocent. She was brazen and un-repentant.

From the moment she'd revealed her identity, flouncing about the astronomically expensive apartment as if it were hers, he'd wondered why she'd dressed as she had. The dark trouser suit was tailored but it hung on her, making her look like a child dressing up, especially with the gamine haircut accentuating her exquisitely pared features and huge eyes.

There'd been nothing childlike about her when he'd ca-ressed her. She'd been all needy woman. Yet with her navy jacket hanging loose around her neck, she exuded an air of fragility that intrigued him.

Now he knew why. That vulnerability, enhanced by the sedate cut of clothes that hinted at mourning, was a deliber-ate act to aid her dealings with the antique dealer.

Look at Giscard! He ate her up with his eyes, like a dog slavering after a bone.

She'd prepared carefully for the interview to play on the Frenchman's sympathies.

And Jonas had doubted she was capable of thieving!

She was as conniving and dangerous as her mother.

More so. He remembered Silvia as having a blatant sensu-ality that made her stand out like a Mediterranean sex god-dess with her flashing eyes, swinging hips and earthy laugh. But her daughter… He narrowed his eyes as he watched the woman so easily manipulating the Frenchman. She had an arresting face, the sort of eyes that a less pragmatic man could lose himself in, and a body that, though slim, made him want to haul her close and discover its secrets.

But there was more. An aura of banked passion and quick intelligence that melded into something that drew him at the most primitive, male level.

He wanted her.

The realisation hit him a solid blow to the belly.

He didn't like or admire her. She was the sort of woman he'd learnt to despise.

And still he wanted her.

He dragged in a deep breath, ignoring the anticipation fizzing his blood at the thought of bedding Ravenna Ruggiero.

It wasn't going to happen. His standards were higher than that.

Instead he would make her pay for what she'd done. He'd make sure she learned the value of the money she'd taken, and when he'd finished with her she'd understand the value of hard work too. She'd repay her debt in full. There'd be no easy escape if she tried batting those long eyelashes at him.

There'd be no police, no trial. He'd looked forward to branding his father's mistress publicly as a thief. But for reasons he didn't want to investigate, that didn't seem appropriate now Ravenna had revealed herself as the culprit.

Yes, he could throw her to the mercy of the courts. But having seen her, touched her, he wanted a much more personal recompense.

She'd stolen his money but the insult carved deeper than the loss of mere money, which, after all, was easily replaced.

Jonas told himself his decision had nothing to do with the heat haze of desire still drenching his skin as he watched her flirt with another man.

Or the feeling she'd somehow bested him in their first confrontation even though he held all the winning cards in this contest.

For there *was* a contest. Of wills. Of strength and, above all, of pride.

Somehow she'd breached the fortress he'd long ago built around his emotions. He was disappointed to discover she'd gone the way of her mother, intent on easy money rather than working for it like any decent woman. He'd expected better of her. It was as if she'd betrayed his memory of her.

His lips twisted as he reviewed his decision to give her a chance to avoid a criminal record. It was almost altruistic of him. Facing the consequences of her crime in the form of hard work might be the making of her.

Jonas' eyes narrowed as she batted those lush lashes at the besotted Frenchman. Something cold and sharp solidified in his belly.

No matter what the outcome, he looked forward to collecting on his debt.

'Now these,' purred Monsieur Giscard, 'are in a different class altogether.' He stood in front of a cabinet displaying a collection of old glassware.

'Really?' Ravenna stepped closer, her hopes rising. So far they'd come across little that could be sold to pay off Mamma's debts, let alone set her up with a nest egg for the future. 'You think they may be valuable?'

She had little expectation of finding anything to cover the money her mother had taken from Jonas Deveson's account but scraping together enough to pay Mamma's immediate bills would be an enormous relief.

'I need to examine them properly, but this appears to be a fine collection of early glassware.' He paused, excitement lighting his face. 'Really, a very fine collection...' His voice trailed as he bent to view a goblet with a long, thick stem of twisted glass.

Ravenna held her breath as he opened the cabinet and reached for the goblet.

'I'm afraid those pieces aren't for sale.' The deep voice came from just behind her and she jumped. She hadn't heard Jonas Deveson approach.

'Do you have to sneak up like that?' As soon as the words snapped out she regretted them, seeing his raised brows and knowing smirk. Maybe it was petty given the enormity of what lay between them, but she'd rather not reveal how thoroughly he unsettled her.

He didn't answer, instead turning to Monsieur Giscard, who held the glass cradled reverentially in his hands.

'C'est magnifique!'

'It is, isn't it?' Before Ravenna could stop him Jonas reached out and took it from the Frenchman, holding it up to the light for a moment, before putting it back in the cabinet and shutting the door. 'But it's not for sale.'

'Now look here—!'

He cut her off as if she hadn't spoken. 'It seems this inventory of yours is flawed.' He took the clipboard from her and glanced down at it. Before Ravenna had the presence of mind to snatch it back he'd taken a gold pen from a pocket and begun slashing lines through her list.

'You'll find the contents of this cabinet are old family pieces. They belong to my father's estate—in other words, to me.' He looked up, his silver gaze skewering her. 'Unless you'd like to try stealing this as well?'

Ravenna's breath hissed in and blood scalded her cheeks. In her peripheral vision she was aware of Monsieur Giscard's sharp, curious look.

'I didn't—'

'No?' Jonas' mouth curled up in a superior smile she'd give anything to wipe away.

'No. And it's strange that your father's solicitor hasn't been in contact about collecting anything entailed. I understood the furnishings belong to my mother.'

'Who is conveniently not here.' His voice was velvet with a razor-sharp edge. 'And who was conveniently not available when lawyers tried to contact her.'

Ravenna shook her head, denying his implied accusation. 'She's upset, grieving. She wasn't ready to handle this.'

'Which is why she installed you with your special...*capabilities,* to wrap up the estate?'

The air between them thickened and Ravenna felt fire spark in her blood. He spoke so contemptuously, as if she were a conniving thief.

Which is exactly what you want him to believe. For your mother's sake.

Caution battled fury as she swallowed a furious protest. She was battered by the intensity of his disapproval, and her need to submit.

Finally she broke eye contact and looked away. Instantly her cramped lungs eased as she sucked in sustaining oxygen.

'Monsieur Giscard.' She turned to the dealer with an apologetic smile she hoped masked her desperation. 'As you see things are not as clear cut as I'd thought. Would you mind—?'

'Of course, *mademoiselle*.' He looked only too happy to go, glancing nervously at Jonas who stood glowering like a disapproving idol, his face carved from unforgiving granite.

'I'll call you when I've sorted this out.'

'Of course, of course.' The Frenchman almost scurried out of the door and he didn't meet her eyes when she farewelled him at the entrance to the apartment.

Ravenna's skin crawled with embarrassment, reliving that moment when Jonas had spoken with such calculated cruelty about her stealing. Her stomach plummeted and she leaned against the wall for support. She'd have to get used to it if she was going to carry this off. She had a disturbing feeling it wasn't just public humiliation Jonas Deveson had planned.

He wanted more. He wanted his pound of flesh.

She shivered, remembering his strong teeth nipping at the erogenous zone in her neck. And that she'd done nothing to stop him.

'Alone at last.' His low voice curled around her like a phantom and wholly misleading caress. She should have guessed he wouldn't let her out of his sight.

Ravenna didn't bother replying. Nor did she have any intention of meeting those judgemental eyes. She turned abruptly and walked away.

'Where are you going?' His tone sharpened in surprise. Obviously he wasn't used to anyone turning their back on him.

'I need a drink.'

Of course he followed her and even in the spacious kitchen she felt that claustrophobic sense of the air thickening. She had the unnerving suspicion that even beneath a wide blue sky she'd feel hemmed in by what Jonas made her feel.

Refusing to acknowledge her burgeoning panic, she busied herself filling the kettle and getting out the cafetière.

'How very domestic.'

She shrugged. 'Well, I *am* the housekeeper's daughter.' She filled the coffee grinder and vented her feelings cranking the old-fashioned grinder.

It didn't make her feel any better.

'So, Jonas. What are your plans? Have you called the police? Am I going to be led off in handcuffs?' Her voice was so brittle the words came out in hard little bites.

'The scenario does have a certain charm.'

Ravenna stiffened, the hairs on her arms rising as she paused in the act of emptying the grinder.

'But?' There was a but in there. At least she hoped there was. Unable to pretend indifference any longer, she swung round. Predictably he lounged against the doorjamb, filling the one and only exit with his broad shoulders and athletic frame.

Ravenna licked her lips as her mouth dried. Fear rather than pride prompted her next words. 'I'll pay you back. I promise.'

'You promise?' He paused as if considering. 'And how will you do that?' He straightened and prowled across the room. She had nowhere to go and stood her ground, but the countertop bit into her back as the space between them closed. 'I'm curious. Do you have a job?'

She opened her mouth to confirm she had, then snapped it shut. She'd been a junior in the restaurant, had only worked there a few months. She'd lost her job when it became obvious she'd need months off work and that she might never return.

'No. I don't have a job at the moment.'

'Somehow that doesn't surprise me.'

'And so?' She refused to be baited. 'What are your plans?'

For the space of four heartbeats he said nothing, then his mouth turned up in a smile that didn't meet his eyes. It made him look lethally dangerous, and, to Ravenna's horror, sexy with it. If you were a woman who liked to live on a knife edge of peril. She told herself she didn't.

'Plans?' He paused. 'Oh, you mean about the theft?'

She clenched her hands. She wouldn't take another swing at him, no matter how tempted. She had no intention of getting close enough again to touch him. 'The arch air of disingenuousness doesn't suit you.'

He shrugged. 'And the wide-eyed air of innocence doesn't suit you.'

She crossed her arms so he wouldn't see how they shook. Behind her the kettle whistled and stopped but she fixed her attention on the man who held her future in his hands.

'I intend to ensure you pay back your debt. It's that simple.'

'Nothing with you is simple.'

This time there was a flicker of appreciation in his smile. 'Ah, you're a quick learner.'

When she said nothing he finally continued. 'I'm reopening Deveson Hall. It's been shut since my mother's death with no one to look after it but a caretaker for the grounds.'

Ravenna frowned. A stately old home like that needed constant attention and upkeep. Not just cleaning but maintenance and ongoing repairs. One of her mother's jobs as housekeeper had been to know exactly who was working where on the rambling old place.

'I'm advised it needs considerable attention.' An undercurrent of emotion coloured his words and, to her surprise, Ravenna saw him scrub his hand around the back of his neck as if to ease sudden tension. His lips pursed and she could have sworn she read concern in his features.

It was the first indication she'd seen today that Jonas Deveson was capable of feeling anything softer than bitterness or contempt.

From the way he spoke he hadn't mourned his father, yet the neglect of his family home moved him?

He was more complex than she'd thought. She'd pegged him as a man who cared for nothing but his own pride.

Ravenna opened her mouth to ask why he hadn't bothered to do something about the house earlier but the answer was obvious. He'd only just inherited the place.

Piers had spent most of the last six years out of England and hadn't visited the estate since his wife's death. Ravenna wasn't surprised to discover he'd decided to spend his money maintaining his lavish lifestyle rather than on the upkeep of a mansion he preferred not to visit.

'That's where you come in.' Jonas' slow smile chilled her anew. 'As well as the renovation work, the Hall needs to be cleaned from top to bottom. Scrubbed till it shines.'

'You want me to be part of the crew that—?'

'Not part.' He shook his head slowly, his smile growing. 'You'll be *it*. Personally responsible for getting the place ready for the ball I'm hosting to celebrate the Hall's reopening.'

Ravenna couldn't prevent herself gaping. Deveson Hall had been built centuries ago when the family employed an army of servants. It was gorgeous, precious, sprawling and the complete opposite of the low-maintenance residences being designed now. It was three floors of steady toil for the team her mother had overseen. Four floors if you counted the attics. Five with the cellars.

She had no doubt Jonas would include the cellars.

'*One person* to do all that? It's impossible!'

'There will be builders working to fix what needs repairing. You'll be responsible for getting the place ready to live in again.'

A flash of something showed in his steely eyes and

Ravenna realised he was waiting for her to refuse, to toss away what she knew instinctively would be her only option apart from prison.

'Is that all?' Somehow she choked the words out.

His smile faded.

'No. If your work is of a high enough standard then you can stay on and work off the rest of your debt as my house-keeper. That's my offer. Take it or leave it.'

The dreadful irony of it didn't escape her. Her mother might have escaped Jonas Deveson's wrath but she wouldn't. He began with putting her firmly in her place, as his servant.

Her insides twisted. She'd vowed never to be anyone's servant after seeing the way her mother had been treated by so many employers. There were wealthy employers who believed service was akin to bonded slavery. Even the sheer hard work of a commercial kitchen was preferable.

Childhood taunts echoed in her ears. Her peers had viewed sharing a classroom with a servant's daughter an insult. They'd made her pay for that insult.

Ravenna had thought she'd escaped all that.

It would take years to pay off the money. Yet she had no choice. She didn't want a criminal record or a stint in prison.

She drew a breath, trying to slow her frantic pulse.

Jonas would make her time at Deveson Hall hell, but she was strong enough to cope. He couldn't throw anything at her that was worse than what she'd already faced. She pushed her shoulders back and looked him in the eye, ignoring the sizzle of heat arcing between them.

Before she could say anything he spoke again. 'Don't get ideas of history repeating itself.' His voice was glacial. 'I don't have a weakness for the hired help like my father.'

Her chin went up. With every word he degraded what her mother and Piers had shared.

'That's a relief.' Ravenna forced the words through numb lips. 'You're not my type.'

His stony face tightened. Yet he said nothing as he waited

for her to reject his preposterous scheme. Then he'd call in the police.

'How could I refuse such a generous offer? You've got yourself a housekeeper, Mr Deveson.'

CHAPTER FIVE

THE BLEAK WEATHER did nothing to brighten Ravenna's mood. Deveson Hall was as imposing as she recalled, sprawling across what seemed acres, its blind eyes reflecting no light on this dreary, damp day.

Ravenna shuddered and wrapped her arms around herself as the drizzle-laden wind tugged her coat.

She wasn't afraid of hard work but this… She swallowed, her throat dry as the enormity of it sank in. He expected the impossible.

No sane man could expect one person to care for all that. Even if the Hall hadn't been neglected for years it needed a team of staff. He couldn't seriously think—

Of course he didn't. Jonas Deveson was no fool. He expected her to throw up her hands and surrender. He wanted to watch her admit defeat before he subjected her to the humiliation of the justice system. He'd shred her of her self-respect and rub her nose in the fact she was at his mercy.

She shuddered at the memory of his merciless gaze.

Again the furtive temptation to run sneaked into her brain. But that would solve nothing. The money had been stolen and if she didn't accept the consequences Mamma would. She was in no condition to do that. Besides, it was Ravenna who'd benefited.

She sent up a prayer of thanks that her mother was in Italy. Face to face Silvia would have known Ravenna lied when she said all was well, explaining she'd left Paris for a promising job in England.

Mamma had been so excited for her, seeing this as a chance to get her interrupted career back on track. She probably thought Jonas with his billions wouldn't miss the money. If she guessed Ravenna had accepted her guilt…it didn't bear thinking about. Ravenna felt sick to the stomach lying in their regular phone calls but she had no choice. She wouldn't leave her mother to Jonas Deveson's mercy.

Reluctantly Ravenna delved ice-cold fingers into her pocket and dragged out the key. Picking up her bag, she stepped through the weeds and up to the back door.

On the step was a carton of supplies. She ignored it as she dealt with the lock and the keypad of the state-of-the-art security system that matched the new high-security perimeter boundary.

There might be no one at the Hall but there was a full-time presence at the gatehouse security centre.

She'd been warned not to try leaving the estate lest she set off an alarm. The implication being that she was a prisoner. The shiver scudding through her turned into a full-blown shudder as she recalled the curious blaze in Jonas Deveson's pewter-hard eyes.

'Prisoner' sounded Dickensian, but that was what she was.

There would be a camera trained on this door now, eyes monitoring the entrances. Apart from keeping the place safe from intruders, Jonas probably suspected her of trying to steal the antique silver.

Was that his game? To tempt her into another theft so he'd be absolutely certain she'd get a prison sentence as a repeat offender? It seemed likely.

She grabbed her bag and entered, eager for privacy.

The flagstone hall was so gloomy she flicked on the light. The place was drear and freezing, far different from her memories. The rest of the Hall had been off limits but she'd been allowed free access to the back of the house.

She made her way to the suite of rooms Mamma had used. Rooms Ravenna had called home during summer holidays. For a weak moment she let herself wish her mother were here. She could do with her trademark optimism and determination.

Ravenna pushed open the door and slammed to a stop.

The smell hit her. A pungent aroma of damp and mouse and something rotting. Her nose wrinkled as she stared at what had once been a cosy sitting room. A breeze eddied and she turned, seeing the half-closed curtains stir as air funnelled through a broken pane.

The caretaker employed by Piers hadn't done much of a job if he'd missed something so obvious.

But the damp wasn't just from rain soaking through the hole. It streaked the walls from the ceiling. The wallpaper had green-brown smears no scrubbing could clean.

Putting down her case, she stepped forward. Debris crackled underfoot as she headed for the bedroom. The smell was worse there and the stained walls too.

Steadfastly ignoring the sound of tiny, scurrying feet, Ravenna headed back to the corridor.

Had Jonas realised the damage was this bad? No wonder he'd looked smug as he offered her this chance.

The place didn't need a cleaner. It needed ripping down and starting again! Except in a heritage-listed building things weren't so simple.

It would be a nightmare to restore, she decided as she opened door after door and found similar damage. She guessed a water pipe had burst upstairs or a drain had become blocked and these rooms had borne the brunt of the damage.

It was criminal that it had been neglected. How could Piers have been so irresponsible?

She thought of the laughing, garrulous man she'd known. He'd loved Mamma as she'd loved him. Ravenna had seen it in his eyes and in his readiness to please her mother.

But she'd also seen his self-indulgence. The way he changed the subject whenever anything unpleasant cropped up. He preferred gaiety and good times to responsibility. He'd had the look of a man who'd indulged himself for decades and he'd been a connoisseur of fine food and wine— one of the reasons he'd approved her career choice.

He'd lived a life of casual luxury. According to Mamma there was only one thing he'd been firm about and that was in having nothing to do with his family or the entailed estate he'd left behind in England.

No wonder there'd been murder in Jonas Deveson's face when he'd talked of the work that needed doing here.

Finally she came to the kitchen and hope kindled. In the grey light from the grimy windows it looked neglected rather than damaged. Ravenna released a breath she hadn't known she was holding.

At least this room was habitable. She cast a professional eye over the outdated range and badly laid out cupboards. She'd worked with worse.

The trip had exhausted her. The enormity of what faced her made her want to curl into a ball and hide.

But Ravenna had learned that the worst had to be faced. Ignoring bad news didn't make it go away.

Imagine Jonas Deveson's delight if she gave up before she'd begun! Squaring her shoulders, she turned and went to get the box of supplies.

'What's the meaning of these?' Jonas let the pile of bills flutter onto his PA's desk.

Unflappable as ever, Stephen turned from his computer. 'You said anything to do with Ms Ruggiero or Deveson Hall should come straight to you.'

'But this?' He poked a finger at the top invoice. 'Glazing?' He stirred the pile. 'Boiler repairs? Why are they coming here?'

He should have known she'd find a way to niggle at him, reminding him of her presence even though she was out of London. She should be busy scrubbing the Hall from top to bottom, too exhausted to do more than worry if he might change his mind and hand her to the police. Instead she had the temerity to interrupt him at work.

Jonas shoved aside the fact that she'd been interrupting him ever since Paris. Too often he relived the cinnamon-scented sweetness of her skin and the arousing sound of her sighs as he tasted her.

The tightness in his belly exacerbated his anger.

'Explain!'

Stephen looked at him in surprise and Jonas realised he'd raised his voice. He never raised his voice. Ever. His calm was renowned.

The only exception had been in Paris. With Ravenna Ruggiero.

He palmed the back of his neck, massaging tight muscles. What was it about her that made him lose it?

Before he could apologise Stephen spoke. 'The building project manager has been held up in Singapore. He can't start yet. I sent you a memo about it two days ago.'

He had, and Jonas, wanting only the best on the delicate job of restoring his family home, had preferred to wait a little longer to get the best in the business.

'But this?' He picked up another bill. 'Twenty mouse traps? What on earth is she doing?'

'Fighting a plague?' Stephen grinned.

Jonas rifled through the invoices again. He'd thought he could leave her to stew in her own juices for a while. But without anyone to supervise her... 'Clear my diary from tomorrow. I'm going to Deveson Hall.'

* * *

Jonas stood at the bottom of the wide front steps, a curious, hollow sensation in the pit of his stomach.

It yawned wider as his gaze crossed the weeds choking the gravel and sprouting in the litter edging the stone steps. An ornamental urn leaned drunkenly near the front door and a couple of window panes were haphazardly boarded with rough planks and even, if he wasn't mistaken, cardboard.

The emptiness in his belly became an ache and then a hard churning that riveted him to the spot. His nape prickled and something snaked through him. A searing hot sensation that wound tight around his vital organs, squeezing mercilessly till the force of it threatened to poleaxe him.

Emotions, turbulent and powerful, rose in a potent, poisonous brew.

Six years since he'd been here.

Six years since his mother took her life and his father—

Jonas clamped a lid on those thoughts, horrified at what he felt.

For six years his life had been satisfying, productive, with challenges, triumphs and pleasures. There'd been no place for emotions in his ordered, busy world.

He didn't waste time on regrets or any other pointless feelings that might distract him from his purpose. Instead he'd focused on moving forward, taking the company to even greater success.

He dragged in a slow, sustaining breath.

That was better. He had himself in hand now.

But that moment of sickening weakness, of horrible vulnerability disturbed him.

For six years there'd been nothing like it. Nothing to shake him to the core of his being. Not until Ravenna Ruggiero. Her theft, her brazen guilt, the conflicting mix of sensations she'd aroused, had unsettled him.

She was to blame.

It was as if she'd opened the sluice gates on a dam of emotion he'd walled up long ago.

He didn't like it one bit.

Another reason to have his revenge and be done with her. Surely now, seeing the magnitude of the task facing her, she'd admit defeat. There would be no more flashing eyes, no sassy comebacks, no dredging up unwanted responses.

Jonas firmed his lips and strode up the stairs.

The past hit him in a rush as he opened the massive door. A sense of long-forgotten familiarity, of childish memories and days gone by.

Of homecoming.

His hand tightened on the old wood as he fought back emotion.

There was nothing welcoming about the dimly lit room. Frigid air misted his breath as he surveyed the vast, lifeless space. Jonas absorbed the scent of dust and old wood, his gaze raking the darkened recesses, as if expecting the spectres of his past to rise up before him.

With a huff of self-disgust he strode to a window and yanked back the wooden shutters. Light spilled across the worn flagstones to the foot of the massive staircase. Overhead the shadowy beams of the high vaulted ceiling were just discernible.

Another few paces and another window, and another. Till the great hall, once the heart of the house, was revealed in its grimy glory. No sign anyone had been here in years. It looked soulless despite the faded tapestries and ancient furniture.

Jonas flung open the doors into a drawing room. More modern than the Hall, this had a fine Regency fireplace, decorative plasterwork and a massive mirror that reflected the wraith-like forms of furniture concealed beneath dustcovers.

Temper rising, he yanked open more shutters and curtains. Daylight revealed no evidence of recent habitation. His hands were grimy from the dust everywhere.

Damn it! Was she even on the premises?

He strode from room to room, letting doors slam wide to reveal neglected spaces of damp, dusty decay.

By the time he'd stalked back to the great hall that strange, unsettling feeling was gone. Instead anger burned bright and hard.

Anger against the woman who couldn't be bothered to lift a finger even to pretend to do the job he'd held out to her as an alternative to gaol.

Anger for the greedy woman who'd stolen from him.

For the woman whose mother had stolen his father, broken up his family, such as it was, and destroyed his mother.

Like mother, like daughter. Both out for an easy life. Well, not any more!

He took the stairs two at a time. If she couldn't make an effort to work on the beautiful reception rooms he knew there was no chance she'd be below stairs.

He found her three doors along, in one of the family bedrooms.

She didn't even stir at the sound of his approach. He slammed to a halt at the foot of the four-poster bed, heart beating double time as his gaze raked her.

She lay on her side, hands tucked beneath her cheek and legs curled—looking the picture of innocence.

Suspicion surged.

Was she aware of him watching? It would be remarkable if she hadn't heard him slamming through the downstairs rooms then marching up here.

His eyes narrowed but he saw no change in her breathing, no giveaway flutter of lashes.

Slanting light traced her features, throwing delicate shadows beneath her eyes and cheekbones. Tiny frown lines marred her brow as if even in sleep something troubled her.

Probably dreaming of a way to escape justice!

Jonas' gaze dipped to her mouth, softly pink and slightly

parted as if in invitation. He remembered the sigh of her sweet breath as he caressed her, the hunger to taste more.

Jonas caught himself leaning closer, hand raised as if to gentle her awake. Jerking back, he grasped the carved bedpost, anchoring himself.

He was no gullible mark like Piers. Jonas had her measure. He knew what she was, as she'd discover to her cost.

'I said it's time to get up.' The deep voice wound its way into Ravenna's sleep-fogged brain and she snuggled into the soft pillow. Just a little longer. It felt so good to let her exhausted body relax, weightlessly floating.

'Much as I appreciate the Sleeping Beauty tableau, it's not working.' The rich voice lost its mellow timbre and turned harsh, yanking her out of her hazy dream of warmth and well-being and the delicious scent of spiced citrus. In her dream strong arms had held her tight and close. Now she was alone, her skin chilled and legs cramped.

Ravenna opened her eyes and swallowed a scream as she saw him looming above her, all but blocking the light.

'You!' It was a strangled gasp, torn from tight lungs as she struggled up, scooting back against the carved headboard.

'You were expecting someone else?' Dark eyebrows slashed down in a ferocious scowl that turned his proud face into that of an avenging angel. He didn't seem to move but she had the impression he stood closer, keeping her within reach.

Panic flared and her heart beat a tattered rhythm as she read the sizzle in those narrowed eyes. Not pewter now, but the luminous silver-grey of lightning. Ravenna remembered his fury in Paris, his lashing tongue and hard, unforgiving hands that turned gentle as they curved around her breast and stroked her nipple till she all but swooned.

Fear sliced her. It had nothing to do with the taut anger in his face and wide, masculine shoulders and everything to do with the yearning that softened her traitorous body. Liquid heat rushed to her womb as she met his gaze and felt again that juddering vibration, like an unseen explosion radiating through the air between them.

Despair filled her. She'd convinced herself it had been a one-off. Some horrible aberration, never to be repeated. She *couldn't* be attracted to him. She *wasn't!*

In a tumble of limbs Ravenna scooted to the other side of the bed and off the side.

But she'd underestimated her exhaustion. No sooner did her feet hit the floor than her knees crumpled. Only her hold on the high bed stopped her collapsing.

A split second later he was there, arms outstretched as if to support her.

If she'd needed anything to galvanise her failing strength that was it.

'Don't touch me!' It came out high and breathless, choked with emotion.

Instantly he reared back, his mouth a thin line and eyes unreadable.

Dragging in a rough breath, Ravenna braced herself and stood straight. She had herself in hand now. Her legs shook like jelly but that was to be expected after the hours she'd been on her feet. It had nothing to do with Jonas Deveson.

'What are you doing here?'

His eyebrows arched high. 'I think that question is my prerogative. What are you doing sleeping *here* of all places? And in the middle of the day?'

Ravenna glanced at her watch. Two o'clock. No wonder she felt wobbly. She'd only lain down fifteen minutes ago, desperate for a restorative nap.

Since arriving she'd forced herself to her limits, ignoring earlier advice about taking things easy and allowing her body time to recuperate.

Terror was a fine motivator, allowing her to push beyond the boundaries of exhaustion day after day, knowing Jonas

Deveson would leap at that chance to accuse her of not being up to the impossible job he'd set.

And here he was. Just as she'd feared.

Ravenna swiped suddenly clammy palms down the worn denim of her jeans, vowing not to let him best her.

'I started early this morning so I was having a short... break.'

'Most people take a break over a cup of tea and a biscuit, not stretched out on a valuable antique bed.'

He was accusing her of damaging the furnishings? She might not be some delicate, petite woman, but she was hardly a heavyweight, especially after her recent illness.

Her gaze swept the bed. It was huge enough to sleep four and she'd barely wrinkled the coverlet. The rich, embroidered coverlet she'd carefully cleaned along with the full-length curtains that just a week ago had been caked in dust.

'If you're waiting for me to tug my forelock you can give up now.' She stuck her hands on her hips in a confrontational pose she hoped hid the way her legs shook. 'If I'm good enough to clean the damned thing, I'm good enough to sleep in it.'

His features tightened. 'Spoken like your mother's daughter. She must have had the same view of Piers' bed whenever she *serviced*...his room here.'

Ravenna felt the blood drain from her face at his crude implication. That Mamma was some greedy tart, using sex to her advantage.

'You b—'

'Now, now.' His voice was maddeningly superior as he raised his hand. 'Don't say anything you'll regret.'

'Believe me,' she bit out between quick breaths, 'I wouldn't regret it.' But the warning hit the mark. She couldn't afford to get him even further off side. It was only at his whim that she wasn't in police custody.

Ravenna drew a shaky breath as the surge of adrenalin dissipated, leaving her feeling ridiculously fragile. 'But since you have such archaic views on class differences, I should warn you that this is my bedroom.'

That shocked him.

Swiftly she surveyed the room she'd so painstakingly brought back to mint condition, from its plaster-decorated ceiling to its delicately shaded carpet. Old wood gleamed after multiple applications of beeswax, the soft furnishings had been painstakingly cleaned and even the crystal drops in the overhead light had been polished till they shone. He hadn't even spared it a glance.

For some reason that galled her almost as much as his high and mighty attitude.

'The housekeeper's accommodation wasn't good enough for you?' His eyes glinted a warning she refused to heed.

'The housekeeper's accommodation wasn't weatherproof or dry.' She watched shock freeze his face and knew an unholy pleasure that she'd punctured his self-satisfaction. Then her mind processed a little further, realisation dawning. 'You didn't know, did you?' Ravenna stared at his still face. 'How long since you've been here?'

Predictably he ignored her question.

'If this is your room then we'll go elsewhere for our discussion.'

It was on the tip of Ravenna's tongue to riposte with some barbed retort when she realised the sense of his words. The last thing she needed was to imprint the memory of him here, in her personal space. As it was the sight of him looming over her in the bed would haunt her for too long.

Abruptly she spun around to lead the way out. But she'd reckoned without her lingering physical weakness. Her limbs still felt like wet noodles, wobbly and uncoordinated, and for one horrible, slow-motion moment she felt herself sway dangerously and begin to topple, her arms flailing.

He grabbed her elbows, his long fingers hard and hot through the wool of her ancient cardigan.

Ravenna stared at the charcoal knit of his cashmere pullover mere centimetres away, rising and falling with each breath. Her nostrils twitched as his scent reached her, the tang of lemon and hot male skin that conjured images of long, powerful limbs, naked in warm Mediterranean sunlight.

A shudder ripped through her and she closed her eyes in denial. *No, no, no.* She was weak from what her body had been through recently, but she wasn't weak for him.

She'd have to be sick in the head to desire *him*.

'Are you all right?' No mistaking the reluctance in his voice. If he'd had time to think rather than act on instinct he'd probably have let her drop to the floor.

Slowly Ravenna lifted her gaze, past the strong contours of his jaw, up to his grim mouth, bracketed now with disapproving grooves that somehow emphasised the leashed passion in those surprisingly soft lips. She remembered the tender way they'd caressed her neck and shivered as that betraying heat swirled and swooped low in her belly again, settling and spreading at the core of her.

A tingling started up between her legs. An edgy sensation that made her want to snuggle up against him and—

'I'm fine.' Her voice was hoarse and she ducked her head rather than meet his scrutiny. Instead she felt it graze the contours of her face.

How she wished she still had her long hair. She could use it as a shield, obscuring herself from his sharp eyes.

Ravenna shook her head. Of all the things to regret, the loss of her hair was the least of them.

She stepped back, moving carefully, giving her body time to adjust. His hands dropped away instantly, as if he was only too eager to let her go.

Ravenna told herself that was a good thing. If he realised the power his physical presence had over her, he'd be sure to use it to his advantage.

They were on the landing when she spoke again. 'You haven't told me why you're here.'

'To check up on you, of course.' The words came from too close behind her. She imagined his warm breath on the back of her neck and hurried down the stairs.

'In case I was stripping the place of valuables?'

'I'm sure security would put a stop to that.' His tone was complacent. 'No, I decided you needed supervision and from what I've seen I was right.' Familiar disapproval coloured his voice. 'That's why I've decided to stay.'

Ravenna clutched the banister as the world reeled.

She'd thought this nightmare couldn't get any worse. How naïve she'd been!

CHAPTER SIX

JONAS SCANNED THE large kitchen. Old-fashioned and functional, it held a homely warmth he hadn't expected to find when Ravenna had led him to the servants' domain.

Bright sunlight revealed a huge, scrubbed table, old-fashioned wooden cabinets and a collection of brass moulds and pots hanging on one white wall. It looked like something out of the past.

His past.

He remembered having cocoa and fruitcake here, presided over by Mrs Roberts, the motherly woman who'd ruled the kitchen in his childhood. He'd often sneak in for a sample of the exotic meals she prepared for his parents' sophisticated dinner parties. She regularly patched up his scrapes and let him help roll out pastry or stir a pudding.

Until his mother had found out and put a stop to it, insisting he had more valuable things to do with his time than hobnob with servants.

Jonas blinked and turned his head, ignoring the sharp, twisting sensation deep inside and the metallic tang on his tongue. He catalogued the scrupulously clean room, the vase of evergreens on the old Welsh dresser and the way Ravenna bustled around the vast space, with an economy of movement that told him she was at home here.

The housekeeper's daughter.

She'd flung that in his face, hadn't she?

But she was far more than that.

Jonas ran a hand through his hair, watching her loose-fitting jeans pull tight and tempting as she bent to get something out of a cupboard.

His pulse thudded into overdrive as he watched her supple body. Gone was the vulnerability he'd seen earlier in her startled dark gold gaze and her clumsy movements.

Her weakness had worried him. She'd almost collapsed and it had been no act. He'd felt the tremors race through her. He'd seen the frustration in her not-quite veiled eyes and watched her work to hold herself upright, moving as if each step was an effort.

He didn't want to feel sorry for her. He didn't want to desire her either! But he'd done both. Every time he came within sight of her his hormones roared into life.

Whatever the problem it was gone now. She moved gracefully, snaring his gaze so he couldn't look away.

Jonas scrubbed his hand over his face and round his neck, massaging the stiffness from his muscles. Fat chance it would erase the stiffness elsewhere!

This wasn't supposed to happen. Not for her.

'Here.' A cup and saucer appeared on the wood before him with a plate of biscuits. Shortbread, perfectly formed and, if he wasn't mistaken, home-made.

'You're feeding me? Should I check for poison?'

She didn't answer, merely settled at the far end of the table and sipped from a cup that matched his own.

Blue and white willow pattern. It had been Mrs Roberts' favourite, brought out whenever he visited.

A jagged splinter sheared off from the twisting screw in his belly and jabbed hard.

Reacting blindly, he reached for a biscuit. It dissolved in his mouth, pure buttery comfort, like those special treats he'd devoured here long ago when his parents' blistering arguments had driven him to seek refuge in the warm kitchen.

A roaring rush of ancient memory sprang to life. Ruthlessly Jonas blanked it out.

'What's the plan? To distract me with your culinary skills?' He sounded boorish, but the alternative, letting the murky past swamp him, wasn't an option.

She didn't even look fazed, though her jaw tightened as if keeping tight rein on her temper.

That only fuelled his anger. Jonas didn't like feeling in the wrong. It was a new and unsettling experience for a man who ruled his world with confidence and authority.

'I thought for once we could have a civilised conversation. Clearly I was mistaken.' She drew a breath that lifted her breasts. Jonas' hands curled, a reflex to the memory of touching her there.

'Come on.' She shoved her chair back. 'Let's get this over with. You're dying to inspect what I've haven't done, aren't you?'

She was right. He'd stormed down here, intent on putting her firmly in her place—under his heel. Yet since arriving he'd been on edge, feeling curiously *full,* as if he barely kept a lid on emotions he'd long pushed aside. His brain teemed with unwanted memories.

Venting his spleen on Ravenna Ruggiero was the perfect antidote to those disturbing feelings.

Except now, following as she marched through the house, flinging open doors on room after room of criminal neglect, he couldn't do it.

He'd read the building report but still hadn't imagined how severe the damage was. It cut him like a blade to the heart. Anger and self-recrimination scored deep.

He'd refused to visit while Piers was an absentee landlord. He'd told himself the Hall wasn't home. Home was London, New York or Tokyo, wherever there was money to be made. He'd avoided the past and concentrated on building Devesons into the country's premier investment company.

Later, receiving the building report, he'd chosen to stay

away till refurbishment started. There'd been no reason for his personal presence.

His mouth twisted. It had been easier to stay away than remember those last months when his mother had been in such despair. He'd almost hated the place then and all it represented. Their failure of a family. His father's betrayal. His mother's depression. His inadequacy. Nothing he did or said could make things better.

He'd failed her. He hadn't been able to save her.

'Well?' The word yanked him into the present. Sherry-gold eyes sparked at him in the gloom of the damp cellar. 'Aren't you going to accuse me of slacking because I haven't fixed this yet?'

Jonas cast a cursory look over the puddles, the evidence of recent flooding, the bulging wall, and knew the sooner he got his building expert on the premises, the better.

He turned back to see her braced for confrontation. The light in her eyes challenged him to do his worst.

'It will take a team of experts to deal with this. There's nothing you can do.'

His response was utterly reasonable yet Ravenna looked stunned. More than stunned, she looked suspiciously annoyed, as if, despite her earlier words, she'd *wanted* another confrontation.

His gaze bored into hers, trying to read her thoughts, and a flush climbed her cheeks. Abruptly she looked away, lashes dropping, hiding her expressive eyes. She looked... discomfited.

Could it be that she too found it easier to trade barbed insults? And if that was a defence mechanism, what was she hiding from?

'Okay. You've shown me the worst, now show me what you've done. Or did it take all your time to clean up the kitchen and bedroom?' Given the state of the other rooms he wouldn't be surprised.

Ravenna's jaw sagged, her mouth gaping as if she'd never seen him before.

Finally he'd stemmed her flow of snarky comments. He'd fantasised about doing just that. But in his imaginings he'd silenced her with his lips fused to hers, his tongue in her mouth, finishing what he'd started in Paris.

The image erupted out of nowhere, of her melting into him as incendiary sparks ignited their bodies. It was so vivid his hands twitched, ready to reach for her. Heat drenched him despite the cellar's chill and blood roared in his ears.

His response was so sudden, so profound, it made a mockery of all the reasons he'd told himself he'd never touch her again. Upstairs, holding her steady lest she fall, Jonas had been abundantly aware of Ravenna Ruggiero as a woman. Not a thief or a parasite. Not kin to the woman who'd destroyed his mother. But as desirable.

Even in faded jeans and an oversized cardigan, Ravenna fascinated him in a way he didn't understand. He liked his women sophisticated and ultra feminine. Ravenna was feminine all right, but with a sharp tongue and prickly attitude that should have been a turn-off.

Instead—

'All right.' She spun away, turning the movement into a flounce of disapproval. 'This way.'

He got under her skin.

At least he wasn't the only one.

By the time they finished the tour Ravenna didn't know what to think. Reading Jonas Deveson when he was in a temper was easy. But now she hadn't a clue what he thought.

'*You* did that?' There'd been surprise in his voice when she showed him how she'd boarded up the windows as best she could, and the new panes the glazier had begun installing.

Did he really think she'd ignore the damage as if it didn't

matter? Deveson Hall was a beautiful old place. It deserved better than what Piers had dealt it.

She'd shown Jonas the attic bedrooms she'd cleared and scrubbed, with some notion of starting at the top and working down. But the rest of the vast attics had defeated her, filled as they were with what looked like several hundred years' accumulation of family memorabilia.

Instead of berating her for giving up on the top floor he'd merely nodded and gestured for her to move on.

She'd shown him the gallery where she'd spent the morning on a ladder, carefully cleaning ornate picture frames, aware all the time of rows of haughty Devesons looking down their superb noses at her as if outraged anyone so lowly should dare enter their presence.

Now they surveyed the bedrooms. Only one other than hers was finished, where they stood now.

'You've done a good job.'

Again he'd robbed her of speech. Praise? From Jonas Deveson?

Ravenna swung round to find him watching her. She should be used to it—that piercing regard so sharp it could scrape off skin. Or carve a needy hollow deep inside.

She blinked and tried to tear her eyes away.

'It's come up well,' she agreed. 'But I'm surprised you admit it.' What was he up to?

He shrugged. 'It's the truth. Besides, if we're going to be here together, I'd rather not have you glaring daggers at me all the time.'

'This isn't about the way *I*—'

'See what I mean?' He was frustratingly superior, as if the thickened atmosphere between them were down to *her!*

'There's no need for you to stay.' The words shot out. 'You've seen what you came to see. You know I'm not trashing the place.'

'No,' he mused, frowning, 'you're not. You're actually making a difference.'

Ravenna's hands clamped her hips. 'No need to sound surprised!'

Again that shrug. It emphasised the broad planes of his shoulders and chest and the way he blocked the doorway, making the spacious room seem too small.

'In the circumstances—' he stepped towards her '—I can be excused for doubting that. You gave the impression of a woman who's never worked in her life.'

Ravenna shuffled back, away from that keen gaze. She walked a knife edge with the truth. If she revealed too much about herself she might inadvertently let the truth slip—that it was Mamma who'd stolen his money.

'I have hidden depths.' She stopped abruptly as her legs came up against the edge of the bed. Something dark and untamed skittered through her belly at the feeling he'd trapped her there.

He paced closer, a dangerous light in his eyes. Ravenna gulped down rising tension and told herself he wasn't interested in her. That...caress in Paris had been simply him illustrating how vulnerable she was.

He stood so close she saw the beginning of dark stubble on his jaw. She remembered the soft scrape of it against her skin and sucked in a breath warm with the scent of his skin.

Flurries of sensation raced across her flesh as she met grey eyes that now looked anything but cold.

'I'll enjoy sleeping here.'

He moved and she stiffened, but instead of touching her he reached out and prodded the mattress. 'A nice, big bed,' he murmured approvingly. As easily as that Ravenna could think of nothing but how it would feel to have that long, strong body flush against hers, naked on the king-sized bed.

'You can't sleep here!' It was too close to hers, connected by a bathroom.

One ebony eyebrow arched and to her amazement she saw amusement in his face. It turned his strong aristocratic features into something potently seductive. 'It's either that or in your bed, Ravenna.'

'I didn't mean…'

He straightened and she sucked in a breath as the distance widened between them. 'Forget it, Ravenna. I'm staying. The place can't be left like this.'

Not in *her* untrustworthy hands. That was the implication. In the circumstances she could hardly blame him, yet his prejudice rankled.

'But you've got a business to run.'

Steely eyes pinioned her. 'You really are desperate for me to leave, aren't you?'

Ravenna tilted her chin. She was sick of lying. 'You can't be surprised. You're hardly pleasant company.'

Instead of glowering as expected, Jonas flummoxed her by laughing. It was a deep, rich sound that eddied and swirled around her like a liquid embrace. Ravenna shivered and rubbed her arms, scared of how much she liked it.

'That's rich coming from the woman who thieved from me.'

Ravenna flinched. She couldn't help it. And she regretted it instantly, when Jonas' eyes narrowed on her face. What did he see there? How much did he guess?

'I propose a truce,' he murmured. 'We'll behave like civilised people while we're under the same roof. Agreed?'

What other option was there? Her nerves were shredded after an hour with him. She'd be a gibbering wreck if he chose to prolong the animosity.

Ravenna nodded but she pretended not to notice his outstretched hand. Touching Jonas Deveson again was right up there on her list of never-to-do experiences, like swimming with sharks and sleeping on a bed of nails.

Two hours later Ravenna emerged into the high street of the nearby market town, arms full of provisions. Jonas had insisted he accompany her since her meagre supplies wouldn't cater for them both.

He's making sure you don't do a runner, a sour voice inside her head insisted. After all, once off the estate there was nothing to stop her disappearing except fear of what he'd do when he caught her again.

A little shiver raced through her. For Jonas *would* find her if she ran. She couldn't imagine him failing at anything he wanted. And he wanted her under his thumb.

He walked beside her, carrying the bulk of the shopping. But it wasn't his role as gaoler that unsettled her so much as his physical presence. Big, bold and aggressively male, his testosterone-charged presence challenged her in ways she didn't like to examine.

He'd been as good as his word—a perfect gentleman during their outing yet that only unbalanced her more. She could cope with his temper, even his disapproval. But there was something ridiculously intimate about the simple act of shopping together, having him insist on carrying the heavy items and even opening doors for her.

Realising how much she liked it made her edgy.

Her eyes lit on the dark red Aston Martin across the street, magnet for a bunch of admiring boys.

'You've got a very showy car.' Conveniently she ignored the fact that she adored its sleek lines and the delicious sense of being cocooned in comfort as they'd driven here.

'You think I should drive something that blends in?' Infuriatingly she heard laughter in his voice. 'A discreet dark Bentley or a battered Land Rover?' He strode towards the car. 'I worked hard for everything I've got, and I'm not ashamed of enjoying it.'

Ravenna huffed as she hurried after him, stopping as he opened the boot and unloaded his purchases. 'You were born with a silver spoon in your mouth. I hardly think—'

He turned and his expression clogged the words in her throat. She almost heard ice crackle at the look he shot her.

'Frankly, I don't care what you think.' He reached for her packages and stowed them with the rest of the food, then closed the boot. 'But for the record, I may have been born with a silver spoon in my mouth but the rest of the family silver was hocked. Piers only married my mother for the much-needed money she brought the failing family coffers. With his spectacularly unsuccessful investments and his skill at spending that disappeared soon enough.'

He leaned towards her. 'Do you know *why* I got a reputation as a *wunderkind* investor?' His breath was hot on her face but she couldn't step away. She was mesmerised by what she saw in those remarkable eyes—passion and, if she wasn't mistaken, pain.

'It was because by the time I was finishing school there was no money left. If I wanted to go to university I had to fund myself.' He shook his head. 'Hell, if I wanted to keep a roof over my mother's head I had to fund that too, since your precious Piers was incapable of doing it.'

'He wasn't my Piers.' The words came out automatically, Ravenna's mind whirling. All these years she'd imagined the Devesons living in easy luxury.

'No.' Jonas invaded her space, head thrust forward. 'He was your mother's. Did she know it was my hard-earned money she lived off all these years? Or didn't she give a damn?'

'Yours?'

His laugh had a razor edge. 'Devesons may have started as a family company but the most Piers did was act as front man. He loved that—preening publicly at our success. At *my* success. Not that he'd admit that. Easier for him to talk of the company's spectacular profits than admit it was his teenage son taking the risks and doing the work.'

'I'm sorry. I didn't know.'

With the knowledge something shifted subtly, like a kaleidoscope on the turn, pieces sliding and settling in an almost familiar yet totally different pattern. It revealed Jonas in a new light.

He'd been the breadwinner all those years, keeping Deveson Hall running and funding his parents' lifestyle? Jonas had striven to accumulate the fortune that supported Piers and her mamma?

What had it been like carrying that weight of responsibility and expectation so young?

Ravenna's teenage problems paled by comparison.

Jonas lifted his shoulders, the movement shrugging away everything but the pair of them, standing close. 'No, you didn't, did you?' he mused. 'How could you know?'

His breath ruffled her hair and suddenly his grey eyes looked soft as mist. Ravenna felt herself heat from the inside as warm treacle spilled and swirled deep in her belly. That skittering sensation was back, drawing her flesh tight.

A whirring sound intruded and Ravenna turned, startled to find a massive lens trained on them.

'Who's the girl, Jonas?'

For a startled moment Ravenna thought it must be a friend asking. But the man with the camera was backing away, camera still trained on them, as if aware of Jonas' big body tensing.

Jonas' hand encircled her arm, drawing her abruptly away and into the car.

'Damned paparazzi,' he muttered under his breath.

'Paparazzi?' Ravenna stared at the man, now two car lengths away. 'Why would they want a photo of us?'

Jonas shrugged. 'Slow news day.' Reading her frown, he added, 'Don't worry. The photo probably won't get used. And if it is—' again that wide shrug '—it's hardly damaging.'

He closed her door and got into the driver seat, apparently unfazed by the press intrusion. Which left Ravenna pondering what it was like to be so influential that even a shopping expedition was newsworthy.

They really were from completely different worlds.

It was imperative Ravenna remember that. Especially as there was unfinished business between her and Jonas Deveson, and she sensed it wasn't all to do with stolen money.

It was easier sharing a house with Jonas than Ravenna had believed possible. They avoided each other.

Yet she was hyper-sensitive to his presence. The rich murmur of his voice through a half-closed door as he spoke on the phone. The spicy scent of damp male skin that clung to the bathroom, evoking heady images of what that solid, athletic body might look like naked.

She found herself cataloguing facts about him. He made his own bed—because he was neat or because he didn't like the intimacy of her touching his bed? His weakness for shortbread and fruitcake. His habit of leaving half-empty coffee mugs about when work distracted him.

Jonas worked ridiculously long hours, running his business from a distance in between a continuous schedule of meetings with conservation officials, builders and others.

Occasionally a young man with a thin, intelligent face and a ready smile arrived, with laptop and briefcase, and the pair closeted themselves for hours. Ravenna took pity on the assistant, Stephen, and supplied refreshments. Jonas never noticed but Stephen would grin and thank her. Ravenna told herself she was glad Jonas never looked up.

She didn't want his notice. She wanted—

A betraying twist of sensation between her legs reminded her of what she'd wanted from Jonas in her dreams last night. What she'd *demanded,* and what he'd so willingly supplied.

Heat suffused her and Ravenna made herself concentrate on the next stack of leather-bound books to be lifted from the shelves.

So she had a libido. She should be glad. It meant her poor battered body was getting back to normal after the long stint of treatment.

She just wished her libido hadn't fixed on the man who'd made it his mission to wreck her life!

Ravenna laid the books on the desk and wiped her brow. It really was warm in here. She'd filled the study with every heater she could find, laying open damp-damaged books to air. But the number of books needing attention was enormous.

If only Jonas would get in staff to help her. She hadn't suggested it again, preferring to avoid him. But that hadn't worked. He was in her head all the time.

Grimacing, she yanked off her pullover. She'd worn extra layers since Jonas arrived as if they would somehow protect her. Ridiculous since he kept to himself. She could work in her underwear and he'd be none the wiser.

Grinning at the thought, Ravenna climbed the library ladder to finish clearing the top shelf.

'Careful up there!' Jonas' deep voice sounded from below, furring her arms and nape with what felt far too much like anticipation. 'I don't want you injuring yourself.'

'Afraid I'll sue for damages?' Gripping the rail, Ravenna turned. Her insides tightened at the picture he made, legs apart and arms folded, hair rumpled.

She'd thought him formidable in bespoke Italian tailoring. In a casual white shirt and faded jeans that clung to heavy thighs, he looked like a pirate. He hadn't shaved and the shadow on his sculpted jaw gave him a dangerous air. Or maybe it was the glitter in his silver gaze.

Sensation scudded through her. Something she preferred not to name. It made her feel hot and achy, needy.

She narrowed her eyes. 'Or afraid I'll squash you if I fall?' She was one of the tallest women she knew.

His mouth quirked in a sexy curl that did devastating things to her. His voice was a deep purr. 'I'm sure I'm up to your weight, Ravenna.'

He moved into the room, his gaze raking from her bare feet, cotton trousers and T-shirt to her flaming face.

She clamped her mouth shut but it didn't stop the shimmer of awareness charging the atmosphere.

'What have you got here?' He stopped by the table and picked up a small volume. Instantly the feeling of pressure in her lungs eased and she drew a slow breath.

'Those were in the small writing desk by the window. And the bigger ones are from up here.'

Jonas stood stiffly as if braced, head bent to the pages of the small book. Colour leached from his face, leaving it starkly pale, skin stretched taut over strong bones. He was so still he didn't seem to breathe. Then the pages began to flutter in his suddenly unsteady hand.

Alarm knifed her. 'Jonas?'

He didn't even look up.

By the time she climbed down he was slumped in a chair and his face was a sickly, greenish hue that made her stomach clutch. He looked as if he was going to keel over.

CHAPTER SEVEN

JONAS WAS STARING.

Ogling was probably a better word, since he couldn't tear his gaze from Ravenna's slender body. With her arms raised, reaching for an upper shelf, her white T-shirt moulded to her breasts. Her enticing, braless breasts.

Damn. He planted his feet wider, needing to ground himself, assert control over his wayward, yearning body.

He'd avoided her all week, telling himself his fascination with her would fade.

That had been a spectacular miscalculation. Every time she entered a room he lost his train of thought. He found himself staring blankly at the computer screen while she traded banter with Stephen, and his PA, still inexperienced in the ways of women, lapped up the attention.

Jonas' mouth set grimly and he yanked his gaze away, turning to the giant desk in the centre of the room. Anything other than Ravenna's distracting body.

'What have you got here?' He grabbed the first book he saw, opening it at random.

As the pages came in focus the world eclipsed.

His skin tightened. A curious ripple raced down his spine as he recognised the handwriting and the import of the words at the top of the page.

He hadn't known she'd kept a diary.

His mother had never struck him as the sort to pen her

thoughts. In later years she'd found solace and company in alcohol. But then—his gaze flicked to the date—this was an old book. Almost as old as him.

His gaze fixed on the line that had caught his eye.

Now I know it's true. Piers is having an affair.

How can he when I love him so?

Jonas couldn't help but read on, scanning the pages where the young woman who'd been his mother had poured out her despair at finding Piers with another woman. A woman who was vivacious, beautiful and confident. All the things Jennifer Deveson felt she lacked.

Jonas' stomach churned. So early in the marriage? He'd thought at least there'd been a honeymoon period. But as he read he realised Piers had had no compunction about pretending affection once the knot that bound him to his wife's money was tied.

Bile soured Jonas' tongue as he read, unable to stop. A pattern emerged. Of Piers seeking out the most gorgeous women and flaunting them. Of his wife retreating into her shell, only emerging to row with her faithless spouse.

Memories rushed back. Scenes he'd witnessed and pretended to forget. The raised voices, the threats, the undercurrent of despair. Despair so profound his mother hadn't wanted to live once Piers left her for good. What sort of sick love was that, clinging on even when it was rejected?

He'd been conceived in such a relationship?

His gut wrenched. His one dream had always been the same. To turn Deveson Hall into what it had never been in his time—a true family home. He'd fantasised about family, a real family, all his life. One that cared and shared and gathered together to celebrate the important things in life. The things his family never did.

Since he was a kid he'd imagined the Hall filled with laughter and companionship. Filled with the family he'd never had but had vowed to acquire. The gorgeous, supportive wife, the brood of happy kids. A generous-hearted matron like Mrs Roberts presiding over the kitchen. A muddle of pets, like the ones he'd never been allowed, to complete the picture.

His lips stretched mirthlessly. His imagination was as corny as a greeting card ad. Yet wasn't that why he was here? Overseeing the refurbishment ready to marry and start that family? Piers' death had been a wake-up call.

Tradition was important to Jonas in a way it could never be to a child who'd known love. He'd absorbed the legends of the house and the Devesons with an enthusiasm honed by his determination to escape the emptiness of real life. He needed heirs to fill that vacuum and share those traditions.

Now, reading his mother's despair, he felt again the helpless emptiness of his childhood.

He hadn't been important enough for her then. Nor had he been able to save her at the end.

Who was he fooling, thinking he could achieve the impossible and create a genuine family? That he could rise above the past that had moulded him? With his family history he was a foreigner to the softer things in life like love and caring. The truth smashed his long-held illusions.

'Jonas?' A hand touched his and he realised the book had fallen from his hold. He watched slim fingers mesh with his. Hers felt warm, roughened by work, but supple and capable. Feminine. She smelt of cinnamon and honey, mouth-watering. 'Are you all right?'

He opened his mouth but no sound emerged.

What could he say? That Jonas Deveson, the man who ran a multibillion-dollar business, whose views were canvassed by investors and leaders worldwide, who lived a life envied by many, was a hollow shell?

There'd been such *pain* in his mother's words. It pierced him in a place that even after all this time was raw and vulnerable.

Guilt swamped him. He hadn't been able to make things

right for her. For all his skill and corporate savvy, he'd never been good at that. He'd failed her.

'Jonas!'

His head whipped up and he saw Ravenna's concern.

He must look as bad as he felt if *she* worried about him!

Her touch was gentle as she hunkered before him. He swallowed, feeling something unravel within. Some of the tightness binding his chest slackened.

'What's wrong?' She leaned closer and he lost himself in the dark gold glow of her eyes. He focused on that rather than the darkness within.

'Nothing.' His tongue was thick and his speech slurred. 'Just an old book.'

'It's obviously upset you.' She looked down as if to reach for it and he snapped his hands around her wrists.

'Leave it. It's just history.' He couldn't believe his reaction—how long-buried emotions had rushed to engulf him as if he were some callow youth.

'I've never seen a history book affect someone like that. You look…ill.'

He felt it. Though the swirling nausea had abated a little with her touch. His hold tightened.

'I really think—'

'No!' He yanked her close, bringing her to her knees before him so she couldn't delve for the book.

'It's my mother's diary.' The words shot out, harsh and uncompromising. 'About Piers' first extra-marital affair. And the next. And so on.' He paused, listening to his blood hammer in his ears. 'Not a book I'd recommend.' He tried for casual but his voice betrayed him, emerging gruff and uneven.

Her eyes widened. 'I see.' And she did, damn her. She read him as easily as he'd read those pages for there was more than sympathy in her eyes now. There was pity.

Pity for *him!*

Everything in Jonas revolted at the idea. He'd spent a

lifetime taking on the world and winning, proving himself stronger, better, triumphant. His name was synonymous with success. He didn't need her pity.

Fury sparked, rising in a searing, seething flood.

There she was, kneeling between his legs, her expression solemn, her lips soft and desirable, the perfume of her skin tantalising and her nipples dark smudges of promise budding against her thin T-shirt. Anticipation was so strong he could almost taste her.

Lust swooped, tightening his groin, urging his legs in hard to trap her where she knelt. He welcomed it, a distraction from emotion.

This he could handle. *This* he welcomed.

Ravenna froze, her expression morphing into disbelief.

'I think I'd better get up.' Her voice was husky.

'I thought you wanted to make me feel better.' He leaned close, meeting those huge sherry-gold eyes.

He didn't want her looking at him like that, as if she could read his secrets.

'I don't think that's possible.'

'Oh, but it is.' Triumph coloured his voice as he cupped her jaw and felt her pulse hammer. Yes! That was what he wanted. Not pity or sympathy. He'd settle for something simpler and far more satisfying. And when they were done he'd feel whole again. Not like some pathetic, wounded...victim.

He slipped his hand round the back of her neck and tugged her to him, planting his mouth on hers before she could speak. And there it was, that raw spiral of heated need, spinning between them, dragging them under.

Her lips were soft as he'd known they'd be. Yet despite a week of anticipation he wasn't prepared for the delicate taste of her. Delicious. Addictive. Perfect.

Using both hands, he pulled her close, locking his thighs against her hips, imagining how it would be with her legs wrapped around his waist.

Heat shot through him and his groin was in agony, constricted by too-tight denim.

He needed her. Now.

Ravenna's head spun as Jonas dragged her into his arms with a ruthless economy of movement that spoke of practice. If she'd been in any doubt about his experience with women, his fierce certainty abolished it.

He knew women. The graze of his hard palm over her budding nipple told her that.

Yet nothing could hide his uneven breathing, or erase the pain she'd read in his face. It was his pain that had lured her close, casting aside caution.

But it was something else that kept her here. Not the taut clench of his thighs that stoked delicious awareness of his masculine strength. Nor the arm wrapped possessively around her back.

Despite the overwhelming sense of Jonas' superior size and power, despite the implacable hunger she'd read in his face as he plastered his mouth over hers, Ravenna had no fear he'd force her. Instinct, and the knowledge she'd gleaned of his pride and self-possession, told her she was safe. *If she wanted to be.*

Her mind whirled as her body responded to his urgent demands.

The truth struck her like a flare of lightning, illuminating what she'd tried to hide.

She didn't want safety. Not with his mouth reducing her to willing compliance, his body flush against hers and that heady rush of arousal in her veins. It didn't matter that they were enemies.

Maybe her response was an outlet for pent up emotions that had weighed on her too long.

Maybe she needed this rush of life-affirming pleasure after coming so close to death mere months before. She felt so *alive* in his arms.

Or perhaps she simply responded to the sheer wanton thrill of being desired by such a man: devastatingly attractive and potently charismatic, if you forgot that cutting tongue.

Right now his tongue was doing things that turned Ravenna's bones to butter.

She clawed at his shirt, relishing the taut, hot muscle beneath, and kissed him back. He tasted like last night's erotic dreams: spicy, delicious and unique. No matter how she worked she'd never create a dish with such a wonderful flavour.

Large hands slid below the drawstring of her trousers, beneath her panties to splay over her buttocks and brand her with his searing touch. He tugged and Ravenna found herself plastered against a solid ridge of denim and rampant male.

For a dizzying moment caution vied with pleasure. But her need was too strong. She thrust her hands through his hair, tugging glossy dark locks then clamping hard on his skull as she ground her hips against his.

Fire shot through her veins and the world juddered.

'Again.' The word was a hoarse rasp in her ear.

Ravenna obliged. How could she not, when the stranger who'd taken possession of her body craved Jonas as if her life depended on it?

Again she tilted her hips. They came together in a move that would have left her impaled on him but for their clothes. Light burst in the darkness of her closed eyes and she shivered at the myriad sensations bombarding her. His body, his touch, the clean smell of aroused male, even the friction of their clothes was erotic.

Ravenna tugged at his shirt buttons, whimpering with frustration when she couldn't get her fingers to work. She needed her skin against his.

'Yes, touch me.' Did she hear the words or just taste them in her mouth?

His shirt disappeared, ripped by strong hands, leaving her free to palm his torso. Blindly she traced the contours of Jonas' chest, the broad weight of hair-fuzzed pectorals, the smoother planes and ridges lower down.

She'd just reached a barrier of taut denim when abrupt movement widened her eyes. She was falling. No, not falling—Jonas' strong arm was at her back, cushioning her as she landed on the floor.

She lay on the rich antique rug as Jonas ripped open the drawstring at her waist and tugged her trousers and underwear down.

A surge of indignant anger would have given her the strength to slap his face and cover herself. But it wasn't anger she felt.

It was excitement.

Her breath came in raw gasps as she watched him wrestle the clothes off her feet and toss them aside. His eyes glowed pure silver, almost molten, and his gaze, raking her from top to toe, was incendiary. Rivers of fire ignited in her blood, searing through anything like caution.

The way he looked at her, as if there were no one and nothing else in the world, as if he'd die if he didn't possess her…she revelled in it. For she felt the same.

She traced his powerful frame with possessive eyes, rejoicing in the heavy rise and fall of his chest and the pulse hammering out of control at his throat.

'Jonas.' His name was an aphrodisiac on her tongue. 'Come here.' She reached out and he planted a brief, fervent kiss on her palm then turned aside.

Ravenna opened her mouth to protest then realised he was tearing open a small packet he'd grabbed from his wallet. Undoing his jeans with the other hand, he moved swiftly, economically. A glimpse of his erection made her inner muscles tighten in a mix of anticipation and doubt. She was tall but—

The weight of his half-naked body on hers obliterated any doubts. He was big, his bare torso burning up, and she revelled in the way he imprisoned her, propped on his elbows to protect her from his weight.

He lowered his head, suckling her nipple through her T-shirt and she arched high, a moan of pleasure throbbing in her throat. The movement produced friction lower, where he waited at the juncture of her thighs, and lower still where her calves slid against the jeans he still wore.

Ravenna clutched his head, holding him to her breast. 'Please.' It was all she could manage, words failing her. She wanted his mouth on her but she wanted far more. She needed—

He must have understood for with one quick movement he centred himself and thrust hard and fast, right to the core of her. It was shockingly perfect, the feel of them joined so completely. For a trembling moment Ravenna felt she hung suspended from the stars, quivering in awe.

Then one large hand pushed her T-shirt up and cupped her breast. Jonas sucked on her other breast, hard and insistent, as he withdrew then surged in again, higher this time.

As easily as that she shattered. Not in delicate ripples of delight but in a cataclysmic upheaval that made her buck and scream beneath him, hands clinging and voice hoarse as she rode out a storm of pleasure so exquisite, so intense, it must change her for ever.

She was floating in ecstasy when he said her name in a voice so deep it rumbled through her, right to her bones.

Eyes snapping open, she was snared by Jonas' hot, silver gaze. In her confused state she wondered if she'd wear the brand of that intense look for life. She felt it like a touch, heavy and erotic, strong enough to mark her.

His face was austere, pared to bone and taut flesh. Then he moved, short, sharp thrusts that sent shock waves through her, re-igniting desire though it should be impossible now. It was his look that held her captive, that intense connection, the throb and push of his body in perfect sync with hers, the raw pleasure and something more, something huge and full of emotion.

Ravenna slid her hands around his hot, damp torso and down, clamping hard on the taut muscle of his backside, pulling him in, needing to share.

'Ravenna!' His voice was a roar, his eyes shocked as he bucked hard, pulsing frantically and she shattered again. This time she wasn't alone. They rode the whirlwind together, gazes enmeshed. His ecstasy was hers. Every throb and quake of delight was shared. Every gasp and groan. Every delicious shudder and squeeze of loosening muscle.

Still he held her gaze and Ravenna held him close. She reached up to those wide shoulders, tugging.

'I'm heavy.' His voice wasn't the clipped, sure one she knew. It burred soft enough to make what was left of her insides melt.

'I know.' She tugged again. 'Come here.'

He let her pull him down so they lay chest to chest, his heart pounding against hers. It felt so right, as if she'd waited all her life for this.

She'd known a man before. Just one. He'd been attractive, fun, nice. Yet she hadn't experienced anything like this feeling of completion with him. As if all was right with the world and at long last she'd found her place in it, not an outsider any more. It was as if with Jonas she was home.

Ravenna took a shallow breath, inhaling the musky scent of sex and the sharp tang of Jonas' flesh. She was barely aware of the trickle of tears down her cheek as she hugged him close.

Ravenna was limp in his arms as he carried her upstairs.

For a tall woman she didn't weigh much. There was a delicacy about her that tugged at him, made him want to keep her close.

His stride lengthened as he marched to his bedroom. Still she didn't stir. The cynical side of him wanted to assert she was playing him, trying to stir protectiveness. But he'd seen her stunned expression as she'd climaxed not once, but twice. He'd felt her convulse around him in great waves of pleasure that shook him to the core.

Jonas had never experienced anything so intense. It was as if her passion had turned him molten and forged him into someone new. He felt...different.

His arms tightened. Was it like this with her every time?

He'd known Ravenna was passionate. Her vibrancy, whether in fury or indignation, had fascinated from the first, drawing him despite himself. If he'd known how that translated to erotic passion he'd have followed through on that kiss in Paris instead of waiting all this time.

Satisfaction stirred as he nudged open the bedroom door. *This* was what he wanted from her. Sex. The sort of passion that drove out anything as corrosive as pity. He didn't need her feeling sorry for him. He was no charity case.

Jonas laid her on the bed, taking in the beguiling curve of her full lips and those lustrous, long dark lashes that fanned her rosy cheeks. Something unfamiliar skated through him as he looked down at her. Tenderness. The need to look after her.

The realisation slammed into him, catching his breath. Already his hand had reached out as if to trace Ravenna's cheekbone, the pure angle of her jaw, the delicate pulse at her throat. His heart skipped a beat as he remembered the look in her eyes as they'd climaxed together. The wonderment and joy. A joy so strong it had branded him.

Jonas snatched his hand back.

Even asleep Ravenna was dangerous.

He assured himself this wasn't different from what he'd experienced with other lovers. It *couldn't* be different. If he felt altered it was only because of the depth of his arousal. He couldn't remember ever needing any woman with such a primitive urgency.

Jonas nodded, satisfied with that explanation. He knew

what he wanted from Ravenna and it wasn't emotion. He'd never felt emotionally bound to a lover and he wasn't about to start with her of all women.

When the time came for feelings they would be for his wife. The perfect woman who would fit his requirements and his world, who'd excel at being a mother, a gracious hostess, a social success and a loyal, supportive spouse.

Jonas frowned. For the first time his vision of the perfect wife to create his perfect future didn't fill him with anticipation.

He looked at Ravenna, noting the graze of stubble rash on her cheek where his unshaved jaw had rubbed and how the damp patch on her T-shirt clung to her nipple where his tongue had laved.

He felt a primitive satisfaction that he'd marked her as his.

His chest tightened and a frisson of doubt snaked through him. No! This was lust pure and simple. Not to be confused with his longer-term plans. Those plans had been all that kept him sane in a world where no one cared for him except as a pawn in the game of his parents' disintegrating marriage or, later, as the goose that lay the golden eggs. His family, his women—all had only wanted what he could give them. They hadn't wanted *him*.

So he'd learned to take.

He let his gaze rove Ravenna's slim legs, bare and supple, to the V of dark hair between her thighs. His sex stirred, eager for more.

That was what he wanted. Physical pleasure and release. He could seduce her awake or have her again while she slept. But he did neither.

His gaze caught on a red mark on her hipbone. It was where he'd gripped her hard as he came. White-hot memory of that glorious cataclysm rocked him. And more, of the soft light in her eyes when she'd tugged him to her and wrapped him close in trembling arms. She'd had nothing to gain from that embrace. It had been about giving, sharing, and he couldn't remember anything better than those moments in her arms, not even that spectacular orgasm.

Silently Jonas shucked off his jeans and climbed onto the wide bed, careful not to disturb Ravenna. The bed shifted beneath his weight and she rolled towards him. Automatically he put his arm around her, tugging her close, her head on his shoulder, her hand at his hip. His breath snared at the innocently erotic pleasure of her touch but he made no move to wake her. For now this was enough.

He wrapped his other hand around her thigh, dragging it over his belly, and sank back into the mattress.

It seemed hours later that she woke. Her lashes tickled his chest as they fluttered open. Her fingers twitched as if testing the surface she lay on. Instead of rearing back in horror she nuzzled closer as if drawing in his scent. All his senses went ballistic.

She blinked sleepily up at him, her lips widening in a smile that knocked a chunk of granite off the corner of his heart. Her gaze was warm and for the first time he saw her smile reach her eyes. They glowed.

Jonas felt something shift deep inside. Something he had no name for. He felt it again when her hand skimmed up and around and he found himself being cuddled.

Hugs weren't common in his experience, even after sex. He discovered he liked them. They made him feel…good.

Who'd have thought 'good' could be so satisfying?

'Thank you.' Her voice was low, shivering through him like a caress.

Another first. How many lovers thanked him even though he put their pleasure first?

Guilt pummelled him. He hadn't been careful with Ravenna. He'd taken her with a savagery that bordered on uncontrolled. Look at the way he'd bruised her.

'Are you okay?'

She blinked at his rough tone and moved as if to prop

herself up to see him better, but he kept her clamped to him. He liked her right where she was.

'Okay? I feel fantastic.' Her smile turned secretive and her lashes lowered as her cheeks coloured.

A woman who blushed and thanked him for taking her with the finesse of a horny teenager? Ravenna was far from the woman he'd imagined.

'I didn't hurt you?'

She shook her head. 'I told you I enjoyed it. Didn't you?' Ravenna's voice was like warm whisky spilling through his veins and pooling low in his belly. She looked him square in the eyes and Jonas' heart give a great thump.

'Absolutely.' *Enjoy* didn't come close to describing what he'd felt. 'But I should have been more careful. I've bruised you.' His hand drifted to her hip, caressing the spot where he'd held her.

Her lashes dipped, hiding her eyes as she shrugged. 'I bruise easily. But it doesn't hurt.'

'Good.' Jonas told himself he should end this, get up and walk away. But he couldn't. His fingers feathered the soft skin at her hip and he heard her hiss of indrawn breath.

'In that case,' he murmured, slamming a door on the voice of caution crying out in his head, 'perhaps we might do it again.' He watched her eyes widen with anticipation and felt satisfaction flare. Satisfaction at the thought of having Ravenna again, of taking his time to pleasure her slowly. Of sharing that oneness again.

'I never thought I'd say this, but you have some good ideas, Jonas Deveson.' Her smile was sexy as she trailed a finger up his throat to his ear.

Arousal jolted through him. Swiftly he rolled her onto her back, capturing her wrists and dragging them above her head. At her moue of disappointment, he leaned in and tasted her mouth, shocked yet pleased to discover her as delicious as before.

'Let me, Ravenna. I want to do this slowly.' He feathered

tiny kisses down her neck, then moved down and licked the underside of her breast, unbearably turned on just by the taste of her and by her uneven breathing.

'I'm not sure I can bear it.' But the look in her eyes belied her words. It was warm like a caress as it locked with his. Again he felt that unfamiliar clenching in his chest.

In that moment it was far more than sex that he wanted.

CHAPTER EIGHT

RAVENNA WOKE IN Jonas' bed. Smiling, she rolled on her side, reaching for him. He wasn't there.

Her stomach dipped. She'd never imagined herself insatiable but an afternoon with Jonas had taught her things she'd never expected.

That she had erogenous zones she'd never known.

That she could make Jonas lose his cool.

That ecstasy made her noisy. Her face flamed at the way she'd screamed his name over and over. But he hadn't minded, encouraging her as if he enjoyed hearing her shout his name.

That she had a weakness for silvery eyes, a broad chest and clever hands that knew exactly how to touch her.

That she had a weakness for Jonas Deveson.

Her breathing quickened. Jonas wasn't the frigid enemy she'd thought. He had his own difficult past. He'd been the one supporting his family and her mother, from the day he left school. Was it any wonder he'd had no time for Piers or Silvia, who'd kept their distance yet lived off his hard work?

As for his mother… Ravenna bit her lip, remembering his wretchedness as he read that diary. Whatever else Jonas might be, he wasn't unfeeling. He'd been raw with pain. It had hurt to see him so.

When he'd made love to her it hadn't been a cheap little wham, bam, thank you ma'am, no matter how fast and furious the first time. She'd felt so much. They had shared more than mere physical coupling. And his tenderness here in his bed—

Ravenna wriggled under the sheets. The next time he'd been gentle, utterly devastating with those careful caresses, until the white-hot urgency overtook them again.

It had been wonderful, far beyond her imaginings.

The explosion of passion had been inevitable. She'd been too inexperienced to understand the frisson of sexual tension from the moment he'd stalked into the Paris apartment. All she'd known was that around Jonas she was on edge, as if her skin didn't fit. She'd put it down to hatred, not attraction.

Ravenna watched the door. Jonas would be back soon. Their relationship had changed irrevocably and they needed to work out where they went from here.

It wasn't so much sex that had changed their relationship, but the sense of intimacy. She knew him for a more complex, feeling man than she'd imagined. And he knew she was more than the grasping thief he'd believed, or he wouldn't have let her get so close. He was too proud to open himself to a woman he disdained. The knowledge buoyed her.

Tantalisingly, Ravenna felt on the brink of understanding Jonas. Not completely, but she realised his original antipathy came from the harsh realities he'd faced. She'd seen a hint of the scars he'd carried since childhood.

In that moment she despised Piers. He'd been good to Silvia and she was grateful, but to ignore his own son…!

Whatever difficulties Ravenna and her mother faced, they'd had each other. She couldn't imagine growing up so alone. Jonas hadn't spoken much of his relationship with his mother but she guessed it hadn't been easy. What she knew of Piers' wife made her seem self-focused rather than maternal.

A shiver passed through Ravenna. She and Jonas still had a long way to go. The money was an almost insuperable barrier. Ravenna couldn't simply blurt out the truth.

Jonas detested her mother and would love a chance to make her suffer if he learned it was she who'd stolen from him.

But surely now Ravenna could make him listen and he'd be more understanding. Things weren't black and white any more. Behind the lord-of-the-world façade was a man she wanted to know better.

Given time they'd work things out. It wouldn't be easy, or immediate, but eventually he'd understand.

Through the bathroom door her mobile phone rang. The insistent ringing grated, high pitched like nails clawing her sensitised skin. Maybe because she'd faced such bad news in the last year she couldn't ignore it—had to check it wasn't something important.

Scurrying to her room, she snatched up the phone and draped a rug around herself, chilled after leaving Jonas' bed.

'Ravenna?'

'Mamma? What is it? Are you all right?' Her stomach curdled at Silvia's tone. They'd spoken only yesterday. What had happened since to put the fear in her mother's voice?

'I'm fine. It's you I'm worried about. What has that man done to you?'

Ravenna stilled in the act of shrugging the rug closer.

'What man?'

'Oh, *Ravenna!*' It was a wail of horror. 'So it's true. I can hear it in your voice.'

'What's true? What are you talking about?' It was impossible Mamma had guessed she was with Jonas. Yet, standing naked, aching in unfamiliar places after his thorough loving, Ravenna felt as if she'd been caught out.

'Don't pretend, darling. I know you're with Jonas Deveson.'

Ravenna sank onto the bed. What on earth was going on?

'I saw it in a magazine. You and him shopping together.'

'A magazine?' It must have been the paparazzi shot that had so surprised her.

'The press have labelled you his secret girlfriend. They

say the pair of you are holing up in a love nest.' Her voice rose in panic. 'Tell me it's not true. Tell me you wouldn't be stupid enough to fall for him.'

Ravenna opened her mouth then shut it again. Everything was moving too fast. She felt dizzy.

'Ravenna?' Her voice was sharp. 'Has he hurt you?'

'Of course he hasn't hurt me, Mamma. You're overreacting. There's nothing to worry about.'

'Nothing to worry about?' She could almost see her mother roll her eyes. 'You're such an innocent when it comes to men. There's nothing innocent about the way he's looking at you in that photo. He looks like he wants to eat you all up.'

Heat scorched Ravenna from her toes to the tips of her ears. That was precisely what Jonas had done, using his mouth on her body to reduce her to quivering desperation.

'Ravenna.' Her mother's voice, now quiet, vibrated with worry. 'Tell me you didn't fall for his lies.'

'Jonas isn't a liar, Mamma.'

'Oh, Ravenna! You did, didn't you?'

Ravenna squared her shoulders. 'I'm twenty-four, Mamma, not a little girl. Jonas hasn't hurt me.' Given her mother's response to that innocent photo, now wasn't the time to reveal the whole truth. Her mother would hotfoot it to England and that would set the cat among the pigeons. Much as Ravenna wanted to see her, Silvia was safer in Italy. 'I'm...working for him, as a temporary housekeeper.'

'That's the job you were excited about?' Silvia was disbelieving. 'You vowed never to work in service.'

It was true. Ravenna had determined never to be anyone's servant after years of being made to feel inferior at school.

But that was before her mother had stolen and put her in a situation where she had to swallow her pride. Mamma had taken the money for *her*. This was her responsibility.

'Jonas is hosting a ball to reopen the Hall and I'm doing the catering. It will be a great opportunity to showcase my skills.' Ravenna was babbling but couldn't stop. Maybe because she was naked, her body tingling from his touch. 'I hope it will be a stepping stone to other jobs.'

Her mother sighed. 'Promise me you'll keep your distance. He hates me and he'd do anything to hurt me. You have no idea how ruthless he is—' her voice dropped '—or how much he despises me. He blames me for his mother's death. But I swear I had no idea she still cared about Piers. While I was at the Hall all she did was snipe at him. Poor Piers—'

'I know.' Ravenna had heard it before, how Piers had fallen in love for the first time ever with her mamma. How happy they'd been. 'But Jonas can't hurt me.'

He already had his retribution. What more could he do?

'Don't be too sure. Even when he was young he had a way with women, a magnetism that drew them even though it was obvious they were expendable.'

Ravenna bit her tongue rather than snap that if he had, he'd probably got that from his father. Her mother hated hearing anything negative about Piers. He was one of the few subjects they didn't see eye to eye on.

'I wouldn't put it past him to seduce you, just to settle the score. He's charismatic and persuasive but beneath the charm he's cold and calculating.'

'Maybe there's more to him than you think. Besides, it was Piers, not Jonas, who ripped that family apart.'

Silence greeted her words. It was the closest she'd come to criticising Piers to her mother. He'd been good to Silvia and he'd loved her in his own way, but she'd never been comfortable with his irresponsible take on life.

'I know.' Her mother's misery caught at Ravenna's heart. 'I'm sorry, Mamma. I—'

'No, don't apologise. It's just I'm worried about you. No matter what you think you know about Jonas Deveson, remember this: he's an aristocrat through and through. He's not easy-going like his father. He's a perfectionist who only settles for the best. To him that means a woman from the right family, with the right connections, the right accent, the right look. You'll never be that woman. To him you'll always be the housekeeper's daughter. Worse, you're a permanent reminder of me and Piers.'

A weight crushed Ravenna's chest as she heard her mother say all the things she'd told herself. But that was before—

'You'll find the right man one day, Ravenna. But it won't be Jonas Deveson. At best he'd offer a brief affair. At worst—well, you only have to look into his eyes to understand the meaning of revenge.'

Ravenna swallowed. She'd seen that look. That day in Paris it had transfixed her with a fear she dared not show.

'I'm sorry, Mamma,' she said quickly. 'I have to go. But don't worry. I'm perfectly able to look after myself.'

So why, when she ended the call, did Ravenna feel shaken to the core? Jonas didn't love her—she wasn't that naïve. But there was something between them stronger than prejudice. Something drew them despite the reasons they shouldn't be together. It was worth exploring.

Tossing aside the rug, Ravenna went to her wardrobe. It was time she squashed those poisonous tendrils of doubt.

She reached for a pair of trousers and paused. Call it feminine pride but she wanted him to look at her with desire. Ravenna pulled out the one decent dress she'd brought.

It felt disturbingly as if she donned protective armour.

Ravenna was back in his bedroom when he returned. At the sight of her tucking in sheets with swift movements, he almost wondered if he'd imagined the last, passionate hours when they'd driven each other to ecstasy again and again.

His gaze dropped to the length of her legs, revealed as she leaned across to plump up the pillows, and the sweet curve of her bottom against the clingy orange dress.

Jonas swallowed over sandpaper as his body stirred.

Then she turned and he saw what she wore. Not the nondescript work clothes he'd fantasised about stripping off her all week. The dress was held in place by a single, provocative tie at the waist. A V neck hinted at her delicious cleavage, but it was the way the dress clung that made his heart hammer. Like lover's hands it cupped, caressed and flowed over proud breasts, the swell of her hips and a waist that he could almost span with his hands.

She was blatantly sexy. Her gaze collided with his and that white-hot blast of connection shimmered in the air.

Hunger slammed into him as if he hadn't already had his fill of her several times. Instead of sating desire, an afternoon spent in bed had turned him into a randy teenager, driven by his libido, not his brain.

It unsettled him. He ruled his world through logic and careful planning. Yet he'd lost a precious afternoon's work and all he could think of was how many moves it would take to have Ravenna naked beneath him again.

He raked his hand through his hair. He'd left her to seek refuge downstairs, needing to gather himself, yet just one look shattered him all over again.

'Jonas.' Her voice had a low, throaty quality that would make him think about sex even if she were wearing a sack. 'I was just coming to look for you.'

She approached then halted as if having second thoughts.

'I was busy downstairs.' Busy revisiting that diary. When that got too much he'd taken refuge in thoughts of Ravenna coming apart in his arms, more radiant and alive than any woman he'd known.

'Oh.' She wiped her hands down her dress, instantly dragging his gaze to her thighs and flat belly.

Jonas drew in a breath redolent with the tang of feminine arousal. He'd yanked his clothes on without bothering to shower. Till this moment he hadn't admitted it was because he revelled in the scent of her on his skin.

He frowned. Why? What made her different from other women?

He hadn't even come back here in the hope of more sex.

She'd been so exhausted he'd expected her to be asleep. He'd simply returned to be with her—she made him feel good.

That was a first. An unsettling one.

'Why did you want me?' It came out gruffly but for once Jonas was incapable of charm.

Ravenna shrugged but the movement was jerky, betraying nerves. 'I thought we should talk.'

He nodded and prowled further into the room. 'Go ahead.'

Her eyes widened before she looked down, lashes veiling her eyes. Silently Jonas cursed the loss of even the most basic courtesy. No morning after had ever been so awkward. He had a horrible suspicion it was because none had ever felt quite so important. He was ridiculously on edge.

'We need to talk about us.'

Every male instinct Jonas possessed hummed to alert.

'Yes?' He noted the way her gaze skated over his shoulder then to a spot below his ear.

'About this afternoon.'

Suddenly her uncertainty made sense. He'd been careful about protection, as always, but that last condom had torn. He hadn't realised she'd noticed and had told himself the chances of it leading to anything were slim.

'Are you on the pill?'

'No.' Her gaze jerked to his. It wasn't worry he saw in her face but something indefinable. Instinct told him it was something she didn't want him to notice.

'I see.' That complicated matters. Suppose she got pregnant? It wasn't what he'd planned, but he'd never walk away from a child of his.

The idea of Ravenna being pregnant with his seed shafted possessiveness through him. 'If there's a child—'

'There won't be a child.' Her expression was shuttered.

'It's possible.'

She shook her head and he read obstinacy in her jaw. 'You don't have to worry about it.'

His belly twisted hard. His mother's diary had revealed

with brutal clarity why he was an only child. After him there'd been an abortion and she'd ensured she didn't have another baby to the man who'd betrayed her. Jonas had thought he'd plumbed the depths before, but that revelation had torn a gaping hole somewhere in the vicinity of his chest.

'Why?' The word shot like a bullet. 'Because you'd terminate it?'

Ravenna's face froze. 'No! Because I know my body and you don't have anything to worry about.'

Air escaped his tight lungs and he realised he'd been holding his breath. 'I see.'

Ridiculous to feel a pang of regret.

'So what did you want to discuss?' He stepped closer but made himself stop at arm's length.

'Us.' She waved one arm in a gesture that encompassed the bed. 'I mean, what happens now?'

Jonas could think of several things he'd like to happen. All involved Ravenna naked. He moved forward but stopped, seeing her draw herself up stiffly. He remembered how demanding he'd been. She could be sore. Jonas tried to feel guilty but couldn't bring himself to regret what they'd done.

'Things aren't the same now.' She fixed him with a keen gaze. 'Are they?'

What did she want? An admission that she'd turned him inside out with her sexuality, indomitable spirit and devastating generosity? That moment in the study when she'd offered comfort had undone him. He was so unused to anyone's concern, he'd repudiated it even as secretly he coveted it.

He hadn't managed to fathom what it was he wanted from Ravenna, except more. Until he understood he'd admit nothing.

'Jonas?' Her tone sharpened.

'What happens now?' He shrugged, not liking the sensation of being cornered. 'We both have work to do.'

Her stare grew fixed. 'Is that all?'

'No, of course that's not all. I want to take you back to

bed.' His gaze dropped to the V of her neckline. 'Hell! I don't even want to wait that long.' Heat surged in his blood and his lower body grew heavy and hard. 'But given the fact you're up and dressed I'm assuming you don't feel the same.'

Jonas enjoyed the fiery colour slashing her cheeks. It reminded him of her full body blush when he made love to her.

'I'm not talking about that.'

'No?' He jerked his brain back into gear. 'What else is there?'

Her eyes widened and he felt a moment's regret. But he refused to be railroaded into discussing *feelings,* if that was what she meant.

'I see.' Ravenna's jaw tightened and she crossed her arms. Did she realise how that plumped up her breasts? 'So as far as you're concerned we'll go on as before, except for bouts of hot sex when the fancy takes you.'

'It's an improvement on what went before.'

She didn't respond to his smile.

He wondered how long it would take to seduce her into breathless compliance. His body stirred. He'd always enjoyed a challenge and despite her frosty attitude Ravenna would welcome him. Look at the way her nipples budded and her pulse throbbed in her throat.

'Let me get this straight.' She unfolded her arms and stepped into his space, her eyes glinting gold sparks. 'After what we shared you think nothing has changed, except you get rights to my body whenever you want?' She shook her head. 'You're in the wrong century, Jonas. The droit du seigneur vanished ages ago.'

He stiffened. 'No one forced you, Ravenna.' Her sceptically raised brows grazed his pride, for he hadn't been gentle that first time. But nor had she been forced. Ravenna had made a choice. She could have refused. 'You wanted me.'

'I did,' she finally admitted. 'But that doesn't mean you can expect me to slave away here under your Draconian conditions and be your sex toy as well. You can't have it both ways. I deserve better.'

Jonas surveyed her defiant face, her pouting lips, fuller from his kisses, her reddened cheek where his stubble had marked her. Anger flashed in her eyes and something like disappointment.

His gaze dropped to the seductive flame-coloured dress designed to bring a man to his knees.

His belly curdled as finally, and far too late, realisation struck. Jonas almost staggered under the impact.

How had he been so blind? Disappointment carved a hollow through his vitals. Disappointment and fury at his naivety. Him, naïve! You'd think with his history he would have expected this. Yet he felt sick with the shock of it.

Just like her mother, Ravenna aimed to sell her body for a rich man's favours. She saw him as an easy target and wanted to buy her way out of debt. She thought sharing her body wiped out her crime.

That put what they'd done together in a new light.

Anger and resentment swamped Jonas—that he should have responded, wanted so much, when all the time it had been a tawdry transaction by a conniving woman.

Ravenna watched storm clouds gather in Jonas' eyes. That leaden stare sent a chill scudding down her spine. It was as if they were back to the animosity of Paris.

Stoically she forced down rising bile. Had she deluded herself? Had the man she'd begun to feel for been an illusion? Had his vulnerability and his easy charm been as her mother had warned—a ploy to make her lower her guard so he could wreak revenge on her family?

She didn't want to believe it.

'What did you have in mind, Ravenna?' His voice was a low purr, but instead of soothing it made her hackles rise. He sounded like a hungry lion inviting her to dine.

She lifted her chin. 'I was hoping to talk. Get to know

each other better.' The words sounded lame in the face of his
cool regard but she plunged on. 'I thought we might come
to a better arrangement too about the work to be done here.'

'Really?' One saturnine eyebrow rose in lofty surprise.

'Yes, really.' His condescension sliced through her caution. 'If you want this place put in order I'll need help.'

'You don't think you should dirty your delicate hands
now you've slept with the boss?'

That sarcastic tone scraped her skin raw. She felt sullied,
pressing a hand to her stomach as nausea rose. Familiar exhaustion struck, dragging at her limbs, making her panic she
wouldn't be able to stand up to him physically.

Not now. Not in front of him!

'In case you hadn't noticed my hands aren't delicate.'
They were firm and capable, bearing nicks from her ap-
prenticeship in a commercial kitchen.

Jonas shifted, looming over her by a head, making
Ravenna feel every inch of the difference between them.
From his chiselled, aristocratic features to his elegant handmade clothes and designer watch he was the epitome of
wealth and authority. She, with her shorn hair and cheap,
chain-store dress didn't fit his world. She'd never been
ashamed of being poor, but she'd always hated condescension.

This was worse, far worse.

'You know what I mean,' he said, his voice low and le-
thal. 'You think because we had sex I'll forget your crime?
Or are you setting your sights higher? Do you think I'll keep
you in luxury now I've had a taste of what you're bartering?'

Ravenna rocked back at the force of his contempt.

'All I *want*,' she ground out between her teeth, 'is a little respect.'

'Is that what you call it? And there was I, thinking you
were simply whoring yourself like your mother.'

Ravenna's hands clenched as she fought the urge for violence.

'You really are a self-satisfied bastard.' He didn't even flinch, whereas she felt as if she were crumbling.

'And I'm sorry to say you're every inch your mother's daughter. I warned you, I don't share my father's weakness for the hired help.' His smile killed something fragile inside. 'But that doesn't prevent me taking what's on offer.' His eyes stripped her bare and she shuddered.

'There's *nothing* on offer.' Not any more. Not when he'd taken her caring and her concern, and, yes, her body, and reduced them to nothing with a few slashing words.

'Let's get one thing straight, Ravenna.' He leaned closer, invading her space. 'If you're aiming for something permanent you're barking up the wrong tree.' His voice was rough, reminding her of the sharp emotion she'd seen in him when he talked of his family. Yet his eyes had the blank look of someone who'd shut himself off from feelings.

She wished she could do the same.

She wished her mother had been wrong and Jonas was even half the man she'd begun to believe him. Mamma had been right—Ravenna had confused sex with caring. Now she paid the price as pain sliced her.

'Don't worry. I get the picture. As far as your family is concerned the Ruggiero women are good enough to be mistresses but never wives.' From some inner reserve of strength Ravenna summoned a shaky smile. 'Frankly, a long-term relationship hadn't occurred to me. I'd like to respect the man I live with. But thanks for the clarification.'

Ignoring his glare, she turned away, careful to keep her balance on wobbly legs. When the door shut behind her it was with a snick of finality.

CHAPTER NINE

JONAS TOSSED THE design portfolio onto his desk and sat back, rubbing eyes gritty from lack of sleep. He couldn't concentrate. He hadn't been able to concentrate since that scene with Ravenna.

Ruggiero women are good enough to be mistresses but never wives.

The look on her face as she'd thrown what he was thinking straight back at him! Defiance, hauteur and a pain that cut to the bone. It was that anguish, etched in her eyes and taut frame, that had dragged him from blind fury long enough to recognise he might have overreacted.

Might have? He'd jumped down her throat without hearing her out.

Because it was easier to dismiss Ravenna as a gold-digging opportunist than believe she could be something more.

Yet it was the something more he'd responded to, not just her sexuality. It was the woman who'd comforted him, her enemy. The woman who, without being asked, catered cheerfully for those working around the Hall, even him, the man set on making her life hell. The woman who had rolled up her sleeves and taken on the ridiculously impossible task he'd set her, revealing a grit and determination he'd not thought possible. The woman who'd fought him tooth and nail but never shied from the consequences of her actions in thieving from him.

He shook his head. Something didn't add up, but he was too befuddled to work it out.

Jonas looked at his half-empty mug and the scatter of crumbs on the plate she'd left on his desk and felt remorse.

Good enough to be mistresses. The pain in her words made him feel two inches tall.

No woman deserved to think that. Especially the woman who'd shared herself so unstintingly while he'd behaved with the finesse of a Neanderthal.

In Paris he'd thought her a consummate liar, a woman totally changed from the earnest, engaging teenager he'd met. But that scene in his bedroom proved him wrong. Ravenna couldn't hide her shame and anguish as she faced him down.

He felt like scum.

As if he'd taken advantage of her.

For the first time he wondered how Ravenna had reacted to her mother's affair.

The teenage Ravenna had seemed heartbreakingly alone in a world that judged merit on status and money. She'd suffered at the hands of bullies who despised her lack of wealth. Yet she hadn't envied their money, just hated their shallowness.

How had she felt when her mother took up with Piers, revelling like a self-satisfied potentate in the furore over his gorgeous mistress? Had Ravenna enjoyed the ride?

Or, the thought struck hard, had she cringed at the gossip about her mother leeching Piers for cash?

Ravenna had developed that shell of pride for a reason.

Once the thought lodged he couldn't shake it. Especially as he recalled the wretchedness she'd tried to hide when he'd accused her of sleeping her way out of trouble.

Guilt smote him. Perhaps it was true. Perhaps not. But the memory of that haunted look discomfited him.

Jonas shoved back the chair and strode across the room.

He halted when he saw Ravenna talking with his garden designer, Adam Renshaw. The man's auburn head was bent towards hers and fire seared Jonas as if he'd been skewered on a spit. He couldn't breathe.

It took a moment to identify the unfamiliar feeling as jealousy.

His jaw tightened. He wanted to stomp out and haul Ravenna away.

As if he had a right to her.

As if she wouldn't simply ignore him after what had passed between them.

Jaw gritted, Jonas admitted that no matter what he wanted, no matter what Ravenna wanted, this wasn't over. They had unfinished business.

His mouth twisted mirthlessly as he registered something like relief at the knowledge.

The women in his life had always been expendable. Even the Honourable Helena Worthington, the blonde beauty with impeccable bloodlines and a sweet disposition whom he'd half decided on as a future bride. She hadn't been important enough to stop him taking Ravenna to bed.

Yet with Ravenna, for the first time in his life a woman seemed infuriatingly *necessary*.

He had to discover why.

Then find a way to free himself.

Jonas swung away, almost knocking over the easel of samples his interior designer had set up. His gaze slid over dark paint and patterned fabrics. He'd wanted traditional but this was… He shook his head. Too predictable?

Then he noticed the sheet of paper Ravenna had brought with his coffee. Concise bullet points listed matters needing attention. Every day she presented him with another list of problems—from damage to wainscoting to cracked tiles, usually with suggestions on how to deal with them. She had an eye for detail and a flair for organisation. Qualities that didn't sit well with his original judgement of her.

Jonas looked from the list to the design portfolio. They

were talents he could use. And they would keep her out of the garden and in here, where he wanted her.

'Sorrel, chervil, sage, fennel.' Adam Renshaw smiled. 'There must be at least three dozen herbs on this list.'

'Too many?' When he'd asked Ravenna, as interim house-keeper, for input to his garden design, enthusiasm had overcome her bitterness about Jonas.

How could she resist the opportunity to help plan what promised to be a superlative cook's garden? She daydreamed about having such a place, with space for not only herbs and vegetables but fruit trees and berries. Just walking in this garden with its mellow stone walls and gnarled apple trees lifted her spirits. Something she needed badly.

The alternative, dwelling on Jonas, was untenable.

'Not at all. It's good to have your input.' Adam moved closer. 'We'll fit them in easily over there. I just need to check the final design with Mr Deveson.'

'Did I hear my name mentioned?'

Ravenna froze as that familiar, rich voice curled around her like velvet on bare skin. Her lips compressed. How could she react that way when the same voice had lacerated her just days ago?

Adam swung round to face their boss. Ravenna took longer, bracing herself before she met his gaze. Would it be coolly dismissive or would he ignore her as he'd done this morning when she'd brought coffee and he'd been absorbed in a huge portfolio?

Neither, she realised with a jolt as she turned. His gaze was as intent as ever but with none of the chill she expected. Nevertheless she moved half a step closer to Adam, aware of those dark pewter eyes narrowing.

She lifted her chin, reminding herself she didn't care what Jonas Deveson thought.

She'd been naïve to believe she could bridge the chasm between them. He'd used her and made a mockery of what she'd felt. The knowledge kept her chin high and her gaze steady.

'Of course,' Adam was saying, when she finally tuned in to the conversation. 'Ravenna and I were plotting the herb beds, but I think we've got it now.' Warm brown eyes smiled at her approvingly and she wished she could summon a spark of excitement for this pleasant, talented man.

Instead her attention focused on Jonas, standing preternaturally still, just watching the pair of them.

Her mouth flattened in self-disgust. No matter how hard she tried she couldn't ignore him.

'Excellent. In that case I'll just borrow Ravenna.' Jonas turned to her. 'If you have a few minutes?'

She raised her eyebrows. Jonas was requesting, not ordering? Suspicion rose but she forced herself to nod, bidding Adam a warmer than necessary goodbye. This was the first time Jonas had sought her out since that scene in his room and her stomach knotted. What did he want?

'You two seem to get on well,' Jonas said, holding open a door for her to enter.

'Adam is good company.' And attractive. And clearly interested. But Ravenna's pulse didn't quicken when he was around. Yet now, walking beside the man who despised her, she couldn't control her racing pulse.

'Do you have a lot in common?'

She swung around to face Jonas, livid at his feigned interest and at herself for being so weak. 'Why do you ask? You're not interested in my personal life. Only my ability to scrub floors or spread my legs.'

A flush coloured those high cheekbones. 'I deserve that.'

His admission did nothing to mollify her indignation or self-recrimination. She took a deep breath and looked away. 'What do you want, Jonas?'

She was so weary. Her chores had been almost beyond her lately as she fought an exhaustion she hadn't known for some time. At the back of her mind lingered the worry that perhaps her illness had returned. That worry gnawed at her, keeping her awake at night. That and thoughts of Jonas.

'In here.' He gestured to the open study door.

Squaring her shoulders, she entered, studiously averting her eyes from the dark carpet on the far side of the room where they'd come together in such urgent passion.

Cheeks flushed, she took a seat by the desk. If he was going to tell her he'd finally decided to call the police to deal with the theft she'd rather be sitting.

'I'm sorry.'

It was the last thing Ravenna expected. She jerked her gaze up to find Jonas standing over her, as tense as she'd ever seen him.

'I beg your pardon?'

'I said, I'm sorry.' He waved one arm in a gesture of frustration. 'I'm no good at this, but I'm trying to apologise for what I said. What I did.'

Ravenna blinked and stared. 'For what exactly?'

Jonas rubbed his jaw and she heard the faint scratch of bristles. Her skin heated as she remembered that roughness against her skin. Just looking at his unshaven jaw made her stomach tighten as erotic recollections filled her head. She shivered. Her thoughts were dangerously self-destructive.

His lips twisted ruefully and despite everything she couldn't help the little tug of attraction deep inside.

'Not for the sex. I can't regret that.' His smile disappeared. 'But for later. The way I acted, what I said about you.' He breathed so deep she watched, fascinated, as his chest expanded. 'I was crass and hurtful.'

Ravenna stared. 'You're saying you don't think I tried to buy my way out of trouble with my body?'

'I'm saying I don't know enough about you to judge.'

It wasn't what she wanted to hear but at least it was honest.

Yet did she want to wait while he took his time learning to judge her on her merits? Why should she?

Because she had no choice. She was trapped here.

More importantly, despite everything, she couldn't turn her back on Jonas.

That spark of fire between them had morphed into something that tied her to him, no matter how she tried to sever the connection. As if she still believed the half-formed hopes she'd harboured when she'd met him, passion for passion, as an equal rather than a bonded servant.

That scared her more than anything.

'I behaved badly, accusing you the way I did.' His voice was deep with regret. 'I should have listened. Especially after...' he shrugged and spread his hands in a gesture that seemed curiously helpless '...after your concern for me.'

He looked as if he were swallowing hot coals. As if he wasn't used to anyone's concern. Or being seen as vulnerable.

That realisation dried the caustic response forming on Ravenna's lips.

As her gaze meshed with his it wasn't the heat of anger or lust she saw there, or his familiar stonewalling expression. She read uncertainty in those grey depths, as if he'd lowered the shutters to let her glimpse the man behind the façade of authority. The man she'd discovered the day they'd shared passion so fierce it had burned away everything else and left her feeling raw and new.

'And so?' Ravenna forced herself not to trust the regret she thought she read in Jonas' features. Only days ago she'd been duped into believing he felt something for her.

'And so I regret what I said.'

Ravenna nodded. He watched her as if expecting a response but she said nothing. Words were easy. It was actions that counted.

'And I've decided to make some changes.'

Here it comes. Ravenna clasped damp palms together. *He's calling in the police.*

'I'm bringing in extra staff. Not just the builders but some local people to help with the cleaning and heavy work.'

Ravenna searched his face for some hint of a catch.

'But you said—'

'I know what I said. Looking after the Hall was to be your penance.' His lips compressed as his gaze swept her. 'I was unreasonable.'

Her jaw sagged as he met her eyes almost defiantly. She couldn't believe her ears.

'There's no need to stare as if I've got two heads.'

'Are you feeling all right?'

Jonas gave a bark of laughter. 'I should have known you wouldn't just say thanks. You wouldn't let me off easily.'

Let *him* off? He was the one in control. Ravenna stared, bemused, as laughter softened the grooves around Jonas' mouth and eased the severity of his austere features.

She swallowed, fighting fizzing awareness.

'And what about me? Are you pressing charges? Is that it?'

Jonas' expression sobered. 'No. Not for now. You'll stay and work as my housekeeper.'

Not for now. He still held that over her. What had she expected? That without evidence of her innocence and in the teeth of her admission of guilt he'd let her go? Impossible!

'But I'm hoping we can continue in a more…civilised way.'

Ravenna sat straighter. 'If by civilised you mean sharing a bed because I'm supposed to be grateful you've brought in staff—'

Jonas' raised hand stopped her. 'I've never had to buy my way into a woman's bed, Ravenna. I won't start now.'

Heat scored her cheeks. Once had obviously been enough for him. Once with the hired help to satisfy his curiosity.

'It's time to take some of the heat out of this situation.' He looked at her long and hard, as if attempting to read her mind. 'I'm trying to be reasonable, Ravenna. We can't continue as before.' He sighed. 'Contrary to what you might think I'm not prone to outbursts of temper.'

She did believe it. She'd learned all she could about her nemesis and there had been plenty. The consensus was that Jonas Deveson was one of Europe's most eligible bachelors, wealthy, charming and urbane. He was known for his incisive mind, impenetrable calm and careful planning. Employees and competitors respected him and his generosity was renowned. As was his drive to succeed. There was no mention anywhere of a temper or strong passions.

Which left her wondering why, with her, he'd been anything but calm and controlled.

A tremor whispered down her spine.

Perhaps it had something to do with the way her emotions undercut caution and good sense when he was around.

'So you'll treat me as your housekeeper and I'll treat you as my employer?'

After what had passed between them was it even possible? The strain of the last couple of days had almost broken her.

'That's the idea.' He nodded. 'To step back from the rest.' His wide gesture encompassed all that had gone before: the animosity, the flagrant desire and the illusion of closeness that had betrayed Ravenna into believing they shared something special.

'How can I refuse?' That was safest. No more dangerous, incendiary desire. No fireworks. She should be thanking her lucky stars, not feeling dissatisfied, as if a rug had been pulled out beneath her.

'Thank you, Ravenna.' Their eyes met and she felt a now-familiar jolt of heat. The awareness hadn't gone away.

Jonas turned away and she breathed deep, searching for equilibrium. He offered a truce and this time she was determined nothing would break it. If she had to stay here with him, it would be strictly on a boss-employee basis.

'In the circumstances I thought you might help me with this.' He turned, the large portfolio in his hands.

'What is it?'

'Come and look.' He put it on the desk.

Ravenna stared from the album to his broad back in charcoal cashmere. She didn't want to stand beside him. It was easier to maintain her poise if she kept her distance.

'Ravenna?'

Reluctantly she crossed to the desk, keeping as much distance as she could from Jonas. He turned the pages, revealing swatches of colour and design, all rich but rather ponderous and dark.

'I told my designer I wanted a traditional feel. But it's not working.'

He stopped at a page showing one of the drawing rooms. There were fabric swatches in deep, rich hues, heavily decorated, and photos of imposing antique furniture. It would be like living in a museum.

'You see what I mean?'

Ravenna straightened, realising she'd been leaning over the page, imagining the finished room and disapproving.

'Why show me? I'm just the housekeeper.'

'You know this house better than anyone, apart from me.' He picked up a sheet of paper and tossed it on top of the portfolio. Ravenna saw it was a list she'd made of repairs. 'You've got a good eye for detail and a feel for the place.'

She raised her eyebrows. 'Where are you heading, Jonas?'

'I thought you might have some thoughts on what would suit the old place.' His eyes met hers then shifted to the portfolio. Because he was up to something or ashamed of his earlier behaviour? Ravenna wished she could read him.

'I'm the housekeeper, remember? This is what you pay a designer for.'

'Most women would jump at the chance to plan a redecoration.' His tone was persuasive.

'I'm not most women.' Her hands crept to her hips. Despite his apology, his earlier accusation still rankled.

'No, you're not. Most women would have run screaming from Deveson Hall the moment they saw how much work it needed. But you didn't.' His deep voice was rich with what sounded like admiration. 'Others might have made a mere token effort at the job, but not you. You've been boarding up holes and drying out damp books on top of everything else. You make lists of repairs. You've even sourced local suppliers so work can begin quickly.'

Jonas paused. 'You've betrayed yourself, Ravenna.'

She started, horrified that somehow she'd given away her mother's secret.

'You've shown yourself to be a woman who cares and takes pride in what she does. I'd like to have you work with me. If we could set aside our differences I believe we'd deal well together.' He spread his hands in a gesture of openness. 'Of course, I'd take your assistance into account when it came to determining how long it takes to pay off your debt.'

Ravenna braced herself on the polished desk, her pulse hammering. She told herself it was relief that her mother's guilt was still secret. Or disappointment that he still held that debt over her head.

The alternative, that it was reaction to Jonas' praise, wasn't an option.

'When you put it like that, how can I refuse?' She tore her gaze away and made a show of concentrating on the samples. 'So long as you don't hold it against me if the result is a disaster. I have no decorating experience.' Furnishing her bedsit with second-hand pieces hardly counted.

'Don't worry, I'll still use the decorator. I just want another opinion on some things. Like this.' His finger jabbed a page showing the study.

Ravenna took in the handsome, heavy furnishings in the design, the deep green colour and the use of dark wood. She guessed nothing in the proposed design was less than a hundred years old. Even the light fittings were modelled on old lamps. Just looking at the page made her feel claustrophobic.

'What do you think?'

She shrugged. 'You said you wanted traditional.'

'But?'

'How honest do you want me to be?'

'I've never had a problem with honesty, Ravenna.'

She met his bright gaze and knew an almost overwhelming temptation to blurt the truth. To explain about the money and her mother's desperation. To resolve the lurking tension between them so she could be free of the burden of secrecy and Jonas' bad opinion. But love for her mamma stopped her. Ravenna couldn't leave her to his not-so-tender mercies.

'It's like something out of Dickens.' She waited, trying to read his expression. 'Or a movie set of what an old-fashioned gentleman's residence should be.'

'My feelings exactly.'

'Really?'

He nodded. 'I couldn't work in a room like that.'

'What *do* you like?' Her curiosity stirred.

Jonas waved his hand towards the long windows. 'Light. Space. A comfortable chair built to take a man's weight and a desk high enough for my knees.'

Ravenna surreptitiously scanned his big frame. She'd never thought of Jonas' height being an issue. He always looked supremely comfortable whatever his surrounds.

'So keep this desk. It's a bit battered but the wood is lovely. I'm sure an expert could restore it beautifully.'

Jonas' mouth turned up at one corner and Ravenna felt a little tug as if someone pulled a string through her insides. 'That's one decision I'd already made. The desk stays. But what about the rest?'

'What colours do you like?' She forced the words out, mesmerised by that half-smile. It evoked intimate memories she'd tried and failed to bury.

'Gold,' he murmured, his voice low as he leaned close,

looking straight into her eyes. 'Old gold, something like the colour of a good aged sherry.'

Ravenna felt his breath on her face like an elusive caress. Her skin drew taut and the tugging sensation in her abdomen became a heavy thrum. Her pulse sounded in her ears as she swayed.

Blinking, she stepped back, wary of the way his low, masculine purr resonated through her. Once bitten...

Deliberately she turned. It was ridiculous to imagine Jonas had been describing the unusual colour of her eyes.

'Tell your designer you want gold.' She surveyed the walls. 'Or maybe lighter. What about a soft straw? Something more neutral so the woodwork doesn't overpower the room?'

'That could work.' From the corner of her vision she saw him finally look away towards the walls. 'What else?'

'You said a comfortable chair. What did you have in mind? Do you mean for working at the desk or a sofa?'

'Both. I like the chesterfields.' He waved a hand at a couple of sofas that needed reconditioning. 'But there's a young German designer who does brilliant ergonomic chairs in minimalist design.' Jonas frowned. 'But would that clash?'

Ravenna read his abstracted look and realised Jonas really wanted her opinion. When he'd suggested getting her input she'd thought it some ploy. Instead he was genuine.

Something softened inside. She hoped it wasn't her defences.

He met her eyes, a hint of familiar impatience in his expression. 'Well? What do you think?'

Ravenna shook her head. 'That's for your designer to advise. How about I make a list? Can you pass me a pen and paper?'

CHAPTER TEN

RAVENNA PULLED HER jacket close and stepped out briskly. Even after a couple of months getting used to the bustle of building work, she preferred early morning solitude.

She surveyed the house, its stones mellow in the early sun, its new glazing glittering. Despite its size the Hall felt welcoming, maybe because she'd come to know it intimately. She'd delved its crannies, supervising cleaning and small repairs, and helped Jonas plot the refurbishment of what would be a marvellous home as well as historic treasure.

Turning, she crunched her way along the gravel path, wishing she could turn her mind as easily from thoughts of Jonas. His presence pervaded the place, even though he spent half the week in London. From London he rang regularly to check progress, his deep voice never failing to send a thrill of pleasure through her.

Life had fallen into an easy, if busy, routine since his apology. A routine Ravenna found a little too easy given Jonas still held her future in his hands.

Surely it wasn't right that she cared so much for a place she'd leave as soon as her debt was paid? Or enjoy Jonas' company? She laughed too often at his dry humour over the restoration's inevitable mishaps and delays.

He was patient, flexible and understanding. All the things she once thought him incapable of. Plus he appreciated her efforts, thanking her when she catered for emergency meetings with contractors and heritage officers, or when she helped him sift decorating suggestions.

She enjoyed the latter most of all. She told herself it was because she loved having input to the way the grand old house would look. It had nothing to do with the camaraderie that had developed between them as equals, rather than boss and servant.

Jonas had never come on to her again—he kept his distance. It was as if that day they'd spent exploring each other's bodies had been a dream.

Except her body remembered the pleasure he'd bestowed so lavishly. It quivered in anticipation when he approached, or when she inhaled his scent of citrus and warm male.

There were times when she'd swear she saw heat in his polished silver gaze. A heat that reflected all the things she told herself she shouldn't feel for Jonas. Since his apology the vicious, vengeful man she'd met in Paris had disappeared, replaced by one she liked far too much.

Ravenna quickened her pace, passing a drift of spring flowers, only to pause at the sounds from the newly restored stable block. Jonas had mentioned animals being delivered yesterday.

The stables had been empty while Silvia worked here and Ravenna had never seen thoroughbred horses up close. She followed the path to the nearest door.

'There now, Hector. That's better, isn't it?' Jonas' voice halted her in mid stride. 'That's my beauty.' The words were a slow thrum of approval. Obviously he was gentling some highly strung stallion, but, even knowing his words weren't for her, Ravenna felt the murmur like a caress on her skin.

Her heart dipped. Most of the time she coped with her situation, telling herself she was almost over the feelings Jonas evoked. But coming upon him suddenly, unprepared for the impact of those deep baritone cadences, her instant response told its own story.

How long before she could shake off this volatile attraction?

'Tim, you're in the way. There will be time for you in a moment.' Jonas laughed and she couldn't resist inching closer.

The sight that greeted her stopped her in her tracks.

There was Jonas in scuffed boots, worn jeans clinging to bunching muscles and a plain black T-shirt that stretched across a torso that was all hard-packed strength and perfect proportion. His dark hair was tousled and his skin glowed. He looked like a pin-up for the outdoor lifestyle.

But it wasn't just his breathtaking male appeal that sent the air scudding from her lungs. It was the joy in his expression. Unadulterated happiness that turned his strong features into something so powerfully appealing it wrapped tight fingers around her heart.

Ravenna had seen him smile, heard his wry humour, had even heard him laugh, but she'd never seen him look so happy.

And the cause of his happiness? A sway-backed draught horse that nudged him as he brushed it and a chocolate Labrador that lurched between man and horse, its tail waving.

'Watch out!' Ravenna darted forward as the horse shifted and the dog wandered into the path of its massive hoof.

Man, dog and horse all turned to stare. An instant later the hoof descended harmlessly as the dog hobbled towards her with a ruff of pleasure.

'He's only got three legs.' No wonder the dog had wobbled so badly. She dropped to her knees so it could sniff her hand then lavish a rough-tongued caress on her wrist.

'Timothy! Back here.' Jonas moved towards them. 'I'm sorry. He's a bit too enthusiastic.'

Ravenna laughed as the dog tried to lick her face. 'No, don't worry. That's fine. I like dogs.' She looked up into silver eyes and felt a jolt right to her core.

'So I see.'

Ravenna blinked, telling herself she couldn't feel Jonas' gaze. As for the way her lungs had constricted… It was as well she was booked for a medical check-up soon.

'Look out!' she warned.

But it was too late. Jonas staggered towards her after being nudged by the draught horse's massive head. He braced himself before her, legs planted wide as she looked up into his laughing face.

'Obviously Hector doesn't like his routine being interrupted.'

'Hector?'

A large square hand reached down to her. Automatically she took it, letting Jonas pull her up. For an exhilarating moment they stood toe to toe, then he let go and moved back.

'Meet Hector.' He raised a hand to the massive animal's neck and the horse whinnied as if in response.

At Ravenna's feet the lopsided Labrador looked up expectantly, tongue lolling.

'I suppose this is Timothy.' The dog barked at the sound of its name.

Bemused, she looked around the stables. The stalls were deserted but for this one.

'*These* are the animals you brought in? They're not yours?'

Jonas shook his head. 'I'm giving them temporary accommodation as a favour to a neighbour. Part of her stables burned down due to an electrical fault and she put out an SOS for Hector. Where Hector goes, so does Timothy.'

The dog hopped over to the big horse, which lowered its head and gusted its breath over the Labrador.

'That's…very nice of you.'

'But not what you expected?' He didn't miss her surprise.

She shrugged. How could she say caring for a lame dog and an old horse wasn't how she saw him spending his spare time? She hadn't known he *had* spare time.

'I thought you'd bring in thoroughbreds to ride.'

'Later. For now Hector needs a home.' He patted the horse. 'Didn't you, old fellow?'

'You know him?' There was familiarity in his tone.

Jonas nodded. 'Hector was saved from the knacker's yard when I was a kid. Vivien, my neighbour, finds homes for unwanted animals—donkeys, goats, ponies, even a three-legged dog and a blind draught horse.'

'He's blind?' Ravenna stepped closer and saw Hector's eyes were cloudy.

'Pretty much. But he's got Timothy, who leads him where he wants to go. Together they make a good team.' He ruffled the dog's ears then picked up the brush he'd been using.

'I spent a lot of time at Vivien's when I was young. She taught me to ride and help out. Hector was venerable then.' Absently Jonas rubbed the horse's neck and it struck Ravenna she'd never seen him so relaxed, except for the day they'd spent sprawled in his bed, boneless and spent from ecstasy.

Fire seared her cheeks and she bent to pat Timothy, who'd hobbled back to her. 'I'd imagined you learning to ride here.' She waved her hand around the enormous stables.

Jonas turned away to brush the big horse, but not before she saw the shutters come down, eclipsing the laughter in his eyes. 'My mother didn't ride and Piers had other things to do with his time.' Wide shoulders shrugged. 'He spent most of his time in the city and when he was here he had interests other than teaching me.'

The edge to Jonas' voice made her think instantly of comments he'd made about Piers chasing women. Not much of a father then.

'So you spent a lot of time at your neighbour's?'

'Enough to learn to ride and to care for animals.' His words were matter of fact but his tone confirmed the experience had been precious.

'Didn't you have animals here at the Hall?' She stepped closer, needing to know more.

* * *

Jonas flicked a warning look over his shoulder. He didn't welcome prurient curiosity. But the sight of her, bent to scratch Timothy behind the ears, even while she looked up at him with serious eyes, gave him pause.

'Pets weren't allowed. My mother wasn't an animal person and Piers…' Jonas shrugged. Piers had rarely been around long enough to express an opinion. As for teaching him to ride! His father had never taken time out from his own pursuits to be with him. Even on those occasions when his parents had temporarily made up, Jonas wasn't a priority.

Jonas watched Ravenna's expressive eyes flick from him to Hector. 'You like horses?'

'I don't know. I've never met one up close.'

Jonas remembered the first time he'd visited Vivien's stables, the excitement tinged with fear that had turned to delight. 'Come and meet Hector. He's very gentle.'

She hesitated for so long he thought she wouldn't come. Why it was important that she did, Jonas had no idea. But it felt good when she approached, as if she trusted his word.

'Here.' He took her hand, fishing in his pocket for one of the sugar lumps he'd brought. He dropped it onto her open palm and drew her in front of him.

Sensing a treat in store, Hector snuffled at her hand. Instantly Ravenna stepped back, her curves enticing even through her jacket.

'No, don't drop your hand.' He held hers up and flat. 'Hector won't bite.'

'He's so big.' She leaned back, her shoulders pressing into his chest, her riot of newly grown dark curls tickling his chin. She smelled of cinnamon and sugar, and beneath them was the scent of her pale skin, an unnamed but heady perfume that he greedily inhaled.

He'd missed her, missed the right to touch her. Every day was a battle not to reach for her, to palm her soft skin, taste her, draw her close and have his fill.

'Oh, you beautiful boy,' she crooned as Hector lipped up the treat then nodded as if in thanks. 'Did you see that? How he took it from my hand?'

'Mmm, hmm.' Jonas strove to suppress the arousal that fired as Ravenna whispered her delight to Hector. She wasn't even talking to Jonas yet the low thrum of her voice and the press of her body almost made him forget his promise to keep his hands off.

'Here.' He found the curry comb he'd been using and sidestepped, taking Ravenna along with him till she stood at the horse's shoulder. 'You can groom him.'

'Can I? How?'

The best way to demonstrate was to put the comb in her hand and cover it with his, moving them both in slow sweeps.

Hector shifted and Ravenna shrank back. Jonas smiled as he wrapped his other arm around her waist to hold her steady. Or perhaps it was a grimace, given the exquisite torture of holding her and not revealing his needy reaction.

'You're safe. Hector is a gentleman.' Their joined hands traced a wide arc across that broad equine shoulder and side.

'And you're here to protect me.'

Had he heard right? The indomitable Ravenna needing protection?

'Did you visit your neighbour and her animals often?'

'As much as I could. It was so *alive* there, always something happening.' He watched their hands move in tandem, telling himself he'd step away soon.

'I'd have thought the Hall would have been busy too. I seem to remember quite a few servants and tradespeople when I visited.'

Jonas dropped his hand, letting her continue alone. 'As son of the house I was kept separate from that.' And he'd hated it. 'My early memories of the Hall were of solitude. There never seemed enough people to fill it and a house like this needs people. When there were visitors it was for formal dinner parties to which small boys weren't invited.'

'You make it sound like you were on the outside, looking in.' Ravenna half turned then seemed to think better of it, leaning in to comb Hector with a long stroke that moved her backside temptingly against Jonas' groin.

He should move away, should drop the arm wrapped around her waist, before she sent him over the edge. But he couldn't shift his feet.

'Not all the time.' He didn't want her sympathy. 'The kitchen was always welcoming and then there was Vivien's and the animals.'

'It still sounds lonely.'

He watched the curry comb slow almost to a stop.

'I was no lonelier than lots of homes.' He had no intention of sharing exactly how bleak his childhood was. 'I remember you here, just behind this stable block, crying your eyes out because someone named Pamela had made your life hell at school. Because you were excluded.'

Ravenna's hand slid to her side. 'You remember *that?*' She'd never thought he'd recall in such detail.

'I remember feeling sympathy for someone else who felt like an outsider.'

Ravenna stiffened as the memory of ancient pain surfaced. He saw too much. Then it hit her he'd made it sound like something they had in common. Both outsiders.

She spun around. Jonas was so close her pulse thudded in response. She saw deep into his eyes, could even count his spiky dark eyelashes.

He was so near one tiny move would bring them together. A half-step, a tilt of her head, and they'd be kissing. The air between them crackled and heat saturated her skin. Her fingers tingled, anticipating the feel of his smooth-shaven jaw. Surely he'd moved closer?

Her breath hitched audibly and suddenly there was distance between them.

Ravenna blinked. Had she imagined that moment of intense expectation? The way their bodies swayed together?

Hurriedly she gathered her scrambled thoughts.

'But you fitted in. Your family has been here for centuries. You were born to all this. You *belonged.*' She waved her hand wide. 'I never did.'

Move back, she told herself. *It's too tempting, too dangerous. You're too close to Jonas.*

But her body wouldn't listen. She stood, looking expectantly into his dark face.

His mouth curved in a half-smile that was poignant rather than amused.

'You belonged, Ravenna. You had your mother, remember? You were close. Even now I can't help feeling that she's mixed up somehow in the reason you're here.'

Ravenna opened her mouth to protest but his raised palm stopped her. 'I'm not asking for your secrets, Ravenna,' he said, surprising her. 'I'm just saying you always had her on your side. She loves you.'

She nodded. That went without saying.

'Then you were lucky. Luckier than a lot of kids.'

Like Jonas.

'Who did you have, Jonas?' The housekeeper he'd spoken of so warmly now and then? His neighbour, Vivien? Everything he *hadn't* said about his parents confirmed what had been lacking in his family: warmth and love.

'I had myself.' Not by a flicker of an eyelid did his expression change. He looked strong, proud and sure of himself. All the things she'd seen in Paris when she'd thought him arrogant and self-opinionated.

But now Ravenna realised there was much more to him. The man who'd lost himself in her body. Who, in his grief, had needed her with a desperation that scorched through every barrier. Who now distanced himself again.

With a fervour that surprised her, Ravenna wished for a return of the intimacy they'd shared. She wanted—

This wasn't about what she wanted.

'Was that enough?' Suddenly it struck her that Jonas' sometimes superior air, his confidence, his determination to get things right, no—perfect, every time, might be traits he'd learned in his youth to overcome loneliness and doubt. Had they been defence mechanisms for a little boy desperately in need of love? Mechanisms that had become habit in the man?

His dark eyebrows rose. 'Every child wants to be at the heart of a big, loving family, don't they? But I was luckier than a lot. I had food and warmth. I had an excellent education.' His stare dared her to feel pity for him. 'And I had this—Deveson Hall. I knew one day it would be mine and then I'd make it right.'

'Right?'

'Absolutely.' His eyes shone. 'I had a lot of time to dream as a boy. I spent my days exploring the Hall, absorbing its history and traditions and planning how it would be when it was mine. The old place became my family in many ways. It was my mainstay.'

'So that's why you're here through the renovations.' Ravenna had wondered why he didn't stay in London and leave the detail to his project manager. She'd thought at first it was because he wanted to keep a close eye on her.

'I want the job done properly.'

There was that perfectionist streak again. Everything had to be done just right before Jonas would be satisfied.

'You wanted it furnished in a traditional style to match what you'd known when you were young?' Or more probably, from what he'd said, to bring it up to a standard he'd never known as a child when money had grown shorter each month.

Jonas shrugged. 'Maybe. Though my tastes have changed. Traditional with a modern twist perhaps.' He strode to the open stable door to gaze at the Hall, automatically stooping to pat an adoring Timothy, who shadowed him.

'When it's done I'll hold a ball. That's a Deveson tradition that got dropped over the years. This year it will be a turning point.' Jonas turned and she read anticipation in his face. 'I'll want you there, Ravenna.'

Her heart fluttered, till she reminded herself the housekeeper had a vital role in any big house function.

'Of course. I'll supervise the catering.'

He nodded. 'It will be a big job but we'll do it.'

Ravenna felt a tiny jolt of pleasure at his 'we'. They worked well together, perhaps because of the unspoken boundaries they'd been careful not to cross.

'But I don't want you behind the scenes.' His gaze collided with hers and her skin tingled at the approval she saw there. 'After all your hard work I want you at the party, not in the kitchen. You deserve to celebrate too.'

Ravenna blinked, a tiny trail of fire flaring in her blood. It was the closest he'd come to hinting he'd forgiven her for the money. Would the celebration signal the end of her servitude? The weight she'd borne so long lightened a little.

Working in service reinforced all the insecurities of her youth. Despite the ease of the past couple of months, it still stuck in her craw to be a servant, especially here.

'Ravenna?' Jonas watched her expectantly. 'You'll come?' So it wasn't an order. It was an invitation. Ravenna smiled.

'Of course. How could I miss celebrating you achieving your dream?'

He shook his head. 'Not quite. This place is my heritage, a part of me. But the refurbishment is just the first step.'

'Really? What else is there?' She reached up to stroke Hector's cheek as he snuffled at her pocket, searching for treats. She could get used to the warm, comfortable smell of horse and hay. In fact, she could get used to life at Deveson Hall with an ease that surprised her.

Jonas surveyed the mansion that had come to life under his supervision.

'I loved this place as a kid but even I could see it wasn't a home. It was cold and unloved, despite the best efforts of our housekeeper.' He paused so long Ravenna thought he wouldn't go on.

When he spoke again it was in a low, musing voice that made her wonder if he talked more to himself than her.

'That's what I want. A home. Something more than the apartments in London and New York. A place with heart.' He shoved his hands in his pockets and rocked back on his feet. 'A place for a family. A wife who'll love the place as I do. We'll fill the old place with children.' He bent to pat Timothy as the Labrador bumped his leg. 'And a muddle of dogs and other animals. I'll make it a real home.'

Ravenna clutched Hector's mane.

Home. A family.

It shouldn't surprise her. Why else renovate Deveson Hall? Jonas wouldn't want to live there alone.

Fill the old place with children.

Her stomach dipped in an abrupt roller-coaster curve that hollowed her insides, turning them queasy.

She'd listened to Jonas' plans for the Hall with an approving smile. Wistfully she'd almost seen herself as part of that, despite her resolve to keep her emotional distance. In a hidden chamber of her heart had lurked the hope that one day they could put the past behind them and start again—pursue that connection she still felt to him just as strongly as the day they'd shared their bodies.

Then he'd mentioned children.

Her hand crept to her cramping belly, over the womb she knew was barren.

Months ago, shocked at the news of her cancer diagnosis and the need for early action, she'd told herself infertility was a small price to pay for the treatment that would give her a chance to live.

She'd always wanted children but she was young, yet to find a man with whom she wanted to spend her life.

Ravenna had concentrated on being grateful she'd survived, refusing to regret what couldn't be cured—the chance to bear her own children.

But now the void within yawned wide and pain poured in.

She was crazy ever to have imagined she could build a relationship with Jonas. Everything stood against it. Their history. The theft. Her background and social status. She didn't fit in his world. She never would.

And she could never give any man children. She was strong, capable and worthy of a good man's love. But she lacked—

Hot tears prickled her eyes and she blinked. She hadn't cried through months of treatment. She wouldn't start now.

Quietly, leaving Jonas to his dreams, she turned and slipped out through the other door.

CHAPTER ELEVEN

JONAS MANOEUVRED THE Aston Martin through the city streets on autopilot. His attention was all for Ravenna, sitting pale and subdued beside him.

These last weeks she'd changed. They still worked well together but that spark of camaraderie, that sense of being *comfortable* together had gone.

Perhaps it was his fault for not addressing the question of how long he expected her to work for him. The money she'd taken was substantial, but the effort she'd put into Deveson Hall had been remarkable. Without her organisational skills, eye for detail and hard work there'd be no celebratory opening ball next week.

Who could blame her for wanting to end their arrangement?

Yet he'd avoided the issue. He couldn't imagine the place without her.

The realisation made him frown.

No one was indispensable in his life. No one except the wife he'd marry once the Hall was ready.

He'd spent the last couple of years considering potential brides, taking his time sorting through likely candidates before settling a few months ago on Helena Worthington. Beautiful, gracious and warm-hearted, she'd make an excellent spouse and mother. Born and bred on her family's vast country estate, she lived in London, working at an exclusive gallery. She had the skills to make him an excellent hostess.

One of the reasons for the ball was to see her in his home and check he'd made the right choice before finalising his plans. They'd been out a few times in the past and she was definitely interested, but he'd kept things light till he was sure.

Beside him Ravenna shifted. He really should talk to her about the future.

He could offer her top dollar to stay permanently as housekeeper. She'd run the Hall with the brisk efficiency and empathy for the place that he required.

But keeping an ex-lover on his staff? It went against every instinct. No matter that they'd proved they could work together and put those few hours of weakness behind them.

Almost behind them.

Jonas set his jaw and confronted the truth. Not a day passed when he didn't remember in glorious detail the incandescent pleasure of sex with Ravenna. He enjoyed being with her. Her quick wit, her indomitable attitude, her pleasure in so many things he enjoyed, like seeing the gardens come to life, celebrating the completion of each room, even smiling over the antics of Timothy and Hector.

Until a few weeks ago. Something had changed and he couldn't work out what. He only knew he didn't like it.

'Where exactly is it you're going?' Jonas asked as she pleated her skirt with restless fingers.

'Just a few streets away. You can drop me anywhere here. I would have been quite happy catching the train. You really don't need to go out of your way.'

Which was the most she'd said on the whole journey. If he didn't know better he'd think she was babbling.

Ravenna never babbled. She was articulate and composed. Except that day they'd been naked together and ecstasy had stolen her voice. Predictably, arousal stirred at the memory, and a deep-seated satisfaction.

Hell! He shouldn't feel anything like this for Ravenna. Not now, not when he was planning to marry. But the sexual attraction between them hadn't yet dimmed, no matter how hard he tried to ignore it.

Jonas forced himself to concentrate on the traffic rather than the past.

Yet something was wrong and he couldn't ignore it. Over the months at the Hall Ravenna's colour had improved—she wasn't pale and fragile as when they'd met in France. But now that healthy glow had faded.

'Where will I collect you?'

Her head swung round, her eyes large and startled. 'There's no need. I'll catch the train.'

'My business won't take long so I can pick you up whenever you like. Just give me the address.'

'Really, I—'

'Unless you want me to wait now?'

'Up here.' She pointed abruptly at a café. 'If you come by and I'm not here, then just go on without me and I'll find my own way back.'

Jonas suspected she had no intention of meeting him and fobbed him off with a place chosen at random. Once he'd have suspected she was plotting to run away and escape the consequences of her crime but now he knew better. Concern filled him.

'Very well.' He manoeuvred the car into a recently vacated spot and watched her fumble with the door. 'I'll meet you in an hour or so.'

Ravenna nodded and got out, walking away without looking back.

Jonas watched her go, telling himself it wasn't his business she kept secrets. She had a right to a personal life. But the tension in her rigid body was palpable.

He waited till she'd rounded the corner before he got out and followed.

* * *

Ravenna pushed open the clinic door and emerged into the open air. She breathed deep, filling her lungs with the city scents of wet pavement and exhaust fumes. It was better than the not-quite-neutral smell she associated with hospitals and doctors' waiting rooms that dredged up bleak memories.

She grabbed the railing at the top of the few steps to the street and gathered herself, feeling the adrenalin still coursing through her system after the nervous wait to hear the results of those recent tests.

Her hands clamped the metalwork as emotion hit.

'Ravenna?'

She lifted her head to find Jonas on the step below, his face level with hers. She blinked moist eyes and drew in a breath redolent with that tangy scent she always associated with him.

'What are you doing here?'

'Waiting for you.' His voice was harsh and his expression grim. 'Come on.' He took her elbow, his grip surprisingly gentle given his expression. 'Let's get away from this place.'

She followed his gaze to the sign beside the door, proclaiming exactly what branch of medicine the staff practised.

He led her down the street and into the sort of exclusive restaurant in which she hoped one day to work.

She hesitated on the threshold. 'There's no need for this. I'm ready to go now.'

'Well I'm not.' He swept her into the beautifully appointed dining room and secured a quiet table before Ravenna could do more than blink owlishly at the expensive furnishings.

'A drink?' he asked as she seated herself.

'Nothing, thanks.'

'Cognac for me,' Jonas said to the waiter before turning back to her, his eyes steely. 'Don't tell me you wouldn't like something after visiting that place.'

He was right. She *was* on edge and had been all day with that appointment looming. At least it was over. She sank back in her seat with a sigh. 'A sauvignon blanc if you have it, please.' Ravenna smiled at the waiter who nodded and passed over two leather-bound menus before leaving them.

'Are you all right?' Jonas leaned towards her across the fine linen tablecloth, his gaze intent.

'Fine, thanks. Just a little tired.' Yet tension eddied in her stomach. He'd seen where she went, which meant she couldn't fob him off with vague answers. She'd have to explain, which meant revealing what she'd kept hidden all these months.

It would be a relief, she decided. It had been a strain, lying all this time.

She opened her mouth to speak but halted when he leaned across and took her hand in his. It was the first time he'd touched her since—

No. She wouldn't go there.

'Why didn't you tell me you were ill?' His voice was hoarse and Ravenna read intense emotion in his silvery gaze.

'I'm not.' She shook her head, her heart lightening. When she'd left the clinic she'd still been numb, just coming to grips with the news, but now she felt happiness surge. 'I'm healthy.' Her mouth widened in a smile that felt wonderful. She'd been so worried her remission might be short-lived, perhaps because she'd felt so depressed these last weeks.

'Thank God!' His fingers squeezed hers. 'When I saw you go in there…' He shook his head.

'You followed me?'

'You were anxious. I knew something was wrong.'

Ravenna stared. Jonas Deveson had followed her because he *cared* about her? Her heart leapt and she had a struggle to keep calm.

It made no difference that he'd been concerned. There wasn't anything between them. There could never be.

'So it was a false alarm? You thought you had cancer?' He sat back in his seat, still holding her hand. She should pull away, but she liked the sensation and it was probably the last time he'd touch her—he was so adept at keeping his distance now.

Ravenna drew a slow breath. 'No, not a false alarm. I had cancer. I don't now.'

'Ravenna?' Shock lined his face.

'I'm in remission. I have been for a while. This was just another check-up to make sure nothing had changed. I've had several, but this time I thought the results might be—' She shrugged, not wanting to admit she'd been so down lately that she'd half convinced herself her illness had returned.

The waiter arrived with their drinks and, at a signal from Jonas, left without taking their order for food. Jonas reached out and grabbed the glass of cognac, his eyes not leaving hers. He tossed the liquid back in one quick movement then put the empty glass down.

Guilt stirred. Not because she hadn't told him about her illness. That was private. But because he'd obviously been worried.

'I'm sorry, Jonas.'

'Don't be.' His voice was gruff. 'That's excellent news. I'm just…surprised to know you've been ill.' He paused, his fingers threading hers. 'How long has it been?'

Ravenna hesitated. But she was sick of lying. Surely now, when he heard her out, Jonas would give up his idea of revenge against her mother. He'd already had his pound of flesh after all.

She hoped she was right.

'Ravenna?'

'Last year I was diagnosed with leukaemia.' She saw his eyes widen. His firm grip tightened. 'I was advised to have treatment straight away. The cancer was aggressive but potentially curable. And they were right. I'm well now.' Joy made her smile again.

'How long before I met you?'

Ravenna's gaze dropped to her untouched glass of wine then up to the flat line of Jonas' mouth.

'When we met in Paris I'd just come from a Swiss sana-
torium. I'd been there, recuperating.'

'I see.' His expression didn't change but his gaze turned
laser sharp. 'Why didn't you tell me when we met?'

Ravenna tugged her hand but his grip didn't ease. It kept
her anchored within his warm grasp. Could he feel her pulse
trip faster?

'It wasn't relevant. It's not the sort of thing to share with
strangers.'

'I was hardly that, Ravenna.' His tone made her nape
prickle. 'Could it be because you didn't want to admit you
needed my money to fund the health resort?'

She sighed. 'You're sharp, aren't you?' Not that it mattered now. He'd have to know it all. She'd just have to do
her best to protect her mother.

'Sharp enough to realise if you were recuperating in Switzerland you weren't in my father's Paris apartment, forging
his signature.'

Jonas felt his gut plunge hard and fast, like a stone in deep
water.

He remembered Ravenna in Paris—proud and defiant,
throwing her guilt in his teeth. To deflect him? Of course.
And he'd been so wrapped up in his hatred of Piers and Silvia that he hadn't stopped to question.

He'd seen how pale Ravenna was, how delicate her wrist
as he shackled it and pulled her to him. He recalled how
fragile her body had seemed compared with her in-your-
face attitude.

Because she'd been ill.

Too ill to fight back?

Guilt was a raw slash of pain to his belly. He'd bullied her
when she was vulnerable. What did that make him?

Jonas dragged his free hand through his hair. No wonder her clothes hadn't fitted. She must have lost weight in
therapy. He'd been sure she'd dressed to project waif-like

vulnerability for that antiques dealer. He'd been so ready to make snap judgements, hadn't he?

Bile seared his throat as he reviewed that day. He'd stormed in, all violent temper and attitude, and nearly ripped her head off when she'd dared stand up to him.

'Your hair,' he croaked, his windpipe tight. 'That's why your hair was so short.'

Ravenna lifted a hand to the sable curls clustering like a dark halo around her face. 'I'm growing it now.'

'I remember it before. It used to be long.' For months after meeting the teenage Ravenna Jonas had wondered why so many women cut their hair short. There'd been something deliciously appealing about long female tresses.

'Another drink, sir? And something to eat?' He hadn't noticed the waiter approach.

'Another cognac.' He didn't drink much but today he needed it. Confronting the truth had never been so unpalatable. 'Ravenna? Something to eat?'

She looked up and after a moment's hesitation engaged the waiter in a discussion of the day's specials. When she'd ordered he said he'd have the same and finally they were alone.

'It wasn't you who stole my money, was it?' Jonas spoke through gritted teeth. How could he have fallen for her story? Hadn't the evidence pointed to Silvia from the first?

After a lifetime keeping a lid on his feelings, they'd finally erupted with the news of the embezzlement, undercutting his usual clear thinking. Why hadn't he questioned her more closely when she admitted the theft?

Because his blistering anger had needed a target and she was handy. Because she was the daughter of the woman he'd spent years blaming for his father's defection, despite knowing Piers had always sought his own pleasure rather than embracing his responsibilities.

It had been easier taking out his long-simmering fury on Ravenna than dealing with the fact that the person who'd been at the root of so much pain—Piers Deveson—was finally beyond either reproach or reconciliation.

'It was Silvia, wasn't it?'

'Please don't hurt her, Jonas.' Ravenna's hand twisted in his, her fingers grasping with reassuring strength. The shock of seeing her entering that clinic still reverberated through him.

'Jonas?' Solemn eyes of old gold fixed on him. 'I know it was wrong. She had no right to the money. Nor had I.'

'Did you know where it came from?'

'Not till you confronted me in Paris.' Her quick gesture discarded that as a minor issue. But it wasn't. Ravenna had been innocent from the first. She'd claimed responsibility only to protect her mother and then she'd worked like a slave to pay off a debt for which she had no responsibility.

Jonas was torn between admiration for her and deep-seated nausea at what he'd done. He'd used and abused her. He'd taken out his ire on an innocent woman.

'Mamma was desperate. She'd been selling off assets for ages, just to live the way Piers expected. She had no money of her own.' Ravenna shook her head. 'Piers had expensive tastes and in the past he'd bought Mamma extravagant gifts, but he'd never spent money on me. I should have known his generosity to me was out of character.'

'You were sick.' Even now the thought of it smote him a hammer blow to the chest.

'But I should have realised.' Her mouth firmed. 'Maybe I didn't want to think too much about it. Maybe—' His finger to her warm lips stopped her words.

'Stop beating yourself up.' He let his hand drop to the table, noting how she slid her hands into her lap, away from him. Who could blame her after what he'd done? 'You weren't to blame.'

Ravenna leaned forward, the subtle, sweet perfume of her skin enticing. 'You have to understand my mother was desperate. She shouldn't have stolen from you, but she was convinced I needed time and care to recuperate fully. She was terrified I'd have a relapse.'

Jonas nodded, his stomach churning in sympathy with Silvia Ruggiero for the first time. He understood her fear too well. He still felt sick from the shock of believing Ravenna ill.

'Please, Jonas. Please be lenient with her.'

'She should have stayed. Not left you to carry her guilt.' That stuck in his craw.

Ravenna's slim fingers closed over his hand, startling him before sliding away. 'She didn't. She has no idea you'd discovered the loss. I suppose she hoped the money wouldn't be missed or you'd write it off as money to your father.'

'So naïve.' When he started out Jonas had risked every penny to invest then invest again. He never took money for granted, given how he'd worked to acquire it.

'Jonas, what are you going to do to her?' The fear in Ravenna's voice brought him up sharply.

'Nothing.' He watched her exhale on a sigh that left her looking limp. 'Here, drink this.' He lifted her wine glass to her lips, waiting till she held it herself and took a sip.

'Nothing? Really?' She looked dazed. He really *had* been an ogre. And now he felt about two feet tall. 'You won't prosecute?'

'There'll be no gaol, no prosecution. I've had enough of revenge.' Jonas grimaced on the word, its taste souring his tongue. 'How could I prosecute a mother for trying to save her daughter?'

'But I would have been all right without the funds.' It was as if still she didn't believe him—had to test him.

Jonas raised his eyebrows. 'Piers would have looked after you?'

'No. He was unwell by that stage, but no one knew how unwell.' Ravenna's eyes dipped to the pristine cloth. 'I'd have come back to London to work.' She lifted her head. 'I'm a chef. I had a promising position before...' She waved her hand vaguely and Jonas' anger fired. She'd lost her job when she got sick?

'So you were going to return straight to work after cancer treatment, doing long hours in a commercial kitchen?' He knew how gruelling that would be. He'd worked as a waiter in his university years. He'd vowed then to make his living the comfortable way—at a desk rather than on his feet doing split shifts till all hours.

The full brunt of what Ravenna had borne hit him. The illness. The slow convalescence. Dealing with her mother's financial crisis on top of what must be worry about her own finances and career. Then facing down an irate idiot hell-bent on vengeance. How had she coped?

He remembered that first day at the Hall, finding her asleep in the middle of the day and assuming she was lazy. His gut twisted as he realised she must have been exhausted.

'I'm sorry, Ravenna.' The words were too little, too late. 'What I've done to you, what you've been through…I had no right to threaten and take out my anger on you. I should never have forced your hand the way I did.'

'You didn't know.' She smiled wearily. How much she'd borne. The knowledge shafted home his guilt.

'I should have made it my business to know.' Instead of jumping in boots and all.

How could she take it so calmly? He winced, remembering his harsh words and actions. 'I said things I had no right to.' Her pain when he'd accused her of being a gold-digging opportunist like her mother! 'I'm sorry, Ravenna—'

'It's all right.' She looked over his shoulder. 'Here's our lunch.'

The waiter didn't linger but served them swiftly, providing another large cognac for Jonas. He reached for it, wanting that quick burn of fine brandy in his throat, then stopped. His father had always avoided the consequences of his actions and responsibilities. His mother had escaped reality in her own world of gin-fuelled disappointment.

Jonas put the glass aside.

'It's *not* all right, Ravenna.' It was all wrong, in so many ways.

'It is if you're not going to make Silvia pay.' She paused as if waiting for him to confirm it.

'Forget the money. There *is* no debt.' He breathed hard, still grappling with the knot of self-disgust in his belly. 'It was put to good use.'

Her eyes flashed pure gold and Jonas' breathing hitched. 'Thank you, Jonas.'

'Stop being so gracious!'

Her eyebrows arched. 'You'd prefer if I made a scene?'

'You think I'm being melodramatic?' Was any woman so infuriating?

Ravenna smiled and something fizzed in his veins. 'We were both at fault. We both jumped to conclusions and said things we regret. Can't we wipe the slate clean?' Her stomach growled. 'Especially as I'm starving. I was too anxious to eat this morning.'

'Then eat.' He gestured to her plate.

'And we're all sorted?' Her gaze searched his face.

'Absolutely.' What else could he say? She didn't want his apologies. He felt…frustrated.

'Thank you, Jonas. That's very generous. My mother will appreciate it as much as I do when she hears.'

He didn't care what Silva thought. It was Ravenna who concerned him.

'You'll want to leave Deveson Hall.' The thought struck abruptly as she lifted her fork to her mouth.

She took her time chewing. 'You want me to leave straight away?'

'No!' The word shot out with more force than necessary. He didn't want her gone. Not yet. 'I'd like it if you stayed on. Not to work,' he assured her quickly. 'But for the ball. You've worked too hard to get the place ready. It would be a shame to miss it. If you want to stay on.'

Ravenna kept her eyes on her plate. What was she thinking? Tension crawled down Jonas' spine, one vertebra at a time.

He was working on blind instinct. He had no plan in the aftermath of the truths that had rocked his complacent world. He only knew he'd feel bereft if she left now. He needed time to adjust. Time to replace her, his sensible self reasoned.

'Thank you.' Still she didn't look up. It was as if, having his promise that the theft had been written off, she didn't want to connect with him. 'I've never been to a ball and I'd love to see the Hall with the renovations complete. I'll stay till then.'

CHAPTER TWELVE

SHE SHOULD NEVER have agreed to stay. She should have left the same day. But the shock of her sudden freedom hadn't been as welcome as she'd expected.

Ravenna strode up the staircase as if expending energy could erase the dreadful weakness she harboured.

Despite Jonas' assurances that she didn't have to, she'd put long hours into getting the Hall ready. But they'd done nothing to extinguish what she felt for him. If anything her feelings were stronger since his apology and the sight of his horror when he realised she'd been innocent.

Jonas was essentially a decent man despite his plot to make her pay for the stolen funds. And who could blame him for that? His prejudice against Piers and Silvia was understandable, and to have Mamma then steal from him... Ravenna guessed it had been the final straw.

She walked along the corridor, checking all was in order. It was easier to focus on the busy work of housekeeping than think of the future. The ball was tomorrow and then she'd leave. She had no reason to stay.

Except she didn't want to leave Jonas.

Ravenna blinked at an arrangement of roses gracing a hall table. Reaching out to a velvety red petal, she was reminded of Jonas' touch, exquisitely tender as he brushed his fingers over her naked body, his gaze luminous as he'd watched her shiver with delight under his ministrations.

Sharply she sucked in her breath. This couldn't go on.

There was no future for them. She'd gone from being the enemy to a reminder of an episode he'd rather forget. She saw the shadow of guilt in his face whenever he looked at her.

Ravenna pushed open the door to her bedroom then halted as she saw the flat box on the counterpane. Only one person could have left it there.

Her heart seized then leapt to a gallop, gaze riveted on the distinctive embossed name on the box. Every woman in the western world knew that name. It belonged to one of the grandest Parisian couture houses, one whose young chief designer had taken the world of fashion by storm.

Ravenna's hands trembled as she moved closer, lifting the lid to pull back layer after layer of finest tissue.

Her throat closed. The dress was a delicate filigree of bronze shot with blue and amethyst as the light caught it. Ravenna had never seen anything so ravishingly beautiful in her life. She lifted it out—full length, with a wide skirt and tiny, jewelled shoulder straps, it was a modern Cinderella fantasy. Wearing this would make any woman feel special.

Twirling, she hugged it close and surveyed herself in the long glass. The woman staring back didn't look like Ravenna Ruggiero. She was a princess. The belle of the ball.

Except she *was* Ravenna Ruggiero. She'd never be the belle of any ball, especially Jonas Deveson's. Pain tugged her insides and her fingers crushed the sumptuous fabric.

The dress was a generous, extravagant gesture, borne of guilt and shame. Jonas wanted to put the past behind him and tried to make it up to her like this. He thought an expensive dress for his expensive party would make everything okay.

The gift was the embodiment of his guilt. He'd been too gracious to insist she leave immediately. But every time he looked at her in this gown he'd be reminded how he'd treated her.

And she'd remember he thought to buy her forgiveness.

She stiffened, her hands dropping.

That was what rich men did, didn't they? Bought what they wanted? It was what Piers had done with Mamma. Her mother had fallen for Piers hook, line and sinker and in his own way he'd fallen for her. But he'd begun by lavishing outrageously expensive gifts on her, blinding her with his generosity, because that was how the system worked.

Rich men married rich women. They only offered poor women expensive treats in return for—

No! That was not what Jonas was doing. He didn't want her in his bed.

But he did want her silence, her forgiveness, a sense of closure over what had happened between them.

The dress dropped from Ravenna's numb fingers and she turned from the mirror. She wasn't for sale. Just touching the dress brought his earlier accusations about her selling herself rushing back.

She didn't need Jonas' gift. Gorgeous as it was, she'd feel worse for accepting it, as if she'd let herself down. Besides, did she want this stunning gown hanging in her meagre wardrobe? It would be a constant reminder of a time, and feelings, she needed to forget.

Swiftly she scooped up the froth of fabric and tucked it back into its box.

'It's delightful, Jonas. You've done a marvellous job restoring Deveson Hall.' Helena smiled up at him, her china-blue eyes bright with approval and her perfectly sculpted lips curving in an enchanting smile.

He held her close but not too close as they danced. The ballroom glittered as the antique mirrors down one wall reflected the brilliant chandeliers, opulent gowns and lavish jewellery.

Over Helena's shoulder he saw Vivien dancing with a cabinet minister, while the local vet stood in earnest conversation with a sheikh in pristine white robes and a minor royal, no doubt discussing horses, given all three were passionate about them.

Everyone was enjoying themselves. He alone was dogged by a sense of anti-climax.

'Thank you, Helena. I'm glad you approve.' He smiled and pulled her a little closer.

This was the woman he planned to marry. Why couldn't he feel more enthusiasm? The Hall was just as he'd hoped, better, even. Nothing stood in the way of him reaching out and making his dream a reality.

Helena's eyes were as bright as the platinum-set sapphires at her throat. She was interested, expectant. He sensed it with the instinct borne of experience.

'What are your plans, Jonas, now you've completed work on the Hall?' Her voice was warm and appealing. She was intelligent, generous, good company.

And holding her in his arms he might have been waltzing with an aged great-aunt. Where was the spark of attraction he'd once felt?

'Plans?'

She tilted her head to regard him better and he inhaled the subtle designer perfume she favoured. It was like her—elegant, appealing—just right.

Except she wasn't. Not tonight. Something had changed.

'Now you've finished will you move in full time? Commute from here to the city? Perhaps allow the public in for viewings?' Her smile made light of the question, but he read her anticipation.

It was a perfect opportunity to talk of the future, *their* future. Except looking down at her he felt none of the satisfaction he'd felt before.

'I'm not sure yet.' Where those words came from he had no idea. 'But, yes, I'm considering opening the gardens once they're established. I've had heritage and horticultural groups already badgering me about open days.

Apparently my designer has done something quite special with the grounds.'

'They look marvellous already.' Helena took his lead, chatting about landscaping. Only the puzzled expression in her eyes hinted she'd expected something else. Jonas was grateful she was intelligent enough not to press.

For suddenly, on the brink of achieving his long-held goals, he found himself hesitating.

The music ended and they pulled apart. 'Let me get you a drink.' He took her arm and led her through the throng to the end of the room where drinks were being served.

At the vast double doors more people were clustered, mainly men, their dark formal clothes contrasting with the slim form of a woman in a dress of soft, buttery gold.

Jonas stiffened, every sense alert as she nodded and half turned. No wonder half the men in the place where there. Ravenna's smile was enough to stop any man in his tracks.

Jonas' chest tightened, squeezing his heart into a racing beat. The arousal he hadn't felt when embracing Helena surged hard and fast in his groin, betraying the need he hadn't been able to banish.

Ravenna looked good enough to eat. Heat swamped him and suddenly his bespoke tailoring seemed too tight. He wanted to rip his collar undone and shrug out of his jacket.

Then what? Stalk across and haul her to him so her audience knew she wasn't available?

To hell with the crowd, he wanted to hold her for the sheer satisfaction of having her where he wanted her.

The realisation hit in a blinding flash.

She turned again and her skirt belled out. Unlike most of the gowns hers ended at the knees, revealing smooth, shapely calves. She wore no jewellery except glittering earrings, but she didn't need any. She looked graceful and gorgeous with her cap of dark curls and pale gold skin.

Jonas frowned. That dress! What had happened to the one he'd bought? He surged forward.

'Jonas? Is everything all right?'

Helena's voice recalled him to sense. He slammed to a halt and turned, fixing on a stiff smile.

'Of course. I just wanted a word with my housekeeper but it can wait.' Though the effort of holding back almost killed him.

'Is that her? In the brocade? That material is just gorgeous. I've never seen anything like it.'

Unaware of their gaze Ravenna left the group and crossed the room only a few feet away. She was deep in conversation with one of Jonas' business associates, who looked far too suave and smug as he separated her from the crowd.

As they passed the light caught the material of her dress. Jonas blinked, not believing what he saw.

'I believe it's quite unique,' he muttered.

Damn! It *was* unique. It had been woven especially to a design by his artist great-grandmother. Until a couple of weeks ago it had hung in one of the massive state rooms.

Ravenna had rejected his gift—the best Paris fashion had to offer—and instead swanned around his home wearing discarded curtains!

His hands clenched in fists that shook with outrage. So much for his conciliatory gift! Did she deliberately try to provoke? And the way she flaunted herself, monopolising the unattached men!

'I should go and congratulate her,' Helena said. 'She's done a fantastic job here.'

'Later, Helena.' With a mighty effort Jonas unclenched his teeth. 'Let's get you that drink first.'

Ravenna paused in an alcove off the ballroom, catching her breath. It had been months since she'd mixed with more than a handful of people at a time. The London restaurant kitchen with its frantic pace seemed light years ago.

She'd enjoyed herself tonight. When she'd admitted she was the housekeeper many had congratulated her on her work and plied her with questions about the restoration. One or two men had even been a little too attentive, which, while awkward, had done wonders for her bruised ego.

There'd been raised eyebrows among the society women though, and pointed looks at her home-made dress and extra height. Those stares reminded her of childhood peers who'd claimed she'd overstepped the line, presuming to socialise with them.

But Ravenna was no insecure child now. She'd responded with cool courtesy and moved on, refusing to let prejudice spoil the only ball she'd ever attend. Yet the experience reinforced everything she'd known. Jonas moved in a different world. She was an outsider here and always would be.

Her gaze zeroed in on the couple at the top of the ballroom. He was tall and commanding while she, in figure-hugging midnight satin, was the epitome of cool, English beauty.

Jonas Deveson and Helena Worthington, looking the perfect couple. Her hand was on his sleeve as she leaned in, wearing a private smile.

A hot knife of jealousy sliced Ravenna's breast. Was that the woman Jonas would marry? The press thought so and guests had speculated about an engagement announcement.

Ravenna couldn't even dislike the woman. She was pleasant and charming, with a down-to-earth friendliness. Ravenna could imagine her here with Jonas and their brood of children. Helena would probably even take to Hector and Timothy.

Ravenna lifted her glass of vintage champagne, trying to wash away the sour tang on her tongue.

What had she expected? That after all that had gone wrong between them, Jonas would feel the same unsettling yearning Ravenna did? That he'd want her over the woman who was patently perfect for him?

She took another sip of the effervescent wine, letting it fizz on her tongue then slide down her aching throat.

Across the room Jonas turned and unexpectedly their

eyes locked. Ravenna's breath stopped as lightning arced through her veins. Her toes curled as if she'd touched a live wire. Her whole body hummed with awareness.

His dark eyebrows came down in a straight line of disapproval.

He couldn't know how she felt. He couldn't! So why was he annoyed? The answer was easy. The sight of her discomfited him. The sooner she left, the better.

Her breath caught on something suspiciously like a sob. She turned abruptly to find herself against a solid chest.

'Ravenna?' It was Adam Renshaw, the horticulturalist. His friendly smile was balm to her tattered soul. 'I've been looking for you. Would you like to dance?'

'Thank you, Adam.' Ravenna was fed up with herself—pining for what she could never have. She had to move on with life. Defiantly she drained her glass and put it down with a sharp click, ignoring the slightly foggy feeling of a little too much champagne. 'I'd love to dance.'

Ravenna switched off the last of the lights and stood in the vast, empty ballroom, revelling in the silence. The ball had been a huge success and she'd enjoyed it, she assured herself, ignoring the pain clutching her chest.

She'd danced for hours and instead of being relegated to the kitchens she'd indulged in champagne and caviar, in a midnight supper on the terrace with Adam and then more dancing. She smoothed her hands down the heavy silk of her skirt, trying to focus on the evening's pleasures rather than the dragging feeling of disappointment that weighted her.

'You've been avoiding me.'

Hand to her throat, she spun towards the door.

A shadow detached from the inky gloom of the wall and blocked her path. Ravenna's heart lurched then thumped against her ribs in a too-familiar needy rhythm.

'You startled me.'

'Did you really expect to keep your distance all night?'

She couldn't read Jonas' expression in the dark but his voice had an edge that cut.

'Why not?' Pride lifted her chin. 'You were busy with your guests. And I didn't need looking after.'

'So I noticed.' He stepped closer, his form growing in bulk as he approached. Even in her heels she felt dwarfed by him, weakened, as if he sucked the energy from the air between them. 'You let Renshaw monopolise you.'

Ravenna stood straighter. 'Adam and I have a lot in common.'

'He'll be moving on to the next job, Ravenna.' Was that a warning in his stern tone? 'He won't stick around.'

'Nor will I.' She'd leave as soon as it was daylight. Seeing Jonas and Helena together had been the impetus she'd needed.

He raised an arm as if to touch her then let it drop. 'You're going together?'

Ravenna frowned, hearing an unfamiliar note in his voice. 'I thought we'd agreed that what I do from here on is my own business, not yours.'

Jonas' breath hissed between his teeth. 'I see.' There was a wealth of disapproval in those two syllables. 'So that's why you didn't wear the dress I gave you.'

'Sorry?'

'If you and Renshaw are an item he'd wonder why you wore clothes bought by another man.'

Jonas' words confirmed her decision not to accept his gift. There was something far too intimate about accepting such a present.

'Adam had nothing to do with my decision. He and I aren't "an item" as you put it.' Pride wouldn't let her hide behind such a deception.

Jonas stalked closer, a hint of his male scent making her nostrils flare.

'You could have fooled me, the way he kept touching you.'

'We were dancing! That's what people do when they

dance.' He was a fine one to talk. She'd seen the way he held Helena. 'I'm going to bed now.'

'Alone?' He moved in front of her as she tried to sidestep and her heart slammed against her ribs. Ravenna sensed tension in him, an aggression that made her neck prickle.

'My movements have nothing to do with you.' Why did that hurt so much, even now? She had to get over this... obsession.

Still he stood unmoving, his bulk blocking her exit.

Ravenna tried to tell herself it was anger stirring butterflies the size of kites in her stomach. 'Instead of giving me the third degree why don't you go to bed? Helena will wonder what's keeping you.' The words shot out on a burst of bravado that left her feeling hollow.

'Helena's gone.'

'Gone? But she was with you, farewelling the guests.' Ravenna had tried not to notice how the blonde beauty had lingered. She'd headed to the kitchens to supervise the packing up so she didn't have to watch the pair.

'Nevertheless, she's gone.' His tone had a ring of finality.

'I should go too.' The air was fraught with tension that sent quivers through her body. Jonas was so close she saw his eyes gleam. If she leaned in they'd touch. She felt his proximity from her tingling lips to her budding nipples and lower, where desire spiralled deep.

His arm snapped out and long fingers circled her bare arm in a bracelet of fire.

'Let me go.' She tried to keep her voice even but it came out in a rush of breathless energy.

'Not till you tell me what's going on. Why aren't you wearing my dress?'

Ravenna tried and failed to tug her arm free. Desperation rose. She needed to get away.

'Because it would mark me as yours, bought as easily as any other commodity.' She shook her head, trying to find her voice in a throat choking closed on a rush of emotion.

'I know you didn't do it because you *want* me. Only because you want to be *rid* of me. But—' she drew a ragged breath and met his eyes '—I am not for sale. You don't need to *buy* me with anything. I told you we were quits. I won't wear your guilt.'

His hand slid up her arm to close on her shoulder. Hard fingers spanned her bare flesh, warming it against the chill inside her.

'You're wrong.' His voice was a low throb, brushing like velvet across her skin and making her shiver. Ravenna squeezed shut her eyes. He only had to speak and she weakened! And his touch...this was impossible.

'Let me go, Jonas.'

For answer he lifted his other hand and cupped her face, his hand engulfing her jaw, imprisoning her so she had no option but to lift her head towards his.

'You're wrong,' he said again and this time she heard a tremor in that deep, rich voice. It mirrored the shiver in his long fingers. 'I do want you, Ravenna. I've never stopped wanting you. Seeing you tonight only confirmed it.'

Stunned, Ravenna stared up at him.

Jonas stared back, committing every detail of her face to memory, his mind supplying the detail the darkness hid. He knew her features as well as his own.

His hand at her shoulder slid down, shaping the supple curve of her back and dragging her in against him.

'That's impossible.'

His bark of laughter was short and humourless. Jonas pulled her closer, higher, cupping her buttocks in an act of flagrant carnality that set his mind spinning. He'd wanted this so long.

'Impossible? Surely this—' he thrust his hips forward, melding them in a move that made his head spin '—proves it.'

Her hands clamped his shoulders. To push him away or

tug him close? He tightened his grip. No way was she waltzing off to her gardener tonight. Not now. Not when her yielding body told him she wanted him too. A sigh escaped her parted lips and it was music in his ears.

Fire coursed through his veins. He burned up with need. Touching her, imprinting her against him stoked the flames.

'Ravenna.' He dipped his head and kissed her neck, triumph filling him as she arched, giving him access to her throat. She tasted sweet as honey, soft and alluring. Impossibly tempting. 'You want me too. I feel it.'

Her hands clutched him. One thigh lifted to slide restlessly along his, inflaming his libido. He shook with the force of standing firm, doing no more than taste.

'No. This isn't right.' But her voice lacked force. It ended on a sigh when he scraped his teeth along the base of her neck and she shivered voluptuously. 'What about Helena?'

'I sent her away.' How could he even think of marrying her when he was consumed by thoughts of Ravenna?

'Away?' Ravenna stirred in his hold and Jonas squeezed his eyes shut, trying to withstand the excruciating delight of her body moving against his.

'It's you I want, Ravenna. All night I've watched you, wishing I was with you. Wishing we were alone so I could do this.' He bent his head and traced the neckline of her dress down to the delicious swell of her breast, fuller now that she wasn't so waiflike. Her gasp of pleasure as he suckled her through the fabric set his blood roaring. He remembered the taste of her naked breast and needed it now.

In one urgent move Jonas backed her against the wall.

'You want me too. Don't you?' Her body responded to his, arching into his touch, but he needed to hear it. 'Ravenna.' His voice shook with the force of holding back. He was on the edge, never so inflamed by desire as now, holding Ravenna's slim form, tasting the musky note of arousal on her skin. 'Tell me.'

'I can't.' Her voice was a thready whisper.

Jonas blinked and lifted his head to look down at the woman he wanted—no, needed. A sliver of moonlight pierced the gloom, revealing confusion on her fine features. But it also showed the slumberous warmth in her eyes.

'Can't or won't?' He let one hand drop to her leg, drawing her dress inch by inch up her thigh, watching her eyes widen then narrow to hooded slits. Her tongue darted out to slick her bottom lip in unconscious invitation.

His groin was tight and hard, needy for her. Only her. He pressed close, imprisoning her against the wall, revelling in the way her thighs parted for him. Yes! She wanted him as much as he did her.

Jonas slid his hand beneath the rucked-up skirt to touch silk stockings then cool flesh. His rough fingers felt clumsy as he circled her inner thigh, drawing another gasp from her.

'Say it, Ravenna.' She drove him crazy! He stroked up to the apex of her thighs, to brush hot silk and feel her quiver. His ears clogged as his blood pounded. His nostrils filled with the scent of arousal. His body grew rigid with the force of holding back.

Fear held him. He didn't trust himself to touch her again. He was too close to losing control.

The brush of her hand against his shirt came out of nowhere, making him start. Her fingers trailed lower and he was stone, set solid with desperate anticipation.

Her voice was a ragged whisper that sounded as if it had been torn from her. 'I shouldn't but I do. I want you, Jonas.'

An instant's shocked stillness then restraint ripped away. Jonas' fingers tangled with hers, fumbling to undo his trousers. The feel of her nimble hands wrenching open his zip almost tipped him over the edge. And when her cool fingers touched his hot flesh...

With a hungry growl he planted his hands at her hips and hiked her up against the wall. Her legs came round his waist in a quick, clumsy movement as between them they hauled her skirt up out of the way. Her breath came in pants that matched his tortured gasps.

Their eyes locked. Jonas never wanted to look away. When Ravenna looked at him like that he could do anything, be anything she wanted.

Unsteadily he reached for her, tracing the lace edge of her underwear, pulling it aside. But he couldn't manage gentle; his hands were too clumsy. He heard tearing and her panties came away in his hand.

Something flared in her eyes. Something that told him she was excited, not afraid. Her legs tightened around him, and suddenly it was too much. He thrust high and hard, burying himself in her heat. She was all around him, hot silk against his erection, long legs circling his waist, hands cupping the back of his neck.

'You're mine.' The words slid through gritted teeth as he thrust again, anchoring her, probing as deep as humanly possible, making her his in the most elemental way.

'Mine,' he growled, feeling tremors begin deep inside her and knowing a fierce, possessive joy that *he* did this to her. He brought her bliss. He saw it in her radiant face, heard it in her hoarse voice, shouting his name, felt it in the pulsing climax that rocked her from the inside out. She came so hard and fast he had no time to think before it took him too, overtaking him with a rush of such force, such violent ecstasy, he doubted he'd survive.

Bracing himself, Jonas rode out a storm of pleasure that wrung every ounce of energy he'd once possessed. It was all he could do to stand. Yet from somewhere he found strength to hold Ravenna. Nothing could have pried her from his possessive grip.

She was his. Nothing in his life had ever felt so right.

CHAPTER THIRTEEN

AFTER ANOTHER URGENT coupling, this time on the newly re-upholstered sofa, Ravenna lay, pulse racing, weighed down by Jonas' solid form. He held her close. His head pillowed on her bare breasts, the dark spill of his hair tickling, and his hand splayed possessively at her hip.

Her heart tumbled in a rush of amazement and pleasure.

Ravenna cradled him as his breathing began to slow, the hot puff of his breath deliciously intimate on her skin.

She couldn't believe what had happened despite the evidence of her own sated body. She could lie here for ever.

But already she saw the sky lighten through the French windows on the far side of the ballroom. Dawn was on its way.

How long had they been here, lost in each other?

Too long. Shocked, she remembered today was the day she left Deveson Hall for good. Left Jonas.

Pain cramped her chest, constricting her breathing.

Jonas stirred. Languidly he licked the underside of her breast, then took her nipple into his mouth, suckling gently. Immediately a fine thread of tension pulled from her breast to her womb, tugging her senses into tingling awareness. Molten heat filled her, turned her boneless all over again.

Her breath caught at the sight of him there at her breast and the thread of pleasure snapped to vibrating tautness.

Yet it was the emotional connection, rather than the physical, that undid her.

How could she bear to walk away?

She had no choice.

The metallic tang of despair filled her mouth. She blinked and looked away, forcing her arms to her sides. They felt empty without him.

'We need to move.' The words rushed out.

'Ravenna?' He lifted his head, silver eyes piercing in the gloom. 'You regret this?'

How could she not?

Yet it was an exquisite memory to hoard for later. Instinctively she knew forgetting Jonas would be impossible.

'This wasn't supposed to happen.' She put her hands on his sturdy shoulders but he didn't budge.

'No. But it was inevitable.'

'Nothing is inevitable.' Except perhaps her weakness for Jonas. The full import of what she felt for him had hit her hours earlier as she'd swayed in Adam Renshaw's arms, trying not to stare at the glamorous couple at the centre of the throng. Trying to tell herself she was mistaken—she could never care for Jonas *that* much. But the hollow in her heart told its own story.

'You're going to marry her.' She saw the shock in his eyes and knew the rumours were true. Pain stabbed.

Again she pushed his unyielding shoulders. 'You need to get off me.' She couldn't bear to look at him now he'd silently confirmed the truth.

'We need to talk.' Still he didn't move.

Ravenna's fingers clawed at his bare flesh, trying to shift him. How could she think when they lay naked together?

'Please, Jonas. Let me up.'

For a moment longer he lay there, then abruptly he was gone.

She'd never touch him again, she realised with a tinge of desperation. Slowly, avoiding his eyes, she sat up, naked but for her suspender belt and silk stockings. Frantically she scanned the floor but couldn't locate her clothes. She couldn't even recall where she'd lost them.

'Here.' Jonas draped something around her shoulders. It was his dinner jacket, she realised as it enveloped her and the scent of his body engulfed her. She wrapped it close, prolonging the moment she had to trust her jelly legs and look for her dress.

Jonas tugged on his dress trousers then turned to her, barefoot and bare-chested. One furtive glance confirmed he looked sexier than ever. And more dangerous, his jaw set stubbornly.

'First up, you're wrong. I'm not marrying Helena.'

Her gaze collided with his, a ripple of shock filling her. 'You're not?'

A frown wrinkled his high brow. 'I'd thought about it.'

Again pain knifed her. 'But you've changed your mind. You've found another bride.'

Slowly he shook his head. 'No. I just realised I couldn't marry her.' His polished pewter stare pinioned her. 'Because of you.'

Elation mixed with disbelief in a potent brew that made her light-headed. Ravenna clutched the lapels of his jacket with stiff fingers.

'I don't understand.' She wanted to hope but something held her back. Maybe the confusion in Jonas' face.

He shoved his hands in his pockets and her gaze dragged down over the bunched muscles in his arms and chest. He'd used that power tonight to pleasure her, taking her with a fervent passion and raw strength that had made her feel positively petite against him. She'd never felt more feminine.

He spread his arms. 'I'd planned to marry Helena. She'd make an excellent wife and mother.' He ticked off points against his fingers. 'We mix in the same spheres. She's intelligent and attractive. Warm-hearted too.'

With each point Ravenna's belly squeezed hard over a

knot of pain. It was one thing to realise she'd been right, but quite another to hear Jonas spell out all the reasons Ravenna would never be right for him.

'I get the picture,' she said before he could continue. 'You want the perfect wife for your perfect life at Deveson Hall.'

'It's not that simple.' He inhaled, his impressive chest rising mightily. Ravenna remembered the feel of it, hot and slick, rough with a smattering of hair that tickled her sensitised breasts.

'No?' She jerked to her feet, unable to sit, listening to his marriage plans. On still-wobbly legs she crossed to one of the French windows, preferring the grey pre-dawn view to Jonas' sharp gaze.

'No.' His voice came from behind her. 'Give me credit for some scruples. How can I marry her when I'm fixated on you? All night my attention kept wandering to you flirting with Adam Renshaw, driving me quietly insane.'

Stunned, Ravenna whirled to find him a few paces away. Big, bold and surly—he was the most intimidating male she'd ever met.

'But you and I aren't…we weren't—'

'Lovers?' His eyebrows drew together. 'Think again, Ravenna.' His look scorched her skin and she pulled his jacket close, as if to hide her wanton eagerness at his possessive stare. He kindled an excitement that turned her bones to water.

'I want you,' he murmured in a voice of rough gravel that abraded her senses. 'I've wanted you from the first and I want you now. I tried to keep my distance, especially when I discovered how wrong I'd been about you. The truth about you only made me want you more.'

He took a step towards her but stopped as she held her palm out.

'That's why I can't marry Helena.' His look was grim. 'Because I want you here, Ravenna, with me. Will you stay?'

His words knocked the breath from her lungs, leaving her

dizzy from shock and lack of oxygen. She put a hand to her thumping heart to stop it catapulting right out of her chest.

He wanted her with him?

He wanted her to replace Helena as his bride?

For a fleeting moment Ravenna pictured herself with Jonas, not just sharing her body, but her life. The picture was so alluring it almost blinded her to reality. For she loved him. She'd fallen for him despite her caution. Fallen for him hard as she learned the sort of man he really was.

Then she remembered what he wanted from life.

She couldn't give him that.

She could never be the woman he needed.

Her knees loosened and she reached out blindly, steadying herself on the window pane, cool from the night air.

Besides, she'd asked if he'd found another bride and he'd said no.

Sheer willpower made her straighten and face him. 'What exactly is it you want from me, Jonas?'

Jonas tried to lock his eyes on her face but they kept straying. Never in his life had he seen a woman so sexy. His jacket hung loose and long on her, but now she'd forgotten to clamp it closed it parted to reveal her satiny skin, a hint of one lush breast and the shadow of her pubis, a dark arrow between her legs. She shifted, inadvertently revealing the suspender strap that secured one of her stockings and his blood thundered in a storm of need.

Twice hadn't been enough. Would he ever have enough of this woman who so intrigued and innocently seduced? From the look on her face she had no idea he fought arousal all over again.

'I want you, here, with me.' The words felt good. *He* felt good, admitting the truth he'd avoided too long. Relief filled him and his mouth tugged up in a smile. He saw emotion flare in her eyes and knew it would be all right. Ravenna wanted him too.

Jonas stepped in, lifting his hand to stroke her cheek. She turned her head and shifted away, making him frown.

'Ravenna?' What was she playing at? 'You feel it too—I know you do. After tonight you can't deny it.'

She swung to face him, her expression guarded. 'In what capacity do you want me, Jonas?'

He shrugged. Lover? Girlfriend? What did words matter?

'As your housekeeper?'

He hesitated. He'd thought about asking her to stay and keep the Hall running as she'd done so admirably, but it didn't seem right.

'Or as your mistress?'

'That's a word I prefer not to use.' It implied payment for services. Ravenna would stay because she wanted to, not because he'd shower her with gifts. He'd been wrong earlier, believing her driven by mercenary motives.

'Or maybe both?' Her husky voice rose half an octave. 'Housekeeper and mistress together? Keeping up the family tradition?'

Jonas shook his head, her words like a smack in the chest. What they shared had been wonderful, incandescent. Why did she twist things?

'I refuse to do to your fiancée what Mamma and Piers did to your mother.' Ravenna planted her hands on her hips, anchoring his jacket wide and inadvertently displaying her nakedness. Jonas' blood pressure soared but he dragged his gaze to her face.

'I'm not Piers.' Her expression remained accusing and he felt anger stir. 'Besides, I told you I have no fiancée. Helena and I have never even discussed marriage.'

Still Ravenna didn't look impressed. What did he have to do to make her admit what was between them? Didn't she realise what a huge decision he'd made, ditching his planned proposal? Had she no inkling of what a momentous concession this was for him, pushing aside his long-held plans? All because of her?

'But you will have a fiancée at some stage, won't you?' Ravenna stepped into his space. She poked an accusing finger into his sternum.

Jonas grabbed her hand, flattening it against his chest. He breathed deep of her sweet cinnamon scent, letting it steady him.

'I want you, Ravenna, and you want me. It's that simple.'

He lifted his free hand to her jaw then let it slide slowly down her throat, between her breasts, to her navel. He felt her skin twitch and she sucked in a huge breath. Pleasure filled him at her responsiveness but he kept his eyes locked with hers. His hand drifted down her belly then slid between her legs to the damp core of her where he'd lost himself so recently. Where he wanted to lose himself again.

Need juddered through him and his body grew rigid. Still she didn't move.

'Remember how good we are together?' His demand emerged gruffly but somehow it sounded more like a plea. Why the defiant look in her eyes? Why hold herself so aloof?

He dragged his hand away but kept her palm planted on his chest.

'I'm not asking you to betray anyone, Ravenna. I'm not talking about some tawdry affair behind another woman's back.' Relief showed on her face and he frowned. 'How could you think that of me? After what my mother suffered from my father's infidelity?'

Ravenna blinked and he thought he read regret in her expression. 'You have your sore spots. Being treated as a mistress, as the other woman, is mine.'

'I'd never ask that of you.'

She shook her head and tried to pull away. He kept her anchored.

'But one day you'll want what you've always wanted, won't you? The dream you've had for years. The perfect wife in the perfect life.' Her eyes were huge and pleading.

'I…' Jonas flattened his mouth. He hadn't thought that

far ahead. 'I just know I can't marry Helena when I need you like this.' He'd never been so honest with a woman in his life. It made him feel raw, almost vulnerable.

'But I'm not the bride for you.' Her voice was cool, devoid of emotion.

Everything in Jonas stilled. He stared into her arresting, haunted face and felt something shift, as if the ground quaked and moved beneath their feet.

He looked at Ravenna and saw something utterly, stunningly new. Why hadn't he seen it before?

'Why not?' His fingers tightened around hers, excitement stirring.

'Oh, Jonas, don't!' Fleeting pain shadowed her eyes before she looked away to their joined hands.

'I'm serious, Ravenna.' He'd been so caught up with the list of wifely attributes he'd compiled that he'd almost ignored one of the essentials: desire for his wife. No, not just desire, he realised as Ravenna's hand trembled against him. Need. A sense of connection.

He'd come to rely on Ravenna in ways that had nothing to do with her work. Being with her completed him—emotionally as well as physically.

His mind raced. Ravenna might not have the social network and impeccable breeding he'd once wanted in a wife, but she had other things: honesty, warmth and loyalty.

With her he felt alive, whole.

'Why not, Ravenna?' The brilliance of it stunned him. 'Don't say you don't want me because I don't believe it. We're good together. We could build a wonderful future.'

She jerked her hand free and spun away, walking with quick, jerky steps to the far side of the window. She wrapped her arms round herself protectively and he frowned. What was wrong with her?

'It wouldn't work.'

'Of course it would.' He started forward but halted, perplexed, at her raised, outstretched hand.

'I'm not the sort of woman you want, remember?' He heard an echo of her old jeering tone. 'I'm not from the right family. I don't move in the right circles. The only reason I know what cutlery to use at a formal dinner is because my mother taught me to clean the silverware!' She hefted a deep breath as if waiting for him to agree.

'I don't care.' It was true. None of that mattered in the face of his need for this warm, lovely woman, who for some unfathomable reason tried to push him away.

'I'm illegitimate. Plus my mother was your father's mistress, for heaven's sake! People would talk.'

'Let them. You're not a woman to let fear of gossip rule your life.' He crossed his arms over his chest. He didn't give a damn what others thought, except for Ravenna's sake, knowing how comparisons with Silvia and Piers could hurt her. He'd just have to protect her from that.

She shook her head and he saw desperation in her face as she moved into the dawn light. He wanted to cuddle her close and make her forget her doubts, but he respected her too much to dismiss her concerns. After all, he'd been the one who wanted a wife who was aristocratic and socially assured.

'Ravenna, none of that matters any more, truly. Not now I've found you.' Why couldn't she understand?

'It will one day. You'll wake up and wonder why you settled for me. Don't you see?' She flung her arm wide in a slashing gesture. 'I've never worn jewels or haute couture in my life and wouldn't know how to start. Listen,' she added when he made to close the gap between them. 'I grew up poor. It's what I know, what I'm used to. All this—' another wide gesture '—isn't me. As a little girl my favourite dressing gown was one my mamma made from a bedspread her employer was going to throw out. I wore handmade clothes and made do with second-hand everything.'

'Which made you resourceful.' Why did she think that counted against her? 'Those silk curtains never looked so good before you wore them.' He grinned, remembering how the fabric had moulded her slim, ultra-sexy body.

'You're not listening!' She stomped her heel, making him smile. He loved her passion.

'I'm listening, sweetheart. But I don't hear anything important.' He stepped closer. 'Nothing you've said makes me stop wanting you. We can build our future together. We'll be happy, I know it. You love the Hall and so will our kids.'

Excitement sizzled in his blood as he imagined it. But a chill scudded through him as she met his eyes. She looked... defeated. In all the time he'd known her, despite everything he'd thrown at her, he'd never seen her look so bleak. She stretched out her arm to ward him off, her hand cool against his skin.

'Ravenna?' Now she worried him.

'It wouldn't work.' Ravenna swallowed hard and her fingers trembled against his chest. 'You want to make Deveson Hall into the home you never had.'

Jonas nodded, bewildered.

'You want it to be a real family home, with your children to carry the Deveson blood and traditions into another generation.' Ravenna's hand fell. Where her palm had been the dawn chill brushed his skin like a premonition of disaster.

'You'd have to give all that up if you married me. I can't be the wife you want. Ever.' She drew a sharp breath and fear drilled deep inside him. 'I can't give you those children, Jonas. Not children of your blood. The cancer treatment left me infertile.'

Her mouth twisted in a pained smile as she took in his silent shock. Then she turned and left the room, leaving him dazed and gutted.

CHAPTER FOURTEEN

RAVENNA WALKED SLOWLY along the meandering street, grateful of the shade cast by the tall houses. With her basket full of market produce she should be planning the lunch she'd cook. Mamma would need it after starting her cleaning job well before dawn and Ravenna needed sustenance before her long shift at the café.

She'd make something special, something intricate enough to stop her thoughts straying to England and Jonas.

Naturally it didn't work. It hadn't worked all week, since she'd arrived to visit her mother, now living in a tiny apartment in this large, anonymous Italian city.

She juggled the basket more securely on her arm, inhaling the scent of basil. Instantly an image sideswiped her—of Jonas tasting her home-made pesto. Of the way pleasure crinkled the corners of his eyes and his rare smile made her stomach somersault.

Ravenna blinked, hating the scratchy heat blinding her vision. She'd done the right thing, leaving that morning. What else could she have done? Stayed on as Jonas' mistress till he was ready to move on to a woman who could give him all he wanted? She'd already broken her heart, falling for a man who she couldn't have. Having an affair with him would have shattered it to irreparable smithereens.

The stark horror on his face when she'd admitted she was barren was something she carried with her every moment.

Her mouth flattened. Had she really hoped she'd reveal the truth and he wouldn't care? Not Jonas. Not the man who'd made it his mission to fill the void in his life with what he'd always dreamed of: a family of his own.

Ravenna knew about his past and guessed at his parents' neglect. She'd heard the tension in his voice as he made light of loneliness and isolation. She'd felt the tremor of guilt rack his body for tragedy he'd been unable to prevent. She'd seen his passion for the estate that was more family to him than his parents had ever been. She *understood* his need to belong there and create what he'd never had.

Ravenna tried to take solace from the fact that he'd *cared* about her. Enough to want marriage.

But that made it all worse. Better if they'd never grown close, never shared—

She shook her head. She couldn't bring herself to wish that. Even now she couldn't regret loving him.

Every limb was heavy as she turned into the old apartment building and dragged herself up the stairs. Crossing the tiny landing at the top, she took a deep breath and worked to twist her mouth into a semblance of a smile.

'I'm back.' She pushed open the door and stepped inside. 'I stopped at your favourite *pasticciera* for a treat.' Money was tight but—

'Ravenna.' The deep voice curled around her, spiralling deep to fill the aching emptiness inside. She froze as the wound in her heart that she'd tried unsuccessfully to cauterise reopened.

He was here, filling the tiny hall.

Searing grey eyes fractured her shell of composure. His dark hair had a rumpled look as if he'd tugged his hands through it. In jeans and a casual, open-necked shirt he looked devastatingly attractive and potently male.

'Jonas!' Was that her voice, that yearning gasp?

'Here, let me.' He dived to rescue the wicker basket that dangled from her nerveless fingers.

The brush of his hand on hers sent her blood racing and brought her numbed brain back to life.

Ravenna snapped her mouth shut, her brain fumbling to take in the fact he was here, not a figment of her needy imagination. 'Where's my mother?'

'She's gone out for a while. Don't worry, she's fine. She just thought to give us time alone.'

Why? What had he said to convince her mother to leave? Questions burned in Ravenna's brain but she couldn't wrap her tongue around the words. Everything was an effort. Her chest ached and she realised belatedly she'd forgotten to breathe.

'Why are you here, Jonas?'

'Shall we?' He gestured to the cramped living room.

Instinctively Ravenna shook her head. 'I can't do this, Jonas. I don't want to talk.'

Something flared in his eyes, turning them the colour of a summer storm. 'Neither do I.' Tingling spread out from her feminine core at the look on his face. 'But we need to. Please, Ravenna.'

How could she walk away? She'd done it once. She didn't have the fortitude to do it again. But did she have the self-control to face him?

'In the kitchen.' If she kept herself occupied maybe she'd be able to hear him out without revealing her feelings.

Her legs trembled as she led the way into the tiny alcove that passed for a kitchen. It shrank to minuscule as his wide shoulders filled the doorway and her heart faltered. This close she smelled his citrus and warm male scent and a pang of longing shafted through her.

'Ravenna?'

She avoided his searching look and lifted the basket from him before scooting back to the corner bench. She busied herself unloading fresh food.

'Why are you here, Jonas?'

'Won't you even look at me?' Her pulse pattered faster and she turned to wash her hands.

'Just say what you have to say, Jonas.'

'I'm sorry.'

She faltered as she flattened garlic with a knife.

'You have nothing to apologise for,' she said finally, her voice scratchy. 'You were honest. That's all I could ask.'

Her hands moved with the ease of long practice as she assembled the rest of the ingredients, peeling and chopping an onion with barely a fumble. Thank goodness for routine! She could pretend to focus on that rather than the man just a few paces away.

She wanted to cup his strained face in her palms and nuzzle that strong neck, feel again the heat of his embrace.

Ravenna blinked. Better if she could thrust him out of the door. But nothing would shift him until he was ready. She remembered his formidable power, how he'd held her weight easily that last night as he took them both to ecstasy. Heat razed her last crumbling defences and she dropped the knife on the bench with a clatter.

'I can't do this.' Her voice wobbled. 'Can you go now?' She couldn't look up, instead bracing herself on the bench so she wouldn't slump to the floor.

'No.' The word came from so close it furred the nape of her neck. 'I won't leave.'

'What?' Her head swung up. His face was so close she could count the tiny lines raying out from his eyes.

'I love you, Ravenna. I'm not leaving.'

She pressed the heel of her hand to her chest, trying to draw in enough air to stop the spots wheeling in her vision.

'You…?'

'I love you.' His eyes shimmered and she felt the warm caress of his breath on her upturned face. '*Ti amo*, Ravenna.'

'That's not possible. You didn't—'

He brushed a curl back behind her ear and her heart contracted at the tender gesture. Heat traced down her throat then dived, arrowing straight to her heart.

'I didn't say it earlier because I didn't realise.'

Ravenna shook her head, unable to summon the words to contradict him. It wasn't love he felt.

'I know that makes me a stupid, slow-witted fool.' His wry half-smile made her unwilling heart flip. 'But you see, sweetheart, I've never been in love before. I don't have any experience to draw on.' His voice hit a deep register, trawling along her bones and insinuating its way into her soul.

Trying not to hear the tension in his voice, she shook her head. 'It's not love. It's lust.'

'Is that all it was for you?'

'No, I—' She swallowed hard, watching lightning sheet across those fathomless eyes. 'You're feeling regret, that's all. You feel sorry for me.'

'Sorry? I'd like to wring your neck for walking out on me like that.' But there was no fire in his words, just pain. 'Do you know how worried I've been? Anything could have happened to you.'

Dumbfounded she stared into his hard-chiselled face. 'I can look after myself.'

His eyes bored into hers and the world quaked.

'I know,' he said at last. 'That's what I'm afraid of. That you don't need me the way I need you.'

'Jonas?' Finally she let herself register what she'd been trying to avoid—the pain drawing his features tight. Without planning it she fitted her palm against his jaw. He clamped it to the roughened silk of his skin, and she shivered as a blast of pleasure hit her at the contact.

'Do you know how I've tortured myself thinking I'd never persuade you to come back? I'm a wreck.'

He didn't look a wreck. He looked more decadently delicious than any pastry she'd ever concocted.

'I love you.' Touching his face, she felt his mouth shape the words, making them real. 'I lust after you, Ravenna, that's a given. But I love you too. I've loved you for weeks, months, I think, but I didn't realise till the ball.'

Her heart pounded on her ribs and she swayed, mesmerised by what she saw in Jonas' eyes. Could it be true?

'And I think you love me too.' His voice was raw with tension.

'Of course I do.' That was the worst of it.

Jonas gathered her close in possessive arms and Ravenna wanted to cry out at the poignant pleasure of it. 'But that doesn't change anything.' She braced herself against his hard chest as he leant in. 'Jonas! Please!'

He nuzzled her neck and Ravenna's world slid out of focus.

'Jonas, you need to listen.'

'I'm listening,' he murmured against her ear, then bit her lobe, sending pleasure streaking through her. 'And it changes everything. The way you invented objections back in England, I couldn't be sure you really cared.'

'I care.' The words slipped out unbidden. She cradled his head as he trailed fiery kisses down her throat and she arched back against his arm, letting herself steal one more desperate moment in his embrace. 'I tried not to but I couldn't help myself.'

'Even after I'd been such a bastard.' It wasn't a question. He held her so tight their heartbeats melded.

The wonder of it, having him here, having him say he loved her, was too much. Her emotions were all over the place. Hot tears leaked down her cheeks. Through the months of tests and treatment she hadn't cried but now—

'Don't cry, my love.' Jonas brushed them away with unsteady hands. 'I'll make it up to you, I swear it.'

'You can't.' She tried to tug out of his embrace but he wouldn't let her. 'Please, I can't think when you hold me.'

Jonas traced his thumb over her bottom lip. 'I'll remember that next time I want to win an argument.'

'There won't be any arguments. We—'

'Of course there will be. You're a passionate, headstrong woman.' His tone turned the words into a compliment. 'And I'm used to getting my own way. So forget right now about telling me we won't stay together. I died a thousand deaths not knowing where you were.' He threaded his fingers through her hair, holding her so she had no choice but to meet his eyes. 'It took far too long to locate you. I'm not letting you go.'

'You're forgetting one thing.' It was the hardest thing she'd ever faced, looking into Jonas' fiercely tender expression and knowing she had to pull back.

'If you're talking about children, stop right there. If it's a choice between children and you, there's no contest. It's you I want.'

For one perfect moment Ravenna stared into his face and knew he genuinely believed that. Wonder filled her, a joy that turned the dingy little kitchen into a grand, sunlit chamber, its pock-marked ceiling into a Tiepolo masterpiece.

She hugged that incandescent moment to herself a little longer then swallowed hard.

'I know you believe that, Jonas. And I love you for it.'

His embrace tightened and she'd never felt safer or more treasured. Finally she moved to pry his hands loose.

'But I can't do that to you. I know how important family is to you.' It was the dream that had sustained him since childhood. 'One day you'll regret tying yourself to me and I can't bear to watch that happen.'

'*You* are my family, Ravenna. You're all I need. How could I give you up?'

She shook her head. 'I won't strip you of your dreams, Jonas.'

His darkening gaze meshed with hers and she felt she looked right into his heart.

'They were dreams, Ravenna, concocted by a needy kid. I'm a man now and I know what I want, what I need. I need *you.* Always. For ever.' He swallowed hard and her heart went out to him. She felt the same way.

'As for kids, we can adopt, or grow old together without them, you, me and a gaggle of dogs and horses.' He shook his head. 'How many people have the chance to be with the one they love, Ravenna? Don't throw what we have away. Don't ask me to. I can't do it.'

For the first time Ravenna dared admit a sliver of hope.

'It's a gaggle of geese, not dogs,' she whispered when she found her voice.

His smile snatched her breath. 'We can have those too. Anything you want.' His smile faltered. 'Just don't send me away.'

'I can't, Jonas. I can't let you do this.' She felt stretched thin by the effort to keep strong.

'You want to see me as a lonely recluse, is that it?'

'You wouldn't be lonely long.' A knife pierced her at the thought of Helena offering Jonas comfort.

'I suppose you're right.' He gave an exaggerated sigh. 'Not with Silvia living in Deveson Hall's Dower House.'

'The Dower House? That's impossible. You hate her!'

'But if I offer her a home you'll visit her, won't you?' He nodded. 'Yes, I'm that desperate, Ravenna. Besides, she brought you up to be the woman you are, so presumably there's more to her than I thought.' He drew a deep breath. 'It may take me a while but I thought I should try to start again with her, if I can do it without the past tripping me up.'

Ravenna shook her head, pride in him stirring. Jonas truly was remarkable. He'd do that for her?

'I can't believe she agreed.'

'She'd do anything to see you happy, love. That made us unexpected allies.'

The idea boggled Ravenna's mind. 'She thought this would mend things between us?'

'It's a start, isn't it?' His eyes searched hers, his expression serious. 'None of us can know the future, Ravenna, but

I know this—I wouldn't be complete without you. I want you as my wife.' He stopped her protest with a finger to her lips. 'You can work as a chef instead of being chatelaine of the Hall. You can shock the county by wearing soft furnishings instead of buying clothes. You can do whatever you like so long as you promise to stay with me.' He hefted in a huge breath. 'I love you, Ravenna Ruggiero. My life could never be complete without you.'

Her heart was bursting. Ravenna swiped her cheek with the heel of her hand. 'That's not fair,' she gulped through a knot of emotion. 'How can I say no to that?'

His blinding smile cracked the last of her defences.

'Say yes. Say you'll marry me.'

'I'll agree to live with you.' Despite the flood of happiness, caution weighed. One day he'd realise what he gave up in taking a barren wife.

'Agreed. Live with me now and in a month we'll marry.'

Despite her battered feelings, Ravenna choked back a smile. 'Don't be impossible.' Jonas leaned in and kissed her throat, her jaw, working his way to her mouth until she gave in. 'Make it five years.' Had she really said that?

'Two months,' he shot back, his eyes gleaming.

'Four years.' Surely by then he'd realise his mistake and she would have a store of memories to sustain her.

'Three months.' Jonas slid his hand down her side, brushing the side of her breast, then letting it rest on the swell of her hip.

Ravenna's breathing hitched and her brain spun dizzily. 'Three years.'

'Oh, love, you drive a hard bargain.' He leaned in, eyes glittering, and kissed her softly on the lips.

Ravenna couldn't resist Jonas at the best of times. When he told her he loved her with every second breath she didn't have the will power to withstand him. Happiness had crept up on her and now it filled her with a blaze of optimism that finally overcame gnawing doubt.

She took his proud, patrician face in her trembling hands and kissed him back with all the urgent passion and deep, abiding love she could no longer deny.

'Don't look so worried, love,' Jonas said later as she sat, cuddled close on his lap. 'We have each other. That's all that matters. And as for the rest—' he shrugged '—we'll take each day as it comes.'

He paused, his lips twitching. 'Now about those three years. I have a counter offer…'

EPILOGUE

RAVENNA SAT IN the shade of a chestnut tree and watched Jonas, blindfolded, tumble to the ground, pulled by eager young hands. Chiara and Josh giggled as their dad groaned theatrically then reached to tickle them. There were screams as they and Vivien's son, Ben, tried to elude him but the five-year-olds were no match for Jonas' long reach.

Gleeful squeals of 'Mamma! Help!' filled the glade and with a grin Ravenna moved to get up.

'No, don't move.' Her mother was already on her feet. 'You look so comfortable. Stay.'

Ravenna subsided, content to bask in the pleasure of watching her family. She'd held out against Jonas as long as she could, eventually agreeing to marry him a year to the day after he'd arrived at the apartment in Italy. He'd used every wile to persuade her and she'd loved every minute of his loving persuasion.

He'd even followed through with his offer of a home for her mother. To their credit Mamma and Jonas were doing their best to put the past behind them and just recently her mother had moved into the Dower House permanently in-stead of using it as a base for short-term visits.

Jonas had mellowed too, as if the love they shared gave him the strength to accept the complexities of his parents' failed relationship and admit the possibility Piers and Mamma had, whatever their faults, genuinely cared for each other.

Every day with Jonas was a blessing. And the blessings had continued when they adopted the twins three years ago. Jonas had insisted they needn't adopt, that she was all he needed. But the love they shared was so deep and strong it seemed natural to share it further. Each day they learned together, finding parenting a challenge and a reward.

'No, Toby!' Jonas collapsed with a huff of laughter as their Basset Hound, a recent rescue dog, launched himself at them, massive ears flopping and tongue licking.

The children squealed with delight, waking a cross-breed pup that had been asleep at Ravenna's feet. With a yelp of excitement it bounded over to join the melee.

'You might have come to save me.'

Jonas stood, smiling down at her. As ever, her heart gave a skip of pleasure as she met his warm gaze. She'd been a fool ever to doubt his love.

'Sit with me?' She patted the blanket beside her.

'I thought you'd never ask.' He looked over his shoulder. 'If you think Silvia can cope?'

'Of course she can. She revels in it.'

Jonas settled himself and warmth seeped through her as he wrapped his arm around her. 'Happy, love?'

'Always.' Ravenna sank into his embrace. She glowed with excitement. She'd been cautious so long, scared to hope, but the doctor had assured her everything was normal. The miracle she'd never looked for had happened.

'Jonas, I've got something to tell you.'

'Something good?'

'Absolutely.' She lost herself in his smile. 'There's a date we need to mark on the calendar.' Her hand slipped protectively to her abdomen and his gaze followed the movement.

A muffled shout drew the twins' attention but when they looked it was to see Mamma and Daddy cuddling. They did that all the time, so Josh and Chiara turned back to the pups.

It was Silvia who watched Jonas stand and gather his wife

up in his arms as if she was the most precious thing in the world. He hugged Ravenna close and her trill of laughter floated on the warm air.

Silvia smiled. Jonas Deveson was the best thing ever to happen to her darling Ravenna.

Life was very, very good.

* * * * *

A NAVY SEAL'S
SURPRISE BABY

LAURA MARIE ALTOM

Laura Marie Altom is a bestselling and award-winning author who has penned nearly fifty books. After college (Go, Hogs!), Laura Marie did a brief stint as an interior designer before becoming a stay-at-home mother to boy-girl twins and a bonus son. Always an avid romance reader, she knew it was time to try her hand at writing when she found herself replotting the afternoon soaps.

When not immersed in her next story, Laura plays video games and, of course, reads romance!

Laura loves hearing from readers at either PO Box 2074, Tulsa, OK 74101, or by email, balipalm@aol.com.

Love winning fun stuff? Check out www.lauramariealtom.com.

Chapter One

Pandora?

One glance at the next name on his nanny-candidate list told navy SEAL Calder Remington all he needed to know. She'd be a card-carrying unicorn lover or flake. He needed a Mary or Hazel. Someone not only dependable, but with impeccable references and the patience of Mother Teresa. The last four women had been nice enough, but they'd lacked experience. Ideally, he needed a grandmotherly type who'd successfully raised her own brood to be doctors, and now looked to pass along her vast parental knowledge to the next generation.

At twenty-eight, how much parenting knowledge could *Pandora* have?

Calder had pretty much resigned himself to not even let her in the house when the doorbell rang. He dropped his list and sighed. In light of the fluid situation, he adjusted his mission to ditching *Pandora* quickly enough to allow time for a nap before the next candidate showed.

Calder glanced at eight-month-old Quinn, who played on the floor with his favorite stuffed whale. "Might as well get this over with, huh, buddy?"

"Gah!"

Calder shook his head. "My thoughts exactly."

He opened the door on a petite brunette whose black-rimmed glasses struck him as too big for her face. "Um, hello. I, ah, was sent by the Earth Angels agency to—"

"Appreciate your stopping by—" the August heat coming in the door already made him break out in a sweat "—but I need someone older."

"Oh...." As if she were a leaky balloon, her shoulders deflated. "Maybe if you would just give me a chance? You know, like try my services for a week, then decide?"

Desperation fairly oozed from her pores. "Kind of you to offer, but—"

He didn't think it possible, but when she glanced past him into the house, her complexion paled. He was shocked when she shoved him out of her way to sprint across the living room as if she'd just caught a Hail Mary pass and was intent on snagging a game-winning touchdown.

He turned to see what kind of nut-job stunt she was pulling, only to go weak at the knees. Quinn had turned blue. Pandora scooped him into her arms and turned him upside down. She delivered five raps on his back, then flipped him over to do the same in the front. No results.

Calder might be a navy SEAL and combat veteran, but he had never felt more helpless. Since May, he'd been meaning to take an infant first-aid class, but between work and single-dad duties, it was almost September and he still hadn't found time.

She repositioned his son once more and then like magic, a grape popped from Quinn's mouth onto the carpeted floor.

While Calder gaped, Quinn wailed.

Pandora hugged Calder's panicked son, rocking him gently, calming him with a soft, sweet lullaby in his ear.

Once his son's cries had been reduced to occasional shuddering huffs, she held out her hand for Calder to shake. "I'm sorry. In all the excitement, I failed to properly introduce myself. I'm Pandora Moore."

Still shaky, Calder shook the woman's hand. This certainly put a new spin on the situation. How did his conscience justify sending her on her way when she'd literally saved Quinn's life? Did he repay that debt by flat out giving her the job? "Nice to meet you. Calder Remington." Pointing to his son, he asked, "Where'd you learn that—the baby Heimlich thing?"

"Basic Infant Care 101. Choking is a leading cause of infant mortality—which is beyond tragic considering most cases are preventable." She took the bowl of grapes from the coffee table, placing them on the mantel.

"Yeah, well, you made me feel pretty stupid." He rammed his hands into his jeans pockets.

"Oh, no, I didn't mean to imply you're a bad parent."

"I get it." Whether she'd meant it or not, her words stung because Calder knew them to be true. He may be good at a lot of things, but raising a kid wasn't one. He tried, but even after having had Quinn for a few months, nothing about it felt natural. Bottom line, Calder had wearied of the whole nanny search. Unable to shake the guilt telling him the least he could do for this woman who'd saved his son was give her a chance, he asked, "How soon can you start?"

Her eyebrows rose. "You mean you want me for the job?"

"Sure. We'll give it a try." He still didn't wholly trust a woman named *Pandora,* but guys on his team were always giving him crap for his name. Didn't seem fair for him to turn around and do the same. "Can you start first thing tomorrow?"

She pushed up her glasses and shyly smiled. "Sure. The agency said it's a live-in position, right?"

"Yeah." He gestured down the hall. "Follow me. I'll show you your room."

STANDING IN THE sunshine-flooded bedroom with its own private bath and even a bay window peering out on the grassy, tree-lined backyard, Pandora fought the urge to pinch herself. A hardwood dresser, nightstand and headboard all matched and the tan carpet was clean enough for the baby in her arms to crawl wherever he wanted—assuming there weren't more grapes lying around. The queen-size mattress was bare, but new enough to still wear furniture-store stickers.

After all she'd been through, this felt surreal. As a bonus, Calder even seemed like a great guy. Though he possessed beyond steal-your-breath good looks, her gut told her he was a gentleman. As for the indefinable jolt of awareness stemming from just shaking his hand? She was determined to push that from her mind.

"Don't blame you if you hate the color," he said in regard to the mixed shades of lavender, orange and lime green polluting the walls. "The last owner went a little crazy with their sponge painting. We'll pick out something more to your liking."

"Yellow," she automatically said. "I've always wanted a room the shade of lemon sorbet."

He laughed. "You got it. As for the bedspread, towels, sheets and everything, I figured you'd be more comfortable using your own."

"Yes. Thanks." Only trouble was, she didn't have her own. But she had managed to save some money. It wouldn't hurt to spend a smidge of her precious savings on the perfect floral comforter set to match her soon-to-be newly painted walls.

Quinn had fallen asleep in her arms.

The sensation of once again holding an infant struck her as sublime.

For the past year, she'd held a steady after-school childcare position until the Norfolk naval family had been transferred overseas. Pandora's charges had been two little girls aged five and seven. During that time and up to the present, she lived at a halfway house in a gloomy basement bedroom no bigger than some closets. The enormity of this job and all the secondary perks it entailed were too great to presently absorb, so she held them close as she might have a secret gift she wouldn't open until she had some privacy. No, she wouldn't even think about the full ramifications until Calder signed the agency paperwork that officially brought her dream one step closer to fruition.

"Want me to take him?" Her new boss nodded to his son before leading Pandora into the hall.

"Thanks, but I'm good." And she was. Nuzzling the infant's downy hair, she drank in his familiar baby smells of lotion and powder. If this angel were truly hers, she'd never let him go. "If it's not too personal, where's Quinn's mom?"

Calder's expression darkened as he said, "Not to be evasive, but that's a long story best told over a few beers."

"Oh." He drank? She'd hoped he didn't, but that was probably expecting too much.

"Come on. I'll show you Quinn's room and the rest of the house. We've only been here a few weeks. My schedule made it tough to nail down the closing date."

"You work a lot of overtime?"

He snorted as he led the way into a surprisingly drab nursery. "Guess you could call it that. Sorry—I'm still off my game from the whole choking thing. I'm a navy SEAL. A big part of my job is being called out with little or no notice. Like, I might tell you I'll be home for dinner, but then get assigned a mission and won't be back for six months—granted, it's usually not that long, but it can happen. Technically, for just that reason, my mom has shared custody of Quinn. But since she's in North Carolina, I need you here for any and all immediate contingencies. That's why it was important for me to hire someone through an agency. I need to know you're not only reliable and great with my kid, but have the kind of stable history and experience in caring for children that allows me to be one hundred percent certain you're doing a great job. That way, I can fully focus on what I do, which makes my life a helluva lot saner."

Pandora wished she were as confident with the trust he placed in her as Calder. Though in her head, she'd put her past firmly behind her, in her heart the fallout still remained.

Rocking Quinn, she asked, "How can you stand being away from this cutie?"

For a split second, Calder looked blank. "I, ah, guess for what I do, I don't have a lot of options. Come on, I'll show you the kitchen."

Pandora followed, trailing her fingertips along white walls. Had Calder already painted the hall? Somehow she couldn't imagine the same person who'd attacked her room with color being satisfied with a vanilla thoroughfare.

In the kitchen, Calder said, "Nothing fancy here. I don't expect you to cook for me. Just make sure Quinn gets decent meals. I set up a household account at the bank. You can use it for groceries, diapers—whatever else we need around here or for Quinn."

She nodded, though inside, she felt as if she may be dreaming. How many nights had she gone to bed hungry because she had no cash for food?

You sure managed to scrape up enough dough for other things, her conscience was all too happy to point out.

Fighting fire with fire, she squelched the seemingly constant voice in her head, reminding her she was destined to fail, by saying, "Thanks again for this opportunity. I'll care for Quinn as if he were my own."

Wrong choice of words considering what had happened to her sweet Julia. She squelched that thought, too.

"I'm pretty sure I should be thanking you." He fished a key from a meticulously organized drawer, handing it to her. "Everyone I know with kids says the agency you work for

doesn't fool around when it comes to hiring the most qualified people."

Pandora knew that to be true. Her best friend, Natalie, put
all of her employees through extensive background checks.
She feared the only reason Natalie had hired Pandora was
because of the friendship they'd struck up at the restaurant
where Pandora waited tables. But no matter how many times
Natalie assured Pandora that wasn't the case, or how much
additional training she'd done on her own, she never quite
felt part of acceptable society—or worthy of receiving good
fortune.

"WELL? YOU EVER going to tell me how the interview went?"

Pandora glanced up from cramming her few books into a
box to find Natalie seated on the halfway house's twin bed.
She may have offered to help, but so far had done nothing
but talk. "Obviously, it was good, or Calder wouldn't have
hired me."

"Duh. I'm the one who filled out the paperwork. I want the
inside scoop. Did you find out what happened with Quinn's
mom? I kept waiting for an explanation, but he never told
me."

"I asked, but Calder said he'd talk about it later." Pandora
purposely left out the part about the beers. No need for her
friend to worry about her returning to the dark side.

"Interesting." Natalie tapped her index finger against her
lips. "Wonder what happened for her to leave? The guy's so
handsome it hurts to look at him. Don't you think?"

"No," Pandora lied. In truth, not only was Calder easy on
the eyes, but her cheeks flamed at the mere memory of the
heat caused by just shaking his hand. "Even if I did, what
would I do about it? Don't you have a strict nonfraterniza-
tion policy with clients?"

"True, and I appreciate you pointing that out, but you'd

have to be a zombie not to have at least noticed that killer grin—and the width of his shoulders. Dear Lord…" Natalie fanned herself.

Pandora pitched a pillow at her usually more serious friend. "Knock it off. All you need to know is that Calder seems to be a great guy, and the fact that he hired me is a miracle." She swallowed hard to keep the tears at bay.

"You deserve every ounce of good that's been happening for you lately." Standing, her friend ambushed Pandora with a sideways hug. "I never would've suggested you for this job if I didn't think you were capable of handling it."

"Thanks." Pandora sniffled and nodded. "But it's hard, you know? And I didn't expect that. For years, I've dreamed of living a normal life and now that I'm getting out of here and moving into this adorable home with an even cuter baby, I…" Her blessings plate felt inordinately full. The only thing missing was her daughter. But not for long, she promised herself.

Pandora woke the next morning at five. Calder said she didn't need to be at his house until seven, but excitement refused to grant another minute's sleep.

She and Natalie had packed all her belongings into five boxes—including her toiletries. Calder had offered to help her move, but she was embarrassed not only about where she lived, but how little she actually owned, so she'd declined.

She took a quick shower, dressed, brushed her teeth, blow-dried her hair and put it in a quick ponytail and carted the boxes to her car, then stripped her bed, swept the floor and wiped down all flat surfaces. Since she'd spoken with the house counselor and completed all necessary release paperwork the previous night, by six, she'd said her goodbyes to the few women who were awake, then turned in her key. Once in her car, headed toward her new home, she never looked back.

That part of her life was over and she never wanted to re-visit it. Never wanted the shame of being forced by her own poor choices to live in a group home again.

She merged onto the highway and made it to Calder's Norfolk neighborhood thirty-five minutes ahead of sched-ule. She passed the time by driving around, admiring the tidy neighborhood and park close enough for her to take Quinn to play. She'd have so much fun caring for him and Calder's home that it hardly seemed fair for her to accept a salary.

Pulling her car into Calder's driveway filled her with a kind of quiet satisfaction she'd never known. The only thing better would be having a home of her own—which she would, but this made a great first step.

The redbrick house featured large-paned windows with white shutters. The postage-stamp-size yard was neat with box hedges lining the foundation, but the flower beds were bare save for a few hardy weeds. She wondered if Calder would mind if she and Quinn planted fall flowers. She'd al-ways loved pansies.

"Hey, you're early."

Pandora had been deep in her daydream when her new boss stepped barefoot and bare chested onto the front porch. Wearing khaki cargo pants, he carried a sleepy Quinn still dressed in footy pajamas. If she'd thought the home a lovely sight, the man and his son were downright mesmeriz-ing. Mouth dry, she took a moment to even form words. It sounded cliché, but she honestly hadn't known men had arms and chests so muscular outside of movies.

Quinn rubbed his eyes and whimpered.

"He's been cranky this morning." Calder took the few porch steps with ease, offering her his son. "You handle him and I'll unload your stuff."

"I—I can get it." Would he find it odd she owned so few belongings? "I don't want you to go to any trouble."

"No worries." Handing her the baby, he said, "We're in this together now." Eyeing the barely full backseat, he asked, "This it? Or do you have a friend with a truck coming later?"

"That's all." She jiggled Quinn, coaxing out a smile.

The infant grabbed her glasses, giggling while trying to shove them in his mouth.

"Whoa," she said with a laugh. "If you want breakfast, I'm going to need those."

Calder strolled past her with a box of books so heavy she'd had to take rest stops every few feet. He eyed her funnily. Longer than usual. Was everything okay? He couldn't tell from just the acrid smell lingering on her belongings where she'd been living, could he? A lot of the women had smoked heavily. Sometimes, Pandora feared she might never rid herself of the stench.

On his way into the house, Calder said, "I left a credit card for you on the kitchen table. Quinn's seriously low on baby food and formula and stuff, so you'll probably need to fix that situation and grab anything you want for yourself. I usually get fast food on the way home. If you run into trouble, just call my cell. Number's on the fridge. What's your number?"

"I, ah, don't have one." Too expensive. She'd made her Saturday calls to Julia on the pay phone outside the halfway house.

"Wow, okay. Well, we'll work on that. Also, while the weather's nice, use my SUV since it has Quinn's car seat and stroller. Keys are hanging on a rack by the garage door. Oh—and you might as well park your car in the garage. There should be plenty of room."

Toying with the bear on the tummy of Quinn's pj's, she asked, "How will you get to work?"

"Motorcycle. Usually only use it on the weekends, but this'll give me a great excuse to ride."

"Oh." His shoulders, chest and arms were so tanned. Did

he do a lot of work outdoors? Was it wrong she had a tough time focusing on anything but his sheer, male magnificence?

"SHE HOT?" Calder's friend and fellow SEAL team member, Mason Brown—also known as "Snowman" because he grew up in Alaska and never got cold— finished his bologna sandwich and tossed the wrapper from three-point range into the trash. He missed.

"Who?" Calder asked as he opened a bag of chips. They'd been stuck in a classroom studying smart-bomb mechanisms all morning. The fresh air felt good. Plus, the day was pretty nice for a change—not too hot. They shared a picnic table with their other friends.

Across from Calder sat Heath "Hopper" Stone, nickname earned from his knack for hopping over any obstacle while at a full-on run.

Next to him, Cooper "Cowboy" Hansen. Rumor had him riding into Basic Underwater Demolition—affectionately known as BUDs—on horseback, but Calder always figured he'd just grown up on a ranch.

The group was rounded out by a bunch of boring-ass married guys who talked about nothing but their wives and kids. Deacon and Garrett used to be fun, but lately Calder had to force himself to even be normal around them. Oh, he loved Quinn because he was his son, but he also loved the life he'd made for himself.

Commitment wasn't his thing.

He sure as hell didn't want to hear about the so-called promised land of marriage. What a joke. Besides, for all practical purposes he was married—to the navy.

He loved his job. He loved how being a SEAL made the ladies go weak in the knees—not that he bragged about being a SEAL. That wouldn't be cool. But they were a different breed and women smelled them from a mile away. Adrenaline rushes and seeing the world were his life. Before Quinn, the apartment he'd shared with Mason, Heath and Cooper had only been a temporary layover between adventures.

"Duh," Heath said, "the nanny. Is she hot?"

Mason groaned. "Nannies rank right up there with kindergarten teachers on the sexy meter. I like to think there's a whole lot of naughtiness going on under all that nice."

Calder crossed his arms and glared. "Show some respect here, people. She's nice—and really knows her stuff around Quinn." And though he sure as hell wouldn't mention it to this crew, when Quinn had helped himself to Pandora's glasses, and she'd laughed, Calder had been forced to do a double take. In that moment, with the morning sun making her complexion glow, holding his giggling son, she'd been genuinely pretty. Wholesome. Exactly the look he wanted for his son. "I'm lucky to have found her and wouldn't even think of screwing up a good working relationship by making it personal."

Mason roared. "Just keep tellin' yourself that, man."

"Keep it down," Garrett snapped from the other end of the table. He and his wife, Eve, had just had a baby boy and Garrett was obsessed with showing everyone his latest cellphone videos. "My son's talking…"

Calder shook his head. As the parent of his own infant, he knew kids were far from expert communicators. Guilt consumed him for not feeling more in regard to his son. What was wrong with him? When Pandora asked how Calder stood being away from Quinn, he hadn't had a good answer. Singlehandedly caring for an infant was so stressful, whenever he got the chance to bolt, he did.

So why didn't he miss his baby and take hundreds of pictures of Quinn? Most days, Calder felt as if he lacked the most basic of dad genes. Probably had something to do with the way Quinn had abruptly entered his world.

But now that he'd finally found a nanny, he could do right by his son while at the same time getting back to what he did best. Killing terrorists with his guns, then slaying the ladies with his looks.

Chapter Two

When Calder left that morning, for Pandora the house took on the almost-reverent peace she'd only previously found in a church. Maybe it was because of the sun streaming through the many-paned windows? Or could it be as mundane a reason as her boss had painted most of the house angelic white? Regardless, she held Quinn on her hip, kicking off her sandals carefully, quietly taking it all in.

She admired the honeyed glow of maple floors in the kitchen, den and entry. In the living room, the carpet caressed her bare feet like crushed velvet. The brown leather couch and armchair still had tags hanging from them. The coffee table and a flat-panel TV sitting atop a wood stand were the room's only other pieces. Calder mentioned he and Quinn hadn't lived in the house long. Was he taking his time finding more stuff? Waiting till he had money in his budget? Or did he genuinely not care whether or not his house felt like a home?

She hoped he didn't want to rush a big decision like finding just the right clock for the fireplace mantel and serene landscapes to hang on the walls. But then why would a rough, tough soldier care about any of that? He'd also admitted how much he worked. Why would a comfortable home even be high on his priority list? All he essentially needed was a place to park.

Which made her sad. Not for her, but for his son.

A survey of the kitchen showed Calder was right about her needing to go to the store. Unless she and Quinn wanted to eat baby-food peaches, carrots or protein shakes for breakfast, lunch and dinner, the day's first priority was a trip to the store.

Noting the blender on the counter, Pandora decided no more bland, premade fare for her tiny charge. "You're going gourmet, cutie."

Quinn giggled when she landed a playful poke to his belly.

At the restaurant where she used to work after first getting her life back on track, she'd struck up a fast friendship with the chef. Huge, funny and French, in his laughable English he'd taught her to prepare most everything on the menu and a few items that weren't. He'd been the only kind father figure she'd ever had, and his sudden heart attack had almost once again thrown her off course. All she remembered of her own dad was him constantly beating the crap out of her mom, occasionally taking a turn on her, then one day never coming home. Pandora would've thought her mom would be happy he was gone, but she'd suffered a meltdown—dying of an overdose near her forty-third birthday. Pandora, sixteen at the time, missed her, but for as long as she could remember, she'd virtually raised herself, doing her schoolwork as well as all the cooking and household chores, so the loss hadn't come as any great shock. The distant aunt who'd taken official custody of her was all too happy for Pandora to remain self-sufficient. The ratty apartment's rent and utilities were covered by her mom's social security check. Pandora's other needs were met through charity or after-school jobs.

The fact that her own mother had fallen apart should've served as the fire in her belly to make a better life for herself, but through counseling, Pandora now realized she'd fallen into the same abusive spiral.

Catching herself staring out the kitchen window, she said to the baby, "What do you think about from now on just focusing on our awesome future?"

He blew a raspberry in agreement.

"We have a lot to do. Not only is grocery shopping on our list, but I'll need you to help me find a really pretty comforter and all the trimmings."

Blue eyes wide, he hung on to her every singsong word.

"I know you're a boy and probably don't think a whole lot about things being pretty, but if you'd spent the past few years living where I have, you'd want to be surrounded by pretty things, too."

Quinn babbled happily in response.

Turned out Calder's car was as dreamy as his home. Her whole life, the closest she'd ever come to driving a new car had been when the mother of the children she used to work for had gotten a Lexus for her birthday and Pandora and the girls rode in the backseat on their way to a country-club party.

The Land Rover's powerful engine didn't sputter when she stopped for red lights and the tan leather upholstery smelled as good as it looked. In the rearview mirror, she regularly peeked at Quinn, all snug and smiley in his safety seat, gnawing on a rattle. Even he seemed to enjoy the ride.

The two of them made a few stops to find just the right floral bed set and fluffy yellow towels to match. Purchasing the items took nearly all her cash, but it was worth it.

With her purchases stashed in the back, she and Quinn headed to the grocery store.

Pandora had never bought so much food at once. Milk and eggs. Fruits, meats and veggies. When Calder said they were low on groceries, he hadn't been kidding. While standing at the checkout, the total felt uncomfortably large. Her pulse raced and her palms were damp. Would the card Calder had given her even work?

The youngish female clerk asked, "May I see your ID?"

"Um, sure, but I'm a nanny and this is my boss's card." With Quinn fussing in his carrier, Pandora fished through her purse for her driver's license.

"Sorry." The woman returned Calder's card to Pandora. "I'm not allowed to accept any credit card without matching ID."

"Please," Pandora begged. "It's way past time for my baby to have his lunch, and—"

"You just said he's not yours?"

"Well, yeah, but you know what I mean. Can we ask a manager?"

"Don't you have an alternate form of payment?"

"No." As this was the only open checkout lane, a line had formed behind her. With nothing else to do, people started to stare.

"Is there a problem?" the middle-aged manager asked.

Pandora explained her situation.

Quinn's fussing morphed to crying.

"Please." She took him from his carrier, jiggling him on her hip.

"Look, I'm sorry." The manager voided her sale. "You seem like a nice lady, but corporate's cracking down on checking ID for all credit-card sales. There's a lot of fraud in this area and if your card turns out to be stolen, I'm losing my job. Can you get in touch with your boss? Have him come down here to show his ID? Then I'll set you up an account and next time you shop, this won't be a problem."

Pandora eyed her cart. It'd taken over an hour to carefully make her selections. Would Calder be upset if she called his cell?

With Quinn crying harder than ever, she took a deep breath and dialed the store's office phone.

"SORRY…" CALDER HUSTLED toward Pandora and Quinn. With a loaded shopping cart alongside her, she'd parked herself on a bench in front of the store manager's office. "I'm an idiot for not seeing this contingency."

"You're not angry?" As if she'd worried about his reaction, her shoulders sagged in relief. "Because I'm sorry I even had to call. But the baby's hungry and I didn't know what else to do."

When Quinn fussed, she hugged him closer, smoothing her hand up and down his back.

"How could I be upset with you when this was my fault? Should've thought this through."

After getting Pandora squared away with the manager to use his card, Calder purchased the groceries, then pushed the cart, following the nanny and his son to the car. He had a hard time not staring at her cute behind because she wore the hell out of her white shorts.

She turned around and said, "Let me get Quinn settled in his safety seat, then I'll unload everything. You get back to work."

"I'm not in a hurry." He already had the back popped open and had placed the gallon of milk and two bulging sacks inside.

"Still…" Finished with Quinn, she fussed with her hands. "This is my job."

Ah, this was some kind of boss issue. "Look, Pandora, technically I might be in charge, but realistically…?" He laughed. "You're the one with all the answers. I might place explosives on moving subs, but navigating the baby aisle in the supermarket is *way* over my head. I never know what kind of milk to buy, and baby food blows my mind. That makes us a team, okay?"

Smiling, she pushed up her glasses and nodded. "At least let me help."

When she brushed past, their forearms grazed and he caught a whiff of her floral-scented hair. Maybe it'd been too long since he'd been with a woman, or maybe he was just appreciative to finally have some help with Quinn—either way, being near her made him feel extra alert. Not so much an attraction as an appreciation. Curiosity, even, to discover more about what made her tick. None of which made sense, considering he barely knew her. But there it was all the same.

A minute later, they'd finished loading his SUV. "I'll follow you home to carry everything in."

"Really, I've got this," she assured him.

But because he'd been raised to always carry in the groceries, he insisted.

DURING THE SHORT DRIVE to Calder's house, relief shimmered through Pandora. Not only had he not been angered by having to interrupt his day to help her, but he'd been downright gallant. And now, offering to help her unload? Amazing. Her ex had declared anything to do with groceries *women's work*.

Once parked in the garage, she took Quinn while Calder handled her purchases.

In the house, she placed the still-fussing baby in his high chair, dampened a paper towel with warm water, then washed his little hands and hers. "Hold on a minute, pumpkin, and we'll get that hungry tummy filled."

She rummaged in the bags Calder had already piled on the counter. Spotting the one item she needed, she removed a box of teething biscuits and handed a cookie to Quinn.

For the longest time, he stared at the biscuit, inspecting it as if he was unsure what to do. When his next logical step was to put it in his mouth, he grinned, oblivious to the drool dripping from his gummy smile.

She wiped his chin with a fresh dishrag before fishing for one of the bibs she'd bought at the store. With it securely fastened to the enthusiastic eater, she set about putting away the groceries and making lunch.

"That's everything." Calder set the last of the bags on the kitchen table. Sitting in the chair next to his son, he asked, "What're you eating, bud?"

Quinn gurgled and waved his hands in the air. *"Bah!"*

"Really?" he teased his son. "Sounds good."

"It's a teething biscuit," Pandora explained. "Soothes his gums. Plus, buys me time to fix him a proper lunch."

"Ah…." Calder nodded. "How'd you learn about babies?"

For a moment she froze, then slipped into autoresponse mode, glad for the distraction of putting veggies in the fridge. "Mostly classes and on-the-job training. This is my first full-time position with infant care, but I've worked part-time for three other families. Little Jonah, an eleven-month-old, was my biggest challenge. He was a jumper. That baby was nearly the death of me. He'd try escaping his changing table, crib, playpen. Can't imagine the trouble he's going to cause his future teachers."

Calder laughed.

Inside, she felt the stirrings of guilt. More and more, he seemed like a great guy. She wished she could've just told him about Julia, but that would only raise more questions—some of which she may not have been able to answer. As Natalie reminded her, she was entitled to her private life. Her only job requirement was giving expert care to Quinn.

"No kidding. I hope Quinn doesn't try to pull that kind of stunt," Calder said, still chuckling.

While putting pork chops, chicken and beef in the freezer, she said, "I'm making Quinn pureed peas for lunch. Would you like the grown-up version with a grilled chicken breast?"

His grin did funny things to her stomach. "Thanks for the offer, but I had lunch back on base. Speaking of which…"

He stood, then kissed the top of Quinn's head. "Guess I'd better head back."

Pandora understood Calder's work was important, but once he was gone she struggled with the oddest sensation. Something akin to clouds blocking the sun.

ALL AFTERNOON, stuck in a stuffy classroom, Calder found his mind drifting to his brief time with Pandora and Quinn. There was so much he needed to learn about his son, but considering how Calder had come to be a father, he'd had a hell of a time adjusting. Sure, he'd read a few baby books, and the first week, his mom had come from North Carolina to help him through the initial crisis, but there were still times he wondered what had happened to his life.

Opening his apartment door to find a wailing, six-month-old baby blocking the way had been a shocker, to put it mildly. Quinn had been bundled in a beaten-up carrier, *talking* to his pinkie finger.

Since then, everything felt upside down. Calder always seemed to be rushing to catch up. Temporary sitters and day care never seemed to work out and, until finding the agency that had provided him with Pandora, he'd feared maybe having to take an extended leave until his kid started school.

Calm, capable Pandora struck him as an oasis in his childcare desert.

Tonight, instead of rushing around trying to figure out formula ratios and how to scrub Quinn without getting soap in his eyes, Calder figured that thanks to the new nanny, he was back to business as usual.

He'd grab a beer with Mason, Heath and Cooper—maybe even chat up a hot blonde.

Four hours later, Calder shared a table at a favorite SEAL hangout, Tipsea's, with his boys. "This is the life, huh, guys?"

Mason ate a pretzel. "I don't know. At lunch, when Garrett

was showing around all his family pics… Made me wonder if we're missing something, but then gazing out on tonight's sea of available beauties, I'm thinking I like my current life just fine. Can I get an amen?"

Calder and Mason clinked longneck brews.

At the opposite end of the table, Cooper raised his beer.

"You three keep living the dream…" Heath fished in a pocket of his camo fatigues. "But it's time for me to move on. Lookee what I bought for Patricia's birthday." He withdrew a black velvet box, flipped open the lid to display a decent-size rock.

"Whoa—you don't mean *move on* as in leaving the SEALs, do you?"

Heath almost choked on his beer. "Oh, hell, no. Just that she means the world to me and I want her to be my wife. We all saw the drama Deacon, Garrett and Tristan went through in their love lives, and I don't need it. She's the woman for me. Done. End of story."

"Good for you, man." Mason patted his back. "I felt that way once." He shook his head and laughed. "Good thing I came to my senses."

Calder laughed his ass off.

Heath flipped them both the bird. "Yuk it up. I'm gonna be the one sleeping on clean sheets every night that I'm home with a good meal in my belly and a nice, soft woman to hold."

"Should we check this guy for fever?" Cooper asked.

"Oh—I've got one." After pushing back his chair, Heath stood. "It's called Patricia Fever. I'm going home to her right now. You idiots are just jealous."

After lover boy took his leave, Calder ordered a burger. Once the waitress left, he said to his friends, "We should stage an intervention. Clearly, Hopper's traveling down a dangerous path."

"No kidding," Mason said.

Calder's dad loved the ladies, but he had this old-fashioned thing about marrying them before sleeping with them. He was now on his sixth wife, which Calder saw as ridiculous. Though his mom had long since happily remarried and Calder viewed his stepdad as a great guy, he still wanted nothing to do with the institution of marriage. To his way of thinking, marriage only kept good men down. Calder enjoyed women too much to ever settle for one. And truthfully—he winked at a saucy redhead—as much as the ladies seemed to enjoy him, it'd be a damn shame to forever take himself off the market. Vowing to remain available was his gift to womankind.

At least that's what he told himself, and anyone else who cared to ask why he was still single. In the dark of night, Calder suspected the real reason, but no way was he ever acknowledging the fact.

He, Mason and Cooper drank in silence for a while, staring out at the crowded dance floor. It was Eighties Night and Duran Duran blared over the sound system about hungry wolves.

Mason was first to break the conversational silence. "I've bitched about Melissa so much, you guys could probably recite my story for me. But in all these years, you two have never told yours."

Calder said, "That's because I don't have one."

Cooper tipped his cowboy hat. "Same here."

Mason twisted to face them. "You're telling me neither of you have ever been serious with a member of the fairer sex?"

"Nope," Cooper said. "Damn proud of it."

"Amen, brother." Calder and Cooper clinked beers.

Mason whistled. "You two are a rare, fortunate breed."

Calder grinned. "We know."

Only after downing his burger and taking a spin on the dance floor with not one blonde but three, Calder spotted a brunette who reminded him of the new nanny. His stomach lurched upon the realization that despite all his bragging, he'd enjoyed sharing a conversation with her in his kitchen, watching his boy chow down on his cookie, more than he had spending the past three hours in this bar.

PANDORA JUMPED WHEN the front door opened and in walked Calder. Almost nine, with Quinn long since tucked in for the night, she'd been alone for so long that the house almost felt as if it were her own.

"What's going on?" he asked, opening the entry-hall closet to set his motorcycle helmet on the top shelf.

"Not much. You?"

He sat in the armchair adjacent to the sofa. Was it her imagination or did he smell like a bar?

Though it was none of her business where he'd been, she asked, "Tired? You worked late." Early in her recovery, the faint trace of booze on his breath would've had her craving a drink. Now realizing how much those drinks had ultimately cost in regard to her daughter...? She was content to stick with sweet tea.

He shrugged. "I'm good. Workwise, it was a pretty slow day, so afterward, me and a few friends stopped off for a burger and beer. I chilled there for a while to be sure I was sober enough to drive."

She nodded.

"Quinn all right?"

"Perfect."

The house's silence that had only a few minutes earlier been comforting now served as a reminder of just how awkward her new position may be. She'd never stayed with a family before and she hadn't thought about the situation from the perspective that for all practical purposes, she now lived with this man.

Drip, drip, drip went the kitchen sink.

Outside, the neighbor's dog barked.

"Well…" Calder leaned forward, resting his elbows on his knees. "Since we're probably both thinking it, I'm going to come right out and say it—this is weird."

She exhaled with relief. "You're feeling it, too?"

"No offense, but the way you're sitting there all prim and proper like my mom, I'm afraid you're going to ground me for missing curfew."

She laughed. "Trust me, I'm the last person who'd judge." Although if she were in his position, she wouldn't waste so much as a second away from his son. She'd learned the hard way what it was like when you weren't able to see your child. The pain was indescribable.

"Now that we've got that dealt with—" he stood, tugging his T-shirt over his head "—I'm gonna grab a quick shower, then study a new manual."

"Um, sure." Her cheeks blazed. Faced yet again with his muscled-up chest, she was grateful he retreated to his room. The part of her craving adult conversation realized Calder's vanishing act was for the best.

He was her boss.

Not her friend—certainly not anyone whose bare chest she should be appraising.

Chapter Three

"Since you're still up, there's something I want to run past you."

An hour had gone by since they'd last talked, but judging by the way Pandora jumped when Calder entered the room, she'd been deeply absorbed in a parenting book.

"Scintillating?" he teased, running his hand over his bare chest.

When she glanced up at him, her cheeks reddened. "Um, not really. Just researching the proper way to introduce Quinn to more solid foods."

He nodded, fighting a flash of guilt for not having read the book he'd bought months earlier. "Last time I talked to my mom, she mentioned that."

"Oh?" Pandora's red cheeks fairly glowed. Ducking behind her book, she added, "That's nice."

What was her problem?

The air-conditioning kicked on, chilling what moisture still clung to his chest from the shower. Then it dawned on him—prim-and-proper Wonder Nanny didn't like him not wearing a shirt. She'd be the first woman in history who disapproved of his eight-pack, but as her employer, he supposed professional courtesy dictated he be fully dressed. Ducking into his room, he grabbed a clean T-shirt from an unfolded basket of laundry. After tugging it over his head, he returned to the living room. "I know I told you I didn't want to talk about Quinn's mother until I had a few beers in my system, but I guess since you're now his primary caregiver, you need to know why I'm not the sharpest tool in the shed when it comes to parenting."

"I've seen worse." She sipped from her iced tea.

"Not sure if that's good or bad."

"Good," she assured.

He struggled for the right place to start. "Until a couple months ago, I didn't know Quinn existed. Back then, I shared an apartment with friends and one morning I opened the door to find Quinn in his carrier. A Post-it attached to the handle pretty much said his mom quit and now it was my turn to be his parent."

Hands over her mouth, Pandora's striking green eyes shone with unshed tears. "That's crazy. Where is she now? What if something had happened to him while he was alone? You don't even know anything about his medical records."

"Yeah," he said with a sarcastic chuckle, "tell me about it. I took him to a pediatrician and he seems healthy. Had a DNA test run and sure enough, he's mine. Only—and I'm not proud of this—I don't have a clue who his mom could be."

"You haven't heard from her? How could she just leave her child without at least reassuring herself that he's okay? What if you hadn't even been home, but off on one of your missions?"

"Valid questions." Running his hand over his whisker-stubbled jaw, Calder said, "I have to assume she knew my car, and when she saw it parked out front, guessed I was home. Still, the whole thing's thrown me off my game. I've been asking tons of questions from everyone I know who has a kid. Bought this house so Quinn would have a backyard. Tonight was the first time I've been out with my friends in what feels like forever."

"Was it as fun as you've no doubt imagined?"

Leaning back in his chair, he stared at the ceiling. "It was all right." What he wouldn't admit was that his good time had been partially ruined by mental images of her. Of wondering what she and Quinn were doing. Was the little guy playing with his plastic boats in the bath? All of which made no sense, considering how grateful he'd been to hand over his kid to a practical stranger.

"Sorry. Hopefully, now that I'm here, you can get back to your old routine."

"Yeah. That'd be good." But would it? And now that Calder had Quinn, was it even possible to revert to the way his life used to be? Before having a kid, he'd had no worries beyond making it to duty on time. Now he had a constant streaming checklist of diapers and baby food and formula. Granted, all of that was now Pandora's domain, but what kind of dad would he be to just let her take over Quinn's parenting in full?

"You ever worry about what you'll do if Quinn's mother suddenly shows up, wanting to take him back?"

"Thought's crossed my mind." In those first rough days, he'd found himself praying for just such a scenario. But as time went on, he'd gotten angry. Calder might not be the best dad, but he sure as hell would never leave his kid on a doorstep. "At this point, I doubt any judge would grant custody to a mother who pulled this kind of stunt. I mean, what kind of woman abandons her child?"

"I don't know...." Was it his imagination, or had she paled?

As much as Pandora cherished Calder's quiet home during her first day, she struggled falling asleep in the still of night. After hours of fitful tossing and turning, she was relieved to hear Quinn cry over the baby monitor.

She went to him, scooping him from his crib for a quick diaper change before making him a bottle. By this age, she was surprised he wasn't sleeping through the night, but after what Calder told her, she suspected the little guy was waking not from hunger, but an innate need for reassurance that while he'd slept, his world hadn't once again fallen apart.

In the kitchen, Quinn on her hip, she said to the sleepy boy, "When your dad told me your mom abandoned you, I felt sad. But then I felt guilty. By choosing to drink over raising my little girl, is that what I did to her?"

Quinn nuzzled his head against her neck. His warmth, the downy-soft feel of his hair, filled her with achy longing for her own child.

Soon, Julia. Soon.

Her next court date wasn't until spring, but that was okay. By then, she'd have saved even more money—enough to provide her daughter with the true home she'd always deserved.

Pandora turned on the overhead light, heated the formula and poured the liquid into Quinn's bottle. But as she tried to add water to the pan with one hand, it slipped, clanging Quinn into instant, startled tears.

"I'm sorry," she crooned, setting the bottle on the counter to free both her arms for soothing. "I didn't mean to scare you. It was just a loud noise. Nothing *really* scary." Like the nightmares she still had of the day her Julia had been taken.

"Everything all right?" Calder, wearing nothing but athletic shorts, hovered on the kitchen's threshold. As was beginning to be habit, her mouth went dry at just the sight of him and her pulse raced. At what point did her body get the memo that as her boss, not only was the man off limits, but she had no interest in romance—period? Her life's sole focus was regaining custody of her child.

"Fine," she murmured, wishing she wore more than a

flimsy, too-short nightgown. "Sorry we woke you. I dropped a pan, which scared this guy."

"Glad it was nothing major." He ambled toward the fridge. "Got anything good in here?"

"There's leftover meat loaf from dinner. If you'll take Quinn, I'll make you a sandwich."

He groaned. "I know making late-night snacks for me is hardly the job description I gave to your agency, but man, does that sound like a good trade."

Laughing, she handed him the baby, trying to ignore the almost electric awareness stemming from an act as simple as brushing against his hands and forearms. Even harder to ignore, though, was the heat radiating from his magnificent chest—and his smell. Manly soap mixed with faint sweat.

Reminding herself of the task at hand, she made quick work of assembling his meal while he sat at the table with Quinn. "Ketchup or mayo?"

"Gotta go with ketchup."

"Warm or cold?"

With another happy groan, he asked, "Woman, how has some lucky guy not snatched you up?"

If he only knew…. "Stick to the question at hand, sir."

"Fair enough." He failed to look remotely chastised. "I'm used to eating pretty near anything, anywhere, but since you asked, warm sounds off-the-chart good."

She nuked the sandwich. When the microwave dinged, she set his plate in front of him. "Be careful. It could be too hot."

"Thanks. If this tastes anywhere near as good as it smells, I might steal you away from Quinn to make you my personal chef."

Pandora held out her arms for the baby, steeling herself to disregard any physical pleasure stemming from the exchange. "Judging by what you've told me about your eating habits, sounds like he needs me more than you."

"Probably true."

When Calder took his first bite, Pandora realized she'd been holding her breath in anticipation of his verdict. It shouldn't matter whether or not he liked her silly sandwich, but it did.

Only when he smiled did she exhale. "All I can say is wow. If the mashed-up food you feed Quinn is half as good as this, he is one lucky kid."

Fairly glowing from Calder's compliment, Pandora had the feeling she was the lucky one.

After his latest bite, Calder glanced at her, then cocked his head. "You look different."

"I'm, um, not wearing my glasses. They're mainly for reading and driving. Long-distance stuff."

He nodded. "You look good—not that I mind glasses, just that…" He reddened. "I'm gonna finish my sandwich."

Mortification didn't come close to describing the emotion surging through Pandora. She looked *good*? What did that even mean? In manspeak, was that a step above ugly, yet beneath homely? Moreover, why did she care?

"So it's the middle of the night," Calder said to his friends during a break in day two of smart-bomb training. "I hear Quinn screaming, only once I find him in the kitchen with the new nanny, he's already settled down. And damn if she doesn't look pretty good in this skimpy naughty-nightie number. Her hair was all down and a little crazy and she'd even lost her glasses. Anyway, so next thing I know—"

Mason whistled. "You two put the baby to bed, then got busy?"

"Get your mind out of the gutter." Calder smacked the back of Mason's head with one of the wiring manuals they were supposed to be studying. "From there, she makes me a meat-loaf sandwich I swear was better than sex."

"Sounds to me like you're not doing it right." Heath high-fived Mason.

Calder shot them both dirty looks.

Cooper never stopped reading.

"All I'm saying is I think I found a keeper."

"Don't you mean Quinn found a keeper?" Deacon asked.

"Who asked you, married man?"

Finishing the last swig of his bottled water, Deacon shrugged. "Just pointing out that for a guy who hates female attachments, and considering this nanny's only been on the job twenty-four hours, you're sounding awfully content."

"What's wrong with that? As long as I keep things professional with Pandora, I can see this working out for a nice long time. I do what I want. Quinn's getting great care. It's a win-win for all involved."

Heath snorted. "What's the nanny getting out of it?"

Calder winked. "The pleasure of seeing me."

"It's a little bare, but it has good bone structure." Natalie, in her official capacity as the owner of Earth Angels, the child-care agency Pandora worked for, finished her walk-through of Calder's home and set her clipboard on the kitchen counter. "I know it's only been one night, but how was it?"

"Good." Pandora held Quinn, waging a playful battle over who had control of her glasses. So far, the baby was winning.

"Care to elaborate?"

"It was very good. Awkward at first, but I guess that's to be expected. Did you know Quinn was literally left on Calder's doorstep? Calder's only had him a few months."

"Whoa." Natalie sat at the table. "Sure your new boss wasn't pulling your leg? He certainly didn't divulge any of that while filling out his paperwork. Sounds crazy."

"Tell me about it. Remember how when I first asked about

Quinn's mother, he put me off? I assumed they must've had a nasty divorce, but I never expected anything like this."

Quinn squirmed to be let down, so Pandora set him on the wood floor she'd cleaned earlier that morning.

"Luckily, Quinn doesn't show signs of abandonment issues."

"He did wake up around two last night. Seemed more interested in having a nice cuddle than a bottle."

"Poor thing...." Natalie shook her head, then sighed. "Well, I've got two more stops, then a mountain of paperwork back at the office, so I'd better go."

When she stood, Pandora gave her friend a hug. "Even though your stay was official, it was nice seeing you. We should do lunch."

"For sure. And didn't you have a visit with Julia last Saturday? How'd it go?"

"I wish. Her foster family rented a beach house, so we needed to postpone until this week."

Just thinking about seeing her daughter filled Pandora with anticipation, but also resentment. To her way of thinking, Julia should've been returned at least a year ago.

"I know that look," Natalie said with another quick hug. "Be patient. Before you know it, you'll be spending every night going over homework and driving to soccer practice."

Pandora crossed her arms. "From your lips to God's ears...."

"YOU'RE HOME EARLY."

In the entry hall, Calder shrugged. "A few guys were setting up a volleyball game down at the beach, but I wasn't feeling it. You two, on the other hand, look like you're having fun." Pandora sat on the floor with Quinn, building a block tower. When she placed the last block on top, he knocked the whole thing down, shrieking and laughing with delight. In the short time he'd had his son, Calder had never seen him this happy, which produced a mixed bag of emotions. Part of him was thrilled with Quinn's smile, but another side of him regretted not having been able to produce the same results.

Pandora grinned up at him. "It's looking more and more like your son is destined to become Master of the Universe."

"Sounds like a noble calling." That was it. The last of anything witty he had to say. Pandora and Quinn were back to their two-person game and Calder stood there like an oaf, not sure what to do with his hands.

Why hadn't he gone to the beach with his friends?

He knew why. Guilt had damn near eaten him alive. The whole point of hiring a nanny—aside from caring for Quinn—was so Calder could get back some semblance of his former life. So why did he feel like a louse each time he tried to do just that?

She glanced his way. "Want to take over for me? I should probably start dinner."

"Sure." Inspiration struck. "But would you rather pack up the kiddo and head down to the beach to hang with my team? They're cooking out."

"Will there be a lot of drinking?" Of all the questions she might have asked, that wasn't one he'd expected.

"Maybe beer. But it's a *school* night, so if you're worried about Quinn being around a bunch of drunk guys, I doubt anyone's going to get hammered."

She fiddled with her messy ponytail. "I don't even own a bathing suit."

"You don't have to go in the water. Come on, it'll be fun." And it sure as hell beat sitting around here, trying to drum up something clever to say.

"I don't know...." The way she worried her lower lip, drawing it into her mouth so a sliver of her teeth showed, struck him as sexy.

"Come on. Think of it as an official duty. I'm making you go, since I'd like to be with Quinn *and* my friends. More important, if you're not there, who'll hold the baby while I play?"

She sighed, but pushed to her feet. "Give me a sec to change into shorts and get gear and a bottle for Quinn."

"WHOA, THIS A MIRAGE?"

"Lay off, Hopper," Calder said to one of the guys they'd just approached. Feeling awkward around more of the hulking SEALs who were similar in stature to her boss, Pandora welcomed the distraction of Quinn making his usual play for her glasses.

Calder made introductions and everyone seemed nice, but once the volleyball game started and she and Quinn were relegated to the sidelines to sit with a girlfriend of one of the SEALs, Pandora felt like the proverbial third wheel.

Which shouldn't have mattered.

It wasn't as if she and Calder were even friends, so why had a twinge of disappointment lodged in her belly over the fact that for all practical purposes, she might as well be invisible? It was ridiculous.

Though she'd worked for her last family over a year, she could count on one hand the number of times she'd spoken to the girls' father. What was it about this position that should be any different?

Calder's team scored and he high-fived the other guys.

As was starting to be an alarming trend, he'd taken off his shirt. His friends had also lost theirs. The level of male perfection, highlighted in the sun's early-evening glow was undeniably heady. Yet, at the same time, it left Pandora feeling all the more lonely. It was obvious these men were a tight family unit.

The woman beside Pandora constantly cheered on her man.

Even Quinn unearthed something more interesting than her. His expression turned intense while studying driftwood he'd found in the sand.

Pandora may have grown a lot over the years, but sadly, without Julia, she was still on her own, yet craving more. Once and for all, she wanted to be part of a real family. But she knew better than to think she'd find that in a man like Calder. Even if they'd met under different circumstances, what would he want with her? They came from opposite worlds. He was college educated, as she'd seen from the framed diploma he'd stacked along with other yet-to-be-hung pictures in the linen closet.

Had he known Quinn's mom carried his child, would he have married her? What qualities would he find attractive enough in a woman to make him want to stick around?

Chapter Four

"I can't get used to the idea of Calder being a dad."

Pandora glanced up from feeding Quinn his bottle to find a pretty redhead sitting beside her. They'd finished grilling hot dogs and the guys had returned to their game.

"I'm Patricia, by the way."

"Pandora. Nice to meet you." She shook her new friend's hand.

The baby grunted at the interruption in his bottle, but soon enough was back to contentedly downing his meal.

The team playing opposite Calder's spiked a ball deep into their territory, and the men erupted into a slew of good-natured name-calling—further startling the baby.

"Rowdy bunch, huh?" Patricia ran her hand along Quinn's downy hair while Pandora comforted him.

"I've seen worse." No way was Pandora prepared to share the number of drug-induced bar fights she'd witnessed. During her blackest moments, when alcohol had no longer been enough, she'd done and seen things that to this day made her deeply ashamed. She may have technically paid for her crimes, but that didn't mean her soul had been cleared from all wrongdoing.

"My guy's Heath—that big lug to Calder's right. If you're like me, it'll take forever to get everyone's names straight."

"I can see why." Quinn had finished his bottle, so Pandora

tucked it into his diaper bag, trading it for a burping cloth she positioned over her left shoulder. She eased the fussy baby upright for burping and soon enough, despite the noise, he struggled to keep his eyes open.

"I can't wait to have kids." Patricia gazed longingly toward Quinn. "My birthday's Sunday and rumor has it, Heath's finally popping the question. We plan to get started on our family right away."

"Want to hold him?" Pandora offered her the baby.

"Yes, please." The switch was awkward and filled with laughing.

"Mmm…" Cradling Quinn, Patricia closed her eyes and smiled. "He's amazing. When Heath told me the story of how this cutie was abandoned, it still makes me mad. Like, seriously? Who does such a thing? That woman was the world's worst mother. Probably strung out on booze or worse."

"No doubt." A knot formed at the back of Pandora's throat. No matter how hard she swallowed, it refused to budge. Would it always be this tough? Remembering the woman she used to be? She had no right judging Quinn's mom, as she'd once been every bit as bad.

"Quinn smells so good. I come from a large family, but since I was the baby, I never got to play with a real live one till my nieces and nephews started coming."

"Must've been amazing," Pandora said, "growing up in a big, loving family."

"Mostly it was." She laughed. "Although, I still cringe when I think of sharing a bathroom with so many people."

Patricia's statement had been innocent enough, but brought still more bad memories of the halfway house where Pandora had spent the past couple years. It had sure beaten living on the streets, but in some ways it had been harder. So many people and rules. So many reminders of how close she'd come to losing it all.

Reminding herself those days were finally behind her, Pandora forced a smile. "How long have you and Heath been together?"

"Two excruciatingly long years." Cradling Quinn, her smile turned wistful. "It's hard enough being with a SEAL—you never know when they're coming or going. Only the wives have any glimmer of real knowledge as to what's going on. We lowly girlfriends never know anything."

"Oh—I'm not Calder's girlfriend," Pandora said quickly. "Just Quinn's nanny."

"Sorry. I forgot. We don't see many of those. How long have you been with him?"

Pandora laughed. "Actually, this is only my second night. So far, so good."

Quinn started to fuss.

"Spoke too soon?" Pandora didn't mind when Patricia returned Quinn to her waiting arms. She'd only been with the infant a short while, but she'd already learned to decipher his basic cries. Hunger. Dirty diaper. Sleepy. Babies were relatively simple to figure out.

Quinn's father, on the other hand…

In the setting sun's orange glow, Pandora made the mistake of looking up to find Calder in all his bare-chested glory rising up to spike the ball. He struck her as powerful and in control—not at all the same man she'd encountered when Quinn had been choking. Assuming Calder worked with the same efficiency in his capacity as a SEAL as he did on the volleyball court, what did that say about his parenting skills? The fact that the only time he appeared truly happy and at peace was when he wasn't caring for his son.

Not that Pandora was judging. Just curious to discover more about him.

Calder's team won, but by the time they'd defended their

victory by besting their challengers in a two-out-of-three se-ries, the sunset's glow had long since faded to dark.

Quinn slept soundly against her, and since Patricia and her soon-to-be fiancé had skipped out a while back, Pandora had spent the past hour staring out at the dark surf. She grew up on the wrong side of the tracks in small-town Virginia, so her only memories of visiting the beach were imagined. Fourth of Julys she'd dreamed of watching fireworks. Run-ning barefoot in the sand with a whole pack of sparklers all for herself. Birthdays she'd envisioned with friends splash-ing with her in the surf and building sand castles. In her rich fantasy life, she'd even had mermaid-themed cupcakes and balloons.

Back to reality, it was hard to believe she'd finally met her lifelong dream of seeing the Atlantic. The faint, briny-scented breeze and the rhythmic crashing of the waves proved hyp-notic, making her think of a life that might've been. Regret upon regret for not at least giving her own daughter the hap-piness she deserved.

"Ready?" Calder asked beside her, jolting her to the pres-ent.

"Ah, sure." It took her a few seconds to regain her compo-sure. But then her boss took Quinn, inadvertently brushing her breasts in the trade-off. Only, the invasion of her personal space didn't feel like an invasion at all. More like the kind of natural thing that happens between a man and woman shar-ing a relationship and raising a child.

But they didn't share any of that. For all practical pur-poses, they were strangers.

"Sorry." He held out his hand to help her to her feet.

"It's okay." She accepted his help, but soon regretted the decision. When their fingers touched, the usual sparks were there tenfold, making her unsure about her next move. Had he felt it, too?

If so, he showed no indication. All polite business, he fastened Quinn into his carrier, then hefted the baby and diaper bag. "That everything?"

"Uh-huh." Except for the irrational part of her wondering what it would be like to have a real connection with a man as decent as Calder.

"THIS WAS GOOD." Over the years, Calder had had many women in his passenger seat, but none who set him on edge quite like Pandora. Why, he didn't know, but he took her prim posture and pressed-lip silence to mean he'd done something wrong. Knowing full well he hadn't and was just being paranoid, he decided to make a game out of coaxing the woman to speak. "You and Quinn have fun?"

"We did. The beach is always a treat."

"Yeah?" He glanced her way to find her fogging her glasses, then wiping them on a tissue she'd drawn from her purse. "What was your favorite thing about spending time at the shore?"

She slowly exhaled. "I liked the smell. The waves sounded just like I've always imagined."

"Wait." Stopped at a red light, he turned to her. "You mean to tell me tonight was your first trek to the beach?"

"Embarrassing, right?"

After checking the rearview mirror to ensure there were no other cars around, Calder made a U-turn.

"What're you doing?"

"Well, hell, woman." He shot her a sideways grin. "You're a bona fide Atlantic virgin—an elusive and mystical creature, to be sure."

"Sure you weren't spiking your cola?"

"Nope." He made a left, aiming the SUV back to where they'd just come from. "We're on a mission."

"To do what?"

"Something we would've done earlier if I'd known what a momentous occasion this was. We need to get those toes of yours in the water."

"Calder, you're being silly." She glanced to the backseat. "It's already late and Quinn's covered in sand. He'll need a quick bath before bed and I'll need to clean his carrier."

"So? It's not like you have to be at a desk bright and early."

"But you no doubt do."

"Haven't you learned it's impolite to argue with your boss?"

He took her shy smile to mean he'd broken at least a small part of her reserve. "Please don't take this the wrong way, but are you mentally stable enough to protect our country?"

For a split second, he thought she was serious, but then he caught her wink and burst out laughing. "You almost had me."

"You've got to admit this whole notion of sticking my toes in the water sounds a bit off the deep end."

Now he winked. "I'm not suggesting you go deep, Ms. Moore. Merely dip your toes in the shallow end. It's a serious rite of passage."

"It's a rite of passage that can wait. Quinn's comfort and needs come first."

"In case you haven't noticed—" he veered into the parking spot they'd vacated only ten minutes earlier "—Quinn is out. I don't think he'll mind the slight detour."

After having a look for herself, she said, "You've got me there." In the glow of the dash lights, her expression morphed from doubt to wary acceptance to anticipation. "But is this really prudent?"

He laughed. "Does it matter? Come on." He almost held out his hand to her, but then thought better of it. He wanted to have a little fun, but not present the image of being interested in *that* way. "Last one in is a rotten egg!"

"Who's getting Quinn?"

"Me, so you'd better hustle."

Pandora kicked off her sandals and ran and ran, laughing until she reached the shore. The water was cold but refreshing and unexpected and hit her as an affirmation her life was finally on the right track. Granted, her current actions may not be dignified, but for at least a few minutes that was okay. She could let her guard down a smidge—just not too much.

Had she denied herself the beach's simple pleasures for so long because she hadn't felt good enough? Like only clean, wholesome people visit such enchanted places?

"How is it?" Calder asked from behind her. Quinn slept cradled against him.

"Wonderful," she admitted. And honestly, if she hadn't had to work so hard to earn her way to this spot, this very moment in time, she might not have appreciated it for the miracle it truly was. As soon as she regained custody of Julia, a trip to the beach was in order.

"If you don't mind my asking," he said above the surf that pounded louder than it had earlier, "how's it even possible you've lived around here yet have never been to the shore?"

"Just one of those things." Though her gut told her she could probably trust him with the truth, her head warned the less he knew about her past, the better off they'd both be.

The nighttime breeze had considerably cooled the air.

Pandora said, "We should get back to the car."

"What's your hurry?"

"I-it's cold." At first, she'd been exhilarated by their fun, but now she was somewhat ashamed. Almost as if being in such a clean, family-friendly place might mark her a fraud. But was she? She'd worked hard to get to the healthy emotional zone in which she now resided. Didn't that count for something?

She wiped tears from her cheeks, glad for the darkness so Calder wouldn't see.

"You okay?"

"Sure." She hoped her exaggerated nod read as convincing.

"It's all right, you know."

"Wh-what?"

"If the sight of moonlight on the ocean moves you." He reached his hand toward her, brushing first one tear-stained cheek, then the other with the pad of his thumb.

His touch affected her far more deeply than it should have. Embarrassed, she looked away. "I'm fine—the wind blew sand in my eyes."

"Locational hazard...." His soft tone told her he knew she was lying. The fact both mortified her and filled her with hope he'd never guess just how much their shared moment had truly meant. Whatever their future, she'd always associate him with the moment she realized her efforts really were finally making a difference. Soon, she'd not only have her daughter returned, but her dignity.

MIDWAY THROUGH CHANGING Quinn's diaper at five-thirty the next morning, Calder was startled by Pandora's appearance at his side. Apparently she'd felt as awkward about her choice of late-night attire at their last meeting as he had. Not that he hadn't been appreciative of her miles of creamy skin, but her current chaste, white cotton pj's were infinitely less seductive.

"What're you doing up?" he asked. "We were trying to be extra quiet to let you sleep."

"That's nice of you," she said as she passed the wipes, "but my job description is to care for Quinn in order to allow you more rest."

"I had to be up anyway. Got a text we're doing early drills." After wiping down his son, Calder tossed the soiled diaper in the trash, then reached for a fresh one.

"Put cream on his bottom."

"What cream?"

She handed him a tube. "Last time I changed him, I noticed he looked a little chafed. No biggie. Just something to keep an eye on."

"Sure." Calder flipped open the lid. "How much?"

"A dime."

"Did you grab this stuff at the store?"

"Uh-huh." She stood near enough for him to feel her heat. Not a good thing, considering he hadn't been as smart as her and still slept in just boxers. "Want me to finish up with him so you can grab a shower?"

"Trying to get rid of me?" He was only half teasing. Ever since the beach, she'd been quiet. He'd meant for their outing to be fun, but he couldn't help but wonder what'd brought on her tears. He'd wanted to ask her on the drive home, and again while they'd bathed Quinn, but the timing hadn't seemed right. Besides, were her tears even his business?

"No." Her smile seemed genuine. "Just trying to be helpful."

"Thanks." The more time he shared with Pandora, the more confused he grew. When it came to the fairer sex, he excelled at the short game. One or two nights—tops. Mornings could be tricky, so he avoided them like brussels sprouts. So here he was on his second morning with the nanny and despite the fact they'd barely even spoken, let alone had sex, he honestly wasn't sure how many more he could take. Something about her had him all riled up and flustered—in his line of work, never a good thing.

With Quinn tucked back into his snap-bottom T-shirt, Pandora scooped him up and cradled him against her.

His son looked happy, and that fact calmed Calder's choppy nerves. Truly, he needed to chill. Pandora was the nanny. Nothing more. No need to rely on his usual shtick, or worry about spending too much time with one woman, because she wasn't his woman. If anything, he should treat her like one of the guys. "Got anything going on this weekend? Thought we might get back to the beach, only this time do it up proper. More volleyball. Soggy sandwiches. It'll be great."

"Um…" She looked to the baby, out the window, to the changing table—anywhere but him. "That sounds amazing, but I have plans."

"Oh?" He'd placed her firmly in the friend zone, so why did he feel shot down? It didn't happen often, which left him needing answers. Only because he was her employer, no matter how much he wanted to drill her about what she was doing that could be more important than chilling with him and his son—he knew damn well he couldn't. Shouldn't. It would be a seriously needy move, and Calder never lacked for female attention.

"Rain check? I've never been on a picnic, so…" As her words trailed off, so did her eye contact. Interesting. What would the nanny be doing on Saturday? Or should that *what* be replaced by a *who*?

Chapter Five

Wednesday afternoon, the computers Calder's team had been using to study the latest Afghanistan satellite-photo-intelligence models were down. Cooper and Heath used the opportunity to nap. Calder and Mason had just finished a five-mile run and sat on a bench, soaking in rays.

"Damn nice day," Mason said. "Reminds me why I left Alaska."

Calder had tilted his head back and closed his eyes. He opened them to glance sideways at his friend. "Thought you bolted because of Melissa."

"Well, that, too. But mainly because of the weather."

"Uh-huh. You've given me so much crap over the nanny, I'm shoveling it back your way."

Resting his arms behind his head, Mason said, "Whatever. Speaking of which, haven't heard much about her today. Everything all right?"

Calder sighed. "I guess it's going good. Both Quinn and the house are freakishly clean, and she's a great cook." That said, the beach rejection stung his manly pride. His rational side knew giving the matter a second thought was ridiculous. The part of him used to women falling for his SEAL charm still didn't get it. What had he done wrong? "Look, I shouldn't even mention this to you, but after the volleyball game, I found out Pandora had never been to the beach."

"What?" Mason scratched his head.

"I know, right? Anyway, I've been meaning to spend more time with the little guy, so I figured we'd do the whole day-at-the-shore thing with him on Saturday, only—"

Mason laughed. "She turned you down, didn't she?"

Lips pressed tight, Calder had never wished more he'd kept his big mouth shut.

Still laughing, Mason said, "Mr. Professional Working Relationship who yelled at us for asking if Pandora was a sex-kitten nanny broke his own rule, huh?"

"Forget it. Sorry I brought it up." Calder had honestly thought it would be a good idea to spend time with Quinn. The beach was always fun. The whole thing shouldn't have been a big deal.

Standing, Calder headed back to the building housing their classroom.

"Aw, come on…." Mason trailed after him. "Don't go getting your panties in a wad. I'm sure the nanny has a perfectly good reason for turning down your date."

"It wasn't a date," Calder snapped. "I don't like her that way. Wouldn't be right."

"Might not be right, but if she's hot and you two share tight quarters, what's your plan to keep things platonic?"

Calder tugged open the metal door, welcoming the rush of cool air. "Drop it, okay? I don't need a plan, because nothing's going to happen."

"Then why are you so pissy over her wanting an afternoon for herself?" Mason stopped off at a vending machine.

Though his friend asked a valid question, Calder didn't have an answer. If pressed, he suspected his true problem stemmed from the simple fact he was scared to death of once again being alone with his son.

CALDER RODE STRAIGHT home from the base only to find Quinn and Pandora heading down the block. He parked his bike in the garage, then hollered in their direction, "Wait up!"

After closing the door, he pocketed the opener, jogging to meet them.

"Hey." She veered the stroller against the sidewalk's edge to make room for him. "How was your day?"

He shrugged. Now that he'd caught up with the duo, he wasn't sure why he'd even tried. All smiles, Quinn kicked and made baby noises. Pandora had been smiling. However, since his arrival, she'd pressed her lips into a telling line of tension. "You two headed for the park?"

She nodded. "They have great baby swings—you know? The one's that are safety seats?"

"Guess I've never much noticed."

"Quinn loves them."

Another dig at Calder's parenting? Or lack thereof?

They walked the last two blocks in silence. The temperature was already cooling off with a hint of approaching autumn in the air. Even from their distance, the sounds of kids playing—laughing—rang clearly through the air. He couldn't remember ever having been that kid—fully carefree. Sure, after his mom had remarried, things settled down, but he'd been past the playground age.

Upon reaching the park, it struck Calder as surprisingly full. "There always this many people here?"

"It's a park. Most times, there's even more." Her sideways look, not to mention her pinched expression, didn't sit well with him. Yet again, he felt inept. He'd lived a few blocks from what was apparently a family mecca, yet it'd never even occurred to him it was anywhere he and Quinn might want to be.

"Sorry. I didn't know."

"It's not a big deal, Calder." She parked the stroller in front of the lone empty bench in a row of five. "Now that you're here, want to put Quinn in a swing?"

Visions of Quinn screaming whenever Calder tried cramming him into his car seat ran through his head. "No, thanks."

Pandora effortlessly plucked Quinn from his stroller to plop him into the rubber swing seat and strapped him in. As if the kid knew what came next, he giggled and kicked. The size of his drool-filled grin tugged at Calder's heart.

From Pandora's first small push, Quinn howled with laughter. He clapped his little hands and bounced and kicked. His eyes shone with what Calder could only describe as pure glee. Burning heat forced his eyes to close for a moment while at the same time he swallowed the knot at the back of his throat.

He'd never seen Quinn like this—truly happy. But now that he had, something in him clicked. Was this at least partially what parenting was about? Not just keeping your child fed and clean, but figuring out what produced adorable grins? Then earning them over and over again?

"You want to push?" Pandora stepped aside, urging Calder to give it a try.

"What if I push him too high? Is he going to fall out?"

Hands on her hips, she cocked her head. "Really?"

"Well…" He forced a deep breath. "Stranger things could happen."

Approaching the swing, Calder couldn't have said why, but his pulse raced and his palms began to sweat. He crouched to reach the little guy, then pushed just enough for Quinn to shriek all over again. "He's doing it!"

"You thought he wouldn't?" Pandora asked. "See? You're doing great. Now whenever I'm not around, you can bring him here on your own. Once he starts walking, he's going to love the rope bridge and slide."

Calder took one glance at the wood-planked bridge hanging between two roofed forts. "No way. Too dangerous."

Now Pandora was the one laughing. "If you think that's scary, wait till he gets his first bike."

AFTER YET ANOTHER delicious dinner, helping with Quinn's bath and tucking him in, Calder fired off a few emails, then tracked down Pandora in the laundry room, folding pint-size T-shirts. A few larger ones he recognized as his own were already stacked neatly beside his son's.

"Need help?"

"No, thank you. Almost done." The faint smile she cast over her shoulder made him almost as confused as he'd been that afternoon when he saw his son in the swing. Pandora was constantly doing things for him, but Calder never reciprocated. It was her job to care for Quinn, but she spoiled them both.

"You know I don't expect you to do my laundry."

"I don't mind. Besides, Quinn's whites barely took up half a load."

"Okay, well…" Suddenly tongue-tied in the cramped space, he crammed his hands in the pockets of his fatigues. "Thanks. You're a nice lady." *A nice lady?* Calder mentally smacked his forehead. What the hell kind of line was that?

Forehead furrowed, she half laughed. "Thanks. I think."

He covered his face with his hands. "Sorry. That sounded like I think you're eighty. Obviously, you're not." Her black yoga pants and pink T-shirt hugged her in all the right places—even her crooked ponytail enhanced her pretty glow.

"I hope not." Laughing again, she glanced down shyly before pushing up her glasses. "At eighty, I'm not sure I'll have the energy needed to chase after your son."

"Okay, well, whatever your age, I very much appreciate

all you've been doing—not only for Quinn, but me. You're an angel."

She turned from him to place the folded clothes into a basket. "I wouldn't go that far."

SATURDAY MORNING, Calder bumped into Pandora on her way out of her bedroom. "You smell good." The second the words left his mouth, he kicked himself for yet again having nothing smoother to say. The more he was around Pandora, the more he sounded like a mooning fourth grader. Now that the weekend had arrived and Pandora was obviously dolling herself up for someone, he was merely taking a healthy interest in her day's plans. Any good friend would, right? Only, were they even friends? To cover his confusion, he blurted, "Seeing someone special?"

Quinn sat in his walker, grinning and drooling while pressing a squeaky frog head. *"Rah gaa!"*

"Very." Was it his imagination, or had her green eyes grown brighter from the size of her smile?

Mom? Favorite uncle? Grandmother? *Boyfriend?* So what if she did have a boyfriend? In the week she'd worked for Calder, she'd proved herself to be not only an excellent caregiver for Quinn but a great housekeeper and cook. Calder had no complaints. He'd never even caught her on the phone. Which meant if she did have a boyfriend, they couldn't be all that serious, right?

Squeak, squeak, squeak.

Calder frowned. Even in his own head, he sounded crazy. "When will you be home? Not that this is your home, but it kind of is—well, you know what I mean." Since she'd started caring for Quinn, Calder had backed way off from his own parenting duties. Aside from changing the occasional diaper or playing with his son, he really didn't have all that much to do with the boy. Probably not a good thing, but it was what it was.

Though in his own defense, Calder had taken Quinn back to the park all on his own—twice. He'd even wrangled the kid into the safety seat. Maybe he'd go again today.

"I shouldn't be later than four. Is that all right?"

"Sure." It was already ten. How hot of a date could she have with that little time? He was more relieved than he should be that she hadn't asked for even more time off—like overnight!

"Thanks." She knelt to kiss the top of Quinn's head. "I'll miss you, sweetie."

What about me?

"WHAT DO YOU THINK she's doing?" Calder's SEAL pal Cooper dragged his chip through store-bought guacamole.

On the apartment's big-screen TV, Florida pummeled Georgia.

"Beats me." Before Quinn, Calder had also shared the apartment with Cooper, Mason and Heath. He'd been in his house a month, but he'd lived here with his friends for over three years, meaning this place felt more like home.

"If she is on a date, the guy didn't put much thought into it," Cooper said.

"That's good, right?"

His friend shot him a dirty look. "Maybe for you, but not her. This woman is caring for your kid. The key to you and Quinn being happy is keeping her happy."

"Good point." What Calder didn't understand was why Pandora's pretty smile and green eyes refused to leave his head.

He grabbed another chip and ran it through the guac. Now that he thought about it, Pandora's eyes were a unique, avocado green. He'd always liked avocados.

Quinn fussed in his carrier seat.

Calder offered him a bottle, but that didn't help. His diaper was dry and the kid pitched the pacifier Calder offered. "What do you think he wants?"

"Pick him up." Cooper shoved several chips into his mouth at once. "When my brother was a baby, lots of times he just wanted to be held."

"Makes sense." Calder squatted, scooping the infant up with one hand.

"You're not doing it right." His friend took the baby, pushing Calder out of the way. "Like this." The fact that Cooper hadn't held a baby in a couple decades, yet instantly put Calder's son at ease, incensed him. "You've got to hold him close. Let him know you care."

Do I? The thought killed Calder. He didn't want to be *that* guy—the kind of dad who never connected with his son. No way could he live with eighteen years passing only to realize he'd screwed up everything and his own kid was a virtual stranger. They'd connected at the park, so why not now?

Calder took advantage of Heath and Mason being out on a beer-and-pizza run. "Mind if I ask you a personal question?"

"Shoot."

"I'm not even sure where to start." He tilted his head back, working the muscles on his suddenly tight neck. "You guys all know how Quinn entered my life, and I guess I'm still struggling to form a connection with the little guy. I feel like I should have this instinctive draw toward him, you know? But most days, I'm not even sure what he likes to eat—let alone how to really be a good dad. My own father was hardly a prizewinning specimen, but you come from a great family, right? Since you had a great dad, I was hoping you might share a few pointers."

Cooper snorted. "Hate to be the bearer of bad news, but

you hit up the wrong guy for that information. My advice?" He returned Quinn to Calder. "Buy a parenting book."

PANDORA HUGGED her daughter for all she was worth, then gently pushed her back for a better look. "You've grown an inch since the last time I saw you."

Julia laughed. "Mom Cindy calls me her pretty sunflower 'cause I'm growing so big and tall and pretty!"

"You're beyond pretty," Pandora said past the lump in her throat. "You're gorgeous."

The social worker assigned to Julia's case sat in the corner of the pale blue room with its one window that was meant to be cheerful, but how many times had Pandora been here, praying one day she'd take her daughter home? How many other parents like her were on the same seemingly sinking ship? She'd taken state-mandated parenting courses. She'd proved herself capable of holding a job. Still, in the court's view it wasn't enough. Would it ever be enough?

"Look what I made on vacation!" Her daughter proudly displayed a leaning tower made of driftwood, pebbles, shells and gobs of glue. "Mom Cindy said it's the most *beautifulist* thing she's ever seen."

"She's right." The admission was difficult when all Pandora wanted was to scratch *Mom Cindy*'s eyes out. Jealousy may have consumed her, but she'd come too far to let it show. She'd learned a good mother puts her child's needs ahead of her own, and given how precious little time they had this afternoon, that's exactly what she'd do. "Tell me about the beach. Was it fun?"

While Julia shared tales of jumping into the waves and building a *humongous* castle with her fun new beach toys, Pandora drank it all in, wondering at the coincidence—the cruel twist of fate—of them both experiencing their first day at the shore with different people.

Hanging on to her daughter's every word, it occurred to Pandora that far from being angry with the foster parents assigned to their family's case, she should be grateful. Julia's *Mom Cindy* was a shining example of how the system was supposed to work.

"What's in there?" Julia pointed to the floral gift bag that had pink curly ribbon cascading from the top.

"Gosh, I don't know…" Pandora couldn't resist tugging her girl into another hug. "I was so interested in hearing about your adventure, I forgot what's in the bag."

"No, you didn't." Julia's giggle acted as a balm to Pandora's weary soul. "Tell me, tell me!"

"Okay…" Pandora handed her daughter her gift. "But I don't know if you'll like it."

"I will! I will!" The little girl added jumps to her giggles while tossing the ribbon from the bag. First, she took out a small Junie B. Jones doll, then three of the first books in the series outlining the turbulent, yet hilarious, tales of the girl's kindergarten experience. Largely due to Pandora's mistakes, Julia was starting first grade, though she should have been entering second grade. "She's pretty! I love her!"

"These books tell all about what happens to her at school. I thought it might be fun to sit and read them together. What do you think?"

Julia nodded. "Mom Cindy reads to me. It's nice."

"I'm glad, sweetie. Always remember, books are your friends." Seated on a too-stiff formal sofa, Pandora made the best of the awkward situation by patting the cushion alongside her. "Come over here and let's find out what happens…"

Turned out the social worker was a Junie B. fan and hadn't heard the stories since her own child had been small. The three of them laughed together until it was time for Julia to meet back up with her foster parents. Though it was harder than anything she'd ever done, Pandora thanked them for providing such a stable foundation for her daughter.

Then the visit was over.

During the long drive to Calder's, she indulged in a nice long cry. Better to get her tears out privately. Quinn deserved her best, and spending the remainder of her day weepy certainly wouldn't solve the many problems of her own making. For those, the only solution was time. At least now she'd pass that time in a comfortable environment where she knew she'd make a positive difference.

The closer she came to the house, the more her pulse raced with the realization that she was excited to see her sweet charge.

What about his criminally handsome father?

Pandora chose to ignore that thought. She also wanted to forget how she'd fought the strangest urge to give Calder a proper hug goodbye that morning.

Madness. But she supposed, given their forced proximity and the fact that they'd essentially become a ready-made family, her reaction was understandable. As long as she understood the reasons behind her feelings, she could ignore them and keep her primary goal in mind—regaining custody of Julia. Nothing else mattered.

Pandora pulled into the driveway and pressed the button on the automatic garage-door opener, her mouth dry, pulse racing as if returning to this happy place was her own special gift—one that Calder had made possible.

Once inside, anticipation filled her to see him and his son.

Only, they weren't there.

Despite the fact that Calder's car was gone, Pandora looked everywhere. Bedrooms. Living room. Backyard.

When her fruitless search led to her sitting alone on the couch, she kicked off her sandals, drew her feet up beside her then resigned herself to wait.

BY THE TIME Calder got home, he had heartburn from too many of Cooper's hot wings, the Gators had lost by ten and Quinn was squalling. All in all, it'd been a less than stellar day. Seeing Pandora's car already in the garage should've made him feel better, but it didn't.

Calder felt stupid for ever even asking her to the beach. From here on out, he vowed to play it cool. Hell, she worked for him, meaning he wasn't *playing* at all.

He always had trouble getting Quinn from his car seat and this time proved no different. By the time Calder held him safely in his arms, he was surprised the kid could breathe through his screams.

In the living room, Calder found Pandora crashed on the sofa.

She woke in a heartbeat, rushing to take the inconsolable baby. "What's wrong?" she crooned in the kind of ethereal-soft tone his son seemed to love. "Poor baby. Your diaper feels dry." To Calder, she asked above the wailing, "Is he hungry?"

"Could be." He dumped the diaper bag on the nearest chair. "Hell, I don't know. He's been crying the whole way home. It hasn't been *that* long since he had his last bottle, but you know how time can get away from you when a game's on."

She cast him an incredulous look.

Her attention back to his son, she said, "Let's get some nice formula in your tummy, then you'll feel better."

Somehow, Pandora managed to not only hold his son, but fix a bottle and hum all at the same time. Once she held the bottle to Quinn's lips, greedy suckling commenced, making Calder feel like the world's most inept father. What was wrong with him? How could he have let his infant son get this hungry?

In under a few minutes, Quinn had almost drained the bottle and his eyes had drifted closed.

Pandora relocated to the living room sofa, cradling Quinn while still humming her song.

In an angry whisper she said, "I left premade bottles for you in the fridge. Didn't you even look?"

"Sure, and I took all of them and he drank them. Maybe I gave them to him too soon, and then he was crazy hungry later? You tell me." Plenty miffed, Calder crossed his arms. "You're the expert."

She shook her head. "You're impossible."

"I'm good—*great*—at a lot of things, but infant care isn't one of them. I never signed on for this."

"Really?" She laughed, but the sound struck him as cold. "News flash—the moment you chose to sleep with Quinn's mom without protection...? You pretty much signed a lifelong contract."

"Sorry I'm not perfect like you."

Calder had expected a snappy comeback—what he got was a whole lot of silence, then tears.

He followed her when she went to the nursery to change Quinn's diaper, brush his tiny teeth then tuck him into his crib. Only when she'd turned out the nursery lights and quietly shut the door did she respond. "For the record, I'm about as far from perfect as anyone can get. Good night."

He wanted to say more—a helluva lot more, but she'd ducked into her own room and shut that door, too.

"IF YOU WANT my opinion, let it go."

With Quinn happily batting at the stuffed cow hanging from his carrier's handle, Pandora paced her friend's office. "I know, but Calder hit a nerve with that one. Worse—here I was lecturing him for being a bad parent when I'm pretty sure I'm featured in the Lousy Parent Hall of Shame."

Natalie left her desk to wrap Pandora in a hug. "Trust me, there are worse parents out there than you. If I hadn't seen with my own eyes how hard you've worked to turn your life around, I wouldn't have believed it. You're a textbook example of how to make lemons into lemonade."

"But am I?" Sitting in the guest chair, Pandora slid her fingers into her hair. "Saturday, during my time with Julia, she kept bringing up her foster mom, Cindy, and I was so jealous I could've screamed."

"I presume you didn't?"

"No, but…" She wrung her hands. "What if I had? What's inside me that makes me want to snap?"

Her friend took the seat alongside her. "Could it be you're human?"

Outside, the day was gloomy. Earlier, there'd been storms, but for now a light drizzle had settled in. The air held just enough of a nip to remind her of the rapidly approaching fall.

The weather suited Pandora's mood.

After Saturday's visit with Julia, she'd been on top of the world. Returning to Calder's empty house had been mood dampening. But then when he had returned with his cranky son, her spirits had gone from bad to worse. She'd imagined them maybe sharing a nice dinner, then watching TV before putting the baby to bed. What really happened had left her on edge and unable to sleep for hours. Why had she let him get to her? Deep down, maybe she feared his belief that she was the image of perfect motherhood might lead to potential disaster when—*if*—he ever learned her truth.

"What're you thinking?" Natalie asked.

"Wish I knew." Leaning forward, Pandora rested her elbows on her knees, covering her face with her hands. "Calder's my boss—nothing more. I owe him zilch but my promise to give excellent care to his son."

"You're not falling for him, are you?"

"No." Pandora laughed. "That's ridiculous. I barely know him. Besides, things between us are strictly professional." *Except for the way my pulse races every time his gaze meets mine.*

"So what's the problem?"

She glared at her friend. "If I knew, I wouldn't be here, would I?"

Lips pressed tight, Natalie seemed to think an awfully long time before she said, "Please don't take this the wrong way, but are you afraid that if Calder finds out you lost Julia, he may fire you?"

"Honestly?" Pandora sighed. "That's exactly what's wrong. This is the best job I've ever had. Assuming I still have it by the time I get Julia back, I suppose I'll tell Calder everything, but until then…?" She gazed outside. "Guess I'd like him to get to know the current me as opposed to the wretched person I used to be."

PANDORA STAYED AT Natalie's office longer than she'd planned. By the time she returned to Calder's house, she noted his motorcycle parked in the garage. Despite still being upset with him for the way they'd left things the previous night, she hated that he'd ridden home from work in the rain.

Entering the kitchen through the back door, she held Quinn in the crook of one arm and her purse and diaper bag with her other.

Calder stood at the kitchen counter sipping from a mug filled with steaming, fragrant coffee. He wore no shirt and a pair of Go Navy sweats. His hair looked damp. His chiseled profile was so strikingly handsome, her mouth went dry and her pulse skyrocketed.

"Why didn't you call me?" was the first stupid thing she thought to say. "I could've picked you up."

"No biggie. I didn't mind getting wet. Besides, it's not as if you were here, waiting by the phone." He winked.

She set her keys and bags on the kitchen table.

Awkward silence between them took on a physical hum.

"About last night," he finally said after a gulp of his coffee. "I—"

"I owe you an apology. That crack about a condom—it was completely inappropriate and unprofessional. Won't happen again." She glanced down at her tiny charge. His grin not only warmed her through and through but made her wonder what she was doing. She knew the only reason she'd been upset with Calder had more to do with her own insecurities rather than anything he'd done. How many times had she been too drunk to pick up Julia from day care? Or too broke to buy milk—let alone cereal? "I just hated hearing Quinn cry and it set me on edge."

"Understandable. His crying had me almost crazy." He sighed. "I'm sorry for that snap about you being perfect. But you have to know, compared to me, you pretty much are." He held out his hand for her to shake. "Truce?"

"Yeah." When she pressed her palm to his, her fingers to his, her every nerve ending pulsed. The attraction she felt for him was unlike anything she'd felt before. Unnerving in the way his lightest touch made her crave more. But Julia was her only priority. Getting close to her boss wasn't even an option.

"Cool." He opened the fridge. "What's your plan for dinner?"

She looked at him, then Quinn, then laughed. "What do you want?"

"Anything that doesn't come from a bag or box. If I pay extra, could I bribe you into making more of your meat loaf—a double batch so there's enough for leftovers and sandwiches?"

"No bribe necessary. Assuming we have all the ingredients, it'd be my pleasure." Her only request was that Calder either leave the room or put a shirt on!

Chapter Six

"Get the lead out, Calder!"

"Yessir, Master Chief!" All afternoon—two weeks after his fight with Pandora—Calder's SEAL team had been practicing counterterrorism drills by entering a suspected terrorist compound and securing the perimeter in under a minute. After three hours of running a simulated rat-hole maze, they'd finally gotten times down to a minute thirteen seconds, but that wasn't good enough. In a real-life situation, those seconds could mean the difference between successfully completing a mission and being shipped home in a body bag.

Over and over Calder ran the drill with the rest of his buddies—his team. The men had become his family. He'd do anything for them and knew they'd return the favor.

The harder he worked, the more he focused on the reasons he did what he did. He had always thought he'd become a SEAL for the cool factor. There was no denying the title carried with it incalculable bragging rights. But the longer he wore his Trident, the more he realized it meant so much more.

Now not only did he want to be of service to his country but he also wanted to protect his son. Before having Quinn, the seedier portions of the world had been his warrior playground. Now he recognized the world's danger zones hid terrorists intent on not only harming his son, but every man, woman and child in America and beyond.

In short, like it or not, Quinn had given Calder a maturity he hadn't before possessed. He used the newfound drive to keep his kid smiling to dig deep, finally busting through the mental wall that had held him back all day.

"Fifty-seven seconds! Good work!" His CO patted his back.

While Heath splashed bottled water onto Calder's over-heated face, Calder dropped to his knees. Damn glad the ordeal was over, but also proud. If the team could accomplish the task here at home, then overseas, with adrenaline pumping, there would be no question about them performing like a well-oiled machine.

While the last few on their team completed time tests, Heath and Calder sat against the base of a mock concrete-block Iraqi apartment building.

After gulping more water, Heath asked, "How's it going with the nanny?"

"Good and bad."

"Yeah?" Calder's friend raised his eyebrows. "How so?"

"On the one hand, the house has never been cleaner, my laundry's always done and as you've probably noticed, I'm headed out early to eat home-cooked meals every night."

"Sounds good so far."

"This is where things get dicey. I pay her for the basics, but the longer she's with me, the more I look forward to more. To just seeing her. And then there are those awkward late-night meetings when she's all mussed and forgets her glasses..." Calder shook his head and sighed. "I have to keep reminding myself she's my employee. Worse, when it comes down to it, I know nothing about her. Sure, her work references checked out, but I'm still wondering where she disappears to sometimes on Saturdays."

"Have you asked?" Heath tugged an energy bar from his right sleeve pocket, tore the wrapper and took a bite.

"Hell, no. It's none of my business."

"Then why are you whining to me about it?"

Calder snatched a pebble from the ground beside him and pitched it at his "friend."

FRIDAY MORNING, PANDORA fed Quinn and his father. Once Calder headed off to work, she tidied the kitchen and the rest of the house—a task that took a whopping fifteen minutes, considering she didn't have much to work with.

She hadn't forgotten that Calder had told her he'd paint her bedroom, but she wasn't sure how to broach the subject without sounding greedy. Most days, in presenting her with the opportunity to save a generous amount of money while at the same time living in a safe, quiet, fresh-smelling environment seemed like blessing enough. Sure, walls the shade of lemon sorbet would be lovely, but they were hardly a necessity when she'd once relocated from a highway underpass to a crack house to a jail cell.

With chores finished, she said to Quinn, "Looks like a gorgeous day. Want to go swing?"

"Rahee..." Quinn smiled and drooled.

"I'll take that as a yes."

Five minutes later, she'd worked his chubby arms into a light jacket, added a pint-size baseball cap then settled him in his stroller.

She left through the garage, netting a pleasant surprise to find the neighbors just east of the house were holding a garage sale. There were even a couple more down from there.

Some of the few happy memories she had of her early childhood were of visiting Saturday-morning sales with her mom and dad. They'd viewed the outings as fun, but also a necessary way to cheaply furnish their home. The items hadn't seemed shabby to Pandora, but well-worn and loved—the furniture equivalent of the dog pound.

During the first months of her marriage, she'd gone to lots of sales, intent on transforming their rented house into a home, but then her ex had lost his job and taken out his every frustration on her. Usually sporting a black eye, she'd been too humiliated to leave the house.

Doubling back inside Calder's home, she took her wallet from her purse and tucked it in the back pocket of Quinn's stroller.

The first sale didn't hold much of interest. Beyond a half-dozen paperbacks she selected for herself, many tables were laden with baby clothes, but strictly for girls. Pandora did snag a stack of picture books for a dollar and an electronic crib mirror for Quinn to play with. There were lots of fun shapes and when he pressed them, they made silly noises. He *boinged* all the way to the next sale.

"Good morning," said an older man, one of Calder's neighbors.

"Good morning." Pandora greeted him with a warm smile. "You sure picked a gorgeous day for a sale."

"Wasn't me but the wife. She's chairwoman of the Neighborhood Beautification Committee. All proceeds go toward sprucing up the flower bed at the development's entrance."

"Thanks. I'll keep that in mind." At first, Pandora didn't see much beyond stemware and yard tools, but then she spotted a painting that would be perfect over Calder's fireplace. In the foreground, the artist had created an angry sea, yet beyond the surf, sun radiated through tumultuous clouds and the water shone with an iridescent calm. The image spoke to her. How her recent years may have been a struggle, but in the future, by the time the storm blew over and she and Julia were immersed in golden sun, everything was going to be okay. Better.

Along with the painting, she found a lovely silk flower arrangement featuring daffodils in a Blue Willow china–patterned bowl. She envisioned it on the mantel, grouped with framed photos of Calder and Quinn she'd snapped with Calder's digital camera the last time they had played blocks on the living room carpet. All told, she'd spent ten dollars—twelve after also finding a quirky strawberry-shaped cookie jar.

She set the painting atop the stroller's sun visor, then stashed the rest of her items in the bottom netting.

To Quinn she said, "Guess we'd better head home to unload before hitting the park, or you'll end up sharing your seat, huh?"

He kicked and gurgled before once again hitting the *boing* button on his new toy.

"You bought the painting." A smiling older woman approached. "Martin and I have had it over our buffet for years, but my new decorator says it has to go."

"I should thank him or her. I love it."

"I'm glad. It's easier to part with knowing it'll be enjoyed. I'm Lila, by the way. Don't you and this cutie live three doors down?"

"We do." Pandora exchanged introductions.

"That man of yours is a sight to behold." Fanning herself, Lila added, "If only I were thirty years younger…"

Martin, the man Pandora assumed to be Lila's husband, called from where he sat on a lawn chair in the garage, "I heard that!"

Lila waved off his complaint. "How long have you and your hunk been together?"

"Oh—we're not a couple." Pandora's cheeks flamed. "I'm Quinn's nanny."

"*Oh*… Forgive me. I assumed you were a family. Have to admit to being old-fashioned about young couples *shack-*

ing up instead of marrying, but that's neither here nor there. Since he's your employer, I suppose it'd be hard not to share the same roof, huh?"

"Yes, it would." Though Pandora laughed, she couldn't help but fear Julia's family-court judge having similar suspicions, which might ultimately lead to disapproval. Her stomach knotted.

Carrying on with small talk as if she hadn't a care in the world proved difficult, but Pandora muddled through a chat about the lovely weather and maybe joining the beautification committee.

Lila's attention eventually turned to another customer, at which point Pandora decided in lieu of the park, she and Quinn were off to the hardware store for a picture hanger sturdy enough to hold the painting.

At five-thirty, Pandora took a fragrant roast from the oven and even lit a few candles alongside the photos she'd placed on the mantel. She felt good about the changes, but feared Calder either wouldn't care for her taste, or would find her presumptuous for taking the liberty of decorating his house.

At the time she'd impulsively made the purchases, longings for a true home had consumed her. Quinn deserved the real deal every bit as much as Julia. For years, Pandora imagined living in homey perfection. Was it wrong she now wanted her physical world to match her rich imagination?

Stomach roiling with silly nerves, she pureed Quinn's portions of the evening's meal. When Calder still wasn't home by six, she gave Quinn his bath, played with him for a bit, read a couple of his new picture books then put him to bed.

By the time Calder did finally come home, she'd curled onto the sofa's end, immersed in one of her new paperbacks.

"Sorry I'm late." He placed his motorcycle helmet on the entry closet's top shelf.

Had he been at a bar?

"Training ran *waaay* long." He yawned. The fact that he smelled faintly of the outdoors and briny sea told her he hadn't been partying. "What smells good?" He stepped farther into the room, noticing the changes she'd made. "Dang, that picture and the candles and stuff look fancy—like something my mom would do."

Even his indirect praise made her soul sing.

"I'm liking the painting—and whoa! Who are these handsome guys?" He picked up the simple wood frame that housed the snapshot she'd taken of him and his son. "Quinn really does look like me."

She put down her book, hovering behind him. "Is that the first time you've seen the two of you together?"

His eyes shone, but he soon blinked them dry. "Yeah. Caught me by surprise. I mean, I know in my head he's biologically mine, but somehow I hadn't made the connection that we share physical features."

"The bigger he gets, the more similarities you'll see. Little personality quirks will pop out, too. Some good, some bad. They all make you look at yourself in a whole new way."

He gave her a long stare. "You sound like you speak from experience, but you don't have kids, right?"

What did she say? The last thing she wanted was to outright lie. On the flip side, she wasn't anywhere near ready for full disclosure.

She settled for forcing a smile. "You must be starving. Why don't you grab a shower and I'll fix you a plate?"

STANDING BENEATH THE HOT water's stinging spray, it occurred to Calder that Pandora had skillfully evaded his question. Why? On the surface, everything about her read perfection. Was he being paranoid or could she truly be hiding something?

Out of the shower, he made quick work of toweling off, then stepping into boxers, sweats and a T-shirt.

He ambled into the kitchen and found the table set for one.

Pandora stood with her back to him at the sink, her arms up to her elbows in suds. If he hadn't been intent on getting an answer to why she'd evaded his question, his mind could have all too easily traveled to erotic places.

Once he sat and took his first bite, she asked, "Is everything warm enough?"

"It all tastes great. Thanks."

Was it just him or did she also sense an elephant in the room?

He set his fork to the plate. "Have a seat."

"I would, but I need to finish up here, then check on Quinn in his playpen."

Calder looked down. Where did he even start? "You misunderstood. We need to talk."

She turned off the faucet. "H-have I done something wrong?"

She'd given him the perfect segue to tell her his suspicions. That he hoped he was reading more into this than there was, but a couple times now, she'd been evasive. On her few Saturdays off, he'd gotten the impression she didn't want him knowing where she was going or even who she was seeing. Then tonight, when he'd asked her about having kids, her whole demeanor had changed. "If you're not happy with my work…" She seemed to take inordinate care with drying a saucepan.

"Did I say that?" *I can't even say why, but my gut tells me you're hiding something.* Solely for himself, because he woke thinking of her smile, he probed, "Do you have a child?"

"You've seen my references. If I've in any way caused you to doubt my ability to care for your son, then—"

"Damn it, Pandora." When he slapped his palm to the

table she not only jumped, but tears filled her eyes. He was instantly sorry, yet at the same time he'd been trained to always follow his gut. What was going on with her that he couldn't see? Whatever it was hadn't affected her ability to give his son expert care, so why couldn't he leave it alone? On a deeper level, what was it about her that had gotten under his skin, making her—at least in his mind—so much more than someone who worked in his home? "What's with you? Some things don't add up. Your first day on the job, when you didn't have a cell or a way to even purchase groceries without calling me for help. The fact that you lived in Norfolk, yet have never been to the beach. Your two mystery Saturdays. All I'm asking is for you to be straight with me. If you don't have a kid, is there something else going on with you that I'm missing?"

"No." Raising her chin, her expression lost its earlier wide-eyed fear and tears to now read steely determination. "But if you're unhappy with my performance, I'll turn in my resignation in the morning."

WHAT JUST HAPPENED?

Pandora had wanted to run, slamming her bedroom door, but she had held tight to her cool, refusing to throw away all she'd gained on a flash of temper.

In a move that took monumental effort, she calmly left Calder for the privacy of her room.

Until Calder had listed her so-called oddities, Pandora believed she'd done a good job of hiding her true identity, but then what did that mean? Though she'd been Quinn's nanny only a short while, she already felt as if she'd grown so much. Living in this nice home with her sweet charge and a true gentleman like Calder made her feel as if she'd been bathed in a pool of light and had emerged a new woman.

The fact that Calder sensed she hadn't been one hundred

percent truthful with him had her worried, but she couldn't lose focus on the fact that he wasn't her friend, but her employer.

In a perfect world, she might have told him everything. He may have even *deserved* to know everything. But selfishly— not just for herself, but for her daughter—she needed this job. Not only was the money important, but so was the consistency of her employment record. Fran, the social worker assigned to her case, reminded her all too often how important it was for her to prove a record of stability to the judge presiding over her next court hearing.

As Natalie was Pandora's true boss, and had told her she was perfectly within her rights to not discuss Julia, then no matter how difficult it was for her to essentially hide her daughter from Calder, she had to.

There was no other choice.

When a knock sounded on her bedroom door, Pandora's stomach knotted. "Yes?"

"Can I come in?"

How would he react if she said no? She lacked the courage to find out. "Sure."

He opened the door, but didn't breach the threshold. "I probably owe you an apology, but I'm not giving it until you assure me my imagination is running overtime and that your story is as uncomplicated as you presented it to be."

"No apology necessary." Seated at the foot of her bed, Pandora wasn't sure what to do with her hands. She'd been so excited for Calder to see the small but pretty transformation she'd made with the house. And he had appreciated what she'd done, so how had their night degraded to such an ugly place? "What I would like—and from your vantage point, I probably have no right to ask—is that I need you to trust me. Respect my wish to keep the part of my life that doesn't concern caring for your son private."

He rubbed his forehead with his fingers and thumbs.

"You're putting me in a horrible position. You know I'd never win Father of the Year. But I sure as hell only want the best woman for the job raising my son. At any given moment, the world could go to shit and my team could be called in to fix it. I have to know if that happens, you're someone I can trust."

How did she prove herself a good person? A worthy person? Why couldn't she come right out and tell him she had a daughter? Simple—because if she did, Calder would never allow her to keep her job. It wouldn't matter she was highly qualified and had worked years paying for what she'd done. What would matter was she'd once been a horrible person and he'd never believe her to be anything else.

How many times had people let her down? How many times had men specifically proved they were her enemy?

In no way did she believe that of Calder, but she couldn't place her entire future with Julia in the hands of a man she barely knew. A large part of her recovery process had been recognizing her tendency to be the victim, but those days were gone. She claimed full responsibility for her actions. What Pandora wouldn't do was jeopardize her daughter's future as she had her past.

"What do you want, Calder? You know my work history checked out or Natalie's agency would never have hired me."

"Do you have a child?"

She stood only to walk to the window, staring out at the dark yard. "Lord, you're like a dog after a bone. Leave it alone. Leave me alone."

His stare grew into a palpable heat, singeing her back.

But then he left, closing the door behind him. And she sank to the floor, snatching a throw pillow from the bed to cover her face, masking tears she feared may never end.

"This is a nice surprise." Natalie, the head of the agency Calder had gone through to hire Pandora, met him at her office door, extending her hand for him to shake Monday morning. "How may I help you?"

"Mind if we have a seat?" Calder nodded toward the corner sofa-and-chair arrangement. It was the same place where he'd flipped through her book of glowing client recommendations.

She gestured for him to lead the way. "I hope your arrangement with Pandora is satisfactory?"

"Actually, that's why I'm here."

"Oh?" Her eyebrows rose.

"I can't put my finger on it, but something about her feels *off*. I've asked a couple direct questions concerning her past and she never answers. Yesterday, she barely spoke at all. It's my job to be paranoid and in this case, when the woman in question spends most every day alone with my son, I have a right to be concerned."

"Of course you do." She left the sofa to open the door and called out to her secretary, "Anna, could you please bring Pandora Moore's personal reference file?" A minute later, she had the pages open in front of him. "As you can see, not only does Pandora have an assortment of exemplary letters from former clients, but she's a close personal friend. I started this agency nearly twenty years ago, and I'm proud to say I've never had one of my employees fired—or even reprimanded. My people are top-notch. That said, if Pandora has in any way engaged in behavior that caused you to feel concern for your son, then—"

"Okay, whoa…" He held up his hands. "She's been a godsend. Quinn adores her and I depend on her to an embarrassing degree, but I know she's hiding something and I need to know what it is."

Natalie stood. "Unless you're prepared to file a formal complaint against her job performance, I'm sorry, but Ms. Moore's personal life is just that—personal."

Chapter Seven

"Hell's bells," Heath said after shooting off twenty rounds on his M16. "Give it a rest."

"But what if Pandora is hiding something?" Calder's team was engaged in target practice—only, rain fell in wind-driven sheets, making their automated moving bad guys a bitch to see. The fact that he was bone-deep chilled didn't make his day brighter. Part of him regretted even going to Natalie, but another part couldn't let his suspicions go.

"Ever think there's a reason she doesn't want to talk about her past that has nothing to do with whatever nefarious reason you've dreamed up, but something more painful?"

It was Calder's turn to shoot, and he fired an embarrassing thirty-eight rounds before hitting his long-range target. That wouldn't cut it in the field, and his CO let him know.

"Another thing…" Heath annihilated his target in three shots. "All this energy you're wasting trying to solve some mystery that doesn't exist could be better spent getting to know your son. From everything you've said, Quinn's a lucky kid to have Pandora in his life. For that matter, so are you. She's not some Friday-night special out to snag a SEAL, but a sweet gal just trying to do her job."

For the remainder of the miserable afternoon, Calder focused not only on his training, but also on Heath's words.

His friend was right.

After Quinn came into his life, Calder's view of women had changed. Before becoming a father, he'd indulged in an admittedly swinging-single lifestyle. He'd made it clear to whoever he was with that his objective on any given night was to achieve the ultimate good time. Now part of him wondered if Quinn's mother had intended to trap him. But was that paranoia, too? Was his real problem with Pandora the fact that she was so good with Quinn that she made him look all the worse in his role as a father?

If that was the case, he was a jackass.

Now the only question was, what could he do for Pandora to make up for his lousy behavior?

The rain stopped and he'd almost made it to his bike when his cell rang. He glanced at the call display.

Crap. His mom.

He loved her dearly, but lately, whenever she called, she lectured and nagged. Still, she was his mother, so he forced a smile, then answered. "Hey."

Twenty minutes later, Calder had been thoroughly chastised for not retiring from the navy in order to find a more stable job. He let it flow in one ear and out the other. His work was his one true love. Lots of SEALs had kids. They worked around them, just as he was learning to do. He told his mother the same.

"But Quinn is a baby," she said. "You talk about him like he's a friend's dog you regret agreeing to watch."

"You're being dramatic. Quinn and I are getting along just fine. Better, even." He told her about Pandora, skipping the portion about his misgivings.

"I look forward to meeting her. It's good Quinn finally has stable, reliable care."

"Agreed." After a few more minutes of small talk, Calder said, "Hate to cut you short, but I need to go."

"I understand. Oh—but before I forget, Harold has a late-

October conference in North Carolina. The resort is in the mountains and he asked me to tag along. How about the three of you come, too?"

"Thanks for the invite, but I'll have to get back to you."

Calder hung up not sure what to think.

A family vacation? Seemed odd, considering only two out of three of them were related. On the other hand, when it came down to it, he felt closer to Pandora than he had to any woman in a long time. A weekend outing would be perfect for Calder to not only mend fences but once and for all solve Pandora's mystery.

"YOU'RE SO KIND to think of us," Pandora said to Lila, who stood on the front porch shaking off her umbrella. The neighbor from whom she'd purchased the painting had brought still-warm banana bread Pandora couldn't wait to taste.

"Don't thank me just yet." The woman withdrew a soggy Neighborhood Beautification Committee pamphlet from her raincoat's oversize pocket, passing it along with the bread. "Mind if I come in?"

"I'm sorry, of course. You must be freezing." Pandora took Lila's offering, then stepped aside, holding open the door.

"Actually, I love the rain. I grew up on the Oregon coast. We moved out here when my husband, Martin, was in the navy and never moved back."

Unsure how to respond, Pandora was glad when her visitor caught sight of Quinn in his walker.

"Look at that cutie!" Lila slipped off her coat and rain boots, leaving them on the tiled entry floor, then aimed straight for the baby. "Our grandkids are in St. Louis. Martin and I have tossed around moving there to be with them, but with the housing market being what it is…" She shrugged.

"Being away from your family must be hard." Pandora

sat on the brick hearth. "You should at least try putting your house on the market. The worst that can happen is it doesn't sell, but if it does...?" She grinned. "You're back to being a full-time grandma."

"I like your thinking." Lila smoothed Quinn's hair, sitting cross-legged on the floor beside him. "Which brings me back around to the reason for my visit."

Pandora waved the pamphlet. "I'm guessing you're looking for warm bodies to pick up litter?"

Laughing, Lila asked, "Am I that transparent?"

"Just a little, but that's okay. I'd love to help."

"I knew I had a good feeling about you." When Lila leaned in close to make a silly face for Quinn, he stole her glasses.

"Sorry." Instantly on her feet, Pandora rescued the plastic frames just after they'd found a new home in the baby's drooling mouth. "Glasses are his favorite toy. Hold on a sec and I'll wash them for you."

With Quinn safely corralled in his walker, and Lila blowing raspberries for him, Pandora swiftly cleaned her guest's glasses, then returned them.

"That was fast." She gestured to Pandora's own glasses. "I'm guessing you could launch a side career of washing eyewear?"

"You'd be right."

After small talk about the still-pouring rain and how the committee's next meeting was Thursday morning for a trash-cleanup walk, Lila caught Pandora off guard. "Not to change the subject, but how are things progressing between you and Quinn's daddy? I know I said I'm old-fashioned about young folks living together, but I've seen the three of you walking to the park and you make the sweetest family."

It took every ounce of Pandora's self-restraint not to scowl. If only Lila had seen the *happy couple* last night...

THOUGH PANDORA HAD POLITELY shrugged off Lila's comment, now that four hours had passed and it was almost time for Calder to be home, she couldn't deny her pulse had picked up or the fact her mouth had gone dry—only this time, not in anticipation, but dread.

When he'd left that morning without saying a word, the tension had been unbearable. What he didn't know was that she'd already lived that sort of life with her ex and now wanted no part of it.

A key to her continued sobriety was steering clear of situations that made her crave the escape she'd once sought in booze and eventually pills. Far from resenting her arrest, she now recognized it for what it'd been—rescue from a downward spiral she wasn't sure she'd have survived.

When the familiar sound of Calder working his key in the lock finally came, Quinn was giggling to a Baby Einstein DVD and she sat on the hearth folding a basket of baby pants and T-shirts.

Tension balled in her stomach, making her afraid to even look his way.

"Hey, bud." Quinn had been lolling on his favorite blanket in front of the TV, but upon catching sight of his dad, the baby crawled to meet him. "Dang, you're getting fast."

Calder swooped Quinn up for a cuddle, then sat opposite her on the sofa. For the longest time he said nothing.

She kept folding until the tension between them felt tangible. Like rogue waves slamming a pier until it leaned and groaned and the wood cried with the effort to hold.

And then, temporary relief came when Calder finally spoke. "My dad's been married five—maybe six times. Can't keep it straight. He's been lied to and cheated on, but considering he gives as good as he gets, I can't work up too much emotion other than pity for the guy." Smoothing Quinn's hair, Calder seemed lost in thought. His introspection struck Pandora as vulnerable. Never having seen this imperfect side of him—aside from his lackluster child-care skills—she found herself admiring his honesty. "When you avoided my questions, I assumed you were hiding something. Automatically, my brain leaped to the dark side. But this morning, I went to the agency where I found you—spoke with Natalie—and pretty much had my ass handed to me on a platter."

"Oh?"

"Your friend told me you hung the moon. Meanwhile…" He shook his head. "My whole adult life, the only thing I've been loyal to is the U.S. Navy. I—"

"Calder, stop." Pandora continued folding, not feeling strong enough for a heart-to-heart. He was her employer. Period. The temptation to confide in him was great, but it was also dangerous. "I'm hardly a saint."

"Yeah, but judging by how nurturing you've been to not only Quinn, but even me, I'm pretty sure what's in your past can't trump the kind of guy I've been." He stared out the living room window. "Aside from my SEAL brotherhood, my policy has been to have fun without getting close."

"In regard to women?" Where was he going? Why had her heartbeat turned erratic?

He nodded. "Now that I have Quinn, I've been forced into commitment. As much as we both depend on you, that makes another commitment. For a guy who doesn't commit…" Shaking his head, he blasted her with a smile so potent it took her breath away, as well as her ability to think. "Hell, I'm in quicksand without hope of rescue."

"I—I understand." How many times had Pandora found herself in a similar position, only for far different reasons? What she didn't understand was why his explanation of why he regretted digging into her past made her feel guilty. And sad. His gut instincts about her were right. What kind of person did that make her to let him go on believing he was wrong?

Snap out it! her conscience demanded.

Plain and simple, her secretive actions had been dictated by circumstance. She was a woman hell-bent on regaining custody of her daughter. Opening herself to this man, no matter how amazing on the surface he may seem, was not an option.

"THANK YOU FOR doing the dishes, but I could've handled them."

"Did I say you couldn't?" Long after dinner and Quinn's bedtime rituals, Calder glanced up from the tech manual he'd been studying. Pandora and Quinn had taken an after-dinner walk in the park. She'd picked wildflowers and used a drinking glass for a vase. The arrangement now sat on the mantel. The flowers were pretty, but not nearly as attractive as Pandora.

"I didn't mean to sound like I was complaining." She sat on the hearth. "Just, well…thanks." She'd removed her glasses, resting them atop her head. She had a simplicity he found intriguing. Never any makeup or high-maintenance hair—just a natural beauty he very much appreciated.

"You're welcome." He placed the manual on the coffee table, far more interested in studying the ten shades of green in her eyes. "Considering all you do for me and Quinn, I wanted to return the favor."

Her smile warmed him through and through. Made him wonder why he'd ever doubted her being anything other than wholesome perfection. But then, even if he weren't her boss, it wasn't as if he had anything to offer. She deserved better than a guy genetically incapable of commitment—even if in Quinn's case he'd been thrust into it.

"Whatever the reason, I appreciate it."

"Sure." Her sweet, simple smile left him tongue-tied. He usually knew just what to do and say around women, but around her he couldn't even think. He met her gaze, which only made him more confused. Lord, he wanted to kiss her. Not the kind of boozy, dance-floor-make-out kiss he'd grown accustomed to, but more of a leisurely getting to know her in a way wholly inappropriate for a boss to know his employee.

Looking away for his own sanity, he found the perfect answer to his conversational dilemma in the sliver of her god-awful bedroom wall visible from his vantage. "Got anything going on this weekend?"

She shook her head.

"Want to paint your room?"

Nodding, voice barely audible, she said, "Sounds fun." Her words were encouraging. Her expression read wistful. Lost. Was it possible she'd craved that kiss as much as him?

SATURDAY MORNING AT Lowe's, staring at hundreds of yellow paint samples, Pandora could hardly contain her excitement. Her heart felt composed of confetti and glitter. The only thing that would make the moment even better was the day she chose wall colors for her own home she'd share with Julia.

"What do you think?" she asked Quinn, who was too busy chewing a teething hippo to do anything other than drool.

"Rah baa haa!"

"He's not a lot of help." Calder had been at the other end of the aisle selecting rollers and paintbrushes.

"That's okay." As many nights as she'd lain awake at the halfway house, dreaming of the day she'd finally live in a place to call home, she'd committed her lemon-sorbet shade to memory. The house she shared with Calder may only technically be her home because she worked there, but for now that was good enough. "I know exactly the color I want."

"Since you spend so much time in the kitchen, want it yellow, too?"

"If it's not too much trouble, that'd be nice."

He waved off her concern, then performed a smile-and-wink combo that turned her legs to mush. The man really was criminally handsome. When he turned on his charm, she craved the kind of physical attention a woman shouldn't want from her boss. She had to remember Julia came first. "You forget who you're dealing with. I've been trained to handle *any* situation with ease."

Famous last words.

Four hours into their project, Calder had more paint on him than the walls. "What am I doing wrong?"

She laughed. "Not that I'm an expert, but you're tackling the job like—" she took a second to think "—I don't know, like you're charging up some hill with a bayonet instead of a paint roller."

"A bayonet, huh?"

There he went again with his slow, easy grin. Her pulse skipped as if she was a little girl holding a carnival balloon. "Here…" She cupped her hand around his wrist, not caring that in the process, her palm got coated in paint. "Like this."

By showing him the seemingly simple movement, her whole world turned upside down. Somehow he now stood behind her, pressed against her in an innocent yet perilous way. The easy up-and-down motion of the roller called to mind other activities men and women do to a similar rhythm and suddenly the heat, the longing was more than she could bear.

She tried turning away, but only made a bigger mess of things by facing him, gazing up at lips she wasn't allowed to wonder about kissing.

"Am I doing it right?"

"Uh-huh…." How was she supposed to answer when he wasn't doing anything at all other than standing there, radiating heat and a foreign erotic hum that rendered her dizzy-drunk as she stared into his blue eyes?

From over the baby monitor, Quinn cried.

"I—I should check on him." Relief wobbled her legs. She had never been happier for Quinn to need her.

"Yeah." Calder stood close enough that his warm exhales landed near her nose. He smelled so good.

For a split second, she closed her eyes, imagining his sweet taste. And then she dragged herself back to reality.

The old Pandora would've ignored Quinn in favor of a frenzied roll in the hay. New-and-improved Pandora forced a deep breath, then, as gracefully as possible when her limbs were oh-so-pleasantly entangled with a hulking navy SEAL and a paintbrush and roller, extricated herself from the situation.

"Duty calls." She ducked under Calder's arm to escape to the hall bathroom where she washed paint from her hands. A glance in the mirror showed dilated pupils and flushed skin. The lovely shade of lemon sorbet marked her breasts where they'd brushed against Calder's chest.

Cheeks superheated, nipples mortifyingly hard, she craved a drink almost as badly as Calder's touch.

The thought scared her.

Brought her down from the clouds to scurry into Quinn's room where she addressed the infant's needs instead of her own.

Chapter Eight

Pushing midnight, with Quinn long asleep, bone-deep exhaustion settled over Calder—only not from the physical exertion of painting, but from keeping his hands off his son's nanny.

Calder sat on one side of the kitchen floor, leaning against the cabinets. He sat on the floor because Pandora said he was too dirty to sit on the furniture and she was right.

She sat opposite him, daintily plucking green peppers from her pizza and setting them in a soggy pile on the edge of her plate.

"When I ordered," he asked, "why didn't you tell me of your apparent green-pepper aversion?"

"If you like them, it's not a big deal for me to take them off." Having finally completed her task, she took her first bite and smiled. "Mmm. I didn't realize how hungry I was."

She smiled again as she chewed. A good three hours earlier, her ponytail had gone crooked, and yellow now streaked her cheeks and hair. Yellow overspray from the roller speckled the lenses of her glasses. He had never seen her looking more lovely. And he had never wanted a woman more, yet been so keenly aware he couldn't have her. Was that the force driving his attraction? The fact that she was off-limits?

"Green peppers aside," Calder asked after his second slice, "when's the last time you did something nice for yourself?"

"All the time." She sipped her cola. He'd offered her a beer, but she'd declined.

"Like what?"

"Last Friday, Quinn and I went to some yard sales again. We had a great time."

"Yeah, but all you bought were things for my house or Quinn."

"I grabbed a few books for myself. And those two throw pillows. And I forgot to mention it, but I met one of the neighbors and even joined her club. Quinn and I are now official members of the Neighborhood Beautification Committee."

"That sounds indulgent," he teased after finishing his brew.

She rolled her eyes. "You sound like one of those morning talk shows where they have some expert talk about how stressed we all are, and how women should indulge themselves by soaking in bubble baths or frolicking in potpourri."

I'd like to see you frolic—naked.

That thought sent Calder reaching for another beer.

"For me anyway, all that's a crock. I wasted a lot of time doing only what I wanted in life and it cost me—dearly." She shrugged, "May sound cheesy, but now I get more satisfaction from making other people happy."

"Makes sense." Whoa. Had the mysterious Pandora Moore actually opened up? He almost asked what specifically she'd lost, but then thought better. Interrogation wasn't his strongest suit, but he knew enough to recognize he'd learn more from carefully listening to her than pressing for answers. Besides, she was a genuinely nice person. Aside from his team members, he hadn't met all that many.

"Thank you for my lemon sorbet." She was back to plucking green peppers. "Once we clean all the drips and put everything back in place, your house will be very pretty."

It was on the tip of Calder's tongue to tell her no house

could be as pretty as her, but even though the statement would've been true, she deserved more than his old brand of clichéd *cheese.* "I think so, too. Might also make it more homey for Quinn."

She nodded, then rose to put her plate in the dishwasher. She held out her hand for his.

"Thanks."

"No problem." She stared at him a moment too long. "You must be exhausted."

"Trust me, I've had worse days." He joined her in clearing the small dinner mess and putting away what remained of their meal. "Tell me about this club you and Quinn joined."

"It's no big deal." She leaned against the counter and shrugged. "Just a friendly group helping to keep the park and main entrance areas clean. I really like the woman who leads it. Her name's Lila. She's a grandmotherly type. Quinn took an instant liking to her, too."

"Nice." He wiped down the counter. "He doesn't get to see much of my mom—which reminds me, we're invited for a long weekend with her and my stepdad at some resort. Interested?"

"When?" Just like that, her mood turned evasive again. She'd darted her gaze and drew in her lower lip.

"Third weekend in October."

She took a moment to ponder this, then smiled. "Sure."

The issue should've been no big deal. So why was he back to wondering what she was trying to hide?

AFTER CALDER HAD gone to bed and she'd checked on Quinn, Pandora found it impossible to sleep. Her room smelled strongly of paint, but she liked the newness. The scent was faint in Quinn's room, but she'd cracked his window just in case.

While pacing her room, she could've told herself she

couldn't sleep because of excitement over their upcoming trip, and it would be true. After all, she'd never been on a true vacation—not that this was, since she'd technically be working, but just staying at the resort would be a new thrill.

She could also claim insomnia over the sheer wonder of her beautiful new room. She couldn't wait to hit more yard sales and thrift stores, finding just the right pictures and knickknacks. She'd decorate it as if it were her own. Sort of a practice run for when she and Julia finally had their own home.

The truth behind her inability to close her eyes, though, was a bit more complicated, centered around a certain SEAL whose mere presence raced her pulse.

Never having been big on small talk, she'd expected their day spent together to be agony, yet he was surprisingly easy to talk to. But maybe that was because he'd done most of the talking. He never ran out of stories and she'd very much enjoyed hearing of his many travels.

So why, then, had she opened her big fat mouth during dinner? *I wasted a lot of time doing only what I wanted and it cost me—dearly.*

Pandora covered her face with her hands.

Had Calder read anything into her statement? Surely not, or he wouldn't have invited her to meet his mother and stepdad. She was acting paranoid, but spending time behind bars did that to a person.

THE NEXT MORNING, Calder watched on while Pandora fed Quinn Cheerios and pinchable-size banana chunks and blueberries. The baby had milk in his sippy cup, but still managed to make quite a mess. He'd learned berries can be smooshed before eating. Each time he *popped* one on his high-chair tray, he giggled.

Realizing his kid had learned something—no matter how

minute—did funny things to Calder's heart. Not the touchy-feely sort, he couldn't tell whether he felt parental pride or the same garden-variety affection he would for any cute kid with purple cheeks. But then, that was also significant, because when was the last time he'd even noticed a kid other than his own?

Then there was Pandora. Hair still damp from the shower and her T-shirt clinging to certain curvy areas, he couldn't help but wonder if this little domestic scene was the real deal. If he leaned to his right, cupping her left breast, would he earn a swat and a dirty look or the sort of grown-up giggle that led to a steamy kiss?

He exhaled sharply.

This kind of thinking wouldn't do.

He shouldn't be consumed by lustful thoughts about his son's nanny. No doubt a night started at Tipsea's and ended with a hottie at the motel across the street would heal his horny afflictions.

Only trouble was he didn't want to go to a bar. He wanted to stay home with Quinn and Pandora. Which made no sense.

"What are your plans for today?" Pandora asked.

"Guess since poor Quinn got stuck watching us paint yesterday, we could do something together today? I mean, if you're available?"

"Yesterday at Lowe's, I noticed the pansies were out. If you feel up to it, we could plant a few dozen in the front flower bed. Quinn loves the park sandbox, so I'm sure he'd get a kick out of gardening."

"Not a half-bad idea. Mom always used to have me help out in the yard. Though it's been years since I've done anything but mow."

Two hours later, supplies were purchased and unloaded.

Only trouble was, when Calder looked to Pandora for guidance as to how they should proceed, she sat on the pile of three topsoil bags with Quinn on her lap, both of them looking at him.

"What next?" he asked.

She frowned. "Sorry. I've never really done anything like this. Always wanted to, but…" She lifted the hood on Quinn's sweatshirt. Clouds had moved in, turning the September day chilly.

"This whole flower plan was your idea."

Along with an adorable grin, she said, "It can't be that hard."

Calder shook his head then whipped out his phone. "I'll look it up." A minute later, he said, "I officially feel like an idiot and you should, too." He smiled to let her know he was teasing. "Pretty simple. We pluck all the weeds and existing dead crap. Dump on the new dirt. Stick the plants in the ground. If we still have energy, we can go back to Lowe's for the mulch the sales guy kept pushing."

"You're right—" another grin shot his way "—I do feel stupid." To Quinn, she asked, "Ready to get to work?"

The baby gurgled.

She sat him on the brick garden path where he proceeded to grab for anything green and shove it in his mouth. "Maybe including Quinn in this project wasn't such a hot idea."

"How about for the weeding part," Calder said, "you two supervise?"

When the old-and-married crowd at work occasionally complained about the household chores their wives had them do, Calder had always been sympathetic. He'd assumed he'd never want to be saddled with that kind of boredom. But it turned out the more he worked, the better the yard looked. His yard. *Their* yard. And for whatever reason, he liked the sound of that. Not cool for a guy who knew he could never handle true commitment.

Finished weeding, he and Quinn broke up the ground a

little with the spade they'd purchased. "There you go, buddy," he urged his son. "Stab it. Get it all nice and loose."

Quinn shrieked every time he slammed the spade into the dirt.

"Aw, he makes me wistful for when my kids were young." A woman about his mother's age approached across the driveway.

"Lila, hi." Pandora rose, giving the woman a hug. "This is Quinn's dad, Calder."

"Nice to finally meet you." She extended her hand for him to shake, but as he was as dirty as his son, they both laughed and air shook.

"Lila's the leader of the cleanup club I told you about."

"Seems like a clean-enough neighborhood." Calder sat back on his heels. "Is there enough litter that you need a whole group?"

Quinn grabbed a clump of dirt, bringing it to his mouth.

"Hold up, bud." Calder grabbed his son around the waist, swooping him onto his lap. He turned to Pandora. "Think he's hungry?"

"For finding trouble," she teased, taking the infant from him, brushing off the soil he'd gotten on his jeans and T-shirt.

"Sorry," Calder said to Lila. "Seems like ever since Quinn landed in my life, I'm always a step behind whatever mayhem he's causing."

"Comes with the territory." Lila warmly smiled. "And to answer your question, you'd be surprised how inconsiderate people can be when it comes to improper trash disposal. But trash isn't our only focus. We also beautify the entries, decorating them for holidays and such."

"That's nice." Not being all that big a fan of holidays, Calder wasn't sure what else to say. He'd spent last Christmas in Afghanistan. It hadn't been a good time.

"It means a lot to some of our older neighbors whose families are grown and far away. Reminds them of happier times."

"Sure."

"Hard to believe the three of you aren't a family." Lila fixed her smile on Quinn, tweaking his sneaker. "You seem so comfortable together."

"Yeah, well—" Calder thumbed toward his still-to-be-finished job, then the sky "—I should finish. Looks like rain."

"Of course." Lila gave Pandora another hug, asking her to stop by for coffee soon.

Once she'd left, Pandora said, "Sorry about that. I didn't mean to involve you in my club."

"Not a problem." Despite Quinn's *help,* he'd spread the fresh soil and now planted yellow flowers. "She seems nice."

"She is. But I know most men don't like to be bothered with these kinds of things."

Once again, alarm bells rang. Not wanting to alert her to the fact he found her statement—her overall behavior—odd, he kept planting. She'd reacted in a similar manner that day he'd met her at the grocery store. As if she'd grown accustomed to appeasing a hothead. Had she once been in an abusive relationship? The thought of a man doing her physical harm made him nauseous. "In case it escaped your notice, I'm not *most* men. I'm guessing it gets lonely for you, here alone all day with Quinn. I'm glad you met a friend."

"Really?"

"Yeah. Really." He glanced her way, pretending not to notice her shimmering green eyes. It took more willpower than he'd known he possessed not to flat out ask her about her past. Instead, he realized no matter what Natalie told him, for his own morbid curiosity, he had to know what Pandora had been through.

ON WEDNESDAY, PANDORA tidied the house in preparation for one of Natalie's regular home inspections. Though Pandora had nothing to be nervous about, she took extra care with scrubbing the backsplash grout behind the kitchen sink.

"Quinn," she said, "do you think all this cleaning will help your daddy want to keep me around for a nice long time?"

The boy cooed from his walker.

"Yes? Awesome!" She knelt alongside him to kiss his chubby cheek.

By the time her friend arrived, the home fairly sparkled and the air smelled rich from fresh-baked lemon poppy-seed bread.

"Wow," Natalie said as she admired the kitchen. "I love this color. Your idea or Calder's?"

Glowing from her friend's praise, Pandora busied her flighty hands by slicing them each a piece of the bread. "Surprisingly, Calder's idea to paint, but he let me pick the color, which I thought was awfully nice. Since the windows are a standard size, I've got my eye out for curtains. Although I've always thought it might be fun to learn to sew. Wonder if the thrift store ever gets sewing machines?"

"Uh-oh…" Natalie drew a chair out from the kitchen table.

"What's wrong?" Pandora redirected Quinn, who had whined when he'd gotten himself stuck in a corner.

"You're sounding awfully domestic. I've been at this job for a long time, and I'm pretty sure this is the cleanest house I've ever seen." She nibbled her bread.

"And? What's your point?" With Quinn once again happily touring the kitchen, Pandora joined her at the table.

"I don't want to see you hurt. I'm afraid you're falling for Calder and his son. This is a job—not your life. You have Julia to consider."

Natalie's words hit Pandora like a slap. "That's a horrible thing to say. More than anyone, I know my place in this house. And I sure as—" she stopped short of cursing "—I know my first and *only* priority is my daughter."

"I didn't mean to sound cruel." When Natalie covered her hand, Pandora jerked away.

"You might not have meant to, but you did." Moving away from the table, Pandora needed to hold Quinn—to remind herself he was the reason she worked so hard to make this house a home.

Really? Then why had Calder's approval come to mean so much? Why did something as simple as his enjoyment of her meat loaf fill her with a quiet contentment she'd never known?

"I'm sorry." Though her friend's tone was sincere, Pandora couldn't get past her hurt feelings—only not because of what Natalie had said, but because she knew her friend was right but didn't want to admit it. Though Julia was her top priority, she could no longer deny Quinn and his dad had taken a close second.

"It's okay." Rejoining Natalie, she rested her elbows on the table, covering her face with her hands. "Sometimes it's scary how well you know me. I do like Calder—a lot. But I swear to you nothing inappropriate has happened."

"I didn't think for a minute it had, but you know what the funny thing is?" She smiled. "I almost wish it would. Calder's a good guy. He seems shaky about the whole instant-fatherhood situation he finds himself in, but who wouldn't?"

"Bite your tongue. You're right, though. I guess I have been trying to make this place cozier than I should, but Nat, considering where I've been, is that so wrong? Jail was…" Refusing to cry, she shook her head. "Jail was a nightmare. The halfway house not much better. Every day here is a dream. Calder is…" How did she begin describing the unexpected role he now played in her life? "Well, Calder's fast becoming my friend. Aside from you, I haven't had many."

"That makes me sad."

"Up until now, I haven't deserved any." But in the almost two months she'd cared for Quinn, she felt transformed. Granted, her current role had come about through plenty of hard work, but she had done it. And now her life was better for it. "But that's changing. I've had a few good talks with a nice neighbor, and in a couple weeks I'll meet Calder's mom and stepdad."

Natalie helped herself to more bread. "They coming for a visit?"

"We're meeting them at a North Carolina resort."

"As in the three of you are going on vacation?"

Pandora couldn't help but smile. "I guess you could call it that—only I'll still be working."

"Of course." Natalie's exaggerated nod only made her smile more suspect.

Eyebrows raised, Pandora asked, "You think I won't?"

"Oh—I have no doubt you'll continue doing a great job with Quinn, but I'm more intrigued by all that alone time you'll have with his dad."

Pandora frowned. "You do realize that as my boss, you're not supposed to encourage the fraternization you keep hinting you'd like to see?"

"Sadly, yes. Which is why I'll now have to walk off the half loaf of your sinfully yummy bread I've eaten to cover my guilt."

Guilt? Natalie had no clue of the true meaning.

Pandora feared the upcoming trip would test her mightily in regard to keeping her relationship with Calder strictly professional.

More and more, the man and his adorable son felt like her new drugs. For a former addict—not a good thing.

Chapter Nine

Monday afternoon, Calder got word his team would ship out that night for Somalia. *Yay.* He had a couple hours off until returning to base, and in the past, before he'd known about Quinn, he'd be psyched about any new op. But his current feelings were more in the realm of resigned. Hopefully it'd be an in-and-out mission. Surgically clean.

It sounded selfish, but he especially wanted to be home before the North Carolina trip.

The more time he spent with Pandora, the more curious he grew. Working together in the yard, he'd sensed she may have been on the verge of opening up. He'd hoped to see even more progress tonight. Which made no sense. He had nothing to offer her in the way of any serious relationship, so why attempt making more out of their working friendship than there was?

"Hi, there!" The smile Pandora greeted him with as he climbed off his bike and removed his helmet turned his supposedly tough SEAL shell to mush. The day was warm and sunny with barely a breath of wind. She stood barefoot on the front lawn, holding Quinn's raised hands while he staggered about, perfecting his walk. "Look, Quinn! Daddy's home!"

His son's giggle raised a knot in Calder's throat.

When Pandora *walked* the baby to him, Calder lifted his

son for a hug. He would miss Quinn, as well as the boy's nanny, when he left for his mission.

Sighing, he asked, "Remember when I told you I sometimes need to ship out with short notice?"

She nodded, and damn if her eyes didn't suddenly shine with unshed tears. "But you'll be home soon, right?"

"Sure." *Home.* Such a loaded word. He used to return from missions to the apartment he shared with fellow team members. It was vacant while they were gone. An empty vessel standing by to once again be filled. Now that he had a home, a son, a woman—a *friend*—who cared for both, he feared the game may have changed.

"Okay, then…" She took a deep breath and forced a smile. "I imagine you need help packing? I just did laundry, so—"

"Thanks, but I'm good. It's not really a traditional packing kind of trip, and my gear's back on base, ready to go." He smoothed Quinn's downy hair. "I just wanted to see this guy." *You.* "Let you know I'm leaving. Make sure you have enough money and stuff."

"There's plenty in the house account."

"Good. I'll add more. And you and Quinn go have fun once in a while, okay?"

"Sure.…"

There was more he wanted to say, but he wasn't sure how. Or even if it was appropriate. He wanted to thank her for all she'd done for him and Quinn. For all she would do in bringing him peace of mind while he was gone. "Look…" He glanced down. Kicked a pebble near his foot. "There's no easy way to say this, so I might as well come right out with it. If something happens and I don't—"

"Stop." She held up her hands. "You're going to be fine."

"Yeah, but if I'm not…"

She childishly put her hands over her ears and shook her head. Calder set Quinn on the grass, then clasped Pandora's wrists, gently tugging her arms down before taking her hands. Easing his fingers between hers felt as forbidden and raw as if he'd slid inside her. In all the missions he'd been on, he'd never experienced such crushing urgency to take care of business that might be left behind. Before Quinn, before Pandora, he'd always called his folks prior to leaving for a mission, then been on his merry way. Now? He gave her hands an urgent squeeze, wanting desperately to kiss her but squashing the urge. For all he knew, she viewed him strictly as her boss—as she should.

"Okay, so look," he began again. "If anything happens to me, my mom has all the necessary documentation to make sure Quinn's legally safe. Her number's in the address book I keep in the drawer under the kitchen phone."

She swallowed hard and nodded.

"I hope to be back before our North Carolina trip. I want you to meet my mom. I think you two will be friends."

"I—I'd like that."

During their exchange, Quinn had nearly crawled his way to the sidewalk. When Pandora released Calder's hands to chase after her charge, for a moment he felt bereft. He knew it was the whole going-off-to-war thing that had him melodramatic, but he couldn't help it. Was this how his pals Garrett and Deacon felt every time they left their families? If so, how did they take it? He and Pandora weren't anything but employer and employee, so why did he feel as if he was leaving not only his son, but a woman who could one day teach him that commitment might not be all bad?

"THANK YOU," Pandora said to Lila, who'd just brought her fourth batch of cookies in two weeks. She opened the front door, inviting her friend inside. "Quinn and I always appreciate your baking, but you do know you don't have to keep bringing us goodies."

"Of course, I know." She made a beeline for Quinn, who

sat on the carpet playing with his jumbo blocks. "But as long as Calder's off fighting for our country, the least I can do is bake for his family."

"I'm not his family," Pandora said for what felt like the hundredth time.

"Maybe not technically, but haven't you ever heard that old saying about there being families we're born into and then there are the ones we choose?"

"Well, sure, but…" Her words trailed off because she realized what Lila said was true. Of course, Julia was still her world, but since taking this job, her world had expanded and blossomed. Quinn meant so much to her, and no matter how vehemently she tried denying feeling anything special for his father, every night when she said her prayers, adding extra for Calder and his team's protection, her thoughts drifted to memories of that sunny morning he'd held her hands.

Had his action been significant? Or was she reading too much into what had in reality been a casual gesture? Having never been around men who weren't either physically or emotionally abusive—sometimes both—she had no experiences with which to gauge what was real.

All she did know was standing in the yard, warm sun kissing her face, she'd wished Calder had kissed her, too.

BY THE TIME Pandora's next visit with Julia rolled around, Calder was still out of town. She could've asked Natalie to watch Quinn for her, but Pandora figured her daughter would get a kick out of playing with a "real live" doll, so she packed Quinn up and took him with her.

"He's so cute," her daughter said. Julia sat in the corner of the visitation room's sofa, holding Quinn on her lap. "I love his chubby belly."

"Me, too."

"Mom Cindy's having a baby!"

"Really?" Pandora's stomach tightened into a knot. Though it wasn't something she liked thinking about, she did worry what would happen should Julia prefer Mom Cindy to her. "That's exciting." And it was. She didn't begrudge anyone else's happiness but was more than ready to claim a slice of her own.

"When I live with you again, do we get to keep Quinn?"

"No, sweetie." Worry vanished, making way for anticipation of the day she finally took Julia home. The fact that her daughter also thought of that time swelled her heart with joy, reminding her to once and for all stop fearing every little thing. "We can't keep Quinn, but as long as I work for his dad, we get to play with him all we want."

"That's good."

"I think so." She toyed with one of Julia's blond curls. Her hair was getting so long and pretty. During her few sober nights, she'd loved brushing it, singing lullabies, dreaming of a better life for them both. "Have you decided what you want to be for Halloween?"

"A princess or a zombie!"

"Oooh." Pandora made a face. "Wouldn't a zombie be too scary?"

"Probably. But Brent in my class says any costume that isn't scary is stupid. Do you think so, too?"

Peer pressure this early? "I think it's important for you to pick a costume you feel super comfortable and happy wearing. If every time you look in the mirror, you get scared, then that doesn't sound very fun, right?"

Julia giggled. "Mom?"

"Yes?" Hearing her daughter call her that was heaven on earth.

"Can you please read more of the book we started last visit?"

"I'd love to." Snuggling closer to both children, Pandora took the book from her bag, then turned the page to where they'd last left off.

ANOTHER WEEK PASSED with Calder gone.

Pandora kept busy taking Quinn for walks and teaching herself to sew using the ancient Singer she'd found for ten bucks at a yard sale. So far, she'd made kitchen curtains and a small, colorful quilt for Quinn. One day, she'd like to create clothes for Julia, but she'd need way more practice first.

Lila and Natalie often stopped by, and though Pandora's nights were sometimes lonely and long, she worked hard to maintain Quinn's schedule and to not dwell on the fact that his father was likely in constant danger.

On a Wednesday night, when she was dicing carrots to boil for Quinn's supper, the phone rang.

It didn't ring all that often, so the noise startled her and Quinn, who burst into tears.

"Poor baby, it's okay." Before answering, she plucked him off the kitchen floor and into her arms. "Hello?"

"Hi, Pandora?"

"Yes?" The woman on the line sounded familiar, but Pandora couldn't immediately place her.

"This is Patricia—we met during the guys' beach-volleyball game?"

"Oh, sure. How are you?"

"Actually, great. Now that Heath and I are officially engaged, I'm on the *wife*-calling circle. I know you and Calder aren't like a couple or anything, but I thought you'd want to know the guys are due back tomorrow afternoon."

"That's great!" Pandora didn't even try hiding her excitement, and her relief. "Thank you so much for calling."

Patricia laughed. "You're welcome. Enjoy the rest of your night."

Pandora hung up the phone and closed her stinging eyes.

"Hear that, sweetie?" She tickled Quinn's tummy. "Your daddy's coming home."

CALDER DIDN'T THINK his commanding officer would ever end their team's debriefing. Finally, it was over, and he was free to go. A long time ago, he would have hit Tipsea's for a wild night out with his single friends, but instead he shared in a few minutes' obligatory handshaking and backslapping on a job well done, then hitched a ride home from Heath.

Heath dropped him at the curb, saying a quick goodbye as he was eager for his reunion with Patricia.

With his ditty bag slung over his shoulder, Calder crossed the yard and mounted his porch steps at a hurried pace. Lord, he couldn't wait to hold his son.

And Pandora?

How did he feel about seeing her?

He didn't have to wait long to find out. She must've gotten the heads-up on his imminent arrival because she dashed out the door with Quinn in her arms. "Hi! We missed you!"

Laughing, tossing his bag to reach for his son, he said, "Not half as much as I missed you. And this guy looks like he's grown a foot."

"How was it?"

He made a face.

"Sorry." She tucked her hair behind her ears. Had it grown longer? He liked it. "Dumb question."

"Nah, I wouldn't say that past missions have been *enjoyable,* and even though this one was relatively short, it felt longer than the fifteen months I spent in Iraq."

"That's a really long time."

"No kidding." The phrase struck him as trite. There was so much Calder wanted to say but wasn't sure how, or if he should. He'd seen kids Quinn's age living in deplorable conditions. Women performing countless hours of hard physical labor to scrape a meager existence from ravaged land. When he'd been on missions before, he'd focused on getting his job done. This time, he'd soaked in the world around him, really took a good long look at the people and what they were even fighting for. It'd been sobering. And more than anything, he wanted to draw Pandora in for a hug, burying his face in her hair.

"Patricia told me you'd be home today, so if you're hungry, I made all your favorites." She gestured toward the door, smiling shyly in a way that twisted him all up inside. He'd be lying if he said he hadn't spent every second of downtime thinking about her and Quinn.

"You didn't have to do that." *But I'm sure glad you did.*

"I know. I wanted to." Tugging him by his sleeve, she urged him inside. "Come on. Quinn and I did some decorating."

Calder trailed after her, trying not to focus on her swaying hips. Looking up, he got a shock to find his living room transformed into the sort of patriotic homecoming usually reserved for the airport welcoming of National Guard units. SEALs operated without a lot of fanfare. So this…

He teared up. "Quinn," he said, locking his gaze with Pandora, "did you do all this?"

"He sure did." Pandora winked. "Although he had to sit on a few phone books to see over the wheel when he was out buying supplies."

"This is…" There were no words to describe how her simple gesture of red, white and blue balloons and streamers, coupled with a giant banner reading Welcome Home, Daddy! made him feel special. As if he'd somehow become part of a family without even knowing it. "This is really great."

When Calder's throat knotted again, he did what he'd been craving from the moment he'd set eyes on her, and gave Pandora a hug. With Quinn squirming between them, there was nothing sexy about the gesture, but it felt great all the same.

"I'm glad you like it." When she stepped back, her eyes shone. "Quinn and I had fun. He made all the handprints decorating the edge of your banner."

Holding Quinn out to face him, Calder took in his son's handiwork, then said, "I'm impressed. Looks like we've got quite the little artist on our hands." *We.* The moment he referred to both himself and Pandora, Calder knew all the time he'd spent thinking about her when he'd been in Somalia was for a reason. He had started to think of Pandora as an integral part of not only Quinn's life but his.

Whether he felt up for commitment or not, something was happening that felt out of his control. For the first time in his life, he cared for a woman. The notion was both exhilarating and terrifying.

After sharing a delicious early dinner, helping with the dishes, taking Quinn for a walk in the park then giving him his bath and tucking him in, Calder couldn't remember having ever felt more at peace.

"Help me with something," he said to Pandora when they'd both settled in the living room before a crackling fire.

"Anything." Her smile warmed him through and through.

"This is going to sound crazy, but hear me out." He leaned forward where he sat on the sofa, resting his elbows on his knees. "When we met, I operated under the assumption that you were Quinn's nanny and that was it. I never wanted anything more from life than to win a few battles for the good guys, then party every Friday and Saturday night, but now? I don't know…." He ran his fingers through his hair. "Feel free to file a lawsuit if this is off base, but…" He looked up to find her staring.

"Yes?" Hands tightly clasped on her lap, she swallowed hard.

"I like you, Pandora."

After licking her lips, she said, "I like you, too. But I can't. I mean, I shouldn't. It wouldn't be right."

"Would I be out of line asking why?"

Her lips curved into what he could only describe as a haunted smile. As if she'd been in this spot before and wasn't sure she wanted to proceed.

Only for him, this was a first. He didn't commit. He acted as irresponsibly as safety allowed, then went on his way. He wasn't proud of that fact, but that's what it was—fact. Now he found himself in the uncharted territory of not knowing where he stood, and he didn't like it.

"Sorry," he blurted, pushing to his feet. "I shouldn't have said that."

She stood, too. And then went to him, shyly easing her arms around his waist, pressing her cheek to his chest. Could she feel, hear, his heart pounding? "I *really* like you, too."

He exhaled sharply, holding her close.

"But there are things about me—my past—you need to know."

Part of him wanted to know everything about her. His more rational side told him to back away. He'd never had a girlfriend and he sure as hell wasn't interested in marriage. Which meant what?

Hands on her upper arms, he pushed her back, just far enough to finally kiss her. He'd almost touched his lips to hers, then suddenly released her to turn away. "Sorry. You're right. I can't do this, either."

Chapter Ten

Tears caught in Pandora's throat. She hadn't realized how much she'd craved his kiss until Calder left her standing dazed and confused. A few years from now—six months from now, she'd have Julia back and everything would change.

"Sorry. Didn't mean to spoil your nice night." Arms crossed, lips pressed tight, he'd become the human equivalent of a moody spring storm.

"Then why the dark look? The one fairly screaming you can't stand the sight of me?"

"You're reading too much into this. I'm regrouping. Trying to keep my distance. You know—like an appropriate boss should." He'd stepped in close again. Close enough for his breath's heat to tickle her upper lip.

If she leaned in a quarter inch, she'd no longer be fantasizing about kissing him but indulging in the real thing. But was she strong enough to continue her fight for her daughter and also abandon herself to another man, even a nice one like Calder?

Summoning her last shred of courage, she asked, "What if right now I need you to be more than a boss?"

He groaned before framing her face with his hands. "Do you have any idea what you do to me?"

The feeling was mutual.

But she'd had enough push-pull. She craved more from this man who'd roared into her life as unexpectedly as a runaway freighter. Meeting him, falling for him, was a game changer. What she felt for him had no rules. Maybe he could even help her in her custody battle.

When Pandora touched her lips to Calder's, she closed her eyes. When he met her kiss with exquisite pressure, she could've wept from dizzying relief. Her whole life up to this moment felt like a spinning coin that had only just settled. Pulse racing, she pressed her hands to Calder's chest, surprised to find his heart racing, too.

He deepened the kiss, sweeping her tongue with his.

She fisted his shirt, holding on for all she was worth.

"Damn...." he said when they stopped for air.

When he released her, she was caught off balance, but he was right there, hands on her arms to steady her and provide balance—only what he had no way of knowing was how much more support he'd unwittingly provided. Since taking this job, everything felt shiny and new. Dreams she'd never thought possible, such as living in a real house and finally regaining custody of her daughter and now, maybe even forming a relationship with a man who didn't hit or yell—all of it was coming true.

Her conscience wouldn't allow her to risk losing it all on a technicality, so she blurted, "I want—*need*—you to know, I used to be an alcoholic. My dad physically abused my mother and I followed the same cycle. One night I left our car's lights on and when the battery died, my husband hit me so hard I spent three days in a coma. I got better and h-he went to prison, but back then, I was all messed up. Making my own living was h-hard and booze made me forget the constant, nagging pressures of medical bills and making rent. Liquor was my only friend. I made horrible choices—did things I'll always regret. But I'm better now. You have to know that with every breath of my being, I want this recovery—this amazing new life to work."

He terrified her by taking a step back. "How long since your last drink?"

"Three years." She needed to tell him about Julia, too, but for her daughter the stakes were too high. Of all her many secrets, Julia was the one she held most dear. As much as she'd grown to adore Quinn and his father, losing them would at least be survivable. To permanently lose custody of Julia was unimaginable. "For that, I alternate between being ashamed and proud. I worked hard to become the woman I am today. Even if you don't approve, I—"

Throughout her speech, she'd managed to hold her tears at bay, but when he stepped toward her, wrapping his strong arms around her, his support was more than she could take.

She broke down—hard.

He held her till she calmed, but then he asked gently, "Are you in AA?"

"Yes—I just haven't felt like I needed regular meetings in a while."

"Does Natalie know?"

Pandora nodded. "I credit her—and a few other people—for saving me. She gave me a second chance and I won't let her down. I did janitorial duties in her day care for a year before she ever let me work with children. Two more years of part-time day care and after-school care before she'd let me even think of applying for a job like yours."

He released a long, slow exhale. "I don't know what to say. On the one hand, you've been amazing with Quinn, on the other…"

"I know." Head bowed, she covered her face with her hands. "But if this—whatever it is—between us hadn't developed, none of what I just shared would matter. Even though she's my friend, Natalie drops by at least once a week to check on me. When I tell you I'm never going back to my old way of life, I mean it. There's truth to the adage of being *scared straight.* I'm living proof."

"I appreciate that." He wouldn't make eye contact with her. "But you have to understand this news is—well, let's just say I had my suspicions about you having been abused, but the rest..."

"If you want me to leave, I will." She raised her chin. For as long as she could remember, she'd considered herself a victim, but no more. She'd made grave errors in judgment, but she refused to live the rest of her life being dictated by them.

After waiting for what felt like forever, with no sounds in the house other than the fire's occasional crackle, he finally slipped his arms around her again. Kissed the crown of her head. "Considering the way my own son entered my life, I'm the last one who should be judging."

Her limbs turned quivery with relief. "Thank you."

He tipped her head back, forcing her to meet his gaze. "I should be thanking you. You've made me rethink the whole family thing."

"Yeah?" Through happy tears, she smiled.

"Yeah. With you," he teased, kissing the tip of her nose, "it might not be so bad."

"How's it going with the nanny?"

"Huh?" Calder had been so deep in thought over that very subject, he'd forgotten Mason was even in the car. Since it was raining, and Pandora told him she and Quinn had no-where to go, he'd taken the SUV over his bike. He and Mason were now on their way to lunch. Though it'd been almost a week since Pandora's confession, and life with her and Quinn was growing almost idyllic, he still couldn't get her former addiction out of his head.

"The nanny? Please tell me you had a hot homecoming.

Mine sucked." He made a gagging sound. "Heath left the bologna and mayo out on the counter. Smelled like a rotting corpse."

Not sure he was up for sharing, Calder shrugged. "Mine was good." And by good, he meant over-the-top awesome. Pandora had cleared away the balloons, but the banner still hung. Every time he passed beneath it, the paper clipped his head. But he wasn't complaining. The notion that someone besides his parents had been glad to see him safely home still filled him with quiet awe.

"Yeah? The nanny do anything special for you? Make her meat loaf, then serve it wearing nothing but an apron and her glasses?"

Stopped for a light, Calder shot a sideways glare at his gutter-minded friend. "Remember the speech we had a while back about respecting the nanny?"

"Sure, but you've gotta let me have a little fun. Hell, if you aren't dating her, maybe me or even Cooper might want a go?"

"She's taken." Calder hit the gas too hard when the light changed.

"I'm crushed." Hands mockingly over his heart, Mason angled sideways on his seat. "How long you been keeping this from me?"

"Not long. And nothing's official. But I kissed her. But then…" He shook his head. "Things got complicated."

"Bad in bed?"

"Seriously?" His so-called friend had earned another glare.

"What? I'm on a dry spell. Since we got back, sex is pretty much the only thing on my mind."

"TMI, man." Calder shook his head. "Pandora told me she's a recovering alcoholic."

"And?"

Stopped for another light keeping them from reaching their favorite Chinese buffet, Calder asked, "You don't think that's a big deal?"

"Well, sure, but have you seen her drink?"

"No."

"Then what's the problem? I mean, I don't want to downplay that it's serious, but my old man took a bad spell when I was a kid. My mom passed, and—" as if remembering a time he'd rather forget, Mason glanced out the window "—let's just say we both had a rough time of it. My grandparents stepped in, convinced him to get help, and he hasn't had a drink since. He's everything I could hope for in a dad."

"That's a relief." Calder loosened the death grip he'd had on the wheel. "Pandora's amazing, but alcoholism is one of those things you hear about on TV, but unless you have first-hand experience…" He pulled into the restaurant's lot. "I just wasn't sure what to think."

"My advice?" Mason unlatched his seatbelt. "Relax and enjoy the ride."

"I DON'T KNOW what to bring." Wednesday night, Pandora stared at the meager contents of her closet, then looked to Quinn and his father. Calder sat at the foot of her bed with the baby on his lap. Despite their heated first kiss, by mutual agreement they'd opted to take things slow.

It was a seven-hour drive to the resort where they were meeting his family, so he'd taken Friday off, as well as the entire next week. To say she found the prospect of spending all that time with him exciting was the understatement of the decade.

Calder asked, "When's the last time you went shopping?"

"Can't remember. I get most everything from thrift stores. There are some really great bargains, you just have to look at it like a treasure hunt."

"While we applaud your frugality—" he clapped Quinn's hands "—once we load this guy's twenty pounds of traveling gear, if you want, we can make it to the mall in time to grab you a few things for this fancy resort."

"No." A familiar knot seized her stomach. "What I have will do."

"I didn't say what you have wouldn't be fine, I said let's go play. I thought chicks love that sort of thing."

"I'd rather save money." Was now the time to tell him about Julia? How part of her case file required her to be gainfully employed with the same company for a year, and how she also had to provide a stable housing environment for Julia and prove she'd been there for six months? It took not only time for all this but money. Yes, if she maintained her current course, all was well. If not, she'd once again be in trouble with the courts.

"What do you need to stockpile cash for? I'm not complaining, but the fee the agency charges for your services isn't cheap. You probably have more money than I do."

"I have legal fees, all right?" She hated that her tone grew defensive, but when backed into a corner, she fought.

His pinched expression led to him scratching his head. "I'm sorry. I really don't mean to pry, but what are you paying a lawyer for?"

Heart pounding scary hard, Pandora had trouble finding her next breath. She didn't want to tell Calder about Julia. Not yet. Not like this. But if not now, when?

"Hey…" He set squirming Quinn on the floor, then took her hands in his. "Talk to me. You're white as a ghost."

"I need the money to get my child back, all right? Her name's Julia and I was a textbook example of a lousy parent. I showed up drunk at my first custody hearing. My second, I got so mad I cursed at the judge. I—I—" she covered her face with her hands "—I'm humiliated by the person I used to be.

That Saturday you wondered where I was going? I went to one of my monthly supervised visits. In January, assuming I stay on my present course, they move up to bimonthly. So see? I need every dime I make to get my daughter back." Her throat ached from tears, but she forced herself to be calm. She wasn't the same woman who'd lost her cool in court. "I've been to AA, to anger-management classes and parenting classes and even a financial course to help me make a proper weekly budget. I'm so ready to put all this knowledge to good use. All I need is my child."

Calder had long since released her. His supportive expression had darkened to pressed lips and narrowed eyes. "So in the meantime, you're practicing on mine?"

"It's not like that."

"Then why hide this from me?" He turned his back on her to stare out the window.

"It wasn't relevant."

"Not relevant that here you are, caring for my kid, when you lost your own? What was Natalie thinking even hiring you?"

No longer able to hold back tears, Pandora dashed toward the bathroom for tissues, and in the process nearly tripped over Quinn, who she'd forgotten was crawling on the floor.

The startled infant cried.

She lifted him for a comforting hug, but Calder took his son. "I'm going to need time to process this."

"Please, Calder..." She tried holding his hand, but he pulled away. "Please give me a second chance. Going to jail was the best thing that ever happened to me. It scared me straight. I promise, I—"

"You've been to jail?" He laughed without a trace of humor. "This just keeps getting better. My gut instincts were right about there being something *off* with you. I just didn't know to what degree."

This couldn't be happening.

As if time had dulled to slow motion, Pandora all but fell onto the foot of her bed. She was aware of tears wetting her face, but lacked the strength to do anything but let them fall.

"I'm, ah, going to take Quinn for a ride." The baby had quieted in his father's arms. "We'll be gone for about an hour. I'd appreciate you packing your things and being gone when we return."

"Calder?" With her eyes she begged him to at least look her way, but his only action was to leave the room.

SINCE PANDORA HAD already packed Quinn's diaper bag for their morning drive, Calder suddenly decided to turn toward the interstate that led to the resort his mom and Harold were staying at. He'd experienced pain, but nothing like this. He felt humiliated and embarrassed, yet at the same time a crushing sense of loss for the woman Pandora had spent so much time portraying.

How could he have been so blind?

How could she have been so duplicitous?

Thirty minutes into the drive, Quinn grew fussy.

Calder pulled over at a truck stop to change his son's diaper, struggling with the sticky tabs as usual. Using the bottled water and premeasured formula Pandora had placed amongst Quinn's things, he prepared a quick bottle, then climbed into the backseat to feed his son.

The trip wasn't supposed to be like this.

He'd looked forward to it for over a month. He'd not only been excited to see his mom, but for his mom to see Quinn and to finally meet Pandora, whom he'd talked so much about.

Now? As much as he wanted to see his mother, he dreaded the lecture she'd deliver on how he hadn't done adequate research before even hiring a nanny who had a prison record.

But hadn't Natalie been in charge of all that? Should he sue her agency to protect other unsuspecting parents from Pandora's lies?

Had she lied? his conscience probed. Or had she omitted? Did the technicality matter?

This was why Calder had protected himself all these years from entering any sort of relationship. They were doomed to fail. His dad had been married so many times Calder doubted he could even name all his in-laws. Sure, Calder's mom was happy, but at what cost? His dad put her through hell.

Quinn finished his bottle and drifted off to sleep.

Calder eased him back into his safety seat, then resumed his drive. He'd like a nap himself, except he feared dreaming of Pandora, so he didn't dare close his eyes.

"HONEY, IT'S OKAY...."

At Natalie's homey ranch-style house, Pandora had blown her nose so many times it felt raw. She knew her friend meant well, but she also knew nothing would be okay. "You say that, but you know part of my Social Services agreement is to maintain the same child-appropriate address for six months *and* have a job. Now I have neither. I'll never get Julia back."

"Hey, now. Try not to worry." Natalie patted Pandora's knee before rising. "I'm making more tea. Any particular flavor request?"

"Tea won't help."

Frozen, eyebrows raised, Natalie asked, "You're not thinking of drinking away your fears?"

"No. *Lord, no.* And it hurts me you'd even think such a thing."

"Sorry. Guess I'm in kind of a panic, too." She leaned against the kitchen wall. "Don't take this the wrong way, but maybe I messed up by even suggesting you for that job."

Pandora looked at her friend a good long while, then

began gathering her purse and the sole suitcase holding all her clothes.

Losing Calder before she'd ever really had him hurt enough. To hear the woman she respected above all others still doubting her was too much.

"You're taking that wrong." Natalie chased her to the door. "I meant I should've protected your past by keeping you on at the day care. No one asks questions there. All they see is you doing a great job."

"Please move."

Natalie blocked her home's entry. "Don't go. Not like this."

"I'm fine." Pandora gently nudged her friend aside. "I'll be even better on my own."

CALDER HAD BEEN on the road a good two hours when his cell rang. *Pandora?*

The dash's caller ID read Natalie Lawrence. Usually when he'd spoken with her, she phoned from her agency—Earth Angels.

"Hello?"

"Calder—I'm glad I found you. Have you seen Pandora?"

"No. I left with Quinn a while ago."

"And she hasn't called?" Was there worry in her tone? He shouldn't care, but he did. In the time it'd taken him to recover from the shock of just how much of her past Pandora had kept from him, he'd seen her silence for what it had been—a defensive maneuver. Regardless, he couldn't have a former criminal caring for his child.

Is that really the reason you're shunning her? Or is it something more? Like you were in too deep, too fast, and her shady past gave you the perfect escape?

"I haven't heard from her." Calder tightened his grip on the wheel. "But she's a big girl. I'm sure she's okay."

"Did she even tell you half of what her ex put her through? She almost died. He's in jail for attempted murder."

An empathetic pang tore through him. "I'm sorry. That doesn't excuse what she did." Out of sheer morbid curiosity, he asked, "What landed her in jail?"

There was a long pause.

"Natalie?"

"Crack cocaine. She was arrested for possession in a sting operation. She claims it was the first and last time she ever used."

Chest tight with frustration, he asked, "You believe her?"

"Yes." Another pause. "Even if she lied about that, there's no way she isn't living her true life now. She's clean. If I thought for one second she wasn't, I never would've linked my own reputation with hers."

IN THE TIME she'd lived in Calder's home, Pandora had managed to add to her financial safety net. Trouble was, that money had been earmarked for legal fees, but more important, her own home—at the very least a nice apartment. As she hadn't yet raised enough for either, she spent a listless night in a cheap motel. Between throbbing bass, breaking glass and a couple fights, it was a wonder she ever drifted off to sleep.

She woke at 5:00 a.m. confused about where she was.

It took a few seconds for the previous night to come rushing back. A few seconds more to find enough composure to not surrender to more tears.

She wasn't hungry, but coffee sounded good.

Maybe if she forced down an egg and toast her head would be clear enough to choose her next move.

Remembering an all-night diner on the corner, she grabbed her coat, purse and room key, opening the door with the chain lock still in place to have a peek outside.

Places like this used to be the norm for her. Now this world felt frightening and alien.

Finding the motel parking lot clear of anything but cars as crappy as hers, she ventured outside, careful to make sure her door was locked behind her. The restaurant was within easy walking distance, so she set off through misty fog made all the more eerie by the motel sign's blinking red-neon glow.

Almost to the diner's door, she got a shock when a scantily dressed teenage girl stepped out from a narrow alley. A much older man followed, tucking in his shirt. The implications made Pandora's stomach roil. But then at her worst, how many nights had she been tempted to do the same—not even for money, but a measly fifth of vodka?

The teen caught Pandora staring. "What're you lookin' at, bitch?"

Ignoring her, Pandora hastened her pace until she reached the diner's overly warm interior.

The place was surprisingly crowded with patrons who she guessed from their jeans and uniformed shirts were factory workers.

"Sit wherever you like!" shouted a waitress from behind a counter.

Pandora found a corner booth.

She looked out the window, but as it was still dark, all she saw was her own reflection. Behind her glasses, her red-rimmed eyes appeared hollow. Dark shadows had formed underneath. She'd long since lost her ponytail, and her long hair hung dirty and wild. She hadn't looked this bad since the night of her mug shot.

"Coffee?" The waitress startled her. "Sorry. Didn't mean to sneak up on you. Rough night?"

Pandora half laughed. "You could say that."

The woman glanced over her shoulder. "Boss would have

my ass for asking, but if you need a little, you know, pick-me-up? I've got most anything you crave."

"Um, I'm okay. Thanks. Just coffee, please."

"You got it."

Pandora wanted so badly to stay strong, but for the first time in she couldn't remember when she'd lost her will to fight. With no job and no place to live there was no way she'd get Julia back.

Natalie might not have technically let her go, but her words refused to leave Pandora's head. *Don't take this the wrong way, but maybe I messed up by even suggesting you for that job.*

If that was how her friend honestly felt, Pandora had too much pride to go back.

Then there was Calder. His kiss.

The waitress's offer intruded on everything else.

...If you need a little, you know, pick-me-up? I've got most anything you crave.

Oh, did Pandora crave.

Chapter Eleven

"I don't even know what to say."

"Not much to say." Saturday morning, Calder topped off his mom's coffee from the carafe room service had left with their breakfast. Harold, his stepdad, had already left for his day's meetings. Calder had spent the past thirty minutes filling his mom in on Pandora's past.

He'd left out their kiss.

That part was too private. Too raw.

Quinn fussed on his grandmother's lap. The poor little guy hadn't been himself since leaving home.

"You can't be cranky when you're with Nana." His mom adopted a singsong tone.

Quinn wasn't having it and broke into a full-on wail.

"Let me take him." Calder reached for his son but didn't have much better luck calming him.

"Hmm…" His mom rested her elbows on the table, framing her mug with both hands. "Do you suppose he misses Pandora?"

"I'm sure he's just hungry."

"I fed him a bottle right before you got up."

Great. There went that theory. Calder checked his son's diaper to find that hope blown, too.

"I can't believe I'm even saying this," Gloria said, "but maybe you overreacted. Your uncle Pete drank and Aunt Melanie's son—you know? Ulie? Well, he was a raging pothead in college. Of course, he's better now—a lawyer in Boston. Your aunt's very proud. So, see? People can make mistakes and get better."

He sighed. "She was in prison, Mom."

"Prison or jail? There is a difference."

Quinn cried harder.

His mom stood, taking the infant. She paced, all the while singing "You Are My Sunshine" in a soft, lyrical tone. The song took him back to his childhood. To when he'd had a bad day at school and he'd come home to her hugs and fresh-baked chocolate-chip cookies.

Quinn finally calmed.

The relief from his crying struck Calder as profound.

Calder said, "You were a good mom. Still are. I'm sorry for what Dad put you through."

She waved off his concern. "That was a million years ago. And while I love you for thinking of me, would it shock you to know I was secretly relieved your father cheated?"

"What?" Calder narrowed his eyes. "That's crazy."

"No, hon, it's called we got married way too young, and I fell for your dad's Paul McCartney imitation but pretty much couldn't stand anything else about him. We worked in the bedroom, but nowhere—"

"Stop." He waved his hands. "I don't wanna hear this."

"You need to hear it." She set Quinn in the portable hotel crib, along with a few toys. "I've been afraid for a while now that you've never gotten serious about a woman because of the example your father and I set. This Pandora intrigues me. You've never spoken to me about a woman the way you did her."

"It wasn't like that between us." He sat at the foot of the bed, trying not to think about the fact that had he never insisted they go to a mall, Pandora would be here with him now. They'd have all shared a meal, maybe spent the afternoon hiking or riding bikes down one of the resort trails.

That was a first—lying to his mother.

"It's okay, you know?" Her arm around his shoulder, she joined him on the bed. "If you did have feelings for the nanny? Sounds fun to me—like the kind of romance you'd see in a chick flick."

He groaned, covering his face with his hands. "All right, so what if it was like that? And she *is* fully recovered? Then I'm the one who's messed up."

"Then I'd say if you stand a chance of wooing her back into your life, you've got work to do."

"THANK YOU FOR seeing me on such short notice." Pandora followed her caseworker into her cubicle. It was Monday. A cold rain had settled in and she felt chilled to her core.

"I'm glad I had time. Please—" Fran gestured to her guest chair "—have a seat."

Pandora did. Her palms were so sweaty, she pressed them to her knees, willing her legs not to do their usual nervous jiggle.

"How can I help you?"

"You know how hard I've been working to regain custody of Julia, right?"

Fran smiled. "In all my years on this job, I don't think I've ever seen anyone work as diligently as you. Not only have you excelled in all state-sponsored parenting classes, but your performance at the day care has been truly remarkable. I had misgivings about you taking the nanny position, but, if anything, you've proved you're ready to resume caring for Julia. By your March hearing, assuming you maintain status quo, I'll wholeheartedly recommend your full parental rights be returned."

"Th-that's just it...." Pandora's stomach churned as if she'd come down with a terrible case of throw-up flu. "I want to be totally up-front with you. Friday, my, um, direct employer, Mr. Remington, released me from my duty of watching his son."

"You mean you were fired?" The caseworker dug through a stack for Pandora's file, then made a notation.

"Yes, ma'am."

"On what grounds?"

"I—I told him about my past problems with alcohol. And about my daughter. And jail."

"I see...." More notes written. Pandora didn't hear the scratch of pencil lead against paper but nails in her coffin. "So you failed to tell him when you were first hired?"

"Well, since I got the job through the Earth Angel agency—" she clasped her hands so hard on her lap that she dug her fingernails into the backs of them "—I assumed he would've asked any questions at the agency office."

Fran nodded. "And what does the agency say about all this? I was under the impression the owner—" she flipped through several pages "—Natalie Lawrence, felt you'd done an exemplary job with all your assignments? Did she also release you from duty?"

"Honestly?" Moments earlier Pandora had been cold, but she was now hot. Resisting the urge to claw at the neck of her sweater, she said, "I haven't spoken with Natalie since Friday. I was so upset, I wanted to see you first—assure you I will find another job and adequate housing."

"Pandora..." Setting the file on her desk, Fran sighed. "You've been with the agency for three solid years. My advice? Go to Natalie and ask her to return you to your previous work in the day care. Unless there's more you're not telling me, I see nothing here in your file that would indicate she wouldn't have you back. Would you like me to call?"

"No, ma'am. I'll do it." Head bowed, Pandora accepted the

fact that yet again she'd be swallowing her pride. For Julia, she'd do it all day long. "But I'm worried about the housing portion of my case plan. It requires me to have lived at the same address for six months. The fact that I will no longer live in the same household where I worked means that by the time of my hearing, even if I find an apartment today, I'll have only lived there four months."

"I see where that could be a problem." Tapping the file with her pencil, Fran said, "You've been frank with me, so I'll return the favor. Most times, the judges who handle our cases want to return children to their parents. That's the primary goal of our job. That said, though you're an exemplary mom now, you and I both know that hasn't always been the case."

Pandora nodded, biting her lower lip to keep from crying.

"In fact, early on, you were one of the most challenging cases I've ever had."

"I—I know. And I'm sorry."

"Don't be sorry." Fran set her pencil on her desk, then leaned forward, taking Pandora's hands. "What I need you to do is secure a suitable place for you and Julia to potentially live—like, yesterday. Assuming you stay with the agency and have no other problems by March, I'll do my best to smooth things over with the judge."

"Thank you," Pandora said. *"Thank you."*

"Don't thank me yet. You've still got work to do, and when it comes to judges, please realize I don't have a magic wand."

PANDORA LEFT SOCIAL SERVICES and drove straight to Earth Angels.

While Natalie was in an appointment with a potential new client Pandora made small talk with Anna, who handled payroll.

The moment the client was gone, Pandora winced when her friend grabbed her by the arm, yanking her into her office before closing the door. "Where have you been? I've been worried sick! And when are you getting a cell?"

"First, I'm staying at the Super 9 off the interstate. Second, I'm sorry I worried you, but you really hurt my feelings. Third, I refuse to spend one dime on anything other than making a stable home for Julia and me."

Shaking her head, Natalie joined Pandora on the sofa and took a bag from the coffee table. "I figured you'd say that about the phone, which is why I bought you this." She handed over the gift. "I literally haven't slept the whole time you've been gone. Open it."

It was a GoPhone.

"No contracts or anything. I put sixty minutes' worth of calling cards in there, too, so you have no excuse not to let me know what's going on with you."

Sighing, Pandora said, "Thanks, but you do realize I'm not twelve?"

"Yes. But do you realize just how much you mean not only to me, but to Fran and Anna and lots of other people whose lives you've touched? Fran called—she wanted me to reassure her you were still gainfully employed."

"What'd you say?"

"Of course." Natalie winked. "Doris called in sick today, so you're desperately needed in the three-year-old room. After that, I've circled a half-dozen apartments for us to check out."

That familiar knot formed in her throat as Pandora asked, "Why are you doing all this?"

"Simple." Natalie crushed her in a hug. "You're my best friend."

WHILE HIS MOM took care of Quinn, Calder ran until his lungs burned from crisp morning mountain air. Then he ran more. Until he couldn't hear Pandora crying. See the pain in her eyes.

He'd made a mistake kissing her.

Leaves crunching beneath his feet, Calder ignored what under ordinary circumstances would've been an awesome panoramic view. If he'd kept things professional between him and Pandora, would her past have mattered as much? He wouldn't have taken what she'd done personally. He wouldn't have wished he'd met her in high school, saving her the pain of ever having been hurt. He wouldn't wonder about her little girl—if she shared her mom's pretty smile. Most of all, he wouldn't blame himself for quite possibly being the one who pushed her back over that alcohol ledge.

But then, how egotistical was he to assume he even had that power? No doubt Pandora was fine. And if she had returned to drinking, that only proved him right and she shouldn't be around his son.

And if she hadn't? And she really was all she'd portrayed herself to be? That meant his commitment issues were as real as the disease she'd once battled.

"Whoa!" Calder damn near mowed his stepfather down. Harold wore his business-casual clothes and had been headed to the conference center.

"Sorry."

"That's okay," Harold said with a wry smile. "Your mom filled me in on your nanny problems. I imagine your mind was on that. Ask me, you dodged a potential bullet. A man can't be too safe when it comes to protecting his family."

Calder reveled in this vindication. "See? That's what I thought, but Mom says I shouldn't have let her go." He couldn't even bring himself to say Pandora's name. "She thinks I have the problem, and then gave me a ridiculous lecture on how she's worried her and Dad's divorce emotionally scarred me for life."

Harold glanced at his watch. "I'm seriously late for this

morning's session. How about I skip it altogether and we grab the breakfast of champions?"

"What's that?"

On their way toward the main lodge, Harold patted him on the back. "Bloody Marys followed by a truckload of bacon and a biscuit-and-gravy chaser—only don't tell your mom. My cholesterol's already through the roof."

By the time they'd finished their meal, Calder was reminded how much he enjoyed his stepdad's company. His real dad may not have always been there for him, but for as long as he could remember, Harold had.

"Thanks, man."

"For what?" His stepdad finished his drink.

"You know—being around. You're a good guy, and best as I can remember, I wasn't exactly fun to deal with."

Harold laughed. "Not gonna lie—there were times you were a mouthy handful, but all in all, your mom and I couldn't be prouder."

"What do you think of Mom's worry that I have *problems* when it comes to dealing with women?"

After signaling for another drink, Harold said, "We could be here all day discussing women and their problems. Way I see it, once you find the right lady, everything else sorts itself out."

Leaning forward, Calder realized a sense of urgency had taken hold. "How do you know if a woman's *right?*"

"From my experience, you just know. To this day, I remember your mom coming into my office with you in tow. She and your father had just broken up and I remember thinking how brave she was—a single woman raising her child. But she gave me the most beautiful smile…" He downed more of his drink. "Don't mean to get all sappy on you, but *you know when you know.* For me, your mom's smile stopped time. Anyway, she wanted to invest her divorce settlement and I was more than happy to help. Whenever she was in the office, she brought you along. You were eight and you refused to sit in any chair. You always wanted to be under your chair, driving Matchbox cars. I'll never forget the first time I showed up at your house to take your mom on a date—you asked if she was now going to cheat on you with me." He shook his head. "For the longest time, you saw me as a threat." His eyes shone and he patted his chest. "Meant the world when you finally let me in. I—I couldn't have kids of my own, so I mean it when I tell you that in every sense of the word, I view you as mine. I loved every one of your Little League games and Boy Scout meetings. When you went off to visit your dad, I worried you wouldn't want to come home."

Calder wasn't sure how to process this information. All this time he'd had a great father, but he'd been too self-absorbed to see Harold for what he'd been—a devoted family man who'd been a faithful, loving friend to him and a great husband to Calder's mom for twenty years. So why did Calder identify more with his cheating birth father than the true father who'd always been there for him?

For all these years, why had Calder assumed he was incapable of commitment when it turned out he'd had the perfect family role models all along?

And what was wrong with him that when it came to women, he couldn't get it right? More specifically, when Pandora shared her story, why hadn't he listened instead of driving her away?

A ROACH SCURRIED across the counter where Pandora had set her purse. She snatched her bag from the cracked and stained beige surface. Would any amount of bleach return it to life?

"It's close to work," Natalie said with forced cheer.

"It also reeks of the former tenant's cigarettes and I'm pretty sure the carpet's *crunching* beneath my feet."

"I don't know…" Arms crossed, Natalie appraised the shadowy living room with its one cell-like window. "If you add curtains and lots of plants, the place has potential."

Pandora sighed. "I appreciate your upbeat attitude, but this is the fourth apartment we've seen and they're all overpriced."

"How about you move in with me?" Natalie suggested. "I have room. You're more than welcome to pay loads of rent, which I will save for you, me and Julia to take a trip to Walt Disney World, then we'll all live happily ever after—assuming I haven't met a man before turning eighty." She sat on the arm of a sagging brown sofa.

"You think we need men to be happy? Obviously, marriage didn't work out for me, and here I finally thought I might have something real with Calder, only to have that blow up, too." She raked her hair into a ponytail, securing it with an elastic band from her purse. "I'm done."

"I'm not quite ready to give up altogether," Natalie said, "but after what Calder put you through, I respect the fact you are. The thing is, you're even younger than me. You never know where life may take you—so what do you say, wanna be my roomie?"

Pandora had to follow her instincts on this. "I can't tell you how much your offer means, but I want a place of my own not only for the judge who reviews my case, but for Julia. I need to prove I'm not just a good mom but a great one."

"Aw…" Eyes shining, Natalie left her perch to wrap Pandora in a hug. "Sweetie, haven't you already proved yourself just by making it past this mess with Calder only to come out stronger on the other end?"

"I did, didn't I?" Pandora couldn't help but smile. "Did I tell you one morning at breakfast, a waitress offered items that weren't on the menu? For a split second I was tempted, but one vision of Julia's face was all I needed to politely decline."

"I'm so proud of you. Geez, you should be proud of yourself."

Pandora was. She just wished another part of her didn't regret not having earned Calder's approval.

"I CAN'T BELIEVE this is our last night here." Even at their table in the resort's main dining room, Calder's mom held Quinn on her lap. "I'm going to miss this angel."

Harold said, "Without a nanny, Calder's going to need help. How about you stay with him another week or two?"

"That'd be great." Calder climbed right aboard that bandwagon. "You'd not only spare me the long drive home alone, but I obviously need help selecting Quinn's new nanny."

"If I didn't know better—" she landed an elbow's to her husband's ribs "—I'd think you're trying to get rid of me."

"Never, sweetheart." Harold put his arm around her shoulders, then gave her a kiss. When Calder had been a kid, that sort of thing grossed him out. Now? He found comfort in the fact that his mom had a great guy.

As for Calder finding a great gal?

He figured the lingering ache in his chest told him he already had but had let her get away.

"THIS IS REALLY NICE." Thursday afternoon, Pandora turned in a slow circle, taking in the garage apartment's leafy view. There were two bedrooms and though the honey-toned wood floor was scuffed from years of use and the yellow walls had faded, they were yellow, and Pandora took that as a good sign. Tall, paned windows overlooked the main home's shady backyard, and in exchange for gathering mail and watching pets while the owners frequently traveled, the rent was ridiculously low.

"No kidding," Natalie said. "Maybe I need to move?"

Pandora gave her friend's arm a playful swat. "Don't even think about it. This place is mine."

After checking out the rest of the apartment and especially admiring the claw-foot tub, Pandora met with the owner in the main house's kitchen, proudly signing a six-month lease, then providing her first and last month's rent in cash. She still had enough in savings to cover at least two more months and purchase a few furnishings at yard sales and thrift stores.

"That felt good," Pandora said once she and Natalie were back in the car with a brand-new set of apartment keys. "I'm doing this. Just like we talked about in all my parenting classes, I'm supporting myself and soon my daughter and it's not scary but empowering."

"I'm so glad for—uh-oh...." Natalie had taken her phone from her purse and was now checking messages. "What's wrong?"

"I have a message from Calder."

Chapter Twelve

Calder left a message for Natalie's cell, then turned off his phone. To his mom, he asked, "You don't suppose she's purposely not answering?"

"You're losing it." She stood at the kitchen sink peeling carrots.

Quinn seemed happy to be home and tooled about in his walker.

"Stranger things could happen."

"You're giving yourself too much credit. From everything you've told me about Pandora and her friend Natalie, both are strong, capable women fully able to breathe without you. If Natalie's any kind of businesswoman, she'll return your call within an hour."

Damn, Calder hated it when his mother was right.

Sure enough, just as he'd taken the rake and a few trash bags from the garage, his cell rang—this time with the familiar Earth Angels number.

After a few minutes of painfully awkward chitchat, he got to the point. "Look, the reason I called is that I want to talk to Pandora. Any idea where she is?"

After a long pause, she said, "Yes. I know exactly where she is. I also know she has no interest in speaking with you. She's doing great, Calder—better than ever. You firing her only made her stronger."

"I'm glad." He truly was. Only, her success proved him an even bigger ass where she was concerned. "So how about you tell her I called, then let her decide whether or not she wants to talk?"

"Ever occur to you she already has your number? Trust me, if she had any interest in reconnecting, she'd have already made the first move."

Calder tried another route. "What if I want to rehire her?"

"Sorry, but I won't send you anyone else. If you don't trust my judgment in only hiring top-notch nannies, then I no longer trust you to treat them in a professional, respectful manner. As far as I'm concerned, Mr. Remington, you're blackballed from the Earth Angels agency."

When she hung up, it took every shred of Calder's self-control not to throw his phone.

His mother asked, "What'd she say?"

"Mind watching Quinn? I need to run an errand."

"Of course I'll watch him, but first tell me what that was all about."

"Mom…" He kissed her forehead. "That was about Pandora's friend Natalie launching a battle. What she doesn't know is I excel at war."

"Not to interfere in your business, but, hon, I thought the whole purpose of your call was to find peace?"

PANDORA WAS ABLE to move in immediately, and just as soon as she hefted all seven of her boxes filled with personal belongings—a marked increase from her previous five—up the stairs, leaving them in the middle of the living room floor, she called Fran from the phone Natalie had given her, leaving her a message about her new address and number.

Finished with that vital task, she took a moment to wander around her new space. Partially furnished, it had a sort of shabby-chic appeal she couldn't wait to embellish with yard-sale finds. In what would be Julia's room, she imagined the sun-flooded space as the quintessential little-girl's room. The twin bed made with a girlie floral, ruffled spread. Lots of cozy, colorful throw pillows and stuffed animals. Maybe a rag rug she'd spend cold winter nights crafting.

In her own room, she made her bed. Her comforter and sheets matched the faded-yellow walls, and her linens smelled fresh from the washing she'd given them while at Natalie's.

She hung her towels in the bathroom and arranged her books on the built-in shelves flanking the brick fireplace.

There were loads of items she'd need to shop for. Plates and silverware. Pots and pans. All were available for next to nothing at thrift stores. She'd take her time, carefully picking exactly what she wanted.

Funny, when Calder had sent her packing, she'd felt nearly as low as the night she'd landed in jail. She'd felt as if everything she'd worked for had been lost. But now she was almost grateful for what he'd done. He'd given her the gift of recognizing her own power and self-worth. He'd shown her she could not only survive on her own but thrive. One day soon, she and Julia would get along just fine without a man.

Even if that first kiss she'd shared with Calder had been magical and each one after even better, she was done mourning what might've been. From here, she vowed to only look forward.

And if her thoughts occasionally strayed to Calder?

Well, she'd view what they'd briefly shared as a lovely, never fully realized dream.

"YOU DID IT!" Pandora said to three-year-old Rose, who'd just written *H, I* and *J* with her chubby index finger on a cookie sheet filled with sand. Lots of times students used crayons or fat markers, but having children correlate writing not only with tools but their hands helped reinforce the whole concept.

"I smart!" Rose beamed up at her, and as much as Pandora missed working with Quinn, for the past few days she'd enjoyed working with slightly older kids.

"You sure are. Now I want you to see Miss Donna at the Magic Marker station. She's going to let you pick your favorite color to use next."

"Okay." The girl ambushed Pandora in a hug. "Thank you, Miss *Pannora.*"

"You're very welcome."

Billy was next in line at Pandora's station. "Hi, sweetie. Do you remember how to use hand sanitizer?"

"Yeah, but it smells bad."

"I'm sorry." Lowering her voice to a whisper, she asked, "Know what?"

He shook his head.

"I don't like it, either. But we need to keep our sand nice and clean so everyone can have a turn. Can you think of a way to get your hands nice and clean without using the goopy sanitizer stuff?"

Nose scrunched, he took a second to think about it. "Wash with soap?"

"You're right." She gave his nose a playful tweak. "How'd you get so smart?"

Grinning, he said, "Mommy says I got her brain and Daddy's poop!"

"Oh?" Kids really did say the darnedest things, and this was one of those times. "Maybe what your mom really meant was that you're as smart as your mom and as handsome as your dad?"

"Nope," he said with a firm shake of his head. "She said Dad's poop!"

"Wow, okay, well, let's wash our hands and in the future not talk about bathroom things unless we're in the bathroom."

While Billy ran to the sink station, Pandora used a hand

brush and dustpan to sweep sand that had fallen on the floor. Feeling a tingling on her neck, she glanced over her shoulder to see Calder.

She jolted upright so fast she hit her head on the table.

A dozen curses shot through her throbbing head, but considering her ultra-G-rated setting, she bit her lower lip instead and rubbed the spot where it hurt.

Calder was instantly at her side, helping her back into her chair. She was now stuck trying to ignore the way the simplest touch of his hand on her elbow ignited her longing for him all over again. "You okay?"

"Fine." If anything, having him near made her heart hurt worse than her head. Her pulse raced uncomfortably and her mouth had gone dry. "What're you doing here?"

"Miss Pandora?" Billy returned from the hand-washing station, only he'd forgotten to use his towel, so he dripped all over the sand. Wide-eyed, he looked at a towering Calder. "Is he a stranger danger?"

Yes! "No, sweetie. Just someone I know." Forcing her runaway heart to slow, she said, "Could you please dry between your fingers so we don't get our sand any more wet?"

"Oops. I forgot!" He was off in a flash, giving Pandora about thirty seconds to get rid of Calder.

"I'm glad I found you." He pulled over one of the miniature toddler chairs. He looked ridiculous seated on it, but at least he was now closer to eye level. "We need to talk."

"Why?"

A muscle ticked in his clenched jaw. "Don't play games. I hate the way we left things."

"We didn't leave anything, Calder. You told me to get out of your house, so I did. End of story."

"Is this enough?" Billy returned, wriggling his now-dry fingers.

"Perfect." Pandora took the child's arm, drawing him back

onto his chair. "Now, remember how to make the letters *H, I* and *J?*"

"I think so." His brow furrowed with concentration.

Pandora found herself resenting Calder's intrusion. He may not see it, but her job was important. Just as she'd made a difference in Quinn's life, she was doing the same for her new charges.

"Good, sweetie. Whenever you're ready, give it a try."

"Pandora, please…" Calder got up from the chair and knelt next to her, his breath warm in her ear. Every wary, weary inch of her hungered for him, yet self-protective instincts kicked in, reminding her the second she'd let down her guard he'd hurt her once and surely would again. "I see you're busy now, but where are you staying? With Natalie? Give me her address and I'll stop by after work."

"The fact that you don't think me capable of finding my own place to stay speaks volumes."

"Miss Pandora?" Billy looked up at her. "Am I doing it right?"

"Just about perfect, sweetheart. Only, I want you to wipe out what you have and try again. This time make your *H* a little fatter."

"Okay!"

"I know I screwed up," Calder whispered for only her to hear. The sincerity of his words, the faint trace of coffee lacing his warm breath, proved her undoing.

She opened Billy's report file, removed one of the blank pages then wrote her new address. "Come over at six. Please bring Quinn. I miss him something fierce."

"He misses you, too."

"Miss Pandora, can you make the H for me?"

"Sure, sweetie." She wiped out what he'd done, then drew him an example. "How about you draw three of them right next to mine. Can you do that?"

"I think so…."

With Billy refocused on his task, she returned her attention to Calder. "You need to leave."

"Sure." As quietly as he'd arrived, Calder was gone.

Pandora hated herself for already missing him.

Above all, she reminded herself nothing mattered more than bringing her daughter home.

"WELL?" CALDER'S MOM all but pounced on him the second he walked through his door. She was still in the kitchen, only this time washing bottles. "Was she there?"

"Oh—she was not only there, but working so patiently with some little kid she looked like a saint."

"She hadn't been drinking? Or God forbid, worse?"

Was it wrong he shot his mom a dirty look? Her question made him feel foolish. "No. She was the same uber-responsible child-care giver I've known. No trace of the druggie I basically accused her of being."

"Good. Never have I been happier to see you proved wrong. And since I'm on a roll, while you were gone, I got to thinking about how much time I've seen you put in with Quinn and I've reached a decision."

"Yeah?" He opened the fridge and grabbed a couple slices of bologna. With his mom temporarily caring for the baby, and once he patched things up with Pandora, she'd no doubt move back in and his life would be on track.

"As much as I love being with my grandson, I think it's you who truly needs to be with him."

"What're you talking about? I'm with him all the time."

"Really? Then how much formula do you use to make a bottle? Do you know what types of foods he's supposed to eat? What happens if he starts crying and won't stop?"

"That doesn't happen."

"Gee, could that be because either Pandora or I have always been around to buffer you from actually knowing your son?"

Heels of his hands pressed to his forehead, Calder asked, "What is this? National Rag on Calder Day?"

"I'm not *ragging* on you, hon, but trying to teach you to be a better father. Just a guess, but I think you were so quick to jump on Pandora because her faults made your own not look so bad. What you don't get is that your lack of connection with Quinn will have lasting results. Don't believe me? Look at your relationship with your father, then tell me how good you are at relationships."

THE WHOLE RIDE to Pandora's new place, Calder wanted to be angry with his mom but couldn't. She'd added vital pieces to his own personal puzzle. The one thing he disagreed with was that he didn't actively participate in Quinn's everyday care.

Hell, he changed diapers. Gave baths. And what was the point of memorizing formula-to-water ratios when they were written on the side of the formula can?

Knowing Pandora's concerns about money, he was afraid she was living in a seedy part of town. What he found himself driving through was a neighborhood far nicer than his own. He knew it was the historic Ghent district but had never paid much attention to the homes—just bars.

The address Pandora gave him turned out to be a full-on Tudor mansion complete with its own small forest protected by ivy-covered, brick walls. Her apartment was above a four-car garage. Age-old servants' quarters?

He parked his SUV, grabbed Quinn and his gear from the back, then mounted the stairs, eager to apologize and get Pandora back to living with him. This place was nice and all, but she belonged at his house.

Hand poised to knock, nerves seized his stomach.

What should he say? It wasn't like him to not have a plan.

At work, he had everything figured out, but when it came to Pandora—even his son—he was a wreck.

She opened her door. The mere sight of her took his breath away. She wasn't wearing her glasses, which made her green eyes all the more striking. Her long, dark hair hung wavy and loose. He remembered holding her, burying his face in that hair, breathing in her sweet floral shampoo. He craved her smile, but instead of gifting it to him, she reserved it only for his son.

Quinn squealed and laughed, holding out his arms and pinching his fingers.

"Hey, handsome! There's my precious boy. Look how big you are!" Pandora took the squirming boy from Calder's arms.

While his son and Pandora got reacquainted, Calder sat on the plaid sofa, feeling about as needed as mosquitoes at a barbecue.

Quinn's smile was so big he drooled.

Of course, Pandora was first on the scene with a dishcloth to wipe him clean.

Calder didn't think of himself as the jealous type, but seeing how much his own son preferred Pandora's company to his rammed home his mom's earlier rant. He truly didn't have a meaningful relationship with Quinn. The knowledge not only hurt but left him more than a little ashamed and confused as to what he was supposed to do about it.

Eyeing a plate filled with neatly sliced cheese and summer sausage circled by crackers, Calder helped himself. Since the woman he'd come to see was ignoring him, he might as well do something with his time.

"Pout much?" Pandora asked. Still-smiley Quinn rode on her hip, grabbing her hair.

"That's stupid. I don't pout."

She laughed. "Look in the mirror."

He growled.

Seated in an armchair opposite him, holding Quinn's hands while jiggling him on her knee, she asked, "Is he walking yet?"

"Nope."

"Said any recognizable words?"

"Not that I've heard."

"I thought he was getting close." She fussed with Quinn's fine hair. "Seems like ages since I've seen him."

"That's why I'm here."

"Oh?" She still had eyes only for Quinn.

Regardless, Calder forged on. "First things first—I owe you an apology. Your confession scared me. I should've given it a while to sink in, thinking about the person you've become rather than giving you a knee-jerk reaction."

She said nothing. Just sat there, holding Quinn's hands, inspecting his little fingers.

"So I was thinking, with that out of the way, let's get your gear packed and we'll have you back in your old room in under an hour. My mom's still here until the morning, so I'll take both my girls out for a nice steak dinner. It'll be fun."

"Are you even listening to yourself? You sound like the one who may be drunk."

"What's that mean?" He sat forward, resting his elbows on his knees.

"It means you're crazy if you think I want anything to do with you."

"I know you don't mean that, any more than I meant to send you away."

"But you did." Her pretty, green eyes welled with tears. "And it hurt."

He slid off the sofa, shoved the coffee table aside to kneel before her for the second time that day. Taking her hands, he said, "I screwed up, okay? I'm sorry. But you have to understand how much you caught me off guard. Jail? Losing your child? Those are some pretty major bombs. What was I supposed to think?"

"I know it sounds bad—it *was* bad. But that's not who I am anymore. I don't like even thinking about those times, so why would I want to talk about them?"

"I get that, but can you understand my shock? I thought we were building something special."

"We are—*were*." She tried covering her face with her hands, but he still had hold of her and drew them down.

"Look at me." He gave her what he hoped was a reassuring squeeze. "I'm sorry. You once asked me for a second chance and I denied you. Well, now it's me needing your generosity, Pandora. Please, come back to my house. Without you…" He bowed his head. "It stopped feeling like a home. *Please*."

After what seemed like a lifetime of waiting, she finally took a deep breath, then softly answered, "I'm sorry…but no."

Chapter Thirteen

Pandora thrust Quinn at Calder, then dashed to the bathroom.

Emotions—ugly and raw—had balled in her chest, threatening her ability to breathe. Why did Calder affect her like this? Why had she given him so much power?

He banged on the door. "Pandora? Please, let me in."

She wanted to—figuratively and literally.

"I ambushed you like I was storming an enemy camp. I didn't mean it. You may not have noticed, but when it comes to women, I'm not exactly the sharpest tool in the shed."

The fact that he'd even acknowledged such a thing softened her frustration. As for her heart? Where she'd once opened it wide for him, like a rose spreading its petals toward the sun, she was now emotionally exhausted. Torn down and beaten and more than a little confused.

"Forget I asked you to move back in with me—us. How about you come to dinner? Do me the honor of meeting my mom? We'll figure out the rest from there."

She turned to the door, curving her hand around the crystal knob. Forehead resting against the varnished wood planks, she searched her heart for an answer, but only found images of his smile after he'd taken his first bite of her late-night meat-loaf sandwich. Her mind's eye saw him excited to witness her first time touching her toes in the Atlantic. She recalled how much fun they'd had painting her room and the kitchen. How patient he'd been when she'd needed his help that first day at the grocery store. How deeply he'd been touched his first time pushing Quinn on a swing. Most of all, she remembered that first kiss.

The kiss that even now she felt all the way from her tingling lips to her toes.

Against her better judgment, she turned the doorknob, letting Calder not only into the room but her heart.

He held Quinn, and his eyes were red rimmed as if he'd been crying. "Dinner?"

Swallowing her own tears, she nodded before drawing both her guys into a hug.

"I CAN'T TELL you how excited I am to finally meet you."

"I feel the same," Pandora said. Calder's mother's sincerity showed in the strength of her hug. She'd gotten to the steak house ahead of Pandora and her son and grandson. "I'm sorry we weren't able to meet in North Carolina."

Calder's mother looked to her son and scowled. "Me, too."

Pandora held Quinn, who'd fallen asleep during the walk from the parking lot. She'd forgotten how good the simple act of holding him felt.

When Calder helped her ease into a booth, then slid in beside her, Pandora tried ignoring the warm tingles flooding through her from his lightest touch, but he was a hard man to ignore.

"Let me have him." Calder took his sleepy boy, settling him into his detachable car-seat carrier.

Calder's mom extended her hand across the table for Pandora to shake. "We've yet to be formally introduced. I'm Gloria."

"Pandora," she said with a laugh and easy smile. Something about the older woman put her instantly at ease. She had her son's eyes, only in a wiser, more at-peace version.

"My guess is Quinn's happy to see his favorite nanny." Gloria took a blanket from the diaper bag Calder had set next to his son's carrier, then draped it over the sleeping infant. "This is the first time I've seen him truly rest since I've been with him."

"I missed him, too." And his dad. But no way was Pandora admitting that.

The waitress came and went.

Small talk ebbed and flowed.

Only after dessert and coffee had been served did Gloria raise the evening's stakes. While stirring cream into her coffee, she said, "I'm leaving first thing in the morning. Calder, since tomorrow's Friday and you're due back on base Monday, what are your plans for your son?"

"I'd hoped to have Pandora back home, but..." As his words trailed off, he ran his left pinkie along hers—just barely. It wouldn't be noticeable to anyone but her. Pandora felt it low in her belly. Somersaults of pure heat rushed through her, robbing her of all rational thought. "She kinda turned me down."

"Can't say as I blame her." Pandora was touched by Gloria's understanding her point of view. "Only, as we discussed, my reasons are different from hers." Turning to Pandora, she said, "For a moment, though, please humor me by considering an alternate offer from what Calder had in mind."

"O-okay...." Pandora wasn't sure what to think, but out of respect for her new friend, she'd be receptive to whatever Gloria proposed.

Hands clasped in front of her on the table, Gloria took a deep breath, slowly exhaled then smiled. "Here's what I'm thinking. Pandora, the nature of Calder's job means he has to have someone reliable in Quinn's life. That said, as long as he's in town, would you be amenable to watching Quinn solely during the day?"

"How much has your son told you about my past?"

"Everything."

Lips pressed, Pandora nodded. Might as well lay it all on the table. "My last chance to regain legal custody of my daughter will be at a March court hearing. In preparation for that, I follow a strict set of guidelines that have been set for me by my Social Services caseworker." Mouth dry, she sipped ice water. "Those guidelines include maintaining a permanent residence that will be suitable for my child, as well as keeping full-time employment."

Calder asked, "Can't you get both of those things with me?"

"Not on my terms." Pandora would've preferred speaking with Calder about the issue in private, but now that it was out there, she wouldn't back down. "As much as I've grown to love Quinn, my daughter is my primary goal. To get her back full-time, I have to be better than perfect—one hundred percent of the time. Until my hearing, I cannot—*will not* move from my current address. In the same respect, I can't take the risk of you discovering something about me you don't like and once again letting me go."

"Don't pull that." He raised his palms as if intent on slamming them against the table, but then thought better of it and calmed himself before losing control. "Had you told me everything you went through right from the start, this whole thing might have played out differently."

"Get over it. You can't deny I ever gave Quinn anything but expert care. As for my private life—it's *private*. The only reason I told you anything was because you made me feel as if I could trust you. Now I know those instincts were wrong. At this point, I can't take any more chances on you, Calder—at least not before my custody hearing."

Gloria appeared crestfallen. "Please, Pandora…"

"I said I wouldn't take a chance on your son, but for your

grandson?" She couldn't help but smile. "I can't get enough of him. I want to be there when he takes his first steps and says his first real words. What I propose is that Calder drop him off at the day care where I work each morning on his way to the base. I'll personally care for Quinn, and honestly, I think he'd enjoy socializing with the other kids." Hoping what she next proposed never came to pass, she said to Calder, "If you're deployed before you find a suitable full-time nanny, I would be honored if you'd allow Quinn to stay with me, in my home, where I promise he'll get the love and attention I wish I could give my own child."

Wiping tears from her cheeks, Gloria said, "I don't know about you, Calder, but that sounds like an ideal compromise to me."

He nodded. "Thank you. I think that'll work fine."

After paying the bill, Gloria left for the restroom.

On their own, Calder fixed her with a stare of such intensity she felt as if he'd kissed her all over again, and just like the last time, her traitorous body liked it. "For the record, I'm hereby issuing you a promise that I'll never again let you down."

I want to believe you, her emotional side wanted to say, but the more rational part of her said, "I wish I could believe you."

"THAT WENT WELL," Gloria said from the sofa when he walked in the door with Quinn after taking Pandora home. "She's a lovely girl. I see why you like her."

He took Quinn from his carrier, holding him on his lap when he all but collapsed into the armchair. Damn, all this emotional stuff was tiring.

Having slept through dinner, Quinn was now wired. He squirmed until Calder set him on the carpet where he crawled to the coffee table and tugged himself up, giggling and shrieking the whole way.

"Glad you had fun." He kicked off his Sperrys, then landed his feet atop the same table. "Personally, I thought it was a train wreck."

"Because you had to compromise?" Gloria sipped wine from a juice glass.

"I apologized. Repeatedly. There's not much else I can do." The whole thing had exhausted him. He was seriously ready for bed, but with Quinn wide-awake and still needing his bath, Calder didn't see sleep in his near future.

"Know what else you can do?" his mom asked. "Instead of just telling Pandora you're sorry. *Show* her."

"How?"

She tickled Quinn's belly. "That's something only you can decide."

AFTER ENTERING HER apartment, Pandora closed and locked the door, then leaned against it

What a night—in many ways.

She couldn't even begin processing the multitude of conflicting dynamics. Part of her had been downright giddy over once again holding Quinn in her arms. Meeting Gloria had been a joy, especially since her own mother was long since gone. But then there'd been Calder.

At times he'd been almost flirty, others defensive, others still powerfully persuasive.

It would've been so easy giving in to him, and she'd appreciated his apologies, but she wasn't ready for *more*.

Would she ever be? Who knew?

Right now, her sole focus had to be Julia.

"DID YOU AT LEAST like his mom?" Natalie asked at the first yard sale of their Saturday morning. Pandora had already given her a play-by-play of how the evening had broken down—skipping the part about Calder's unfair tactics with his pinkie finger.

"A lot. Oh—and you should be hearing from Calder about him enrolling Quinn in the infant class."

"Nope." She flipped through a stack of CDs. "After what he did to you, I blackballed him."

"I appreciate your mama lion instincts, but I'll be the first to admit my past isn't exactly popular résumé material. A part of me can't fault Calder for being concerned as to who's caring for his son. And why should Quinn be penalized? He deserves the best care."

"You raise interesting points." Holding out a CD, she asked, "What're your thoughts on *A Dean Martin Christmas?*"

"Never too early to bring a touch of class to your holiday playlist."

"Exactly."

By lunchtime, Pandora had found two poppy-colored throw pillows for the living room couch, a fairly decent oil painting of a sunset she thought would look great over the mantel, more books and a gorgeous set of dishes. She'd even picked up an older-model TV for fifteen bucks.

Pandora said her goodbyes to Natalie, then returned home to arrange her purchases. After a shower, she fixed her hair in preparation for her three-o'clock visit with Julia. Their meeting time was later than usual, but she wasn't complaining.

She'd just finished blow-drying her hair when a knock sounded on the door. She drew back the curtain to find Calder holding Quinn.

The moment the infant caught sight of her, he bucked and kicked, struggling to reach her.

She opened the door, took the baby then shot Calder a dirty look. "May I help you?"

"Sure hope so." He held up a bag of groceries, then brushed past her as if he was a man on a mission. "Mom ended up not catching a flight till this morning, and since Quinn's been mopey, I thought you might want to help cheer him up."

"Where are you going?" She closed the door.

"To your kitchen. While you're playing with the baby, I'm making my world-famous spaghetti."

Hands on her hips, she cocked her head. "I wasn't aware you know how to cook anything."

"I don't." His wink and sexy slow grin had her regretting her earlier decision to steer clear of him. "Mom gave me her recipe. Can't be too hard, right?"

She couldn't keep from grinning herself. "While that sounds great—especially the part about me cheering this little darling—" she kissed the top of Quinn's head "—I'm meeting my daughter in just under two hours. I usually leave an hour early, though. If a wreck or traffic caused me to be late, that could potentially hurt my case."

"Can I go?" He brushed past her, setting the groceries on the kitchen table. "I'd love to meet your Julia."

"No." She sat on the hearth, setting Quinn on the floor in front of her, holding his hands to help him walk.

"That was fast."

"Sorry, but Julia's visits are sacred. I would never introduce a man to her unless we were in a committed relationship—even then, if she so much as utters one syllable about not liking him, he's out."

"Knowing kids, isn't that unrealistic?" He unpacked the food.

"After what my ex put her through—no. For a while, she was afraid of all men. Counseling has finally helped. And why are you putting Parmesan cheese in my fridge? I don't have time for you to cook anything."

"I was thinking while you have a nice visit with Julia, Quinn and I will hang back here making you a meal. You have to eat, right?"

Sure, but being around him set her so on edge, she'd lost her appetite. No matter how much she denied it, she was still hopelessly attracted to the man—she craved another kiss like Santa craves cookies. "All right, you can stay, but first you have to tell me your endgame."

"What do you mean?" He'd set Italian sausage on the counter, using a steak knife to slit open the package.

"When you asked me to leave, you made it clear you wanted nothing to do with me and now you're cooking dinner? I'm a recovering alcoholic. I served time—not much, but more than enough to know I'm never going back to that place. Worst crime of all? My child was legally removed from my home."

"Knowing all that, then seeing the woman you are today?" He shook his head. "Hell, I admire you. Sure, I still have a lot of questions, but mostly I just kick myself for letting you get away."

WHILE WAITING IN the Social Services lobby, Pandora couldn't get Calder's words from her head. Was he sincere? Or was he panicked over not having her around to help watch Quinn? He'd mentioned still having questions. Once he learned her ex could one day be eligible for parole and occasionally sent letters begging to see Julia, would Calder want nothing to do with her all over again?

She might have a squeaky-clean new life on the outside, but on the inside, even she knew she had miles to go before being fully healed. For that matter, did anyone ever fully heal from an addiction?

With still twenty minutes to go, she folded her arms and paced. She was always excited to see her little girl, but even more so today. She couldn't wait to tell Julia about her bedroom. The way sunshine would be her new alarm clock.

Calder? Where does he fit in? And Quinn?

Hands to her temples, she almost wished Calder had never entered her life. He'd made her yearn for the kind of Ward and June Cleaver normalcy she'd only dreamed existed. It wasn't practical for her to believe magic could strike twice.

"Mommy!" Julia entered the building with her foster parents, but from her first sight of Pandora, she released Cindy's hand and made a beeline for her.

Heart swelling with happiness, Pandora crushed her daughter in a hug. "You smell good. Like sugar cookies. Been baking?"

"Uh-huh!" She looked to her foster mother. "Mom Cindy got new cookie cutters and we practiced for Thanksgiving. I made a turkey!"

"That's awesome!" Pandora rewarded her clever girl with another hug.

"Ready?" asked the social worker who supervised Pandora's visits.

"Where's Quinn?" Julia asked when they settled at a table to color the new princess coloring book Pandora had brought her.

"He's with his dad today."

"Is he nice?"

"Quinn's dad?"

"Uh-huh…." Julia concentrated so hard on staying inside the lines that she'd drawn her lower lip into her mouth.

"He's very nice."

"My dad scared me. He was mean to you."

Where had that come from? "Yes, sweetie, he was. I'm sorry."

"Mom Cindy's husband is real nice. He fixed my bike tire and learned me how to climb trees."

"You mean he taught you?" she corrected, smoothing Julia's ponytail.

"Yeah. It was fun. I didn't know dads could be fun. I thought they were all scary."

A too-familiar knot formed at the back of Pandora's throat. Honestly, until meeting Calder, she hadn't known, either. But she was learning....

"Done!" She held up her completed princess picture.

"It's beautiful," Pandora said. "Could I please keep it to put on my new fridge?"

"Only if I get to keep yours to put on *my* fridge!" Julia hopped and clapped after her request, reminding Pandora of the lighthearted banter they'd occasionally shared when she'd been very young.

"That's a deal."

As usual, two hours passed way too fast, but when the social worker asked Pandora if she'd like a special Christmas visit, Pandora felt she was definitely on track for winning her March case.

"Dude, seriously?" Calder was already having enough trouble following his mom's recipe. Not only couldn't he read her handwriting, but he'd bought the wrong tomato stuff. Who knew there was a difference between paste and stewed and just plain old sauce? It all looked the same to him. Now Quinn had helped himself to Pandora's lower cabinets, tugging out all the pots and pans, laughing and squealing with each clang. "Sorry, but this isn't going to work."

Calder made a makeshift baby corral from the sofa cushions and coffee table, then set Quinn in the middle with a few toys from his diaper bag.

He'd barely made it back to the kitchen before his son let loose with a wail that sounded as if he'd been stabbed.

Calder ran back in, picked up his bawling son. "Don't you want me to impress Pandora with this fancy dinner?"

Quinn answered with more ear-piercing screams.

What to do? What to do?

The usual panic set in when Calder couldn't calm his son. He was hardly ever fussy with Pandora, but he had been with Gloria. What had Pandora done to appease him?

Remembering her pacing and singing with the occasional rocking motion thrown in, Calder tried cradling Quinn close to his chest.

"I'm not Sinatra," Calder said, "but here goes…"

As best as he could, fudging at least half the words, Calder sang and rocked his son.

PANDORA TRIED SQUELCHING the seed of excitement growing inside her when she saw Calder's car still in her driveway.

With Julia's picture and her purse in hand, she locked up her car and climbed the stairs leading to her apartment. At the top, instead of slipping her key in the lock, she stopped to listen.

Was Calder singing?

Peeking through a part in the curtains, she found him not only crooning to his son, but on his knees, holding Quinn's hands, dancing with him. The best part was that Calder wasn't even going with a nursery rhyme, but vintage Journey.

Judging by the smile on Quinn's face, he loved it.

She soundlessly opened the door, wanting to view more of the adorable scene, but Quinn caught sight of her and dropped to his knees, crawling her way. "Hey, cutie!"

Grabbing onto her slacks, he raised himself upright, pinching for her to lift him.

"How'd it go?" Calder asked. Was it her imagination or was his face a shade redder from getting caught being a not-so-manly SEAL? What he didn't know was that she found this softer side infinitely more attractive—not a good thing, considering her intent to remain man-free.

Chapter Fourteen

Fanning herself from the heat just looking at Calder raised in her cheeks, Pandora asked, "Do you have the oven on?"

"No. Why?"

"I'm warm." She removed the hat and gloves the blustery day's temperature had called for, set them on the nearby kitchen table then picked up Quinn. "Did you have fun exploring?"

"Gaa! Baa!"

"Well, that sounds interesting," she teased.

"How was your daughter?" Calder asked.

"Wonderful." She tilted her head back and closed her eyes, remembering her little girl's smile. "I know that old saying about not wishing your life away, but in this case, I'd give anything for it to already be March."

"Is your hearing early March or late?" He picked up sofa cushions from the floor.

"Early. What happened?" She nodded toward her pillaged couch.

"Thought I might outsmart my Tasmanian devil by corralling him, but turns out he's way smarter than me."

"I know the feeling." She kissed the infant's nose. "So where's this fabulous meal you promised? I'm starving." Walking the ten feet to the kitchen, she explored the stove and oven.

"Um, yeah… Have you ever tried cooking while a Tasmanian devil circles your feet?"

"As a matter of fact, I have. Welcome to my world."

They shared a laugh, which surprised Pandora. When Calder sent her away, she'd honestly feared never laughing again.

Neither of them had the energy to figure out where Calder's sauce had gone wrong, so he ordered a pizza and Pandora scrambled an egg for Quinn to go along with his bottle.

After eating, the baby drifted off to sleep, leaving Pandora achingly aware that she and Calder were alone. The sensation reminded her of their nights back at his house. How sometimes they'd watch a movie or just hang out in the living room reading. What they hadn't done was spend a lot of time talking—no doubt largely because of her unwillingness to open up about her past.

"Here we are again." Calder shot a slow grin her way. "Seems like we always end up just sitting."

"Sure sign of parental exhaustion—not that I'm Quinn's parent, but you know what I mean."

"Yeah." After a few more seconds' silence during which she wasn't sure what to do with her hands, he asked, "If it's not too personal, tell me about your ex."

"Wow…" She shook her head. "Talk about jumping straight from the shallow to the deep end."

"You don't have to answer. Guess I feel like I know you better than anyone else, yet when I really think about it, I hardly know anything about you."

"Feeling's mutual." She reached across the sofa to jab his shoulder. He was all muscle to the point his skin hardly had any give. Eyes briefly closed, she struggled to forget the sight of him doing a towel-wrapped shower dash to his room. His bare chest still glistening from the water.

"All right, ask me anything. I'm an open book."

Where did she start? Careful to avoid any more thoughts of his pecs—not to mention those six-pack abs—she asked, "Why is a guy like you still single?"

"I assume you mean such a handsome man?" There he went again with the grin that never failed to stir needs she'd believed long gone.

"Among other things." Squelching the familiar urge to fan herself, she said, "I'm serious. You've got a great job. You seem reasonably smart—except when it comes to caring for small children…." She winked.

Now he was jabbing her. "Watch it. I resent that statement." He rubbed the back of his neck, then groaned. "Where do I even start? When I was in North Carolina, I had a great talk with my stepdad. Mom, too, but it was Harold who unwittingly lit a lightbulb in my head."

"Oh?" Intrigued, she kicked off her loafers to sit with her legs tucked beneath her, angling to face him.

"My folks split when I was eight. Dad cheated, but oddly enough, there wasn't much fighting. I think I was more upset than my mom. He moved to Nebraska and on school breaks I was required to stay with him. Seems like every time I went, he had a different wife who made a big deal out of being my stepmom. By the time I was in high school, it was ridiculous." He shrugged. "I didn't understand the point of marrying someone—or even being in a relationship with her—if it would only end badly. Easier to avoid the issue altogether, you know?"

"Interesting…." She couldn't help but draw comparisons to their lives. "Even though I watched my mom live in a horrible marriage, after she died, I wanted my own marriage so badly that right after high school I ran off to get married—to a man who treated me worse than my father. You, on the other hand, did the opposite of what you'd seen as a child.

Maybe a few years from now I'd like to take a few online college psychology courses."

"You'd probably be good at psychology. Since you've experienced so much, I think you'd be able to help a lot of people."

"Really?" No one had ever said something like that to her before—that she might be good at something. Oh, sure, Natalie told her all the time she was good with kids, but this was different. Her interactions with children felt more like play than a job.

"Of course." He edged sideways to better face her. "I wouldn't say it if I didn't mean it. Now that I realize you're the real deal—you actually beat the kinds of addictions that haunt people their entire lives—even kill them—I'm impressed."

"Thank you." Fairly glowing from his kind words, she found herself not wanting the night to end. How differently would things be between them now if she'd been open with Calder from the start? Would they be holding hands? Kissing? *More?*

She snatched a magazine from an end table, back to fanning flaming cheeks.

"You okay?" he asked.

"Really good."

"Me, too."

He smiled.

She smiled. "There's a swap meet at the fairgrounds tomorrow. I thought I might go. Pick up a few things for the apartment. Think you and Quinn would want to tag along?"

"Sure. What time?"

"It starts at ten. Is that all right?" Her heart galloped while awaiting his reply. Would she ever feel normal around him? Did she even want to?

"Perfect. Quinn and I will pick you up. In the meantime…" He looked to his son. "Guess I'd better get this guy to bed."

After helping Calder gather Quinn's baby gear, she walked him to the door.

For the longest time Calder just stood there with his hand on the knob. He acted apprehensive, as if he wanted to say something but couldn't quite make the words come. "Well…"

She flashed a nervous smile, willing her runaway pulse to slow. Why, when he'd hurt her so badly, would she have given anything right now for him to kiss her?

"Guess I'll see you in the morning." He tried hugging her, but with Quinn's carrier bumping their knees, much to Pandora's everlasting regret any closeness proved impossible.

A good thing? Pandora honestly didn't know.

"AGAIN?" QUINN HAD slept the entire ride home, only to now be wired. "I've got to get you on a schedule, bud."

"Gaaaaah!"

"My thoughts exactly."

Calder bathed his son, having a little too much fun with Quinn's impressive boat collection. After drying him, just as he'd seen Pandora and his mother do, he rubbed lotion on Quinn's bottom, then diapered him, concentrating extra hard on keeping the adhesive tabs even.

"Hungry?" he asked.

"Goooooo bah!"

"Dad-dee."

"Gaaaaaah bah!"

"Dad-dee."

Instead of speaking, the kid blew a raspberry containing enough drool to send them back to the bathroom for a fresh face wash.

For the life of him, Calder couldn't remember if Pandora and his mom fed Quinn right before bed or not. Personally,

Calder was always sleepy after a big meal, but maybe that wasn't the case with kids.

How was it possible that he'd had Quinn since summer and he still didn't have his schedule nailed down? Was that what his mom meant about forcing him to get to know his son?

"How about we both get a snack?"

In the kitchen, he foraged. He found plenty for himself, but he wasn't sure about feeding a protein bar to a baby.

"I'll sure be glad when you can just say what you want."

"Bah!"

"You want a bottle?"

"Dah!"

"Dad-dee?"

"Goooo dah!"

"You do know you're making me feel crazy?"

Quinn grabbed his father's nose and squeezed.

Calder was exhausted, but considering a certain hyper infant showed no sign of sleeping any time soon, Calder popped the original *Total Recall* in the DVD player, settling in for a long night.

"What do you think Pandora's doing?"

"Paaaah?"

"Pan-dor-a."

"Pah hor!"

"Pan-door-rah."

Though his favorite movie played on TV, it'd become much more entertaining trying to get Quinn to say Pandora's name.

WHEN CALDER YAWNED for the tenth time in five minutes as they strolled the bustling flea market and Quinn slept soundly in his stroller, Pandora asked, "What'd you two do last night after you left?"

"I wanted to go to bed, but Mr. Party Animal refused."

"I had him on a great schedule. What happened?" The moment she asked the question, Pandora regretted it. What had happened was Calder sent her on her way. Despite bright sun and the party atmosphere provided by a local swing band, her mood plummeted.

"We both know I screwed up." He sidestepped three boys wielding squirt guns. "You don't have to rub my nose it."

"That wasn't my intent—even though that is what happened. And for the record—" she veered the stroller toward a towering oak, its shade protecting a picnic table "—I understand why you sent me away. If our roles had been reversed and I'd hired you to watch Julia, I'd have done the same. Bringing up the schedule was an honest mistake. I didn't mean anything by it."

He'd shoved his hands into his jeans pockets. "While we're talking about issues probably better left alone…" He sighed and picked at the bark on a nearby oak. "In retrospect, I'm not entirely sure my reaction was all about you. Your past."

"What do you mean?" She brushed crumbs from the table's bench, then had a seat.

"I don't even know how to say this." He looked to the cloudless blue sky, then to her.

"Good grief, Calder, whatever it is, spit it out. Lord knows I've spilled enough of my dirty secrets."

"Looking back on it, your news relieved me. What I felt for you—" he sat beside her, easing his fingers between hers "—it happened too fast. My whole life I shied away from anything real, yet there you were. You scared me. My own feelings scared me."

He straddled the bench, cupping his hand to her face, brushing her cheek with his thumb. Though the crowded sale went on around them, Pandora felt sheltered on an island created by Calder's confession. He cared about her.

"Hell…" He chuckled, leaning close enough to send her

pulse deep into the danger zone. "I'm scared right now, but apparently not smart enough to run."

"Maybe it's time to stop running?"

He kissed her deliciously slow and sweet. He kissed her until she was tilting her head to allow him deeper access and closing her eyes with a sigh.

"Pandora? Is that you and little Quinn?"

Still in a kiss-induced fog, Pandora glanced up to see Lila with her husband in tow.

"I told her to leave you two alone," Martin grumbled.

"Oh, hush." Lila gave her husband a swat. "I haven't seen you in forever, and you missed last week's beautification meeting."

As high as Pandora had been moments earlier, she was now that low. What did she say? Lila knew nothing about her past.

Calder settled his arm around her shoulders. "Quinn and I are so proud of her. She landed a great new job at the day care her agency runs. Quinn starts there Monday."

"How exciting." Lila gave her a quick hug. "But does this mean you're no longer living in the neighborhood?"

"No," Calder again answered for her, "but, hopefully, she'll be over for lots of visits."

Lila hugged her again, and after more small talk, the elderly couple ambled on.

"Thanks," Pandora said to Calder. "I didn't know what to say."

"Like you once told me, there's really nothing to say. The past is past." He kissed the tip of her nose. "Let's keep it that way."

THE NIGHT BEFORE Thanksgiving, Calder coached his son during bath time. "Pan-dor-a."

"Paa gah!"

"Pan-door-rah."

"Ah gah roo!" Splash, splash.

Calder rocked back on his heels. "Dude, you're killing me. Do you know how much it would mean to Pandora if you said her name?"

"Goo goo goo!" Quinn was too busy with his boats to pay any more attention, and to be truthful, this had also become Calder's favorite part of the day. Though he now *played* with boats of a much larger scale, he'd forgotten how much fun small boats could be.

As frustrated as he'd been with his mom for abandoning him to care for Quinn on his own, Calder was now thankful. He'd mastered almost every aspect of infant care, though he still struggled with the tiny snaps now and then.

He gave Quinn a good scrub, then readied him for bed.

Back on the schedule Pandora had written for him, Quinn now had a small bottle before bed, then Calder cleaned his son's teeth before settling him into his crib.

While Calder liked the feeling of accomplishment caring for his son all on his own gave him, he also sorely missed Pandora being with him in the evenings after Quinn drifted off to sleep.

Never in a million years would he have thought he'd envy his friends Deacon and Garrett, but he found himself wanting to share his time with Quinn with Pandora—not because he expected her to perform any of the work, but because he missed sharing small milestones he knew she'd enjoy.

One day soon, Quinn would say his first word, take his first solo steps. Calder wanted Pandora to be there, sharing each and every one of those special moments.

What about her daughter?

The thought hadn't escaped him that Pandora and Julia were a package deal. It'd taken months for him to adjust to being a father to his own child. How would he cope with parenting another man's daughter? One who no doubt carried a staggering amount of emotional baggage?

On autopilot, he reached for a beer, but then put it back in the fridge. He didn't need liquor to deal with this issue; he needed to open his heart. Julia was the same age he'd been when Harold had become a true father to him. Was it time for Calder to pay forward the favor?

If so, how would he know?

Chapter Fifteen

The only way Pandora could be happier would be if Julia had shared this beautiful day with her and all her friends. With a fire crackling in the fireplace, the traditional Thanksgiving meal devoured and her small kitchen cleaned, her apartment's living room had been transformed into a casino. The makeshift dining table they'd assembled from plywood and sawhorses with everyone bringing their own folding chairs was now the scene of a poker tournie using candy corn for chips. So far, Martin was beating the pants off everyone.

Holding Quinn, Pandora watched Cooper and Mason go all in while Heath and Patricia folded. Natalie and Anna conferred on what to do with their poker hands.

Calder spied them. "Hey! No fair playing in teams."

Lila sipped her wine. "What does it hurt? You guys are trouncing the ladies."

The game continued with plenty more good-natured ribbing.

A year earlier, Pandora wouldn't have believed it possible for her life to now be so full. Yet here she sat, surrounded by friends who felt more like family than her real family ever had.

Turning in his chair, Calder said, "How about letting me hold Quinn and you get in on the next game?"

"Thanks, but I'm right where I want to be."

The night wound on, with Martin claiming bragging rights until Lila informed him it was time to go.

The remaining guys disassembled the big table, moving their game to the kitchen table while the women got a jump start on the next holiday by watching *Christmas Vacation,* which Pandora had picked up at a thrift store, along with a secondhand DVD player.

Pandora shared the sofa with Natalie. Quinn lounged between them, plinking on his toy piano. Patricia and Anna sat in armchairs closer to the TV.

"How's it going between you and Calder?" Natalie asked in a conspiratorial tone.

"We're friends."

Eyebrows raised, she asked, "*Just* friends?"

"We've kissed…." Boy, had they kissed. Home from the swap meet, things had grown heated, but that was it. She wasn't sure she was ready for *more,* and being a gentleman, Calder had agreed to take things slow.

"I'm glad things are working out." Natalie jiggled Quinn's hippo rattle. "In my professional opinion, you two would be good for each other."

"Your *professional* opinion?" Grinning, now Pandora was the one raising her brows.

"Now that you've worked out your kinks, the three of you make a nice family. When Julia comes home, I'm sure she'll like him, too."

"Hope so." Pandora looked in Calder's direction. His dark hair had grown long, but she liked it. When he kissed her, she weaved her fingers through it, pressing him closer.

"He's gotten a lot better with Quinn, too. I haven't seen you attending to a single diaper all day."

"I know. He's a changed man."

"Just like you're a changed woman." Natalie took Pandora's hand, giving her a squeeze. "See what I mean? Match made in heaven."

"I want to believe that, but I'm afraid."

"What else could go wrong? He knows more about you than I do. Once Julia moves in here and she gets to know him, I predict wedding bells by next summer."

"Stop." She cast her friend a warning look.

"I'm just sayin'…"

"Yeah, well, quit sayin'. I got my hopes up once, and you saw where that led. For now, I'm taking life day by day."

Mason startled Pandora by shouting, "You're such a cheat, Hopper! No way did you just get dealt a royal flush."

"The hell I didn't!"

"Hey, whoa…" Calder broke them up. "Keep it down, I've got a kid over there." A kid who, thankfully, hadn't been spooked by his friend's outburst.

Cooper sighed. "I miss the good old days when it was just us guys playing for cash."

Heath dealt new hands. "You're just jealous you don't have a good woman. Me and Calder got it all figured out."

"You and the nanny are back in business?" Mason asked.

"Think so." Calder spread his cards. Nothing. Not even a lousy pair.

"Don't leave us hanging." Mason leaned in, making sure the women didn't overhear him. "So you're finally hooking up with the nanny?"

"Drop it," Calder said more harshly than he'd intended, but hopefully it got his point across. "She's way more than just Quinn's nanny."

"You're serious about her?" Heath asked. "If so, man, you need to elope. For me and Patricia, this whole wedding thing is out of control."

Calder slapped his cards to the table. "There's no wedding. We're just friends."

"With benefits?" Mason might be one of his best friends, but at the moment, Calder was on the verge of calling him outside for a *talk*.

"She's a good woman. My kid loves her. End of story." As to how Calder felt about her, all he knew was that even the simple act of staring across the room at her made his chest swell with anticipation for when they were finally alone.

"WHAT A GREAT DAY." Pandora plucked a few stray candy corns from the kitchen floor. "Hope everyone had as nice a time as I did."

Quinn had conked out in his carrier.

"Pretty sure fun was had by all except Mason, who'd better be glad we weren't playing for real money."

She smiled. Bone-deep contentment didn't come close to describing the way her body hummed when Calder drew her into his arms.

"While we were playing, the guys raised a few legitimate questions."

"Oh?" she said against the warm wall of his chest.

"Mason asked if we're an item. I didn't know what to tell him. I mean, we've never really talked about any of this."

"Define *this*..." She skimmed her free hand along his ridiculously chiseled abs. What would they feel like without his shirt?

"Where do I begin? I wouldn't know how to define it. Are we going steady? That sounds so fifties-era high school. Are you my girlfriend? See what I mean? Do we even need a definition? Can't we just have an understanding?"

"I suppose, but then you'd have to define that. What are your terms?" she asked.

"For starters—" he kissed the crown of her head "—I don't want any other guys within fifty feet of you."

"That might be tough," she teased, "considering my favorite student happens to be your son."

"You know what I mean. I want you strictly for myself."

"That's all good and well, but what happens when you find a sitter and decide you need a night of barhopping? What if I have a problem sharing you?"

He tipped her head back, kissing her slow and breathless and dizzy. "I suppose a mutually beneficial agreement could be arranged. Any further demands?"

"More of this...." To make sure he got the message, this time she was the one kissing him, only the day's heady pleasure left her hungry for more than the leftovers stocking the fridge. Emboldened by happiness, she slid her hands under his shirt, finally sampling those abs she'd been dreaming of. His warm, sinewy strength didn't disappoint.

He groaned. "What're you doing to me?"

"What we've both been craving...."

Braver still, she undid the button on his jeans, then lowered the zipper. He'd gone commando and her actions set him free.

Giggling, she said, "Oops."

"Now, that's embarrassing." There was no doubt about him being on board with whatever came next—assuming that meant a long-awaited trip to her bedroom.

"It shouldn't be." Caressing the swollen length of him, she knelt to give him further pleasure, but he stopped her, drawing her up. "What's wrong?"

With a hand on her chin, he forced her gaze to his. "Are you sure this is what you want?"

Nodding, she smiled. "All I really know is I want—need— this closeness. I've lost so much in my life. I can't lose you."

"I'm not going anywhere." He kissed her forehead and cheeks and nose and finally, finally, her lips before taking her hand. "Come on. The kiddo's down for the count. Let's take full advantage of that situation." Taking her hand, he guided her to her room.

Once there, she began unbuttoning his shirt, but he again halted her progress. "The second part of the speech I started a minute ago was that this first time is especially for you." He kissed her soft and slow and thoroughly, all the while tugging up her sweater, pausing only long enough to drag it over her head. He tossed the garment to the floor and lowered his lips to her throat and collarbone and the tops of her breasts before also removing her bra.

The heat from the fire hadn't made it to her room. The sudden chill hardened her nipples, but he soon had her warm by rubbing his palm over one and suckling the other.

By the time he'd lowered his seeking mouth to her abdomen, then lower still to unhook her skirt's waistband and let it pool with a whisper around her feet, her breathing had become ragged.

He removed her leather pumps, rolled down her navy tights. When all that remained of her clothing were the lacy scrap of her panties, he opened his mouth against her sensitive mound, exhaling tantalizingly warm air against her most private area. He made her shiver, but not because she was cold.

Hands pressed to the back of his head, she spread her legs, inviting him—needing him—to explore farther. He dragged down her panties before backing her against the bed. Pushing her back until her calves dangled against the edge of the bed, he lowered his mouth again, this time trailing a line of shiver-inducing kisses from her ankle to the growing hum between her legs.

By the time he kissed more, then inserted one finger and then two, she could scarcely control her fevered emotions. She bucked against him, all at once needing release, yet never wanting the building, budding waves of pure sensation to stop.

"I—I need you inside me," she barely found breath to say.

"Shh…" Ignoring her, he performed more wicked tricks with his tongue before sensations transformed to even more paralyzing pressure. Thrashing her head to and fro, she thrust her fingers into his hair. Higher and higher waves of pure pleasure carried her until she could no longer think and barely even breathe. When release finally came, it manifested in a white-hot explosion behind her closed eyes.

Shivering, sweating, exhausted yet eager for more, she drew him up, begging him for additional sweet release.

He fished a condom from his jeans pocket, then whole-heartedly obliged.

THE WEDNESDAY AFTER Thanksgiving, Pandora had just disinfected the last of the three-year-old classroom toys when she saw Calder headed her way. He hadn't yet grabbed Quinn from the infants' room, and her kids were all gone for the day. Was it wrong to be so excited for their few minutes alone?

"On my lunch break," she said, pressing her hands to his chest before sneaking in a kiss, "I found the cutest decoration idea for a boy's room. My visitation with Julia is early on Saturday, so after that, do you want to see if we can tackle building a battleship bookcase in Quinn's room?"

"I would love to, but I've got bad news."

Nerves seized her system. What else could he possibly have learned about her to turn him against her? "I've told you *everything*.…"

"Baby, no…" Framing her face with his hands, he pressed his lips to hers with an urgency he hadn't before shown. "You're all I've ever wanted. I'm shipping out in the morning."

She'd expected his news to concern her—not him. Now that she knew the truth, she'd have almost rather it had concerned her. At least that way he wouldn't be in danger.

"I want to spend the rest of my time here with you and Quinn. Stay the night with me?"

Unable to speak past the fear knotting her throat, she nodded.

"THIS IS NICE." The November night was calm and not too chilly. By the light of a nearly full moon, they'd packed a picnic and headed for a deserted beach, where Calder built a small fire for hot dogs and marshmallows.

Calder held Quinn a safe distance from the fire, helping him hold his marshmallow stick. "Okay, bud, the secret to a great marshmallow is catching it on fire, then sucking out the gooey insides."

"You can't let him eat that charred stuff," Pandora protested.

"I've eaten it all my life and look how big and strong I am. You want him to be a man, don't you?"

"Well, sure, but not if it means his poor belly's going to be filled with charcoal."

"Hear that, buddy? Your mom thinks we don't know what we're doing." He pulled the flaming ball from the fire and blew it out, waiting for it to cool a few seconds before eating the crispy outer layer, then letting Quinn lick the gooey part.

"Calder?"

"Hmm?"

"Did you mean to say what you just did?" She loaded her own marshmallow onto a stick, poking it into the fire.

"What?"

"You referred to me as Quinn's mom. Is that how you really feel?"

He met her gaze to find her sincere, which left him wondering about his own intentions. Honestly, the slip had been unconscious. Above all, he wanted to keep the mood light. Mellow. He didn't want to cover anything heavy. He needed this mental image to keep with him during the endless black nights ahead. He needed to know normalcy waited for him as soon as he got home.

"Calder?"

"Yeah?" He shrugged. "Sure. I guess that's how I feel. Think about it. Since Quinn's arrival, you're the only mom he's known. It makes sense."

"It also implies we're a heckuva lot more involved than simple boyfriend and girlfriend."

"That what you want?" He dug through the diaper bag for the wipes to clean Quinn's sticky face and hands. "To make things official?"

"You mean get married?" Her eyes widened.

"I suppose that's what people do. You don't have to look so shocked."

"I'm not. I guess I haven't really thought about it—wait, that's not true." As if dazed, she shook her head. "Of course I've thought about it, but in daydreams, you know? Guess I never believed someone like you would want someone like me."

"You know how crazy that sounds, don't you?" With one arm still holding Quinn a safe distance from the fire, he shifted her glasses on top of her head. "You're beautiful."

Ducking her head, she said, "Thanks, but we both know this goes deeper than looks. Calder, I have a child you've never even met. When Julia comes home, she'll have a lot of adjusting. What happens if you two don't get along?"

He snapped his stick in half, tossing it into the crackling fire. "Think I haven't thought of that?"

"I'm sorry. I know this isn't how you wanted our night to go."

"It's okay." He released Quinn just long enough to pick up the boy's hat from where the infant had tossed it a couple feet away.

"Calder, look…"

"I know we'll eventually hash this out, but can't it wait till I get home?"

"Um, this isn't about us, but your son. *Look*."

Calder turned his attention to Quinn only to gasp. "I'll be damned…."

Quinn stood all on his own, pointing at the fire. *"Gah!"*

Arching his head back, Calder looked to the heavens. He'd never been much for church, but he had to believe someone was up there looking out for him tonight. If he'd missed his son's first solo steps, he'd have been devastated.

TOGETHER, PANDORA AND Calder bathed Quinn. While Calder fixed his son a bottle, Pandora dressed the boy in his fuzzy pj's. She'd missed this most special part of each day. To know she'd now get Quinn to herself each night was small consolation considering his father would be in danger.

Calder returned with Quinn's snack. "Mind if I feed him?"

"No. Of course not." She passed Quinn over to his dad and when Calder settled into the nursery rocker, cradling his son, Pandora struggled to control her runaway emotions. As Calder softly sang "Lullaby and Goodnight," she didn't even try hiding silent tears.

Calder had come such a long way as a parent since they'd first met. Quinn was a lucky boy.

Quinn fell asleep before finishing his bottle.

His father tucked him into his crib. When he turned away, it was to wipe his own tears.

In the hall, Calder said, "I never thought it was possible to hurt this bad. How do you stand being away from your daughter? Knowing she's so close yet untouchable."

"It's not easy. But I get by." She slipped her arms around his waist. "You will, too."

"My commanding officer warned this could be a long one. What if Quinn doesn't remember me by the time I get home?"

"If you'll record that beautiful song—" Pandora stood on tiptoe, pressing a simple yet heartfelt kiss to his lips "—I promise I'll make sure Quinn hears you every night."

"You'd do that for me?" he asked into her hair.

"Yes." *I'd do anything for you.*

"Ready to call it a night?" He held her and she nodded against him.

Taking her hand, he led her to the bed.

He faced her, settled his hands on her hips, nuzzling her neck until she feared her knees would buckle from desire. "You have no idea how much I want you."

"I—I feel the same." She unbuttoned her blouse, and this time he didn't try stopping her.

"I know this'll sound crazy, but I want—need—this to be different from other times. Slower, more deliberate. I need every detail burned to memory so I can call it up during especially dark nights."

"Of course," she whispered with a kiss.

Their lovemaking was as he'd requested—slow and beautiful and poignantly, painfully sweet.

After, they showered together, taking turns washing each other, ending up making love again beneath the hot spray.

Finally in bed, when Calder spooned her, and she knew their precious last few hours were ticking away, Pandora's heart shattered. "I don't want you to go," she said in a voice so quiet she wasn't sure she'd spoken at all.

"Likewise."

But when Pandora woke, Calder was gone.

Along with part of her heart.

DECEMBER WAS A BLUR.

Gloria and Harold, Calder's stepfather, had driven over

to spend time with Quinn. They were staying at Calder's house, and on Christmas they watched Quinn for Pandora so she could visit Julia.

The waiting area was surprisingly full. Carols played over the intercom and there was a table laden with cookies and punch. A new, softer side to Social Services? Pandora didn't mean to come across as bitter, but just as she was frightened for Calder, she was terrified something could go wrong at her hearing.

She was tired of this place. She'd done everything the judge and her caseworker had asked, and damn it, she wanted her child.

Julia bounded in, holding Mom Cindy's hand and wearing a red-velvet holiday dress with a black sash designed to look like Santa's belt. Everything about her was perfection, from her specially curled hair to her shiny new black-patent shoes. A pang ripped through Pandora. Even if she won her hearing, would she ever be able to provide a life as rich and full for her daughter as Mom Cindy and her doctor husband had?

While Julia excitedly rambled off the long list of toys Santa had brought, Pandora absorbed every word, wishing with all her heart she could scoop up her daughter and run. But where would she go? Calder and Quinn had also become her family. Only, with Calder now in Afghanistan and Julia still with her foster family, each day it became more of a struggle to get out of bed.

"Mommy?"

"Yes, sweetie?"

"Am I ever gonna live with you, or is Mom Cindy my mom now?" Her daughter's question not only caught her off guard but renewed her fighting spirit. Calder would eventually come home. So would her daughter.

"You know what court is, right?"

Julia nodded.

"In March, we go see a judge and he's going to let you come home with me. I have a nice new apartment and right now Quinn is even staying there until his dad comes home."

Julia brushed her new doll's blond hair. "Where's his dad?"

"A long way away. He's in the navy, and it's his job to protect us." Pandora refused to cry—not on what was supposed to be a happy day.

"Will I ever meet him?"

"I sure hope so. Right after you come home with me."

"Is he nice?"

Pandora's mind drifted to her heartbreakingly beautiful last night with Calder. "Yes, sweetie, he's a very nice man."

"Good." Her daughter snuggled against her. "I like Mom Cindy, but I love you. I miss you real bad."

"I miss you, too, pumpkin." She kissed the top of her curls. "Not much longer and I'll bring you home. We'll never be apart again."

"Promise, Mommy?"

Confident her third trip to court would be a charm, Pandora gave a playful tug on one of Julia's curls. "Promise."

Chapter Sixteen

After Christmas and New Year's and Quinn's sweet, simple January 3 first birthday celebrated at the day care with his grandparents and all his little friends, for Pandora each passing day, then week, that Calder still hadn't returned became studies in keeping herself busy. She'd bought a cheap digital camera and started scrapbooking her many photos of Quinn for Calder to have when he came home. She'd tried knitting but failed miserably. Baking was fun, but after an early February filled with heart-shaped cookies and cupcakes, Natalie gave her a well-meaning but firm lecture on the kids having had too many sweets.

Her hearing was scheduled for Friday, March 7 at the Norfolk Juvenile and Domestic Relations District Court.

She spent the days leading up to it working extra hard, trying to prevent having dreams or nightmares. The nightmares were always the same. She showed up in court and the judge found some excuse not to grant her custody. The dreams were even worse because she walked out of the courthouse into beautiful afternoon sun, holding hands with her little girl, only to wake in predawn darkness, realizing she hadn't truly been reunited with Julia. It had been a dream.

By the day of her hearing, Pandora was a mess. She hadn't slept, had no interest in eating and her stomach was knotted 24/7.

Natalie and Lila accompanied her.

Lila held her hand when they stepped into a courtroom crowded with other parents like Pandora. Somewhere in the large building, Julia and her Mom Cindy waited in a holding room. Was her daughter scared? Was she old enough to grasp the gravity of the day's importance?

Lila said, "Everything's going to be okay."

Incapable of speech, Pandora nodded.

It took ninety minutes before her case was called. She approached the judge's bench on legs so rubbery she was surprised she could even walk. Her heart adopted an unnaturally fast rhythm.

"Ms. Moore." The judge peered down at her from over his reading glasses. "First, let me commend you on not only making it to my court sober and in a timely manner, but for all the work you seem to have done to prove yourself a worthy mother. Your caseworker gave you rave reviews. I see a lot of cases run through here, and the way you've turned your life around is indeed impressive."

"Thank you, sir." Pandora had her hands so tightly clasped behind her that her nails dug into her sweating palms. She was afraid to hope his compliment meant her nightmare was nearly over.

"Actually, I'd like to thank you for being a shining example of how our system can work. You've followed everything on your case list to the letter—with the exception of housing. You were to have six months residing at the same address, but you only have four. Why is that?"

Pandora's mouth was so dry she feared not being able to speak. "Prior to that, sir, my job was as a live-in nanny, but my employer discovered my past and let me go."

"You mean you were fired?" The judge's bushy gray eyebrows shot up.

"Yes, sir, but not by the agency I work for. Just my boss.

Th-that's why I found a new home. But everything's fine now. He's currently deployed in Afghanistan, and I'm once again caring for his son."

Slapping her file on his bench, he removed his glasses, setting them atop her file. "Let me get this straight. This court removed a child from your custody, yet you're now caring for another child in an unsupervised manner?"

"Yes, sir, but I haven't had a drink in three years. I'm sorry for what happened last time I came before you. I really have turned my life around. Please, please give me back my child."

"Ms. Moore, I was fully prepared to return custody of your daughter. Now you've raised questions. Questions I believe at the very least merit further study of you and your perhaps too-lax caseworker before I can with clear conscience wholly declare you a fit mother. Your caseworker may be impressed by your improvements, but considering you've not fully met the requirements outlined on your case list…" Sighing, he turned to a woman seated at an adjoining lower desk. "Please schedule another hearing for Ms. Moore six months from now." He stared at Pandora. "Good day, Ms. Moore."

Pandora sat, stunned. Then she shouted, "Are you kidding me? I've done everything I possibly could to prove I'm a good mom. Yes, I made horrible mistakes, but I've paid for them over and over. Send my caseworker to my house to supervise me every day if that makes you feel better, but please, I'm begging you, don't make me wait another six months."

"Ms. Moore…" the judge warned.

"Please," Pandora begged, not bothering to hide her tears. Why was this happening? "You can't do this! I *promised!*"

The judge stood. "Do I need to call security?"

Pandora was barely conscious of Natalie and Lila charging up behind her, taking her by the arms and practically dragging her from the room.

"GOT BIG PLANS for tonight?"

Late March, Calder looked up from the spy novel he'd only been skimming to find Mason grinning—never a good sign.

"If you don't, I was thinking we'd hit Tipsea's? Find a couple blondes? Or brunettes? Hell, doesn't much matter as long as they're wild and willing." He elbowed him from his seat in the noisy belly of their C-130.

"Sounds good, but I'll leave that to you and Cowboy. I want to surprise Pandora and Quinn."

"Loser."

"For wanting to spend time with my kid? And my—" What was Pandora? His girlfriend? Was he ready to take the next step and make her his fiancée? Guess in large part that depended on Julia. He couldn't even imagine how happy Pandora must be now that her daughter was back with her.

"Your what?"

"My girl—Pandora."

"I knew you were into her, but has it gone that far?" Though his friend's pinched expression clearly read he thought Calder was nuts, Calder didn't care. She meant the world to him. Being without her and his son all these months taught him he didn't want to leave again without knowing they'd both be waiting for him when he returned.

"If things go the way I think they will, pretty damn soon I might just make her my wife."

IT WAS WITH that thought in mind, Calder approached his home—excited to see Quinn and Pandora, and of course, to finally meet Julia. He instinctively knew he and the little girl would become great friends. Hopefully, if he was lucky, she might even view him as her father one day.

It was 8:00 p.m. when Mason dropped him at the curb. Calder grabbed his gear, then mounted the front steps double-time to ring the bell.

He'd given Pandora his keys, just in case she decided it would be more practical for her and Quinn to *unofficially* live in Calder's home while he was deployed.

"Oh, my gosh! Harold!" Calder got a shock when his mom opened the door instead of Pandora. "Harold, come quick! Calder's home!"

"I'll be damned...." Harold rounded the corner from the living room to take Calder's ditty bag. "Welcome back. You've been sorely missed around here."

Inside, he found Quinn standing alongside the sofa, *eating* the remote. "Hey, bud, let's not do that, okay?" He swooped his son into his arms. "Man, you've grown." To his mom he said, "Bet he's walking real good now, huh?"

"Gah! Gah!"

"He walks a little too well. He still isn't formally talking, but he's into everything all the time. I'm exhausted."

"Phoooa!"

"Where's Pandora?" Calder checked the kitchen, then glanced down the hall.

"You haven't heard?"

"Heard what?" He was almost afraid to ask.

"Her court hearing went terribly. The judge put her off for another six months."

"That's ridiculous! Why?" Calder couldn't fathom the amount of pain she must be in.

"The judge didn't like the fact that she hadn't maintained a continuous address for the full six months he'd requested. Then Lila from down the street told me he got all bent out of shape about Pandora caring for your child when hers was taken away. What'd he call it in his written statement?" Finger to her mouth, she paused a moment to think. "Oh—duplicitous."

Sick didn't begin to describe the nausea building in Calder's stomach. Had he caused this? By overreacting to her past, forcing her to find a new place to live then making her look wishy-washy by so quickly leaving Quinn in her care upon realizing his mistake, had he ruined her court case?

"Her friend Natalie says poor Pandora has been inconsolable ever since. That's why she called us to watch Quinn."

"Sure," Calder said. "I understand." Doubling over, he braced his hands on his knees. "Wow, gotta say this is the last thing I expected."

"You should go to her. Don't worry about Quinn."

"Yeah. Thanks." He gave his son an extra-long hug, then hugged his mom and stepdad before heading to the garage for his bike.

PANDORA SAT ON her sofa alone in the dark.

No—wait. She wasn't entirely alone. As he had every night since she'd lost her hearing, her friend Jack sat on her lap—

Jack Daniel's, that is.

So far, the bottle was unopened, but in an odd way, holding it each night gave her strength. It proved that at least in one area of her life she still had control.

Had it really just been Thanksgiving when this very room had been filled with laughter and joy?

Her caseworker, Fran, had been as shocked by the hearing's outcome as she was and vowed to try breaking through red tape to expedite the legal process, but that was a pipe dream. Somewhere in all Pandora's newfound happiness, she'd forgotten the cardinal rule that had applied to most every day of her life up until finding her sobriety—she was a born loser. A societal outcast. She thought she could rise above her past, but at every turn, no matter how hard she tried, there it was, slithering right back to suck her down.

Car lights shone through the front window.

Having grown accustomed to the dark, she squinted at the intrusion.

When footfalls sounded on the steps, she cringed, praying whoever was there would go away.

The doorbell's peal offended her ears.

Then came banging. "Pandora! I know you're in there. Open the door!"

Calder?

"Go away!" It didn't matter how many nights she'd spent on this same sofa, praying for him to safely come home. Now that he was here, she'd say new prayers for him to leave.

"Open the damn door or I'll kick it in."

"I said, *go away!*"

He made good on his promise—only her flimsy lock hadn't needed much more than his powerful shoulder's nudge.

Rushing to her, he fixed his eyes on the bottle. "Oh, no, baby. Please, tell me you're not drinking again."

Clinging to the bottle, she looked up at him with tears in her eyes. "I—I want to."

He gently took the bottle from her, setting it on a side table. "I'm sorry I wasn't here for you, but I am now. I heard what happened with Julia. We'll fight this. There has to be a way."

"I—I *promised* her," she said with halting tears. "How many times can I let her down before she doesn't even want to be with me?"

"She has to know this isn't your fault."

"I w-wanted to talk to her, but the judge wouldn't let me. He said I was d-disorderly. B-but how would he feel if someone took his kid?"

Seated next to her, Calder lifted her onto his lap, holding her, cradling her, smoothing her hair. "We'll figure this out. That's a promise I'm making you. I wanted to wait for this, dream up some over-the-top surprise proposal—even ask Julia for her advice, but I say screw it. Let's get married right away. Tonight. Then, first thing in the morning, we'll get started on this as a united front." He kissed her tear-stained cheeks. "I know some pretty big names. They get things done. Trust me, baby. We'll get your daughter back."

She wanted to believe the fairy tale he was spinning, but trusting him was what first landed her in trouble.

"I—I want to believe you, but I c-can't." Pushing off him, she strode to the other side of the room, hugging herself, wishing he'd go away. "I want to blame you for all this. You firing me, making me move—I want to say that's what raised a red flag for the judge. But I'm a realist, Calder, and deep inside—" she patted her chest "—I know there's no one to blame for any of this but myself. I should never have even thought I could take on the responsibility of becoming a full-time nanny. How could I have been so stupid as to think the judge wouldn't have a problem with my holding that sort of position? And I should never have viewed working for you as anything more than a job. I shouldn't have fallen in love with Quinn."

"What about me?" Calder asked, striding her way, look-ing perilously handsome even in the shadows. "Did you fall in love with me, Pandora? Because I sure as hell feel that way about you."

"No, you don't," she said with a violent shake of her head. "You're in the business of saving people. You might think you love me, but all I am is one more mission for you to sweep in and fix. Nothing more. I wish I'd never even met you. Then I wouldn't have gotten the stupid idea in my head that the two of us ever stood a chance."

Calder had taken enough psychology courses in college to realize she didn't mean what she said and was only push-ing him away out of fear he'd leave her, but that didn't make her hurtful words easier to bear.

He tried wrapping his arms around her, but she swatted him away. "Please, go. I don't need you. I don't need anyone. I'll buck up, get my head back in a good place then return to court in six more months and once and for all get my little girl."

"Okay. That's a great plan. But why not let me help?"

"Don't you see? I tried, Calder. I tried letting you in and it was a huge failure. Here you are, proposing marriage—in an incredibly lame, half-assed way—when what did we ever really share other than a few hot nights? You're a stranger. A stranger I made the mistake of falling for, and look where that's left me. For all I know, the only reason you even want me back is because you miss having a full-time sitter."

"That's B.S." Calder clenched his teeth so hard a muscle ticked in his jaw, and he found himself well and truly at a loss for words. Though he didn't just want her as an instant mom for Quinn, in other concerns, she was right. They did barely know each other. He'd never even learned the most basic facts—her favorite color or even her birthday.

What he had learned was that... *you know when you know.*

Calder had known Pandora was the woman for him all the way back from the day she'd literally saved his son's life. He'd known back when she'd first come to live with him and Quinn and she'd made him that delicious meat-loaf sandwich in the middle of the night. Pandora hadn't just saved Quinn but Calder, too. She'd taught him it was okay to commit. Because sometimes the people you love wind up loving you right back.

Only, where had all that newfound knowledge left him now?

"Calder, please," Pandora said, "I'm begging. Leave me alone. I got into this mess on my own, and I'll see my way out the same way. Whatever we shared, you know neither of us really meant it, so let's just end it now before our lives grow any more messy."

"You sure that's what you want?" Though she refused to make eye contact, she nodded.

He didn't have to be told twice.

Fighting his own tears, Calder granted Pandora's wish.

Chapter Seventeen

When Calder left, Pandora went to the window, watching him go. Had she just made the best or worst decision of her life? Maybe he could have helped bring Julia home. But if he couldn't? What if the judge perceived Calder's attempts to help as meddling? Pandora couldn't take the risk.

Without her jacket, Pandora grabbed her keys and purse.

She needed to get out of here. Speak to someone she trusted before making a grave mistake.

You don't trust Calder?

The real issue was not trusting herself around Calder.

It'd be so easy to lose herself to him. To abandon her every trouble, welcoming him to find solutions, but in the end, what would that say about her? She'd clawed her way from the edge of sanity to finally be in control. She couldn't come this far only to surrender to a man who may or may not stick around.

Her hands trembled so badly she had a hard time inserting her keys into the ignition.

Finally, she managed to get her car started, then she drove straight to Natalie.

"Get in here," her friend said when Pandora stood shivering at her front door.

To save money on utilities, Pandora had kept her heat low. Entering Natalie's home was what she'd always imagined the tropics must be. Balmy and serene—only with reggae playing instead of the latest TV ad from a Virginia Beach Chevy dealer blaring.

Natalie wrapped an afghan around Pandora's shoulders, ushering her to the sofa. "What's wrong?"

Tears began anew. "C-Calder's home. H-he asked me to marry him, but I can't. I have to stay strong to get Julia back. But to do that, I have to pull myself together." Covering her face with her hands, she admitted, "I can't eat or sleep. I'm so scared I'll never get Julia back."

"Calm down," Natalie urged. "I didn't want to say anything until we have a firm answer, but Anna and I, along with Lila and Martin and Gloria and Harold, have all chipped in to hire a *really* good lawyer who specializes in your type of case. We just need a smidge more money for his retainer, then—"

"No," Pandora said. "Please, don't give the judge any more cause to be upset. I need him to know I'm a good mom."

"You are," Natalie said. "You've learned your lesson. Everyone who loves you and has watched you grow into the woman you are today is ready for you to finally receive your ultimate reward—Julia."

"I will." Nodding, Pandora knew she would one day bring Julia home. She wouldn't have been able to survive without that core belief. "But look, I didn't come here to form some crazy takeover plan. I'm mortified by what happened in court. From here on out, I have to be perfect. I can't give that judge reason to believe I'm anything other than a textbook mom."

"That's all well and good," Natalie said, "but there's one problem."

"What's that?" Pandora sniffled.

"Outside of governmental guideline handbooks, I'm reasonably sure parental perfection doesn't exist. Parents make mistakes—granted, you made some doozies, but lucky for you, kids are resilient. Their most basic need is love. As long as you've got that covered, the rest will fall into place."

"Swell, but it doesn't change the fact that whether there's such a thing as a perfect parent or not, that's the standard I'm being held to."

CALDER SHOULD'VE GONE home after his blowout with Pandora, but knowing Quinn was no doubt in bed, as well as his parents, he wanted to kick back with his friends and a pitcher or two of beer. But then, how could he really even enjoy that, knowing alcohol sure as hell hadn't solved any of Pandora's problems?

Tipsea's was one of the last few places where a man could smoke in Norfolk, and Calder bought himself a cigar and two shots of whiskey at the bar. He'd seen the bottle at Pandora's and had fought a craving ever since. If he'd been with her, of course he'd have abstained, but since she'd booted him out on his ass, he figured why not get rip-roaring drunk?

What did he have to lose, anyway?

When it came to Pandora, everything was already lost.

"You're the last person I expected to see," Mason said.

Cooper trailed behind. "Why aren't you with Pandora and Quinn?"

"Kid's asleep and my woman dumped me." Calder signaled the barkeep for another shot.

"No way." Mason took the stool alongside him. "Thought you were about to propose."

"Me, too. But then I found out the court hearing for her to get her kid didn't go so great, and the night went downhill from there."

"Sure she's not just hurt and overreacting?" Cooper suggested.

Mason laughed. "Who appointed you the sensitivity police?"

"Shut up." Turning to Calder, Cooper said, "From the looks of you two at Thanksgiving, you were the real deal. Guess all I'm sayin' is I wouldn't just give up."

Calder clipped off the end of his cigar, then lit it. "Thank you, sir. I shall take that sage advice under advisement. Until then…" He raised his latest shot. "Let's toast to having the best damn night this side of Kandahar!"

IT WAS PUSHING 4:00 a.m. by the time Calder was sober enough to drive. He thought he was sneaking into the house, but as though he'd been caught in a time warp that had zapped him back to high school, his mom sat in the living room, awaiting his arrival.

"Big night out?" she asked, resting one of Pandora's old paperbacks on her lap.

"It was all right."

"Thought you were going to see Pandora."

"I did." He raked his fingers through his hair.

"And?"

Sighing, he said, "I don't mean to put you off, but it's been a seriously long day and I'm ready for bed." He headed for his room.

"Harold's in there. He snores so loud we've been sleeping separately. I set up camp in Pandora's old room."

"Where am I sleeping?"

His mom patted the couch.

He groaned. "Seriously?"

"We assumed you'd be staying with Pandora. We didn't just fall off the turnip truck, you know. We are acquainted with the birds and bees."

Blanching, he said, "Last thing I want to talk about with you is my sex life."

"Or lack thereof?" She laughed. "Why does everything seem so funny this late at night?"

He just shook his head.

"So really, what happened at Pandora's? She doesn't blame you for what happened in court, does she?"

"No." He sat hard on the sofa and scratched his head. "Mom, I opened up to her. I said we should get married, hire the best attorneys and tackle this thing together. But she's got a mile-long stubborn streak and insists on getting Julia back on her own."

"I meant to mention this to you earlier, but you ran out of here so fast I didn't have a chance. Pandora's friend Natalie has taken up a legal-fund collection. She planned on asking you to join as soon as you got back. What do you think?"

Sighing, he said what he most feared. "I think whatever demons Pandora's got inside won't let her accept what she deems charity. She takes full responsibility for the person she once was, and as such, seems to feel she's the only one who can bring Julia back into her life."

"The whole thing is awful. She's paid her dues and then some. Do you know she only spent six weeks in jail before being selected for the program that eventually helped turn her life around? I can't imagine how many parents drink themselves silly every night, yet they don't lose their children."

I was exactly that kind of parent tonight.

Calder asked, "What chance do you think we'd have of secretly helping her? Think the lawyer would talk to just us?"

"Seems to me we'll never know unless we ask."

"But, Mommy, why?" Julia asked on Pandora's first visit since losing her case. They cuddled together on the visitation room couch. Pandora had been reading, but Julia soon tired of that and instead wanted to talk. "You promised I could come home with you."

"I know, sweetie." Never had Pandora fought harder to maintain a bright smile. "But look at it this way, now you get to stay with Mom Cindy a little while longer. You like her, don't you?"

She hung her head. "Yeah, but not as much as you. She doesn't check around my bed for spiders."

"I'll bet if you asked, she would."

Julia said, "I guess. But I wanted to see my new room. And where's Quinn? Can't you bring him to visit?"

Where did Pandora begin to explain what had happened between her and Quinn's dad? How she'd give anything if whatever she and Calder shared could've worked? But it hadn't. And if she were honest with herself, Pandora had known from the start it wouldn't.

Men like Calder didn't fall for disasters like her.

"Mommy?"

"Yes?"

"Why does that judge hate us?" The knot in Pandora's throat threatened to seal off her vocal cords.

"Sweetie, he doesn't hate us—especially not you." She swept hair from in front of her daughter's eyes, tucking it behind her ears. "Remember how I told you I made bad mistakes?"

"Uh-huh...."

"Well, like when you do something naughty at school and need a time-out—"

Julia looked up. "I'm never bad at school."

"Okay, well, you know how some kids are bad at school? And they get in trouble, but then everything's okay? Well, the judge says I'm still in trouble."

"But it's been a long time. I'm tired of you being in detention." Her daughter snuggled closer. "Please, take me home with you. I don't like coming here."

In her peripheral vision, Pandora caught the woman supervising their visit jotting something in her notebook.

Her stomach sank.

WEEKS PASSED.

Each day when Calder brought Quinn to the day care and then returned to pick up his son, Pandora scurried to avoid him. She dashed for the bathroom or ducked into the supply closet. The few times he'd caught her off guard, she'd found herself instantly overcome by sadness and grief and the kind of longing that stemmed from knowing she'd once almost had something special but had lost it.

Luckily, today she'd made it to the janitor's closet in the nick of time.

She stood in the dark, slowly counting to five hundred, which she figured should be a reasonable enough time for Calder to be on his way.

Finished, she opened the door to find him there, facing her with his hands tucked in his pockets.

"How long are you planning on playing this game, Pandora?"

"I—I don't know what you mean." She fussed with her hair, certain after playing with the kids all day she must be a mess.

"Can you honestly tell me you're better off without me? That you don't think about how great the two of us could've been?"

"Calder, please…." She looked at her chipped nail polish.

"Please, what? Hold you? Kiss you?" He'd stepped close enough for his warm breath to fan her cheeks. He smelled of the chocolate-chip cookies Pandora had baked for the front entry's reception counter.

She notched her chin higher. "I meant, please go." *Before I lose my last shred of resistance where you're concerned.* Did he have any idea how many nights she'd lain awake, staring at her ceiling, struggling with her decision to let him go? Of course, she'd done the right thing. Her sole focus in life must be centered on getting her daughter back. But every once in a while, on particularly cold, blustery nights, her thoughts drifted to him. That one magical night he'd held her, and how for those precious few hours everything had seemed okay.

"Today," he said with a funny smile she couldn't recall ever having seen, "I'll do as you ask, but one of these days, Pandora, you're going to be begging me to stay."

Unable to meet his intense gaze, she looked at her feet, mumbling, "Please, Calder, no more teasing. You really need to go."

CONTACTING A HIGH-PRICED attorney had only gotten Calder so far. To achieve the results he truly needed, he'd have to call in the big guns, which is why he now sat somewhere he never thought he would—in one of the base commander's two burgundy leather guest chairs.

"As a matter of fact, I do know someone who may be able to help." The white-haired man spun his enormous old-school Rolodex, stopping it on the *T*s. "Let me see...." He fingered through card after card. "Ah—here he is. Old buddy of mine from Annapolis. Thought he might be SEAL material, but he broke his leg skiing in Vermont and that was that. Glorious career down the tubes before it even started. Anyway, give him a call, explain your situation. He's the type who gets things done."

Calder took the proffered card. "Thank you, sir. Keep me in mind if you ever need a favor."

The commander laughed. "Don't let my wife hear that."

THE FIRST WEEK in May, Pandora grabbed the mail, then climbed the stairs to her apartment, tilting her face to the last of the day's warm sun.

It'd been a rough day at work. There'd been a fight in the three-year-old room over a toy truck and she'd noticed a speech therapist had come to see Quinn, who still hadn't said a formal word beyond *uh-oh*.

She'd had Natalie speak to Calder about working with him at night. Dinner or bath times were great for word reinforcement—pointing at specific items and repeating the name at least three times.

Inside, she set the mail on the counter and made a quick trip to the restroom, then her bedroom to change.

Back in the kitchen, she filled the kettle with water and set it on the stove to boil. While waiting for her steaming mug of chamomile tea to cool, she finally got around to flipping through the mail.

An envelope with the return address of Judge B. Thomas Thornton in the top left corner sent her pulse racing. She tore into it, fearing a further setback to her case, only to instead release a squeak.

How had this happened? What had happened?

The judge wanted to see her in his chambers to discuss his ruling—in two days!

She called Natalie to ask if she'd ever heard of anything like this before. She hadn't.

Her next call was to Lila, who also reported that the letter sounded odd, but that Pandora should cross her fingers for something positive to happen.

The next two days, Pandora wasn't sure what to do with the emotions balling in her stomach. On the one hand, maybe the judge had decided he'd been too hard on her and figured she should regain custody of her daughter. The more realistic view was that he'd discovered a bureaucratic loophole that would assign permanent custody of Julia to her foster family.

The mere thought made her nauseous.

More than anything, she wanted to phone Calder. Hear his take on what the judge could possibly want.

No matter how sad she might sometimes be over losing him, she had only to envision her daughter to realize no sacrifice was too big when it came to bringing Julia home. Calder had become a distraction when every ounce of her energy needed to be focused on her beautiful little girl.

FOR PANDORA'S NEWEST court date, she'd asked Natalie for the afternoon off. That morning had been never ending, and when the time came to leave, her friend was nowhere to be found.

Odd. Since Natalie had been with her for most of her legal journey, why now, when anything could happen, would she be MIA?

She tried Lila, thinking she'd like to have at least one of her friends there for her in case she received even worse news than she had her last day in court, but not even Martin answered their house phone.

Alone and frightened, Pandora proceeded to court.

Should something truly awful happen, she'd deal with it then. For now, she had to stay strong. She could not suffer the kind of emotional breakdown she had the last time she'd been here.

The judge's chambers were located on a different floor from the courtroom. Pandora found it odd her meeting would be there.

She announced herself to a secretary who pointed her to a row of wooden chairs. "The judge will be with you momentarily."

Dozens of thoughts raced through Pandora's head. What if she lost permanent custody of Julia? What if she'd broken some arcane law she wasn't even aware of and was being carted off to prison? What if—

"Ms. Moore, the judge will see you now."

With her pulse racing, her breathing erratic and her palms sweating, Pandora smoothed her dress, then followed the middle-aged woman into a heavily paneled room.

"Ah, the famous Ms. Moore." The judge rose, gesturing for her to have a seat. "I've been on the bench twenty years and never have I heard such a ruckus."

"I don't know what you mean." She sat primly with her hands neatly folded on her lap, praying her galloping pulse could only be heard by her.

"You're not spearheading this campaign?" He tapped a file she presumed was hers.

"No, sir. I honestly don't know why I'm here."

"Humph." He shook his head. "Might as well get on with it. Ms. Moore, whether you're aware of it or not, you have quite a few friends in high places. They've convinced me to take a second look at your case and I'm ashamed to admit, upon closer inspection, you truly are the kind of woman many in the system should aspire to be."

"Th-thank you." The judge's praise made Pandora's chest squeeze with apprehension. He wouldn't be building her up only to tear her down again, would he?

"In light of this, and my earlier mistake, please accept my heartfelt apology and know your pain has at least filled one purpose—I'll now be taking a more common-sense approach to all my hearings. You really are a wonder. Ms. Pandora Moore, I hereby grant you full and permanent custody of one minor child, Miss Julia Elizabeth Moore." He lightly slammed his desk with his gavel. "Case dismissed." Rising, he pointed toward a door. "You might want to greet the lot hiding out in there."

Dazed, unsure if she could be dreaming, Pandora asked, "Really? I'm done? Julia's mine?"

"She's really and truly yours." After patting her back, he

opened the door to a secondary waiting area for her. "Job well done, Ms. Moore."

"Mommy!" Julia was first into her arms, then Natalie and Anna, Lila and Martin, even her caseworker, Fran. Everyone was laughing and talking and Pandora couldn't stop happy tears.

"Sweetie," Pandora said while hugging her daughter, "I love you so much."

"I love you, too."

Once the initial excitement wore down and they all left the judge's chambers, Pandora caught sight of two familiar, dear faces. Calder and Quinn.

They'd reached the lobby where Julia said her goodbyes to teary Mom Cindy.

Pandora said to Calder, "You did this, didn't you?"

He shrugged. "I helped, but so did everyone else. We *all* love you. When you told me the judge denied you custody, I refused to believe for one second we couldn't turn this around."

"We?" She was almost afraid to ask.

"Woman, if you're going to be in a relationship with a SEAL, there's one thing you need to learn up front."

"What's that?" As much as she'd tried telling herself she no longer wanted him, she did. Being near him brought on a fierce longing she was no longer capable of denying.

"We *never* quit. We're like human bulldozers—mowing down anything—anyone—in our way to make the seemingly impossible happen."

"Mommy?" Julia asked, hopping up and down. "May I please hold Quinn?"

"You know my son?" Calder asked Julia.

Her daughter nodded. "Mommy brought him to see me. He's cute. I love babies. My foster mom, Cindy, just had a baby girl and I helped her a lot."

"That's nice of you." He extended his hand. "I'm Calder. I've heard an awful lot of nice things about you."

She giggled. "Mommy says you're nice, too."

"Really?" He raised his eyebrows, glancing Pandora's way.

"Yep!" Julia gave an exaggerated nod.

Pandora gathered their group together as she stood with Julia's backside against her, hugging her arms around her daughter's chest. "I'm not sure what part each of you played in making this miracle happen, but I don't know how to begin to thank you." She was crying again, but happy tears sure beat the heck out of her usual despondency. "For as long as I live, I'll never forget what you've done."

Her speech was ended by more tears and hugs and smiles.

An impromptu party popped up at Pandora's apartment, making her glad she'd long since finished Julia's room.

While Natalie and Anna ran out for burger fixings and Lila and Martin went briefly home to let out a vacationing neighbor's dog, Pandora showed Julia her new room. "Do you like it?"

"It's so pretty! I love the stuffed animals!"

"We still have to find a place for the nice things your foster family bought, but I'm sure we'll manage."

Julia explored the rest of the apartment, ending in the kitchen, where she spotted her coloring page on the fridge. "Hey! I made that!"

"You sure did, angel. Think you can make more?"

"Yeah! Want me to start now?"

Pandora laughed. "If you'd like. But don't forget it's a school night. Do you have any homework from missing today?"

She sighed. "A little. Do I have to do it now?"

Pandora hated jumping right into the least fun part of parenting, but she'd worked a long time to be in this position and she wasn't about to ruin it now. "Yes, I really think it'd be best to get it out of the way. Come on—" she patted the table "—I'll help. Then you'll have it over with and can enjoy your party."

"Okay." While Julia ran to her room to gather books and supplies, Pandora fixed a small snack tray of apple slices and peanut butter.

Being a mom again made Pandora feel as close to being whole as she had in a while. The only thing missing she wasn't even sure could be replaced. One thing was for certain. Now that her primary dream had come true, it was time to start on another....

That is, assuming Calder and Quinn were amenable.

CALDER MOUNTED THE stairs to Pandora's apartment, not quite sure why he was even there. The last time he'd visited her in her home she'd pushed him away. He'd understood her reasoning, but that hadn't lessened the hurt embedded by her words. The doubt that'd always been with him now dogged him even more.

"Remember what we practiced?" he asked his son, who'd insisted on climbing the stairs on his own. "Pan-door-rah?"

"Eee-boo!" Quinn called.

Calder held his hand, reminding Quinn on each new step of the word he was supposed to say. Each night there were also many other words—boat, soap, peas, pig, dog—the list went on and on.

The screen door shot open and Julia popped out. "Mommy! Quinn's here and his dad!" She bolted down the stairs. "Hi!"

"Hey. I sure am glad to see you here. Having fun with your mom?"

Quinn grunted his way up the last few steps.

"Uh-huh. But I had to do my math for tomorrow. But she helped, so it wasn't too bad."

"I used to hate homework. But then I figured out the faster I got it done, the faster I got to play."

She laughed. "I never thought of it like that! Can I play with Quinn?"

"Sure. But let's get him inside first."

"Okay!"

Calder found Pandora at the sink, peeling potatoes.

"Hey." To keep from pulling her into a hug, he rammed his hands into his pockets.

"May I play with Quinn now?" Julia asked.

"You certainly may," Calder answered. "Be careful with him, though."

"I will. Come on—" she took Quinn by the hand "—come see my room. It's really cool."

Alone with Pandora, Calder felt tongue-tied.

"I'm making potato salad," she said. "Would you mind grabbing a couple pots—one big and one little—and filling them with water to boil?"

"Have you always been this bossy?" he couldn't resist teasing. It'd be so easy falling into their old comfortable routine. He'd missed that closeness. The sense of having someone who knew him inside and out—only, that was the funny thing about him and Pandora. On the surface, they hardly knew each other, but deep down he felt as if he'd known her a lifetime.

"Probably not." She shyly ducked her gaze, in the process spilling her hair forward, baring the spot on her neck he used to love to nuzzle.

There was an awkward shuffle as he did her bidding, trying not to touch her but wanting to so badly.

"Calder?" She lifted her glasses, resting them atop her head.

"Yes?"

She blew out a deep breath. "I'm sorry. I said horrible

things to you, but I was so afraid." She bowed her head again, but then looked up, dazzling him with her sweet, unaffected smile. "I told you I didn't blame you—*us*—for my court hearing going wrong, but deep inside, part of me did. That was wrong. Bottom line—I wasn't thinking. All I can say is being without Julia made me temporarily insane."

"And now?"

There she went again with that smile. "I once asked you for a second chance…" She flopped her hands at her sides. "Here I am again. Y-you asked me to marry you, and I'm not ready for that—it wouldn't be fair to my daughter—but breathing one more second without you and Quinn in my life isn't fair to me. Today at the courthouse, when I saw you and realized what you'd done, it hit me how stupid it was of me to ever think I wanted to live the rest of my life alone. Why, you know? When it's so much better with friends."

Calder pulled her into the hug he'd craved since that morning, and then he slid his hands into her hair, kissing her with an urgency he didn't bother trying to hide.

"I love you," she said. "I think I've loved you from the day you rescued me at the grocery store."

He kissed her again. "I've loved you since you saved my baby from choking on that grape."

"Quinn choked on a grape?" Julia wandered in with Quinn in tow. "Is he okay?"

Sniffling from still more happy tears, Pandora said, "He's amazing."

"When we were in my room," Julia said, "Quinn was trying to talk. Has he said any words yet?"

"Nope." Calder slipped his arm around Pandora's waist. "What did he say?"

"It sounded like pan. Does he like playing with pots and pans?" She ran to a cupboard and pulled out a pan and its lid. Clanging it, she asked Quinn, "Pan? Were you trying to say pan?"

Calder crossed his fingers. *Kid, if you ever wanted to wow a crowd, now would be the time.*

"Well, mister?" Pandora knelt in front of him, taking his hands. "Do you finally have something to say?"

"Pan! Pand!"

"He did say it!" Julia gave her pans another clang. "Do it again!"

"Pando!"

Puzzled, Pandora asked, "Is he trying to say panda? Calder, he doesn't have a stuffed panda, does he?"

"Not that I can think of."

"Pandor! Pando!"

Julia clapped. "He's so cute!"

"Calder?" Pandora asked. "Can you make out what he's saying?"

He shrugged. *Come on, little guy. Say it. Say it.* "Beats me. Wouldn't have a clue."

Quinn ran from Julia to Pandora, then he held up his hands, pinching his fingers. *"Pan-door-ah! Pan-door-ah!"*

She covered her mouth with her hands and tears shone in her eyes. "No way. How would he ever have learned my name?" She looked to Calder, who couldn't hide his smile. "Have you been coaching him all this time?"

"Pan-door-rah!"

She lifted him, spinning around and hugging him. "You're such a brilliant boy!"

"Takes after his father," Calder noted.

"Yes, he does." Pandora, with Quinn still in her arms, leaned close to Calder to kiss his cheek. "You've already given me one amazing gift today. Now two? How am I ever going to repay you?"

"That's the thing about gifts—" he pulled Pandora, Julia

and Quinn into his arms "—there's no need to ever repay them. But if you'd want to be my girl, I am accepting applications."

"In that case…" She winked. "I'd better grab a pen."

Epilogue

"Three, two, one! Happy New Year!" Pandora danced and cheered and hugged with Julia and Quinn, but she saved her kiss for her husband.

"I love you, Mr. Remington."

"I love you, Mrs. Remington." Because of her bulging baby bump, Pandora struggled to reach her arms all the way around Calder. At the end of her six-month lease, they'd moved back into Calder's home, but because of their still-growing family, they were in the process of selling that house and looking for something larger.

All their friends had squeezed inside for the night. Natalie and Anna, Lila and Martin, Gloria and Harold, Patricia and Heath, Cooper and Mason, along with many of the other men on Calder's SEAL team, as well as their wives.

The biggest surprise of all was realizing what a small world it was when encountering her former counselor Ellie, who'd married Calder's friend, Deacon. She and Ellie hugged it out, with Pandora apologizing for having given her such a hard time. Ellie warmed Pandora's heart by thanking her for proving her volunteer work really did make an eventual difference by touching lives.

"Where are you?" Calder asked as they danced to "Auld Lang Syne."

"Just thinking what an amazing life we've built in such a short time. I feel reborn." She kissed him. "All thanks to you."

"You've done a lot for me, too, you know." With his hands low on her hips, she wouldn't be too sad when the party was over. If the kids cooperated, they'd finally be alone.

"Oh, yeah?" she teased. "Like what?"

"Let's see." He stopped dancing to touch his finger to his lips as if feigning deep thought. "I'll always be grateful for your meat loaf...."

That earned him a swat. "I'm trying to be serious."

"Oh, Mrs. Remington, I'm very serious. And to prove it, look what I found under your snowflake ice sculpture—it chipped off." He slipped a sparkling square-cut gold-and-diamond solitaire onto her left-hand ring finger, nestling it alongside her gold wedding band.

"Calder?" She released him to put her hands over her mouth. "You're crazy! I don't need this. We talked about how all our savings needed to go into the new house."

"Unless you're planning on leaving your hand behind, by that definition, the ring will move right along with us."

Pandora hated how her pregnancy had her crying more than ever, but she'd say this was just cause. When they'd married, the legal fees incurred from bringing Julia back into her life had prevented Calder from affording an engagement ring.

"Besides, Heath took me to the same guy he bought Patricia's ring from and he gave me an awesome military discount."

"I still say you're crazy."

He grabbed her left hand and tugged at her new sparkler. "Want me to take it back?"

"No." She kissed her ring, then him. "I love this ring,

but most of all, I love you. Thank you, Calder, for saving my life."

He winked before flashing his slow, sexy grin. "I'm a SEAL. That's what I do."

*****

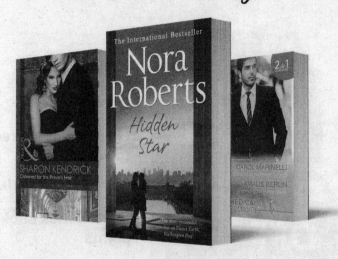